Praise for Anna Jacobs:

'Catherine Cookson fans will cheer!'
Peterborough Evening Telegraph

'Anna Jacobs' books are deservedly popular. She is one of the best writers of Lancashire sagas around.'
Historical Novels Review

'She is a gripping storyteller'
Sunday Star Times, New Zealand

'An exciting book of immensely brilliant character portrayal and a great storyline'
Bangor Chronicle on *Our Eva*

'Another cracking read with a vivid insight into family relationships' *Coventry Evening Telegraph* on *Our Eva*

'Jacobs weaves another magical Lancashire saga that will delight fans and newcomers alike.'
Lancashire Evening Post on *Our Mary Ann*

ANNA JACOBS

Tomorrow's Promises

HODDER

First published in Great Britain in 2007 by Hodder & Stoughton
An Hachette Livre UK Company

First published in paperback in 2008

11

A CIP catalogue record for this title is available from the British Library

ISBN 978 0 340 84080 1

Typeset in Plantin Light by Palimpsest Book Production Limited,
Grangemouth, Stirlingshire

Printed and bound in Great Britain by
CPI Group (UK) Ltd, Croydon, CR0 4YY

Hodder & Stoughton's policy is to use papers that are natural, renew-
able and recyclable products and made from wood grown in sustainable
forests. The logging and manufacturing processes are expected to
conform to the environmental regulations of the country of origin.

Hodder & Stoughton Ltd
338 Euston Road
London NW1 3BH

www.hodder.co.uk

It's about time I thanked Gavin Dwyer and Todd Galvin, the computer gurus who've been building and servicing my computers for a good few years – not to mention answering dozens of questions from me. Couldn't manage without you, guys!

Prologue

November 1918

At two o'clock in the morning of Tuesday, November 12th, when everyone else in the house had gone to bed after celebrating the end of the war, Lady Daphne Bingram sat alone in the library sipping a final glass of brandy and wondering what her life would now become. She wasn't sad that the war was over, never that! But she was sad at the thought of disbanding her 'girls' because she'd miss them dreadfully.

Her thoughts inevitably drifted back over the war years. She'd formed her group of aides as a personal contribution to the war effort – and what a splendid bunch they were! They came from all sorts of backgrounds from maidservants to prim, ageing spinsters and privileged daughters of the rich, and were of all ages, with the majority in their mid to late twenties now and the oldest fifty-four.

She'd started with twelve of them, picking women she'd met here and there who seemed to have more gumption than most. Twelve were all she and her husband could afford to support and buy uniforms for, since they were comfortable rather than rich.

She'd had the aides taught to drive and learned with them – such fun! – then borrowed several cars from friends who were also keen to support the war effort. Ready at last, she'd offered her aides to the War Office to replace the soldiers who drove senior officers from the armed forces around London or further afield. Jolly well the girls had done it, too. Later she'd bought a couple of motorcycles, one with a sidecar.

And her original group of aides had been so appreciated that the government had given her money to employ and train more of them to do special clerical and other work, women prepared to go wherever they were needed. Now the group numbered over fifty.

Later she'd opened a canteen in her London home, a place where men from the armed forces who were recuperating or on leave could spend a few hours at no cost, without the need to buy alcohol.

What would become of her aides now that the war was over, though? Many of the men coming back would be treated as heroes, but what about the unsung heroines who'd also contributed a great deal to winning the war? And once the men reclaimed their jobs, what would happen to the women who'd been doing them? She'd had enough experience of the unfairness of life to be sure that women would not be given the credit they deserved. Would they even be allowed to continue using their new skills in the place of men who'd died, or would they be pushed back into their former narrow lives?

She'd keep in touch with her girls and always be there to help them – well, she would as long as she lived. She was getting on for seventy now, though she didn't feel it.

Raising her glass, she drained the last few drops of brandy in a silent toast to 'Lady Bingram's Aides', as everyone called them.

I

November 1918 – March 1919

Those aides not on duty had just finished breakfast, which was rather late today because of the celebrations of the previous day. Ellen saw Lady Bingram standing in the doorway and nudged the woman next to her. As usual, everything stopped when her ladyship came in and stood waiting for their attention at the head of the table.

'My dears, now that the war is over, I'm afraid we shall have to start thinking about the future. It won't happen overnight, because there is still the influenza epidemic and we can help there. But when we have no more purpose as a group, we shall have to disband. I'm mentioning it today because I want to give you as long as possible to think about what you're going to do with your lives from now on. And if any of you needs help, come and see me. Even after you leave, well, you will always know how to contact me if I can do anything for you. Be sure I shan't forget you . . . ever.'

There was utter silence, then one girl sniffed and pulled out a handkerchief.

'No tears!' her ladyship said sharply. 'We shall hold our heads high until the end.'

She gave them a smile and walked briskly out.

Ellen was rostered to clear up and noticed that her companion in the kitchen was quieter than usual.

'I don't want to go back home, do you?' Tessa said as they washed and wiped the dishes together. 'There's nothing for me there but a dull life looking after Father.'

Ellen looked at her in sympathy. They all knew what a bully Tessa's father was, how angry he'd been when his daughter joined Lady Bingram's Aides and left his care to an elderly cousin. 'You don't have to go back to living with him.'

'What else can I do? He's nearly eighty now.' She sighed. 'But you at least are free to find a more interesting job. Have you got any idea yet what you're going to do?'

'I only wish I had. I don't know what I want and that's the truth.'

When they'd finished, Ellen hung the tea towel over the drying rack and went outside to clean the motorcycle and sidecar that she had used more than anyone else to deliver important documents and messages all over London. She loved driving round on it, would miss it dreadfully.

She'd always planned to return to Lancashire after the war but didn't intend to live at home. She didn't get on with her stepfather, never had, and though she tried to be polite to him, he didn't pay her the same courtesy, ordering her around as he did her mother and expecting her to 'jump to it' and serve him like a lord.

When she was fourteen she'd been glad to leave home and live in at the Hall, and she knew she could return to her old job there, because her mother had said so several times in her letters. 'No, I'm *not* going back to being a housemaid!' Ellen didn't realise she'd spoken aloud until she heard a chuckle just behind her.

'First sign of madness, talking to yourself.' The cheeky young delivery boy from the grocer's winked at her as he lugged a big basket of provisions down the steps.

She smiled. He was sixteen and undersized, so hadn't been able to feign being older as some had done in order to volunteer for the Army. Now he wouldn't have to face the horrors of war, he and many lads like him. But her smile soon faded and her thoughts returned to her own problems. She'd go mad stuck indoors, cleaning the same rooms day after day so that a rich family could live in an immaculate house. Surely she'd be able to find a job where some of her new skills would be used? But try as she might, she couldn't think what that job might be in peacetime.

She'd learned so much since becoming one of Lady Bingram's Aides. She'd arrived in London a quiet, rather shy girl of twenty who had met Daphne when her ladyship came to visit her employer in Lancashire and then had been given a lift in Daphne's motor car when walking back from town on her day off. After her initial shyness she'd enjoyed chatting to her mistress's guest and had told her about the books she borrowed from the library about far-away places.

She could never have guessed where this meeting would lead until a letter arrived from her ladyship inviting Ellen to join her Aides and do important war work. She'd accepted because by that time she was fed up with working at the Hall.

Her stepfather had been furious, as had her employer, but Ellen knew this was her big chance to see something of the world, possibly the only chance she'd ever have. Before she went to London she knew only about housework and life in a village in Lancashire. Now, she not only knew her way round the nation's capital but could drive both a motor car and a motorcycle, service their engines and do simple repairs too. She was comfortable talking to people from the highest to the lowest, could do paperwork and simple accounts. She'd even worked for a time as a stewardess on a ship bringing Belgian refugees back to England. She liked to think she could turn her hand to just about anything because of these experiences.

As she stood lost in thought, Daphne Bingram strolled out to join her in the mews, looking tired, as if she hadn't slept very well.

'I'll miss this old girl.' Ellen indicated the machine, which was now gleaming and ready for use. It was an A.J.S. model 'D' passenger outfit, sturdy and reliable, and she preferred driving it to motor cars, if truth be told, loved to feel the wind on her face.

Daphne studied it. 'The cars I borrowed can go back to their owners, but I had to buy the motorcycles.

It'd be a waste to leave the two of them standing idle, so I suppose I'll have to sell them.'

It was then that the idea came to Ellen, such a bright, wonderful idea. 'How much would you want for this one?'

That urchin's grin that they all loved to see lit up Daphne's face. 'Ten pounds if it's going to a good home.'

'That's not a fair price. It's worth much more.'

'I know how you love this machine and I think ten pounds is very fair, given the circumstances.'

Ellen looked at her uncertainly.

'It'd please me very much to see the bike go to you.'

And she couldn't resist it for a moment longer. 'Done! And thank you so much. I can't tell you how grateful I am.'

Solemnly they shook hands, then Ellen turned and stroked the machine. *Hers*, now. It would cause a sensation in the village and her stepfather would throw a fit, but she didn't care.

It was a symbol of her new life, owning a machine like this. It seemed to promise that she didn't need to give everything up, that she could do anything she chose in the bright new world they were promised.

Sergeant Seth Talbot got up very early the morning after the war ended, just wanting to enjoy a few minutes' peace and quiet. None of the men was awake, so he got his wish and though it was chilly, he went outside the hut where twenty new recruits were still sleeping and sat down on the wooden steps. He was more relieved than words could ever say that he wouldn't have to turn another group of dewy-eyed, enthusiastic boys into cannon fodder.

He stayed there, enjoying the silence and fresh taste of the morning air, until he heard voices. Then he went inside to begin his day. But for the life of him, he couldn't summon up his usual fierceness. It had been alien to his nature, but the only way he knew to frighten the duller lads into learning enough to perhaps save their young lives when they were out there in the trenches. He knew all too well what conditions were like in that hell on earth, as he had been there himself for two long, weary years until he was injured and then transferred to training duties.

'It's all going to be different now, Sarge, isn't it?' one lad said as he made his morning round, inspecting their beds and kit to make sure all was in order. 'We won't have to fight. Will they send us home again, do you think, or keep us in the Army?'

He looked across at the lad and smiled, enjoying the thought that this one wouldn't be killed. 'Well, you won't be going to fight, but it'll take a while to demobilise everyone. And it never hurts to learn what you can, so we'll carry on with our lessons until we're told otherwise.'

They'd go away with more than fighting skills. In every group of new recruits there were lads who had never had a proper bath in their lives, who accepted being lousy as normal, and who didn't know how to use knives and forks properly, others who couldn't read and write properly. He and the elderly corporal were used to teaching many other things than how to fight and look like a well turned out soldier.

For the next few days Seth kept wondering what his life would be like as a civilian. Did he want to go back into the police force? He'd fought against his family's wishes when he'd joined it in the first place, because they'd wanted him to continue working in his uncle's corner shop, which was considered a step up from being a carter like his father. His uncle had no children, so getting their eldest son well in with him was regarded as a prudent move by his parents.

He'd gone to work in the shop when he was fourteen, because no one had given him a choice. He'd lived in an attic bedroom there and acted as general dogsbody, both in the house and in the shop. It was better than he'd expected, because his uncle was a kind man, but this wasn't the sort of shop that delivered to customers and he absolutely hated being penned up all day indoors. But his uncle liked his food and fed them both well, so Seth had grown tall and strong while living with him.

The person he'd admired most in his new life was the police sergeant in charge of that part of Manchester, a man who could control naughty lads in the street with no more than a glance, yes and grown men too.

As soon as he was old enough, Seth apologised to his uncle and joined the police force. His next brother took his place in the shop, but poor Ben had been killed in '16 in France at some obscure skirmish. Now Seth's youngest brother was working in the shop, had been due to be called up, but would escape that, thank goodness.

Seth had enjoyed being a policeman. He'd believed in what he was doing – fighting crime and maintaining public order in Manchester. He'd been ambitious, hoping one day to rise to Sergeant or even higher.

He wasn't ambitious in that way now.

It was seeing the scars on his chest and arm as he got washed that did it, brought back pictures of wounded men, dying soldiers, mangled bodies. He doubled up, trying desperately to hold back the agony. But he couldn't and found himself weeping helplessly into his towel. So many good men dead, friends lost, others maimed. Why had he been saved?

When he recovered from the unmanly tears, his brain seemed clearer and he knew exactly what he wanted to do with his life. No more turmoil, if he could help it. No more ambition, either. All he wanted now was the peace and quiet of a small country town or village, preferably somewhere in the north of England, where he'd grown up.

He longed quite desperately to leave this crowded camp and go home.

They asked him to stay on in the Army but he refused. The Captain pressed him hard to reconsider, so he said quite simply, 'I need some peace and quiet now, sir. I've had enough. The sooner I can get out of the Army, meaning no offence, the happier I shall be.'

The Captain looked at him long and hard, seeming to understand what he was feeling, because he nodded.

'Very well. I'll set things in motion. You can be proud of what you've done for your country, though, Talbot, and the regiment is proud of your bravery in rescuing those men in Flanders.'

Seth shrugged. 'Anyone would have done the same. They gave me a medal, but it should have gone to everyone, because we all stuck together out there.'

The Captain held out his hand. 'I've been happy to serve with you.'

They shook hands solemnly then Seth watched the Captain walk away with that slightly stiff gait. He'd lost a leg at Passchendaele but had talked his way into a desk job, because he came from an army family and had never wanted any other sort of life.

Seth knew it'd take a while for the Army to spit him out again, so he thought about his future for a week or two longer before writing to his former Police Sergeant and doing something that would have been unthinkable to the fiercely independent young man he'd been five years ago: asking a favour.

What did pride matter now? The only thing that mattered was building a world in which war could never, ever happen again. He wanted to be part of keeping the new peace, but only in a minor way. Mostly, he just wanted to enjoy it.

The next day Ellen went to the savings bank to withdraw some money to pay for the motorcycle. It was a daring thing for a woman to do, own and ride a vehicle like that, and she knew her mother and stepfather wouldn't approve, but she was old enough at twenty-six to make her own choices.

At the bank there was a man behind the counter instead of Miss Phipps and Ellen asked where the usual teller was, worried that the kindly elderly lady she'd chatted to every week for the past few years might have fallen victim to the influenza.

'She's gone back to the office where she belongs,' the new man replied in a snappy tone. 'This is *my* job and now I'm doing it again. Anyway, women don't understand money like men do.'

Ellen wasn't being talked to like that by anyone. 'Oh, and who do you think manages the housekeeping money in most homes?'

'I'm talking about real money, the sort we handle in banks, not pennies. Now . . .' He picked up her form and frowned at it. 'You're withdrawing rather a lot of money. Ten pounds! Are you sure you haven't made a mistake?'

As he pushed the paper back towards her she saw that his hand was badly scarred, as if it'd been burnt, and guessed he'd been wounded and discharged from the forces recently. But that was no reason for him to speak so slightingly of poor Miss Phipps, who had once said wistfully how much more interesting it was to meet and talk to customers. And his war service was certainly no excuse for speaking to Ellen as if she was stupid.

'Well?' the teller repeated, tapping the piece of paper impatiently with his forefinger. 'Are you sure about this withdrawal?'

She shoved the paper right back at him without

even glancing at it. 'What I do is not your concern and I'll thank you not to make my business public to the other customers.'

He drew himself up, scowling. 'I wouldn't be doing my job correctly if I didn't double check. Lady customers can make some foolish mistakes and ten pounds *is* a lot of money for a young woman like you.'

'What do you mean by "young woman like me"?'

The Manager came out of his office. 'Is there a problem, Johnson?'

'No, sir. Just checking that the young lady's slip has been filled in properly.'

'Good, good.'

Ellen found her voice. 'Well, *I* have a problem. I wish to complain about this new teller of yours, who's been telling the whole bank my business and talking to me as if I'm five years old. What sort of way is that to treat a customer?'

They both looked at her in shock and two male customers who were waiting their turn rolled their eyes at one another.

Ellen had met this patronising attitude all too often before the war and had been powerless to do anything about it while she was a housemaid except grit her teeth. But she'd hoped that women's contribution to the recent victory would have earned them more respect. It hadn't with the men here today, that was obvious. She could feel the hostility of all four of them. 'I've changed my mind.'

'Ah!' The teller nodded at her. 'I knew you'd made a mistake.'

'I hadn't made a mistake. And I do still need that money because I'm buying a motorcycle.' Oh, the joy of seeing the shock on his face as she said that! 'But now I've decided to close my account and draw *all* the money out. I'm not leaving my savings in a bank where people treat me so rudely.'

'My dear young lady—'

'Please don't speak to me in that patronising tone.' She kept her voice calm, in spite of the anger simmering underneath, trying to achieve the same icy tone she'd heard Lady Bingram use.

Both men behind the counter sucked in their breath in shock, then the manager stepped forward, saying in the same sort of soothing tone people use to small children who have been naughty, 'Shall we discuss this in my office . . .' he glanced down at her left hand, 'miss?'

'No, thank you. I'll just draw out my money and deposit it in another bank where they treat me with more courtesy.'

'You're being too hasty. And you'll be losing some interest if you close the account before the end of the month. Perhaps you could discuss this with a male relative – your father or brother perhaps? – and come back tomorrow? And surely you don't mean it about buying a motorcycle? I should hate to see *my* daughter even riding on one of those things, and as for driving one, well, I'm sure it's unsafe for a woman.'

'No one complained when I used a motorcycle to serve my country during the war, carrying messages and documents round London for the War Office,' she snapped. 'Nor did General Mortonhoe complain when I rushed him across Lodon sitting in my sidecar to get to an emergency meeting.' She waited a moment for that to sink in, then said quietly, 'Please close my account at once and give me back the money I've earned working for the war effort!'

As the sulky-faced teller began to count out the notes, she added, aiming her words at the manager's back as he walked away, 'And you can be sure that I'll write to your head office and tell them exactly why I've withdrawn my money from this bank.' She'd learned about that sort of thing too from Lady Bingram. Don't just accept bad treatment. Complain about it to whoever is in charge and do so confidently.

As she walked home, Ellen's anger faded and she admitted to herself that she'd acted hastily. She should have waited to close her account until she'd found another bank. Oh, well, she could easily do that when she had an hour free. She'd only chosen that one because it had a branch near the place where she lived and worked. Banks were all pretty much the same, after all.

But would other returned soldiers be the same as that teller, acting scornfully towards the women who'd worked so hard to keep things going on the home front? Surely not?

That evening Lady Bingram joined the other women at their meal. Her husband was a semi-invalid now and rarely came up to London, so she often ate informally with the aides, refusing to stand on ceremony or even allow them to address her by her title. 'I have some news,' she said once the pudding had been eaten. 'The influenza epidemic is putting a great deal of pressure on hospitals, which are already busy catering for wounded servicemen, and Major Bradley has asked me if I'll turn this house into a temporary nursing home for those with no family to look after them once they start to recover. So I'd appreciate it if those of you who are able to will stay on and help me look after people.'

Several of the women cheered and one called, 'We didn't want to go home anyway.'

Lady Bingram smiled. 'I didn't want to lose you, either. But you realise you'll be putting yourselves at risk by doing so? I'm told this particular influenza kills more younger people than old.'

'Just let it try!'

Once again they were a team, serving their fellow citizens, and there was great satisfaction and pride in that.

They were so busy the next day reorganising the house that Ellen didn't get a chance to go out and find a new bank. So she asked her ladyship to put the money in her safe and knowing it would be all right there, promptly forgot about it, because almost immediately they were working day and night to care for the sick.

The influenza epidemic got worse and worse. Many people in the streets were wearing gauze masks, some smaller shops had closed 'Due to illness' and two of the aides had to rush home to nurse family members. One aide's young brother died.

There had never been an influenza epidemic as bad, people were saying, and certainly Ellen and the others saw for themselves how it seemed to turn quickly into a severe form of pneumonia for some sufferers. Even when it didn't, many of those who'd been sick were weak and took a long time to recover.

Christmas passed in a blur. The aides were too busy to celebrate, though Lady Bingram bought each of them a dress length as a present, in beautiful fine wool, each piece the exact colour needed to bring out the best in its recipient. How she'd found such material in wartime was a mystery, but then she always had been good at finding things when no one else could. 'I've engaged a seamstress to make them up and I'm choosing the styles for you,' she said with one of her mischievous smiles. 'Mrs Clarence needs the work now that she's not helping to make uniforms, so you can't refuse.'

In February one of the aides caught the influenza and died so quickly they were all shocked rigid. Ellen and Mary Ann were chosen to go with Lady Bingram to the funeral. They stood in the bitterly cold church during the short service, which was limited to a brief ten minutes because there were so many being buried each day.

Her ladyship drove the car herself and was unusually quiet. 'I think we've all had enough of death,' she said as they stopped in the mews behind her house.

Both young women nodded.

When Ellen woke the next morning, her head was thumping with pain and she felt weak and achy. She called out to the girl in the next bed, 'Jenny, I've got the flu.' Her voice was little more than a croak and Jenny didn't stir, so she leaned across and pulled the covers off her friend. 'I've got the influenza.'

She was so dizzy the other girls had to help her down to the makeshift ward and put her in a bed there. It felt strange to be so helpless and she wondered vaguely if she was going to die, but couldn't even raise the energy to worry about it, because her whole body was aching.

Seth was woken a few mornings later by the elderly corporal coming into his room. 'What's the matter?'

'Jim's not well, Sarge.'

It took only one look for Seth to realise that it was the influenza. He'd had a mild dose a few months ago and had thought nothing of it. There was usually some sort of influenza going round most winters. But this one had turned into an epidemic, then into something worse: a pandemic, which was a new word to him. The influenza was sweeping the country, killing hundreds of people, disrupting the normal life they'd all been longing for.

He got up and tied a handkerchief round his face then went to look at Jim. The poor lad had it badly, with dark marks on the skin of his cheeks and a sunken look to his eyes. Seth raised his voice. 'Don't come near him. Get dressed as quickly as you can and assemble outside.'

'But Sarge—'

'*Do as I say!* And on the double! Don't even think

of making your beds.' A doctor had told him once that influenza was passed on by aerial droplets that were inhaled, so he felt it urgent to get the others out of reach.

When he was dressed, Seth went to the door and bellowed. 'Fetch the Medical Officer. Wake him if necessary and tell him it's urgent. And no one is to come in here without my express permission. Corporal, a bit of marching will soon warm them up.'

He waited by the door, knowing he could do nothing to help the poor lad. A friend of his worked in a military hospital and had written him a horror story describing the outbreak, the full details of which were being kept quiet for fear of alarming the rank and file.

And now the scourge had come to their camp.

The MO came hurrying across the parade ground and Seth explained the situation.

As they looked at Jim, the MO shook his head. 'We've got two men down with it in C Squad as well. But he's worse than they are.' He gazed round. 'I think we'll turn this hut into a temporary hospital, because it's well away from the others. Will you run it for me, Talbot? I'll not hide from you that it's a dangerous job, so I'm only taking volunteers.'

'Yes, of course I'll do it, sir. I had the influenza a few months ago, so I may have some resistance to it.'

'Good man. I'll get the gear sent across for nursing them and assign orderlies and nurses as necessary.' He hurried off, looking as if he had the cares of the world on his shoulders.

During the next few weeks, Seth found himself

in charge of an ever-changing set of nurses and orderlies, some of whom became patients themselves, in spite of the masks they all wore over mouth and nose in an attempt to avoid transmission of the disease. Day blurred into night and he slept when he could.

All too many times he sat by the bedside of boys, for most of the lads in this camp were very young, and watched helplessly as they died struggling in vain for breath or drowning in bloody froth.

One day they sent him no new patients, the next day one, then gradually no more, so that the temporary ward emptied. When the last lad had been discharged to finish recovering at home, Seth sat numbly in his office, too exhausted to think what to do next.

A hand on his shoulder made him suddenly aware that the Captain was standing beside him, but he couldn't even find the strength to stand up and salute.

'It really is over now, Talbot. No, don't bother to get up.'

They were both silent for a moment or two.

'Nearly as bad as the trenches,' the Captain said gruffly.

'Yes. I can't believe it's over.'

'As far as you're concerned, it is. Any new cases can go to the regular hospital. I'm going to arrange an immediate discharge for you. You've earned it, if anyone has. I want to offer you the Regiment's thanks for all you've done.'

'Yes, sir. Thank you, sir.'

Seven days later he was on his way home to Manchester, wearing civilian clothing.

The Captain had hinted that his name had been put forward for another medal for his 'selfless work caring for the sick'. As if he wanted it!

2

Ellen was one of the lucky ones and didn't get the influenza too badly, but she was slower to recover than she'd expected. By the end of March she was feeling more her old self again, however.

In early April a letter arrived from her stepfather.

Dear Ellen,

It's about time you stopped being so selfish and thought of your family. Your mother isn't well and needs your help. Now that the war is over she worries about you racketing around London with a bunch of giddy girls. And so do I. We shall expect to see you soon.

Bevan Halsopp

P.S. Jory Nelson's just got demobbed. He asked me to give his regards to you.

After reading and rereading it, she took it to show Lady Bingram.

'You must go and see your mother, of course, but don't let them bully you into staying in Shawcroft if that's not what you want. You can always come back here if you need to until you find your feet, or to our house in Hampshire once I've closed this place down. You know that, I hope?'

'Yes.' Ellen smiled and suddenly dared to give her ladyship a hug, finding to her surprise that it was reciprocated. 'I'm going to miss you. You've been wonderful.'

'So have you. All I had was a bunch of untrained girls and women when we started, who couldn't even drive. Look at you all now.'

'I don't want to leave.'

'The emergency is passing. You'd have to be going soon anyway, like a fledgling leaving the nest. I'll give you a letter to show to any prospective employers, who may also contact me for references, naturally. And I'll make sure the War Office does the same.'

'Even with that, it's going to be hard to find an interesting job. Other employers aren't like you, Daphne. They not only pay women less than men but keep them in the background.'

'I always was a rebel. Don't let them crush you, Ellen dear. Mr Lloyd George may talk about "a fit country for heroes" but I'd like to see a fit country for heroines too, even if we have to fight another sort of battle to win it. What shall you do about the motor-cycle?'

'Drive back on it, of course.'

'Good girl.' She glanced at the letter again. 'Who's this Jory Nelson?'

'I was engaged to him once, but I broke it off.' She didn't explain why, had always refused to explain that to anyone, her stepfather included. He'd been furious at her treating the son of his old friend so badly but she'd never change her mind about Jory.

Ellen sent a letter to her mother to say she was coming back to Lancashire later in the week and hoped they could put her up for a day or two, but wasn't quite sure exactly when she'd arrive as she'd be driving. She decided to travel in her aide's uniform, because it was more practical, consisting as it did of boots and trousers with a knee-length tunic coat over them and a very smart cap, all in a dark, practical brown. She'd wear the matching waterproof raincoat and leggings over it all to drive and tie the cap on very firmly with a scarf.

But oh, she didn't want to go! If it wasn't for her mother, she'd find somewhere else in Lancashire to live, far away from her stepfather – and from Jory Nelson and his cronies too. Trust *him* to have survived the war, when so many better men had been killed!

In the small Lancashire village of Little Fairworthy, Veronica Gresham hurried through the milking, clearing everything up with her usual scrupulous attention to cleanliness, then left her boots on the back porch and ran up to her bedroom to get changed. She intended to wear something far more attractive tonight than her Women's Land Army uniform of green jumper, corduroy trousers and mud-spattered leggings. She was going out with Giles Covington again and had been looking forward to it all day.

When she was ready she looked at herself in the

mirror, took off the spectacles, then shook her head and put them on again because everything was blurred without their help. She had no need to pretend with Giles, didn't want to.

The other land girl who shared the bedroom with her came padding up the stairs in her stockinged feet and stopped in the doorway to smile across at her. 'Going out with him again tonight, Ronnie?'

'Yes.'

'You look nice. That blue really suits you and these shorter skirts show off your ankles. When are you going to bring him back to meet us?'

'Never. I'm keeping him to myself.' It wasn't exactly a joke. She didn't feel at all confident about her own ability to keep a man's interest and felt a deep sense of relief every time Giles asked to see her again, even after three months.

'He must seriously like you and yet you're still afraid of losing him, aren't you?'

Ronnie shrugged. You couldn't hide things from someone when you lived and worked so closely together. 'I'm not pretty like you. I've never been successful with men.'

'But you *are* successful with Giles.' Cora came across to stand behind her and smile down at their joint images in the mirror. 'It only takes one man, you know. He's a widower, isn't he?'

'Yes. His wife died of TB early in the war. He has two sons, and his wife's mother looks after them. He wants me to meet them all next Sunday.'

'That's a good sign.'

'Yes. Only I don't know anything about children, so I'll probably make a mess of it.'

'Oh, Ronnie, what are we going to do with you? I'd hug you, but I'm all dirty. You're a kind, lovely person and I'm not surprised this Giles is courting you. He's lucky to get someone as nice as you.'

Those words heartened Ronnie as she hurried down the lane to the village pub and went into the lounge bar. They'd been meeting here all through the influenza epidemic, sure somehow that they'd not catch it. And they hadn't.

Giles rose to greet her, tall and rather bony, straw-coloured hair thinning, but with the widest smile in the whole world. 'Good. You got away early. What do you want to drink?'

'Lemonade, please.'

'No G and T tonight?' he teased.

She smiled as she shook her head. She had no head for alcohol and never touched it if she could help it. The drink was only an excuse for sitting here with him.

When he brought her glass across and sat down again, he clasped her hand in his and gave her another of his wonderful smiles. 'It's all arranged for next Sunday. Bernice is putting on a special lunch for us. I'm borrowing my friend's car again and I'll pick you up at eleven o'clock.'

'Giles—' She hesitated, then confessed, 'I feel nervous about meeting your sons. I've not had much to do with children. My sister sends hers to boarding school and anyway, they live in Hertfordshire now.'

'I'd never do that to my pair, send them away I mean. I want to be with them, see them growing up, make sure no one hurts them. And it's great fun playing with them. You'll see.'

Imagine having a father who cared so deeply for you. She could barely remember her own, who'd died when she was five. And in her world nearly everyone sent their children away to be educated from the age of eight. She'd hated her own school with a passion. They'd said she was stupid and she felt it sometimes because she was so desperately shy she never dared ask the teachers for extra help. And she got things wrong because she couldn't see the blackboard properly. She knew now that she should have been wearing glasses from an early age, but her mother said they made her look ugly and weakened the eyes, so had refused to let her have them, even for reading.

'Now where did you just go?' Giles asked softly. 'Your eyes glazed over and you looked – hurt.'

'I was thinking about school, how much I hated it, how bad I was at everything.'

'No wonder if you weren't allowed to wear glasses.' He peered at her face. 'Actually, I think they suit you, draw attention to your eyes, and pretty eyes they are too.' He shook his head and waggled one finger at her. 'No, I'm not just saying that. I'll never lie to you, my darling. Your mother must be mad to forbid you to wear them.'

'I sometimes think she is. She didn't believe school-work was important anyway, only riding and knowing how to behave in company and that sort of thing.'

She hesitated, then added in a small voice, 'I'm terrified of her, always have been. Even now. She's so big and loud and bossy.'

'So I've gathered. But once we're married I'll be able to protect you from her.' He took her hand. 'You *are* going to marry me, aren't you, Ronnie darling?'

She bowed her head, her eyes filling with tears of both joy and despair. 'I want to – oh, so much! – but Mummy would never agree.'

'You don't need her permission. You're twenty-five years old.'

'She always finds a way to get what she wants.'

'Darling, we can get married first then tell her, if you'd prefer it.'

'She'd find a way to annul it.'

He laughed. 'You can't do that when two consenting adults over twenty-one marry because they love one another and then consummate the marriage.'

'In that case she'd ruin you, and she *can* do that, especially if you're going to set up your own practice. She's ruined others who've upset her. I've seen her do it. I couldn't bear that to happen to you, Giles. Think of all the people who depend on you, your sons, your mother-in-law.'

Tears ran down her cheeks and splashed on to their joined hands as she desperately tried to make him understand. 'You don't know how ferociously determined my mother is when she wants something. And what she wants now that my brother is dead is for me to marry Algie St Corbin and for him to take over the family estate because he's a gentle sort of person and she'll be able to boss him around. I sometimes think the estate is the only thing she truly cares about in the whole world, which is strange because it comes from my father's side of the family.'

Giles took out a handkerchief and wiped her eyes, kissing her cheeks as he did so. 'I think I can stand up for myself, darling. And I'm a lawyer, a professional man, so not quite beyond the pale as a husband, surely? Now that I've been demobbed, I'll be able to find somewhere to set up shop – I'm not staying where I am now old Henderson is dead – then I can make a proper life for all of us. I'm sure your mother will come round when she sees that you won't change your mind.'

Ronnie shook her head and repeated, 'You don't know her.' She took the handkerchief and blew her nose. 'Now, let's not talk about *her* any more tonight. I don't want to – spoil things.'

'We'll have to talk about her sometime, about this whole situation. Make plans.'

'Later. Tell me about your children now. I don't want to say or do the wrong thing. And then I want to hear if you've had any luck in finding a new practice to join. Weren't you going to see somewhere at the weekend . . . ?'

Seth arrived in the north and felt instantly at home. In Manchester it was raining. He smiled at the shiny grey slate roofs and the water-darkened pavements, cocked his head to listen to the slow Lancashire voices – it was just like the scenes of his childhood.

He was going to see his old mentor, who should have retired from the police force by now but had stayed on because of the war and then the influenza.

Sergeant Roswell was behind the desk in the police station, smiling benignly at the world. He had a little less hair and a little more stomach than the last time Seth had seen him, but didn't look anything like his age. His smile broadened when he saw who had just come in and he raised one eyebrow as he looked at the civilian clothing. 'Have they let you out of the Army at last, then, Seth lad?'

'Yes, sir.'

'Where are you staying? With your family?'

'No. They've no spare beds. I'll find a room for a night or two.'

'You'll come home with me, then. Millie's already got the spare room ready in case.'

'Thank you, sir. That's very kind of you.'

'I think you could call me Bert now, don't you? As one sergeant to another.' He saluted and there was no mockery in his face.

Seth returned his salute and nodded. 'Bert it is, then.'

The Sergeant lifted the desk flap. 'Come through to the back and have a cup of tea. I've only an hour to go before the night officer takes over, and it's usually quiet at this time of day.'

Sitting in the small office sipping tea from an enamel cup made Seth feel he was really home. Oh, he'd go and see his family and his uncle and youngest brother, but Phil was too young to have served in the Army and his uncle had been too old, so none of them understood what it had been like in France. And he had a feeling that Bert did, because he'd fought in the Boer War and anyway, he was a very wise man.

'I got your letter. So you want to be a village bobby now, eh?' Bert stirred three spoonfuls of sugar into his tea.

'Yes. I don't know if it's what I want for ever, but I need some peace and quiet.' To his embarrassment, Seth's voice wobbled.

Bert patted his arm. 'There are a lot of chaps in the same boat, nothing to be ashamed of, lad. I'd think worse of you if the war hadn't left its mark on you or if you'd been brutalised by it. I give you three years, five at most as a village bobby, then you'll be wanting to come back into the City.'

Hope rose in Seth. 'Back from where?'

'Shawcroft. Wes Cobbley came out of retirement for the war, but it's time he handed over to a younger man. So I put in a word for you with an old friend of mine.'

From the tone of his voice, Seth immediately realised that Bert didn't like this Wes Cobbley, but he didn't ask why because he knew Bert wouldn't tell him. His friend never spoke ill of anyone, except for the most hardened of criminals.

'The appointment's been approved already?'

'It has.' Bert smiled into his tea. 'I knew Inspector Dunham, the chap in charge of that district, when he was a little lad, knew his father too. He didn't refuse me a favour and he trusted my word that you're a good policeman.'

Seth closed his eyes and a long shudder of relief went through him. Then he opened them again to say, 'Thank you,' in a choked voice.

'If I was you,' Bert said, 'I'd go and poke around Shawcroft for a day or two before introducing myself. Get to know the place, meet a few people, that sort of thing. You could say you were looking for somewhere to settle. There are a few lads who've been demobbed wandering round the countryside, wondering where to live now. They've not all got jobs to come home to – or they don't want their old jobs. It scars everyone, war does, one way or another.'

After a wonderful meal and a lot of motherly fussing from Mrs Roswell, Seth slept better than he had for months in the comfortable back bedroom of their neat terraced house.

On the Saturday Veronica scalded and tidied away the milking equipment and went to tell her employer that everything was done for the morning. She was intending to wash her hair and do her nails, because she wanted to look her best the next day when she met Giles's family. Just as she was about to sit down for a cup of tea with Mr and Mrs Tilling and Cora, there was the sound of a motor car in the lane and they looked at each other in surprise.

'Who can that be?' Mrs Tilling wondered aloud in her placid voice. 'We're not expecting anyone, are we, love?'

'No. It'll be someone who's lost their way, I dare say.'

The car stopped and there was the sound of footsteps crunching on the gravel.

Mr Tilling got up. 'I'll go and see who it is. You girls have earned your rest.'

He was back a moment later, tight-faced, as if annoyed about something. 'It's for you, Ronnie love. Your mother. She wants you to join her in the car. She won't come in, wouldn't even speak to me, it was the chauffeur who gave me the message.'

She looked at him in horror. 'My mother? Whatever can she want?'

'Only one way to find out.'

It was a minute before she could force herself to her feet. Cora squeezed her hand as she passed and whispered, 'She can't eat you.'

But nothing would lighten the feeling of apprehension that sat like lead in Ronnie's chest. Outside, Tadwyn, who had been with the family as a groom and made the change to driving a motor car reluctantly, opened the car door for her so that she could get in next to her mother.

When she tried to talk standing beside the car, her mother said irritably, 'Do get in. I don't intend to sit here in a draught.'

Ronnie did as she was told, feeling like a condemned prisoner being locked in a cell.

'You look a perfect fright, Veronica.' Edwina Gresham frowned as she ran her eyes up and down her daughter. 'Ruddy cheeks like a milkmaid and what are you wearing *those things* for?' She gestured towards the spectacles and reached out a hand to take them off.

Ronnie put up a hand to protect them. 'Because I can't see properly without them.'

'Of course you can.'

'No, I *can't*! It's worse now than when I was at school. Everything's a total blur without them.'

'That's because your eyes have grown weaker, dependent on them. They'll soon improve if you stop relying on them. And you'll look so much better. Men aren't attracted to women who wear spectacles.'

It was typical of her mother to start by attacking her and making her feel ugly. Ronnie didn't waste her time trying to argue. Once her mother had made up her mind about something, that was that. Her heart was fluttering in her chest and she felt physically sick.

'You haven't asked me why I'm here.'

'Why *are* you here, Mummy?'

'To take you home, darling.'

'I can't go home yet. I'm still needed here.'

'If I'd had my way, you'd never have joined the Women's Land Army in the first place, but no, you sneaked out and signed up. Well, you've been putting me off for long enough with silly excuses about the problems Mr Tilling is having finding a replacement, so—'

'I was *needed* because of the influenza!'

'Don't interrupt, please. I suppose your manners have slipped along with your appearance. So anyway, I decided to come and fetch you. You're to come home with me this very day and I'm not taking any excuses.'

Ronnie stared at her in horror, unable to speak for a moment in shock. 'But – what about my work here?

Who'll do it? Mr Tilling's son hasn't been demobbed yet, he's still overseas.'

'Who cares? The war's long over and they ought to have found someone else to do the job by now, a man. Farm labouring is no job for a woman. Your skin is horribly windblown. We'll have to work on getting it soft and white again.' She paused to stare at her daughter. 'I'd have thought you'd be pleased to come home.'

She wasn't, but didn't dare say so. 'They rely on me. I *can't* just up and leave.'

'I'm not taking no for an answer. Go and tell this Tilling person that you're leaving then pack your things. And don't be too long about it. It's boring sitting here in this foul-smelling yard.'

'I can't leave today. I've got ... things to do, a luncheon engagement tomorrow. I'll come home next week – or the week after.'

'That'll be too late. Algie's been demobbed at last and he's been asking about you. If you play your cards right, you can catch him before anyone else does.'

'Catch him?'

'Oh, darling, don't be so obtuse!' She tapped the third finger of her left hand. 'Get his ring where it belongs, on your hand not another woman's.'

'*Marry Algie?* I couldn't. He's like a brother to me.'

The smile vanished from Edwina's face and her expression became vicious. 'You'll do as I tell you, young lady. And this time I'll make sure you don't mess things up. I intend to have you married to him within six weeks. I've already spoken to his parents and we're all in favour of the match.'

'Has anyone asked Algie what he wants?'

'He'll do as his family tells him, just as you will. He's only a second son and marrying you is the best chance he'll ever have to get an estate of his own. If your brother hadn't stupidly volunteered, I could have found him a war job, then he wouldn't have got himself killed. If he was still alive, the matter of you marrying wouldn't be so urgent, though I'd never approve of anyone who wasn't the right sort. But as it is, we need to get an heir for Gresham Park, a male heir, and the sooner the better.'

'I can't marry Algie. I've met someone else.' As soon as the words were out of her mouth, Ronnie regretted it.

'Then you can just un-meet him. I know best what's good for you, and I always have done, you're so stupidly weak.' Her eyes narrowed. 'Who is he? Another farm hand?'

'He's perfectly respectable. He's a lawyer.'

'Do I know his family?'

'I shouldn't think so. He's frightfully clever, won a special scholarship to Oxford and—'

'If I don't know his family, he won't *do*.'

Ronnie screwed up her courage. 'He'll do just fine for me. He's asked me to marry him and I've said yes. I'm going to meet his children tomorrow.'

'*Children?*'

'He's a widower with two little sons.'

'Then you're definitely not marrying him. You fool, the sons will inherit, not your children. Have you no sense? Go and pack your things at once.'

Ronnie shook her head. 'I'm sorry, Mummy, but I'm not coming back yet and I *am* going to marry – him.' She changed what she had been going to say, because she didn't want her mother finding out Giles's name.

Edwina Gresham glared at her daughter, then grasped her wrist with one hand and took the speaking tube in the other. 'Drive home at once, Tadwyn, and pay no attention to what happens here in the back. My daughter is not well.'

Ronnie fumbled for the door handle, but her mother was so much bigger and stronger than her and not only kept hold of her wrist but somehow managed to twist her arm behind her back, so that it was excruciating to move.

She screamed for help and continued screaming as the car reversed down the lane. As the car turned, she saw Cora at the farmhouse door, with Mr Tilling behind her, staring open-mouthed at the car. But before they could come to her help, the vehicle had gathered speed and turned into the main road.

'Get home as fast as you can!' Edwina shouted.

Ronnie tried to wriggle round, but her mother put so much pressure on the arm that she cried out in pain. Her mother didn't let up the pressure for the whole hour it took to drive back to the Hall, by which time Ronnie was in agony.

Only when they stopped did Edwina let go of the arm and call, 'Help me, Tadwyn! Miss Veronica is unwell. I think she's delirious.'

As soon as she was free, Ronnie hit out at her

mother with the arm that hadn't been twisted and scrambled out of the car. But Tadwyn was waiting for her and her mother called over the farm manager, who was working nearby. Between them, he and Gerry held her firmly while Mrs Gresham mopped her bleeding nose, stared at the red stains on her handkerchief in incredulity, then got out of the car.

She came across to where the two men were holding her daughter, took the spectacles from Ronnie's face, dropped them on the ground and stamped on them. Then she slapped her daughter hard across the face, first one cheek then the other. 'Bring her into the house.'

She led the way, snapping 'Get out of the way! My daughter's ill,' to the middle-aged housemaid who opened the front door. 'We'll put her in one of the spare bedrooms,' she said as they got to the first landing.

Throwing open the door to the sparsely furnished bedroom on the floor above she said to the two men, 'Keep her here till I fetch some medicine. As you can see, she's very disturbed.'

Then she went for the sleeping drops she used regularly herself. 'Hold her nose.'

As her daughter gasped for breath she dripped enough liquid into Ronnie's mouth to send her soundly to sleep. She held her lips together in a vice-like grip until Ronnie had no choice but to choke it down.

'Please stay here until she falls asleep. I must go and call Dr Hilliam, tell him that my poor girl has had a nervous breakdown.'

When she'd gone, Gerry looked at Tadwyn, who shook his head in a silent warning not to speak.

'How can you let her do this?' Ronnie sobbed. 'It's kidnapping.'

'She's your mother,' Tadwyn said.

'I'm twenty-five! She has no rights over me now, none at all.'

He sighed. 'You of all people should know, Miss Veronica, that it does no good to go against the mistress's wishes. You should apologise tomorrow then do as she says. You know you will in the end.'

'Not this time, I promise you. Please, if you have any kindness in you at all, send a message to the farm where I was working. Mr Tilling, Overlea Farm, Little Fairworthy. I have friends there who'll be worried. They don't even know what's happened to me. *Please!* At least let them know.'

'You know I can't go against your mother, Miss Veronica,' Tadwyn said quietly.

She began to sob. 'I hope you can both live with your consciences.'

When Ronnie was asleep, the tears drying on her cheeks, Tadwyn looked at the farm manager. 'You can go now, Gerry lad. And not a word to anyone about this.'

'It doesn't seem fair to do this to the poor lass.'

'You've an estate cottage as well as a job here. If you want to keep them both, you'll hold your tongue about what's happened.'

Shaking his head, Gerry went away. Tadwyn turned to look at the still figure on the bed. Miss Veronica was a fool. Mrs Gresham was one of the most determined and cunning people he'd ever met, always able to get what she wanted, even during a war. He had no patience with fools, never had had. And he knew which side his own bread was buttered on.

Still, it did seem a pity to treat her so harshly. She'd always been a nice lass, as civil as you please to the servants.

But you did what you had to in this world, not what you wanted, and he didn't want to jeopardise his job until he had enough money to retire in comfort.

On Sunday morning Giles drove up to the farm, humming under his breath, looking forward to seeing Ronnie and introducing her to his family. *She* might be nervous about the meeting, but he was sure they'd love her. She was so gentle and kind, how could anyone not?

Since Ronnie didn't come hurrying out to greet him as usual, he rapped on the front door. It was opened by the other land girl. 'Ronnie not ready yet?'

'No. You'd better come in. I'm afraid there's some bad news.'

'She's not ill?'

'We don't think so, but . . . Look, come in first. We can't talk on the doorstep.' She led him into the kitchen where Mr and Mrs Tilling were sitting, both looking very uncomfortable.

He joined them. 'Just tell me.'

Cora cleared her throat. 'Well, Ronnie's mother turned up yesterday just after we'd finished the morning chores. She wouldn't come in, insisted Ronnie go out to speak to her in the car. The poor girl looked so worried and upset. And then suddenly we heard Ronnie screaming and shouting. When we got to the door, the car was driving away and she was struggling with her mother in the back. Her mother's a very large woman and you know how tiny Ronnie is.'

'No way of catching up with it,' Mr Tilling said apologetically. 'And that was the last we saw or heard of her.'

'All her clothes and things are here still,' Cora added. 'So she can't have been expecting to leave. We don't know what to do. You can hardly go to the police about a mother taking her daughter away.'

'Oh, can't you!' he said grimly. 'Ronnie's terrified of her mother. I thought she was exaggerating about the woman, but apparently not.'

'What are you going to do?' Cora asked.

'I don't know yet. No use rushing in until I know exactly what the situation is. But at least we can guess where she is. I'm not letting Ronnie go, so will you please tell me everything you can remember about her family . . . I know roughly where they live, but I don't have their exact address.'

'It'll be among Ronnie's things,' Cora said.

'Take him upstairs,' Mrs Tilling said. 'Maybe you'll be able to find some clue about what's happened.'

As they entered the bedroom Cora said, 'She was terrified of that mother of hers.'

'So I gathered.'

'She kept writing to Ronnie, ordering her to go

home.' She hesitated then pulled a bundle of letters out of the bottom drawer. 'Ronnie never threw anything away. These made her cry sometimes.'

Together they read the letters. Giles found them harsh, full of orders and angry complaints about Ronnie not returning home. 'She told me about Algie once. He's the younger son of a neighbour. Mrs Gresham wanted her to marry him, so did his parents, but he joined the Army before they could force it through.'

Cora nodded. 'That was one of the reasons Ronnie didn't want to go home when the war ended.'

'I shouldn't have waited,' Giles said. 'I should just have married her out of hand and told her mother to go hang.'

'I'd have helped you, but you know Ronnie. She doesn't like to hurt anyone, always tries to do the right thing.'

'That mother of hers doesn't sound the sort of person to be hurt easily.'

'No. But you could never persuade Ronnie of that.' Cora began to tie up the letters again. 'What are you going to do?'

'I don't know.'

'I don't think it'd be any use writing to Ronnie. She once told me her mother used to open and read all her mail.'

He went to stare bleakly out of the window. 'I think I'll go and visit this Shawcroft place, see what I can find out about the occupants of the Hall.'

'Do you want me to come with you?'

He looked at her in surprise.

'Well, if we seem to be a couple, maybe no one will realise you've come about Ronnie.'

He thought for a moment, then nodded. 'Thank you. Can you get away?'

'If we can find someone to replace me here.'

'I'll pick you up the day after tomorrow, if that's all right.'

When he was down the road he pulled in to the side and thumped his clenched fists against the steering wheel several times. 'I'll get you out of it, my love,' he promised. 'Whatever it takes, I'll get you out of her clutches.'

3

Ellen took three days to drive back to Lancashire. She could easily have made it in two, but she wanted to enjoy the beginnings of peacetime and see something of the countryside on the way. As she'd expected, people commented on a woman driving a motorbike on her own, some of them in a very disapproving way.

But younger women envied her and at a country pub where she stayed one night, she gave the landlord's daughter a spin on the motorbike.

'I wanted to join one of the women's organisations,' the woman said wistfully, 'but I had a baby instead, and since its father was killed before he could marry me – which he would have done! – I just had to count myself lucky that my parents didn't throw me out. They love my little Alan now, though, so it's all right.'

Strange that she was so envious of their guest, because when Ellen saw the lovely three-year-old boy, she envied the landlord's daughter. She had always expected to be married by twenty-one, but had wasted her time with Jory, then the war had intervened.

She wished she didn't have to meet him again. After what had happened, she'd as soon spit in his face as be polite to him.

Well, she'd be arriving in Shawcroft the following day, so had better steel herself. It was too small a place to avoid somebody. It called itself a town, but it was really a slightly overgrown village, a long narrow place nestled in a valley on the edge of the moors.

It was with mixed feelings that she set off again on the final leg of her trip on the Saturday morning.

On the Saturday, since it promised to be fine if chilly, Seth took a train to Rochdale with the intention of walking over the tops to Shawcroft. It was a roundabout route, and he could have got closer by going to Littleborough, but he wanted a good long tramp to fill his lungs with bracing moorland air. He took a small knapsack with a change of clothes, because he would probably be staying overnight.

He wasn't going to introduce himself to this fellow Cobbley, because he reckoned he deserved a few days' rest before starting work and anyway, he wanted to see what the man was like.

He took a bus to the edge of town, then followed a track across the tops, stopping for lunch and a pint of ale at a tiny pub looking down on Rochdale. Then he struck out towards Shawcroft. It had clouded over now and looked as if it might rain later, but he hoped to get there before it started. If not, well, he'd been wet and cold often enough before. At least no one would be shooting at him this time.

It was as he was approaching the road that led down into Shawcroft that he saw the motorbike and sidecar stopped by the roadside, with a young woman on her knees beside it, trying to untangle the chain, which had come off.

She didn't seem to have noticed him approaching, so he called, 'Hello, there. Can I help?' before he got close, not wanting to startle her.

'Not unless you happen to have a spare chain in that knapsack of yours,' she said ruefully untangling the last few links. 'I drove all over London during the war and this only happened to me once before. I knew the chain was getting a bit slack but I thought it'd get me here. I was going to get my Uncle Martin to replace it. He's a mechanic.' She held out the chain in an oil-stained hand, a firm, capable looking hand. She had a cheerful, rosy face and didn't seem to mind that she was dirty.

'It's unusual to see a woman driving a motorcycle.'

'I've been doing it for years. I was a member of Lady Bingram's Aides until recently and we drove bigwigs and messages all over London during the war. I loved it.'

'Some of those voluntary groups did wonderful work to support us,' he said.

'You're an ex-soldier.' It wasn't a question.

'Is it that obvious?'

'Yes. There's something about the way soldiers hold themselves.'

He gave the motorcycle a fond look. 'I've driven quite a few of these. Very reliable if they're well looked after.' He flourished a salute at her. 'Sergeant Seth Talbot at your service.'

She held out her hand, then looked at it and grimaced. 'Better not shake or you'll get dirty too. I'm Ellen Dawson.'

'Pleased to meet you, Miss Dawson. What brings you to these parts?'

'My mother and stepfather live in Shawcroft. He says she's ill, but I want to see that for myself.' She looked at the sky and fumbled in the sidecar for a rag. 'It looks like it's going to rain shortly. I'd better walk to the nearest farm and ask if they can take my motor-cycle into Shawcroft on a cart. Pity I didn't break down a bit further along because it's all downhill from there.' She pointed to the crest of a hill about half a mile ahead.

'I could help you push it to the top of the hill if you like, then you can freewheel down. I'm going to Shawcroft myself.'

'That'd be a wonderful help.'

She beamed at him and there was something so wholesome and attractive about her that he found himself not only returning the smile but studying her. She was tall for a woman, not much shorter than himself, with brown curly hair cut short in one of the new styles. And when their eyes met, he didn't want to look away, so continued to smile at her, noting the colour rise just a little in her cheeks.

'Do you have relatives in Shawcroft, Mr Talbot?'

'No. I've never been there before. I'm going to be the new village constable when Mr Cobbley retires, but I hope you won't tell anyone that, because I came to have a quiet look round before anyone knows who I am.'

'Reconnoitring?'

'Yes. Seems a wise thing to do in a new situation. Well, let's start pushing. Is it all right if I put my knapsack in the sidecar?'

'Of course.'

It was a stiff push to the top of the hill and they paused for a rest by unspoken consent when they got there.

'You'll be all right now,' he said.

'Why don't you ride in with me? It'll be quicker than walking and it's going to rain soon.'

He looked at her quizzically. 'I think that might give people the wrong idea about us, don't you?'

'I've stopped caring what narrow-minded people think. You might as well have a ride. You must have had a long walk across the moors from the direction you were coming.'

'I enjoy a tramp. But I will ride with you if you don't mind.' He checked that the sidecar roof was fastened down, waited for her to get on the motorcycle then mounted behind her. Which wasn't a good idea, because when pressed against the closeness of a soft, female body, his own body started getting the wrong idea. But it was too late to say anything, so he helped paddle the motorcycle into position with his feet then let her guide them as they freewheeled down the hill.

She drove competently, he could tell that at once, not allowing the bike to gain too much momentum and guiding it just as he would have done himself around the curves.

As they came into the town, he called into her ear, 'You could let me off here.'

'Can't. If I lose momentum I'll not get where I want to go.'

Even so they had to push the bike again up the last slope towards a workshop.

'It's still open, thank goodness!' she said. 'I was afraid he'd have closed up shop for the day, then I'd have to leave the bike and walk round to his house.' She entered confidently, calling, 'Uncle Martin? Are you there?'

A man with receding grizzled hair, wearing stained overalls, came out of the back of the workshop wiping his hands on a bit of rag. 'Ellen! Nice to see you again, flower.'

She went across to give him a hug. 'My motorcycle has broken down. It's just the chain, but it needs replacing. Can you get a new one for me?'

'*Your* motorcycle?'

She nodded. 'It's the one I drove round London during the war. They let me buy it when they didn't need it any longer. Come and see it. Oh, and this is Mr Talbot, who was walking over the moors and kindly helped me push her till we got to the top of the hill. He's just back from the war too.'

The two men studied one another, sizing each other up in that wary way strong men have, then, as if something had been settled between them, shook hands firmly.

'Good thing she found someone to help her,' Martin said. 'Buying a motorcycle! What will you do next, Ellen Mary! I remember you riding my son's bicycle down that hill when you were ten and coming off it.'

She laughed. 'Don't tell Mr Talbot about my childish misdeeds.'

They went outside and stood looking at the motorcycle.

'Nice machine,' Martin said approvingly. 'Been well looked after.'

'I do the servicing myself.'

'You never!'

'Women learned to do a lot of things during the war. How's Paul?'

Martin stared at her in shock. 'He was killed just before the war ended. I told your Mum, asked her to tell you.'

'Oh, no! Why didn't she let me know? I'd have written to you. You must have thought me so heartless! Oh, Uncle Martin, I'm sorry beyond words. I was looking forward to seeing him and . . .'

Seth watched as she hugged the older man again and held on tightly as his shoulders shook. Then Ellen patted his shoulder and stepped back, her own eyes bright with tears.

Seth judged it time to take his leave. 'I must be

going now. I have to find somewhere to stay tonight.'

Martin looked at him. 'Are you on the tramp? You don't look like that sort of fellow.'

'No, I'm just getting some fresh air into my lungs for a few days. I have a job to go to, but I've been running an emergency influenza hospital in the Army for the past few months and I felt I'd earned a few days' rest before I start my new life.'

'You can stay with us if you like. Paul's room is very comfortable and the wife is a good cook.'

'Are you sure?'

'Yes. Jeanie likes to help other soldiers.'

'All right, then, and thank you. But you'll allow me to pay for my board.'

Martin shrugged. 'If you want. We can discuss that later. Now, Ellen love, do you need help carrying your bag?'

'It's not only my bag, but a trunk and a few other things. I've left Lady Bingram's Aides now, so I thought I could leave my things at my mother's while I look for another job.'

He grinned. 'Not going back to work for Mrs Gresham?'

'No! Definitely not. You know how I hated that job.'

'She hasn't changed, still thinks the world revolves round her and her damned estate.'

The two men walked with Ellen along the main street, with Seth pushing her things on a trolley.

'It's a nice motorcycle, that one,' Martin said. 'That

stepfather of yours won't be happy to see a woman with her own vehicle.'

'I don't care what he thinks.'

'That Jory's back and lording it over everyone because he got a medal. He talks about you as if you're still his girl.'

'He can talk all he likes. I finished with him long ago and the reason will always stand between us.'

Martin nodded, his expression going tight, as if he understood the reason and agreed.

Seth had been looking from one to the other, sensing that there were undercurrents in this exchange, but he didn't ask what they were, just wondered who the man was and what he'd done to upset Ellen so greatly. She didn't seem the sort to hold a grudge.

'Your mother will be glad to see you, love. She's not at all well.'

'How bad is she?'

Martin spread his hands helplessly and didn't say anything.

She knew then that her mother was very ill because Uncle Martin would never lie to her. She and Paul had been good friends, closer than most brothers and sisters, since each was an only child, and the Pughs had been like an aunt and uncle to her. Indeed, she couldn't remember a time when she hadn't called them that, though there was no blood relationship involved.

'Want us to carry the things inside?' Seth asked.

'Just into the hall.' She knocked then pushed open the door without waiting. 'I'm back, Mum.'

A voice called from the front room. 'I'm in here, love.'

Martin patted her shoulder and the two men left.

Ellen pushed open the first door to the right in the narrow hall, to find that it'd been made into a bedroom. When she looked at her mother, who was lying in a bed, her heart sank. Her mother had always been thin, but now she was skeletal. Ellen hurried across to hug her and stayed there in the embrace for a minute or two, fighting to control herself. When she was sure she could, she moved gently away.

'What have you been doing with yourself?' she scolded

'I'm dying, Ellen. Let's not pretend, *please*. Bevan won't face it, so I have to pretend I'm getting better, but I know I'm not.'

'Oh, Mum.' She shook her head helplessly, not knowing what to say.

'We all come to it and I'm so tired all the time, I'd be happy to fall asleep and not wake up, not have to struggle . . .' Dorothy's voice trailed away.

'How are you managing the house?'

'Bevan pays Madge to come in every morning, and we always did send a lot of the washing to the laundry. Madge comes in again later to cook the evening meal. We manage fine, love. I told him he'd no need to send for you. I didn't want to spoil your lovely new life.'

'The Aides were disbanding anyway, now the influenza epidemic is dying down. And I'm glad I've come to see you . . . while I can. Bevan said you were worried about me racketing around London, which didn't sound like you.'

'It's him who was worried about you. He's very old-fashioned and he's got a bee in his bonnet about young, unmarried women.' Dorothy sighed and clasped her daughter's hand. 'I know he has his faults, especially where you're concerned, but he's been a loving husband to me.'

'He's a bully.'

'Not with me.'

She disagreed, but then her mother had always been the docile sort and didn't seem to mind being told what to do. Ellen took after her father, she knew, and was far more independent, which had caused a lot of trouble between her and Bevan Halsopp, whom she had obstinately refused to call father, even though he'd thumped her for it.

Dorothy's expression brightened. 'You'll stay for a while then? I asked Madge to get your old room ready in case.'

'Yes, of course I will. I've not come all this way just to take tea with you.' Rain suddenly began to patter on the roof. When she looked out, the sky was black and it was teeming down, rain driving so hard against the window panes that it cut off the world outside.

'Take your things up to your old room,' her mother said.

'I'll need help with the trunk, but I'll take the other bag up.'

'Bevan will be popping home soon so he'll be able

to help you. He always pops home to see me in the afternoons. That new lad of his is very capable.'

Ellen pulled a face as she carried her bag upstairs. She felt sorry for the lad, whoever he was. Bevan had a butcher's shop and was a fanatic about how he wanted things done. Mind, she didn't fault him for wanting things kept clean, just for the way he kept his lads in line with blows and curses. She'd hate to work for him.

She was sitting with her mother when the front door opened and Bevan erupted into the hall, as noisy as ever, shaking his umbrella out of the front door as he called, 'It's only me.'

'Our Ellen's here,' Dorothy said.

'I can see the trunk.' He came in, staring at his step-daughter with a frown. 'There aren't any trains at this time of day, so I suppose some of your fine friends drove you all the way here. Spoiled, your generation are. And were they too fine to take tea with your mother?'

It had started already. Why did he always have to make slighting remarks about her and her new life? 'I drove myself actually.'

'Actually!' he mocked, then realised what she'd said. '*Drove yourself*? Have you borrowed a car then?'

'No. I bought a motorcycle and came on that.'

His colour darkened as he stared at her. 'A motorcycle! How could *you* afford one of those?'

'I saved my wages carefully and bought it second hand from her ladyship.'

'Where is it, then?'

'At Uncle Martin's. The chain broke, so he's repairing it.'

'I don't believe in women driving, *especially* those things. It's indecent sitting astride them with your legs showing.'

Same old tale, she thought, suppressing a sigh. He'd really hated her acquiring new skills, especially ones he didn't possess like driving, and the few times she'd come home for a visit, had told her she should be ashamed of trying to act like a man, even in a war.

'Women don't understand mechanical things,' he stated in that infuriatingly certain way he had.

'We do if someone bothers to teach us. I drove round London all through the war, drove some important people to and from meetings, too, and I was the one who serviced the motorcycle when it needed it.'

'Well, you're not racketing around Shawcroft on it. It's not *decent*.' He looked down and his mouth fell open, then he stabbed a finger at her. 'And you can change out of those trousers before you go out of this house. I'm ashamed to see you wearing them.'

'They're more practical than skirts when you're driving a motorcycle – more decent too.'

But she was wasting her breath, shouldn't even have bothered to answer him back, because he never listened to her.

After expounding for a few minutes on the faults of the current generation of young women and what he expected her to do, he stood up. 'I'll get back to the shop now that you're here to look after your mother. The customers have been very understanding, but there's no need to put them out. And I'll tell Madge she won't be needed.'

'I'm not stopping long,' Ellen said.

'You're needed here.'

'I'm *not* stopping.'

His eyes narrowed and he breathed in deeply. 'We'll talk about that at teatime. I suppose you do remember how to cook?'

'Of course I do. Can you help me with my trunk before you go back, please?'

'I thought you weren't stopping?'

'I need to leave it somewhere. But if you don't have room for it, I'll take it round to my Uncle Martin's.'

He scowled at her, always had done when she talked about the Pughs. 'You'll leave it here, in your home, not with strangers. That man isn't your uncle and well you know it.'

Still grumbling, he helped her lug it up to the attic.

When he'd gone back to work, Dorothy leaned her head back with a weary sigh. 'I'd forgotten how badly the two of you always rub one another up.'

'What did *I* do to rub him up?'

'Wear trousers. I should have noticed and warned you to change into a skirt. It's like a red rag to a bull for him, seeing a woman in trousers. Go and do it now, before you forget. Please, love.'

Ellen opened her mouth to continue her protest but saw how white her mother's face had become and said nothing. It was only for a few days, she told herself. She could put up with his overbearing ways for that long. But even that first encounter had taught her that she couldn't stay in this house for long.

Suddenly she remembered something. 'Why didn't you tell me Paul had been killed?'

He mother stared down, fiddling with the edge of the sheet. 'Bevan thought it was better not to upset you, you were so busy.'

Bevan had been trying to drive a wedge between her and the Pughs, more like. He'd been attempting to do that for years, she had never understood why. But he'd not succeeded. The reason was quite simple. She cared about them and she detested him. She'd forgotten just how much, but it hadn't taken long for her old feelings about him to re-emerge.

If it wasn't for her mother, she'd leave the very next day.

Martin took Seth home via the main street, Rochdale Road, so that he could see the town centre. 'I don't envy her,' he said as they walked past a butcher's shop where a burly, red-faced man was shouting at a lad wearing a blood-stained apron. 'That's her stepfather, Bevan Halsopp. Good butcher. Brute of a man. Only person he cares for in this world, apart from himself, is his wife, and he does care about her, I'll give him that.'

'Ellen told me she's only here for a few days and will be looking for work elsewhere.'

'Her mother's dying. I think she'll have to stay for longer than that. She'd not be our Ellen if she left Shawcroft at a time like this.'

'You're sure Mrs Halsopp is dying?'

'Everyone in town's sure except Halsopp, who insists Dorothy will pick up again once the weather gets warmer. But she'll be lucky if she even sees midsummer.'

'That's sad.'

'Yes. She's a good lass, Ellen. Did you know her in London?'

'No, I only just met her.'

They arrived at a three-storey terraced house just then and Martin led the way inside. 'We timed it well. It's going to pour down any minute now. Jeanie, love, I've brought a visitor.'

A plump, attractive woman came out of a door at the back of the hall, wiping her hands on a cloth.

'This is Seth Talbot. He's just been demobbed and he's walking the war out of his system. He helped our Ellen when her motorcycle broke down.'

'Ellen's back? Oh, that is nice! And she's got a motorcycle? There's a thing. I hope she'll give me a ride on it. If I were young now, I'd have all sorts of adventures before I settled down.'

'I told Mr Talbot he can stay a couple of nights with us. That's all right, isn't it?'

'Of course it is. I'll enjoy having someone around who doesn't fall asleep in front of the fire after his tea.'

Martin gave her a sheepish grin. 'I'll be all right when I can find a mechanic to help me.' He turned to Seth. 'It's not just motor cars, but farm machinery these days. Everyone who can is getting a motor vehicle.'

'My Martin is the best mechanic in the district and

everyone knows it,' Jeanie said, smiling proudly at him. 'That's why he's always busy. Maybe now the war is over he can find a young man to train. Now, Mr Talbot, let me show you your room.'

'You must let me pay you.'

'Certainly not. If we can't cosset our brave soldier boys when they come back, it's a poor lookout, it is indeed.'

Her voice wobbled a little as she spoke, so Seth didn't press the point. 'I'm very grateful.'

'Here you are.' She flung open a door to show a comfortable room that looked out on to the back gardens of the houses, with the moors sloping up steeply beyond them. 'I'll fetch you some warm water to wash in, then you can join us in the kitchen for a cup of tea afterwards.'

'I'll come down and bring the water up myself,' he said firmly. 'I'm not having you running up and down after me.'

When they were sitting in the kitchen, he decided to explain why he was in Shawcroft because they weren't the sort of people he wanted to deceive. They both exchanged glances that made him think there was something going on in connection with the present police constable.

'It'll be good to have some new blood in the place,' was all Martin said, however.

Seth thought it best not to ask what Wes Cobbley was like, but already he trusted Martin Pugh, and if his host shared the same opinion of Cobbley as Bert did, then Seth knew who he'd believe.

What was the town's only police officer doing, then, to make decent people speak of him in that tone of voice?

4

Ellen unpacked her clothes and found a skirt and blouse to wear, with a jumper coat that matched the skirt. She'd knitted the jumper herself and was pleased with how it looked.

When she went down, however, her mother looked at her in dismay. 'Oh, dear, that skirt's very short. It's nearly halfway up your calves.'

'That's the fashion now. All my skirts are this length.'

'Bevan won't like it. And he didn't notice how short your hair was earlier, but he will this evening. Isn't there any way of disguising how short it is? Or perhaps you could say you had to have it cut short in the Aides and now you're growing it.'

'I won't tell lies, Mum. And anyway, I like my hair this way. It's so much easier to manage when it's as curly as mine.'

When the door opened she braced herself for further arguments but it was Madge, come to make the evening meal. She was carrying a package of meat, which turned out to be steaks, one large one and two much smaller ones. Ellen was feeling tired, so let the daily helper do the cooking, boil some potatoes and use an Oxo cube to make the gravy. She smiled at the sight of the red and white tin. Soldiers had been given these as part of their supplies and many said how welcome the savoury drinks they made had been. She sat chatting quietly to her mother, telling her about her life in London, pleased to see how the wan face lit up with interest.

After a while Dorothy glanced at the clock. 'I'd better get up now. Bevan likes me to sit at table for the evening meal.'

'Should you? You look so tired.'

'I shall do it as long as I can. It makes a change for me, too, you know.'

'I'll help you, then.'

'Thank you, dear.'

Helping her mother dress made her realise just how thin the older woman was. Dorothy was badly bruised in places too. Ellen tried not to let her shock show, but her mother had always been able to read her mind and glanced at her quizzically.

'You knew I was ill.'

'What exactly is wrong with you, Mum? You look as if you've been in a fight.'

'It's some disease of the blood. There's nothing they can do about it. It makes me bruise very easily and I'm getting weaker all the time.'

By the time Ellen helped her into the kitchen, Dorothy was panting and her forehead was beaded with sweat.

'I'll just – sit down – rest.'

So Ellen helped Madge to set the table, talking

quietly to her while keeping an eye on her mother. 'I can serve the meal, so you may as well go home.'

'I'd rather stay, love. He pays me by the hour and I've only got another ten minutes to go to make up an hour.'

'Oh. Yes. Of course.'

Shortly afterwards the front door slammed and Bevan came into the kitchen, his face ruddy and scrubbed, his big hands clean and pink. He looked at Madge then back at Ellen. 'Too much for you, was it, to make the tea for your mother?'

'I was tired. And Madge had everything sorted out, knew what you wanted.'

Dorothy intervened. 'I'm to blame, Bevan dear. I was enjoying my daughter's company. Oh, so much.'

His face softened. 'Had a good chat, did you? That'll brighten you up. You'll soon be on the mend now she's back.'

There was dead silence as the three women avoided each other's eyes.

Madge broke it. 'Shall I serve tea now, Mr Halsopp?'

'Yes. Then you can get off home. Ellen will do the washing up today.'

He went to sit next to his wife, leaving his step-daughter to get her own chair out. She had, she realised suddenly, become used to good manners from the men she'd worked with or helped to entertain in the canteen. But at least Bevan was gentle with her mother. Indeed, his whole face changed when he spoke to her or looked at her.

Ellen cleared away the plates and set out smaller ones for the apple pie, which looked as if it had been bought in from a baker's. When she heard an exclamation from Bevan, she turned round to look at him. His face was ruddy with anger, a familiar sight to her. But now her heart didn't jump with fear, she just wondered what she'd done to upset him now.

'I've been trying to work out why you look different. You've had your hair cut short!'

'Yes. It was much more convenient. We were working very hard.'

'I don't call riding round on a motorcycle hard work. Well, you can just start growing your hair again. Decent women don't go around pretending to be men.'

She dug her fingernails into the palms of her hands and refrained from answering him. For her mother's sake, she must try not to let him provoke her. Not that she intended to do what he asked. She knew that shorter hair suited her better.

It was not until she was clearing the table that he noticed her skirt.

'And you can let down that skirt as well. Showing off your legs like a hussy! What will people think of you?'

'There are a lot of women wearing shorter skirts these days. They allowed us to do more active things during the war and we're not going back to the old ways. Some of the richer women in London are wearing their skirts far shorter than this.'

'Well, no one who lives in my house is going to

dress like a wh—' He broke off with a guilty glance at his wife. 'Sorry, dear. I forgot myself.'

'Her skirt isn't all that short, Bevan.'

'It's shorter than *I* like and she's in *my* house, so she'll dress as I say.'

Ellen wasn't giving in on this. 'I can't change the skirt now. There isn't enough material to let it down.'

'You always have an answer, don't you? Are you *trying* to upset your mother? You can put some braid on it or – or something.'

'I'm only intending to stay for a few days, so the skirt can remain as it is, a suitable length for the sort of life I now lead.'

'Mrs Gresham won't approve of it, either.'

'As I'm not going back to work for her, I can't see how it matters what she thinks.'

'Oh? And what other sort of job will you find here?'

'I don't intend to stay in Shawcroft.'

He opened his mouth, saw his wife's agonised expression and drew in a deep breath. 'We'll discuss this later after your mother's gone to bed.'

'I shan't change my mind, or my appearance.' Ellen turned to her mother. 'What time do you go to bed, Mum?'

'Quite soon. I'm a bit tired today.'

'I'll help you undress, then I'll nip round to see Auntie Jeanie.'

There was silence for a moment or two. From the way her stepfather looked at her, there were things he would have liked to say and she in turn felt angry that he should try to interfere in her life like this. She was twenty-six, had seen life and death in London, had narrowly escaped being killed herself in the air raids, had even travelled overseas. She could make her own decisions about such details. They were a symbol of standing on her own feet and she was not prepared to back down.

As she was helping her mother get ready for bed, Dorothy said, 'Why must you always defy him? You could easily put a bit of braid on your skirt.'

'Why should I?'

'To keep the peace.'

'I've bitten my tongue a dozen times already and I've only been back a few hours, Mum. *He* hasn't held back once. And I'm a visitor here, not a dependent child.' She saw tears come into her mother's eyes. 'I'm sorry, but even for you, I can't behave subserviently.'

'Did you mean it about not coming back to live with us?'

'Yes. You know it wouldn't work. There'd be nothing but quarrels because we're chalk and cheese, him and me.'

'I suppose you're right. I'd hoped you'd meet someone in London, be married by now,' Dorothy said forlornly. 'How will you ever find a man when so many have been killed?'

'I can live a perfectly happy life without getting married.'

'Didn't you meet *anyone* in the south?'

'I met lots of nice young men, but no one special.

Most of them were in the forces – and quite a few were killed, poor things.' She stared into the distance for a minute, remembering one in particular who might have suited her, but had died in '16, then shook her head to banish that memory and tried to smile at her mother.

Dorothy put one hand up to cradle Ellen's cheek. 'Having a husband and children is the reason women were put on this earth, the thing that brings them the most joy. Without us women there would be no nation. It's the most important job of all, being a mother. How can you not want children?'

Ellen sighed. 'I do, Mum. Of course I do. But not at any price. I must like and respect the man I marry, and he must respect me, or I can't—' She broke off, not wanting to bring up the past. But she might have known her mother would pursue the very path she wanted to avoid. Dorothy Halsopp, for all her fragility, wasn't easily fooled.

'What did Jory do to you? You would never say. Whatever it was, I'm sure he's learned his lesson and grown more sensible now that he's been through the war. He's a fine-looking young man and still single.'

'And he can stay single for ever, if it's up to me. I shall never change my mind about him.' Ellen moved away from the bed. She had no intention of distressing her mother further by explaining her reasons for breaking off her engagement. 'I'll go and visit Uncle Martin and Auntie Jeanie now if you don't need me any more.'

She went to get her handbag and put on her coat,

hesitating about the umbrella, then leaving it behind. The rain seemed to have stopped now and the moon was sailing in and out of the clouds, winking up at her from the puddles. Even if it rained later, she didn't have far to go. Well, nothing was very far in Shawcroft, except the big estates to the south of the town, places like the Hall where she used to work, or Daphne Bingram's old home Clough Lodge, a place she'd never visited, strangely enough.

Seth felt instantly at home with the Pughs. He ate a wonderful meal and sat back with a smile afterwards. 'I'd get fat if I ate like that every day. Lovely beef, that was.'

'Halsopp's. He's a good butcher, I'll give him that. Even Mrs Gresham gets her meat from him. But he's tight with his money, could afford to live far more comfortably but never has done.'

Later there was a knock on the front door. Martin went to open it and came back beaming. 'It's our Ellen, Jeanie love.'

Seth stood up. 'I'll go up to bed and leave you in peace.'

'No need to do that, lad,' Martin said. 'We enjoy having young people around. It reminds us of . . . better times.'

Jeanie was holding Ellen's hands, keeping her at arm's length. 'Eh, love, your hair looks so pretty like that, instead of screwed back in a knot.' She patted her own bun self-consciously. 'I did think of having mine cut. It must be so much easier to manage.'

Ellen studied her. 'Why don't you, then?'

Jeanie blushed. 'Martin likes it long.'

When they all sat down, Ellen sighed without realising it, because the atmosphere was so different from that at her mother's.

'What's up, love?' Martin asked.

She shrugged. 'My stepfather, laying down the law as usual. He seems to think everyone will be going back to the old ways – and me with them. I've been ordered to grow my hair and lengthen my skirts. He's also expecting me to go back to work for Mrs Gresham and start seeing Jory Nelson again.' She blew out an angry puff of air. 'I shouldn't let him make me angry. I knew what to expect before I came back. Only . . . I found out it was him who stopped Mum telling me about Paul. I'll never forgive him for that. You do know I'd have written to you, don't you?'

'Of course we do, love. If me and Jeanie hadn't been so upset we'd have written to you about it ourselves. It took us a while to . . . accept it.'

Jeanie changed the subject. 'Are you intending to stay in Shawcroft, Ellen?'

'I wasn't. But my mother . . .' She was unable to finish the sentence.

'Then there's only Mrs Gresham to work for, love, what with all the young men starting to come back and take over their old jobs.'

Ellen sighed. 'Maybe I can get a job and lodgings in Manchester, then come out to visit on Sundays. I hadn't expected Mum to be so bad. She's only forty-eight.'

Watching her, Seth couldn't help admiring the brilliance of her eyes, even though that was due to unshed tears. He'd always preferred blue eyes. He didn't say anything. He felt he should leave them to talk in private, but couldn't think how to get out without making a scene. They seemed to accept him being there, though. He'd never felt so quickly included in a group. He became aware that Ellen was looking at him with a wry smile.

'Sorry to bore you with my troubles, Mr Talbot. When you've met my stepfather you'll understand what he's like.'

They looked at one another and the world seemed to go quiet around them, as if they were alone in the room. She gave him a quick, shy smile then looked away. It was as if she'd broken a spell and it took him a minute to pull his thoughts together.

'Tell me all the latest gossip, Auntie Jeanie. I'm relying on you. Don't leave out a single thing.'

Jeanie smiled at her. 'What makes you think I know what's happening in Shawcroft?'

'You always do.'

'Well . . .' her face grew solemn, '. . . we had a murder last month nearby. No one knows who did it, either. Think of that, eh?' She looked at Seth. 'I hope when you take over, you'll not let such dreadful things happen, Mr Talbot.'

So Seth had told them about being the next village policeman. Ellen was glad about that. She didn't like deceit, even in a good cause. She leaned back, enjoying hearing about the doings of her former school friends, most of whom were now married with babies, one widowed, because a few lads from the town had been killed as well as Paul.

'There's talk of building a war memorial to the lads who died,' Martin said. 'It'd be nice, that. We ought to remember them.'

'Yes, we should. And the women who died, too. There were nurses killed in France as well as soldiers, you know.'

'Nay, I never thought of that,' Martin said. 'You're right though. It was a nurse who wrote to tell us how Paul died and sent us his last words.' He fished out his handkerchief and blew his nose loudly.

There was sadness in the silence that followed that remark, but also a feeling of something shared and agreed on.

When the clock chimed ten, Ellen stood up. 'I'd better get back or he'll be locking the door on me.'

'I'll walk with you, love.' Martin hauled himself to his feet, yawning.

'Why don't I do it?' Seth said. 'I always enjoy a breath of fresh air before I go to bed.'

'Yes, you do it,' Jeanie said quickly, nudging her husband.

Seth looked at Ellen. 'If you don't mind my company, that is?'

'No. No, of course I don't mind.' But she felt a bit breathless as he helped her on with her coat and held the door open for her. *He* had good manners, that was obvious. He seemed . . . a lovely man, just the sort you wanted for the town constable. And just the sort she was attracted to as well. That thought amazed her and she was glad her blush wouldn't show now that they were outside.

The air had that fresh smell that comes after rain and the night wasn't too cold, so they strolled along.

'I used to dream of peaceful villages like this one,' Seth said.

Ellen chuckled. 'Don't use that word again or you'll upset people. Shawcroft regards itself as a town, not a village.'

His chuckle echoed hers. 'Thanks for the hint.'

'When shall you be starting work here?'

'Probably next week. I'll stay for a couple of days this time, get to know the place a bit, then ask the authorities to write and say I'll be taking over.'

'Wes Cobbley won't like giving up the reins.'

'No one would. But he's quite old, isn't he? Nearly seventy, I think they said.'

'Yes.'

'Why does everyone clam up when they mention him?'

She sighed. 'Best you find out for yourself. And I've been away, so I don't know much about what he's been doing lately.' Only what Wes Cobbley had been like before, how he'd refused to believe or help her on the worst day of her whole life. She'd never forgive him for that. Never!

The following morning Ronnie woke up with a heavy, thumping headache, wondering where she was. After fumbling automatically for her spectacles and not finding them, she squinted round. She must be back at the Hall, but this wasn't her old bedroom. Tears welled in her eyes. It wasn't a nightmare, then.

She got up hastily, wondering if she could get dressed and run away, but the room spun round her and she had to clutch the bed's footboard for a moment or two. Then she tried again and this time managed to walk across to the window.

Even before she got there she heard the rain pelting down, blurring the world outside.

She turned and looked for her clothes, but couldn't find them. There was nothing on the dressing-table chair and the wardrobe was empty of everything except an old dressing-gown. Her mother's doing, no doubt. Well, it wasn't going to stop Ronnie from getting away. She shrugged into the dressing-gown and belted it round her before going across to the door.

It was locked.

What was she to do? How to get away?

She sat on the bed and waited, but it was a long time before she heard a key turning.

'So you're awake.'

'Yes.'

'I hope you're not going to continue with this foolishness.'

Ronnie opened her mouth to say she definitely wasn't going to marry Algie, then thought better of it and pressed her lips firmly together. At the moment she had no money, no clothes and couldn't see clearly without her spectacles. If she did get away, people would think she'd gone mad, walking the roads barefoot wearing only a nightdress and dressing-gown. They'd no doubt contact her mother who would call in Dr Hilliam and spin him some story about her having a nervous breakdown.

But she couldn't be seen to give in too easily either.

She realised as those ideas tumbled through her mind how much she'd changed in the past year. The old Ronnie would have caved in and done as she was told, weeping as she did so. The new Ronnie had learned to think ahead and make plans.

She definitely wasn't going to stay here and she definitely wasn't going to marry Algie, whatever her mother said or did.

Then it occurred to her that she didn't know how Algie felt about her. Her mother had spoken to his parents, not to him. If he didn't want to marry her, perhaps he might help her get away. She could think of no one else who might go against her mother.

Covering her face with her hands, she pretended to weep, shrugging her mother's hand off her shoulder. 'Go away!'

'I'll send you up some breakfast then we'll have a chat.'

As the door closed and footsteps faded into the distance, Ronnie stopped pretending to cry and went to stand by the window. She stared out and as the rain had eased to a fine drizzle, she was able to see things that weren't close. All the meadows near the house except for one hayfield had been ploughed up. She'd forgotten that. She smiled grimly. Even her mother had had to contribute to the war effort. Most of their horses had been requisitioned earlier in the war as well. And of course, there was the dreadful problem of all the younger maids going off to do jobs men had done before the war, jobs which paid a great deal more than working here and gave them a lot more free time too. She doubted any of them would come back unless they had to.

It seemed ages until the key turned in the lock again. Her mother came in, accompanied by Tadwyn. He set down the heavy tray on the small table in the bay window and went to stand by the door. As if she could get the better of her mother physically!

'I'll return in half an hour for the tray. Don't waste good food.' Her mother went out, Tadwyn followed her and the door was locked again.

Ronnie sat down and made a hearty breakfast. Her appetite had increased once she started doing heavy farm work and she was far stronger than she used to be, for all she was only five foot tall. She sighed with satisfaction as she cleared the plate.

When her mother returned, she locked the door behind her and sat on the small armchair in the bay window. 'I am very determined that you will do as I have planned, Veronica. And I shall not change my mind.'

Thinking of Giles was enough to bring the necessary tears to Ronnie's eyes.

'Tell me the name of this man you've been seeing.'

She shook her head.

'I'll find out.'

Ronnie had no doubt of that, but she hadn't given up hope yet of getting a message to him. Perhaps she could persuade one of the maids to post a letter for her.

'I've brought up some face cream. We can start doing something about your dreadful rough skin.'

'What about clothes?'

'Not yet, not till I'm more sure of you. Now, let me put this cream on your face.'

'I'll do it.' Their eyes met in a challenge but on this Ronnie wasn't giving way.

'Very well. I'll sit and watch, make sure you do it properly.'

But as she was creaming her face Ronnie felt her head begin to spin again. She stopped and put up one hand to her forehead.

Her mother's voice seemed to echo. 'Is something wrong?'

'I feel dizzy.'

'Oh dear. I wonder if I put too many sleeping drops in your food.' She smiled.

Ronnie felt sick with helpless anger. She continued to cream her face and neck, telling herself it was for Giles, not her mother. 'I won't make much of an impression on Algie if you keep me doped.'

'Just for a couple of days. A little lesson in behaving yourself. Let me help you into bed. Unless I miscalculated badly, you should be awake again by teatime.'

Ronnie shook her hand off and put her feelings into words, not caring if she upset her mother. 'Don't touch me. Don't *ever* touch me again! I won't be answerable if you do.'

Her mother took a hasty step backwards, then shrugged and left without another word.

Maybe that remark had given too much away, Ronnie thought, but it was how she felt. She didn't want those firm plump hands on her skin again. How she came from such a tall, buxom mother had always surprised her, but her father had once said that she looked like his mother, so perhaps she took after that side of the family. And thank goodness for that!

As her thoughts grew tangled she realised that though she had not lost her fear of her mother, she had also grown to dislike her and to despise the tricks she employed to get her own way. And she was the most selfish person Ronnie had ever met, not caring for anything but her own comfort and convenience. During the war, Edwina had bought a lot of black market food and other things, which seemed unpatriotic to her daughter. Now that the war was over, she was continuing to bulldoze her way through life with only her own desires in mind, no thought of how she hurt others.

Ronnie had no idea how she was going to escape, but she would find a way, somehow. There was no way on earth anyone could force her to marry Algie St Corbin.

On the Sunday, Seth attended church with the Pughs, who introduced him simply as a young friend of theirs. He didn't know why he went, because the horrors of war had shaken his faith, but he still enjoyed the ceremonial of a Sunday service. He liked to watch the congregation, to know he was standing in a building that had outlasted many wars and would, he hoped, continue to outlast such horrors. But most of all he enjoyed the singing, always had. He had a decent baritone voice and wasn't normally afraid to use it, but today he sang quietly because he didn't want to be noticed.

He saw Ellen sitting nearer the front on the other side next to her stepfather. The two of them weren't chatting, didn't even look at one another, just sat waiting for the service to begin with well over a yard of space between them.

There was a row of people further back, opposite the Pughs, who looked like servants. He amused himself by trying to decide what job they did at the big house where they must work. The most smartly dressed woman was obviously the housekeeper, definitely a superior sort of servant. The man beside her was about sixty, dressed in an old-fashioned suit that didn't look as if it had been worn much. Definitely not a butler. The next woman must be a housemaid. She was middle-aged and weary looking, with a sad excuse for a hat crammed on her head. She didn't look confident enough to be the cook. Was the bony woman next to her the cook? Well, it definitely wasn't the young lass at the end of the row, who was probably a kitchen maid, no older than fourteen, he'd guess.

Then the service began and Seth turned his attention to the first hymn. After that the cleric gave a mercifully brief sermon and a small choir led the way into a second hymn in thin, elderly voices, mostly female. Parish announcements brought the proceedings to a close.

The better class of people from the front pews filed out first and he studied them as they passed. Not landed gentry, even of the minor sort, he thought, but professional people and superior tradesmen. Did this Mrs Gresham from the Hall not attend church?

When he and the Pughs went outside, the clouds had cleared and it was sunny, the sort of beautiful spring day that is full of shyly nodding flowers, breezes too gentle to do more than ruffle the foliage and caress the skin, delightful bursts of birdsong and the occasional humming of an insect. That filled him with quiet joy. England at its best – and at peace. This was what he'd fought for.

He watched the group of servants squash into a luxurious Austin Landaulette and the man who'd puzzled him started it and drove off. So he must be the chauffeur, then.

Then Seth forgot everything else as Ellen Dawson began to make her way across the churchyard towards them. He watched as she stopped for a word here and there, smiling and being smiled at. Clearly she was well liked. He was surprised how glad he was to see her. Hoped she was as glad to see him.

Her stepfather wasn't with her now. He had joined a group of men at the far side of the churchyard, though he'd positioned himself to keep an eye on her. Seth wondered why. Didn't he trust her?

There was another man in that group who was also watching her, a tall younger man with a shock of coarse dark hair and the sort of skin that never looks clean-shaven for long. You couldn't mistake the look of lust in his eyes, though he made no effort to approach her. It was an affront to a decent woman to stare at her like that and made Seth feel angry.

And then he forgot to watch people because Ellen was there beside him, kissing Mrs Pugh's cheek then turning to greet him. The word to describe her, he decided as he clasped her hand, was bonny. She was a typical 'fair lass of Lancashire', just like in the old songs.

'Did you enjoy the service, Miss Dawson?' he asked, more to keep her attention than because he wanted to know.

She grimaced. 'Not really. I only accompanied my stepfather today because he makes such a fuss about going to church.'

There was a stir behind them and a man spoke rather loudly, asking someone to let him pass.

She glanced quickly in that direction. 'I must dash now. I've got the dinner to finish.'

She was off before Seth could say anything else and when he looked round he saw that the loud voice belonged to the dark-haired man who had been staring at her. Was she avoiding the fellow? It seemed like it. Seth watched as unobtrusively as he could and saw the man stop moving and stand gazing after Ellen as she hurried off down the main street.

'Who is that man?' he asked Martin.

'Who? Oh, *him*. Jory Nelson, son of the town's main carter. Just back from the war.'

'You don't like him.'

'I didn't say that.'

'You didn't have to. Your tone of voice said it for you.'

Martin shrugged. 'I'm trying to leave you to make your own mind up about people, son.'

'I'll do that, don't worry. But I don't have to know you for long to realise that I'd trust your judgement.'

Martin flushed and smiled at him, after which they both changed the subject.

Ronnie didn't eat her evening meal, not wanting to be drugged again. When her mother came to remove the tray she scowled at her daughter.

'This only means you'll go hungry and I shall bring the men in to hold you while I put the drops into your mouth.'

Ronnie shrugged, saying loudly in case anyone was nearby, 'I don't want you drugging me again.' She watched carefully and made a sudden dash for freedom, but her mother pounced on her. She fought back with all her might, kicking and scratching like an alley cat she'd once seen defending her kittens, her main objective to get out of the room.

They fought in silence because Ronnie didn't intend to sound like a madwoman. But it was hopeless. In the end her mother shoved her to the floor and hurriedly backed out and locked the door behind her.

'See how you like going without food!' she called from outside the door then marched away, her sensible lace-up shoes drumming on the thin carpet.

Ronnie sank down on the bed, more thirsty than hungry.

When everything was quiet, Glenys crept out of a nearby bedroom. She'd darted into it when she heard Mrs Gresham coming up the stairs because maids weren't supposed to come down to the kitchen this way, even though it was a much shorter route. They all did, though.

What was going on with Miss Veronica? Mrs Shipton might say it was none of their business but Glenys liked to know what was going on and she couldn't believe what she'd heard. She'd peered through a crack in the door after that to see the horrifying sight of two women fighting. The mistress had always bullied poor Miss Veronica, they all knew that. Why was she locked in this bedroom now, not even her own bedroom? Had she really been drugged?

If Glenys had ever been fortunate enough to have a daughter, she'd not have treated her so unkindly. She'd have loved her, as she'd been loved herself. But having a family wasn't to be. No one had ever courted her, with her plain face and stick-thin body, and never would now.

Thoughtful, she crept downstairs to the kitchen, not saying anything about what she'd seen and overheard because she wanted to keep her job. She'd been a housemaid here for fifteen years and she didn't have anywhere else to go, was a bit afraid of the outside world, if truth be told.

5

Bevan opened up the shop the following morning with his usual attention to detail and cleanliness. Mrs Shipton, who had been housekeeper at the Hall for many years, was always driven into Shawcroft on Mondays to place her weekly orders at the local shops and he wanted to make sure everything was just so.

Before the war he would have driven out to the Hall in his pony trap to take her weekly order, as all the better-class shopkeepers did with important clients, then delivered the meat to her. But because of staffing and supply difficulties caused by the war, not to mention the death of his elderly pony and his inability to find a replacement due to requisitioning of so many horses, he'd had to stop making these calls. He now used Nelson's Cartage Service to deliver to the outlying districts.

He still missed the outings, though.

In fact, the war had not been at all good for business. He had been furious when the government called for meatless days and incensed by the shortages of legal meat supplies. It served them right if a man turned to other ways of supplying his customers. He didn't feel guilty about what he'd done because it stood to reason that people couldn't fight a war on empty stomachs.

It was a good thing Wes Cobbley liked a decent piece of meat, though, and was willing to turn a blind eye to what was going on. It'd have been a lot harder if they'd had the sort of policeman who followed the rules, whether they made sense or not.

Business hadn't improved all that much this year, either, though the war had been over for several months. There were still too many regulations hampering a man from earning an honest living and too many shortages. Many folk had lost their jobs or their loved ones because of the influenza, and there were a few respectable families in the town being secretly helped by the Ladies' Auxiliary from the church.

He put a sign in the window saying, 'Killing a bullock tomorrow. Taking orders.' Standing back, he looked at it with approval. That would bring the customers in.

An hour later the large black motor car from the Hall drew up outside the shop and he hastily finished serving an unimportant woman, leaving the apprentice to wrap up her meagre portion of meat and take her few coins. By the time Mrs Shipton came in he was ready to give her his full attention.

She discussed what would be available that week, placed her order then hesitated and asked in a low voice, 'Is there somewhere more private where I could have a word with you, Mr Halsopp?'

He stared at her anxiously, hoping this wouldn't be

bad news, because Mrs Gresham was one of his biggest customers. 'If you wouldn't mind coming into the kitchen at the back, Mrs Shipton? It's not suitable for a lady like you, but it's clean at least.'

'Everything about your shop is clean, Mr Halsopp, and the meat well hung, which is something Cook and I appreciate.' She followed him into the rear, looking round with interest. 'Do you not use the upstairs?'

'Just for storage. I don't want strangers traipsing dirt in and out of my premises.'

She sat down on the chair he pulled out for her, smoothed her gloves over her fingers as if uncertain how to start, then said abruptly, 'I saw your step-daughter in church. Has she left Lady Bingram's Aides now?'

'Yes, and about time too. I never approved of her going off to London, as you know.'

'It would have been hard for her to refuse a titled lady. I did understand that when Ellen gave notice. Lady Bingram hasn't been up to Lancashire for a while, but she still owns Clough Lodge, which isn't far from the Hall. I can understand and applaud her using it to house men injured during the war . . . even though they weren't officers, just rankers! Mrs Gresham was rather concerned that they weren't kept under control, but allowed to wander all over the grounds. Some even came on to our land. There's only a caretaker in residence at the moment, though. Perhaps her ladyship will rent the house out or sell it. She's not lived there since her second marriage, after all.'

He nodded, suppressing his impatience as he waited for Mrs Shipton to come to the point.

'Anyway, what I wanted to say was that we are, as I may have mentioned before, very short of staff at the Hall. And if your daughter is back, she may perhaps be interested in resuming her old job. I didn't want to approach her without making myself aware of the – the likelihood.' She began to fiddle with the strap of her handbag.

He chewed the inside of his cheek, wondering what to say. 'I'm not sure what Ellen will be doing, but as her mother's ill, we're hoping she'll stay around for a while.'

'How is your poor wife?'

He shook his head. 'No better, I'm afraid.'

There was another silence then he said, 'Leave it to me, Mrs Shipton. I'll speak to Ellen. I know it'd set her mother's mind at rest to have her daughter working nearby. Of course, wages have gone up since the war . . . Ellen was getting a pound a week and all found in London, I believe.'

'That much? It's outrageous. We can't possibly match that. And anyway, the war is over now. Wages will settle down again, I'm sure.' She stood up. 'You'll have a word with Ellen, then?'

He nodded.

'I know we can rely on our own butcher to do the right thing.' Mrs Shipton paused to let her hidden threat sink in, then met his eyes. 'I was sure *you* would understand our need, Mr Halsopp. You'll let me know what she says? Or better still, send her out to see me.'

He nodded and showed her out with the flourishing courtesies he reserved for well-heeled or influential clients.

When he went back into the shop there were no customers waiting, so he slammed the cleaver down on the wooden block. He wished he'd never written to Ellen asking her to come back. *He* didn't care if he never saw her again. He'd only done it for his wife.

But now that Ellen was here, he was going to see she toed the line. No member of his family was going to refuse a request like that from his best customer. Mrs Gresham could not only withdraw her custom but speak to her friends in the neighbourhood if she was displeased with him and influence others to shop elsewhere. She could ruin him, had ruined others who'd upset her.

No, Ellen would have to go back to the Hall and the sooner the better, because he didn't intend to put up with her impudence in his own home for much longer. They'd keep a careful eye on her out there. It was a mercy Ellen hadn't come back from London with a swelling belly, the way these young women behaved once they were away from their families. And she wouldn't be able to come into town easily, because he was quite sure they wouldn't allow her to keep her motorbike.

Maybe he could use it for deliveries and calls? It couldn't be hard to drive one if a woman could do it. He was sure he could learn to drive it.

A smile crossed his face as something else occurred to him. Maybe this would kill two birds with one stone.

After working at the Hall for a few weeks, Ellen would surely be more inclined to treat Jory's attentions with the respect they deserved. That was another sign of how the past few years had gone to her head. She should be grateful that a fine young fellow like him was willing to marry her after she'd broken up with him once, not to mention gone cavorting off to London. Jory would come into his father's carting business one day, so it was a good match and the young fellow would be able to provide well for her.

Best of all, it'd please Dorothy to see her daughter married, something she'd spoken about wistfully several times. He wanted her to die happy.

He sucked in a deep breath at that thought and clenched one fist tightly. He'd tried every way he knew to make Dorothy better, spending a fortune on doctors . . . and he still pretended she was going to get better when he was with her, because he couldn't, just couldn't talk about it. But he knew she was dying, hadn't needed the doctor's warning that she had only months to live.

On that thought he went back to find the juiciest, most tender piece of fillet steak for Dorothy's tea. She didn't eat enough to keep a bird alive, but surely this would tempt her? No need to die before you had to, not when you could have good red meat every day of the week.

That same Monday the weather was fine so Giles borrowed his friend's motor car again, paid a returned soldier he knew was out of work to go and do Cora's chores at the farm and took her for a drive. As he explained to Mr and Mrs Tilling, it'd look less suspicious if a couple turned up in the town. A man on his own asking questions, with no obvious purpose for being there, would attract a lot more notice.

They drove into the centre of Shawcroft and to his relief there was a very nice pub there, the Royal Fleece. Before the war, he'd not have taken a decent woman inside any sort of public house, but things had changed and now females were increasingly seen in the lounge bars of the better ones, though not usually in the public bars. He escorted Cora inside and asked if the publican's wife could make him and his young lady some sandwiches to go with his glass of beer and her shandy.

'I don't want to take her home till I have to,' he added, which brought an understanding smile to the other man's face.

They sat together, trying to look like young lovers as they ate. When the landlord came to clear the table, Giles complimented him on the quality of his beer then got him chatting.

The ease with which he extracted information about the local gentry and Mrs Gresham in particular would not have surprised the men he'd worked with during the war, men who were also in the business of gathering and sifting information, but it made Cora exclaim as they went outside, 'No wonder you got to know our shy Ronnie!'

'I fell in love with her on sight,' he said simply, 'and I didn't have to draw her out because we've never had any difficulty talking to one another. And no one, no one at all, is going to stop me marrying her.' He let out a sound between a sigh and a laugh. 'Sorry. I'm supposed to be looking like *your* young man today, aren't I?'

'It doesn't matter.'

'It does if anyone is keeping an eye on strangers.'

He took hold of her hand and raised it to his lips, but he kissed the air, not her skin and she could tell he was still thinking of Ronnie. 'Did I tell you about the new girl Mr Tilling has found to replace Ronnie?'

'No.'

'She doesn't want to go back to her old job in service, likes working in the open air. So when the war ended she got a job with a farmer in Cheshire and you can't believe how badly they treated her, not even feeding her properly and housing her in a shed. The very first evening with us she said she must have gone to heaven because Mrs Tilling cooks like an angel.'

He laughed. 'Ronnie always said what a good cook the farmer's wife was. Look, I'll just visit the gents' then speak to the landlord about where to take you for a nice drive round.'

Cora took the opportunity to visit the ladies', staring wistfully at her reflection in the tiny square of flyspecked mirror. She wasn't ugly, but she wasn't pretty either. Her husband of four short weeks had been killed in '17 and she hadn't met anyone she fancied since – or anyone who fancied her, either. As far as she could see, she and a lot of other young women were doomed to remain single because there simply wouldn't be enough men to go round now that so many had been killed.

'I have directions for a nice country outing,' Giles said quietly as he rejoined her. 'We'll drive past the Hall today and I'll come back on my own later to reconnoitre. I think I'll have to buy myself a motor car, if I can get hold of one. I can't keep borrowing my friend's.' He stopped and looked round. 'It's a pretty little place, isn't it, Shawcroft? I've heard that the local lawyer lost his only partner last year and is looking for a new man in the practice. Would you mind if we had a quick walk up and down the main street?' He had an ulterior motive for this, one he couldn't share with Cora – or even with Ronnie.

'Not at all.'

He walked slowly, not saying much but studying the shops and business premises. At one stage he popped into a sweet shop and came out with a packet of sweets and directions to Mr Monnings' rooms.

'I'll come back another day and see this chap. If we can just walk a bit further, I'll get the exact address of his rooms and be able to drop him a line. Ah, there it is.' He pulled out a little notebook and scribbled in it, then smiled at Cora. 'Sorry about that. Trying to kill two birds with one stone.'

'I'm not sure Ronnie would want to live so close to her mother.'

'There's probably no chance of him wanting a junior partner anyway. But if he did . . . well, we'll cross that bridge when we come to it. Let's go back to the car now.' He offered her his arm again.

They were soon outside the town. At first the country lanes were shut in by drystone walls then, as they headed south-west, away from the moors, the stark landscape softened slightly. When they stopped on top of a small rise, they found themselves on the lip of a shallow circular valley, sheltered and showing a range of healthy-looking crops.

'I think that's the Hall.' He pointed. Below them, halfway up the slope, stood a large house built of grey stone with a slate roof. It was a square and uncompromising sort of place, with two short wings going backwards, obviously the residence of a gentleman's family. The fields around it had mostly been planted with crops like potatoes, cabbages and turnips, probably because of the war, but there was still an imposing avenue of trees leading to the front door.

'Get out and walk to and fro,' Giles said suddenly. 'Pretend you've got cramp in one leg.' He crammed his trilby down on his head to hide his face and stayed in the car.

A man came striding across the field towards them with a large black and white dog frisking round him. 'Can I help you, sir? If your motor car has broken down, we do have a telephone at the house and there's a very good mechanic in Shawcroft.'

Giles, who had stayed in the car to conceal his height, saw Cora stare at him in surprise when his reply came out sounding very affected and upper-class. 'That's dashed civil of you, old fellow. But it's my young lady who's broken down, actually.' He let out a high whinny of a laugh, then explained, 'She's got cramp, poor girl.'

Cora obligingly grimaced and waggled her left leg about. 'I must have been sitting too long in one position, darling. Just give me a few more minutes.'

'Crops look to be doing well,' Giles offered.

The man turned to look at the fields with pride. 'They are, sir. We've done our bit for the war effort, I can tell you, even if we weren't able to fight.'

'Peter was in the Army,' Cora confided, leaning against the car and waggling her foot some more. 'He served in France.'

'Ah. I lost a cousin at Ypres. Shot through the heart, his Captain said, so at least he didn't suffer.' The man sighed and looked into the distance for a moment.

Giles knew those letters. He'd written quite a few himself. You always said 'shot through the heart, didn't suffer' to spare the feelings of the family, but it wasn't often true. Death could be a great deal messier than most civilians realised. 'I was there too. Bad show, that. We lost a lot of good men.'

He still remembered his time in the trenches as one of the worst periods of his life. He'd suffered through eighteen months at the front, expecting every day to be his last. When they'd offered him a chance to transfer to Intelligence work, he'd felt sick with relief and guilty at escaping the carnage when others couldn't. Several of his close friends had been killed after he went back to England.

The dog jumped up at the car, nudging his arm

with its nose, and he fondled it absent-mindedly, wishing the man would go away.

'My Tinker doesn't often go to strangers.'

'I like dogs. Missed them when I was out there.'

'Good thing it's all over now. The war to end all wars, eh? I wouldn't like Walter to have died in vain.' The man touched his cap and walked off again.

'You did well, Cora,' Giles said when he was out of earshot. He looked at the house again, eyes narrowed, working out the best way to get to it without being seen. 'Let's have a gentle drive round the district now. Doesn't look as if there's anywhere big enough to have a teashop, unfortunately.'

That afternoon, Jory came into the butcher's at closing time.

'You can finish up and go home now, Cedric,' Bevan said abruptly.

'Yes, Mr Halsopp.' The apprentice pulled off his apron and went into the back to put it into the linen basket and wash his hands noisily at the sink.

Jory started to speak, but Bevan shook his head and touched one fingertip to his lips before asking how his father was. Not until the door bell had danced on its spring and tinkled merrily behind young Cedric did he cut short the flow of small talk, slip the two bolts into place and hang the CLOSED sign on its little hook. 'Come into the back.'

When they were there, he took two bottles of beer out of the pantry. 'Keeps it nice and cool, that stone shelf does.' He unscrewed the stopper of one bottle and poured its contents into two glasses, taking care to get a nice head on the top. Then he set the amber bottle carefully down with some other empties by the back door, ready to be returned to the off licence and the deposit money collected.

Jory knew Mr Halsopp's fussy ways of old so waited patiently until the ritual was finished and his host picked up his glass before he drank from his own.

'Cheers.'

Neither man spoke until they'd taken a good mouthful, savoured and swallowed it.

'Good beer, that,' Jory said. 'I missed English beer when I was over in France.'

'It's a decent, healthy drink,' Bevan allowed, lingering over another mouthful. 'I tried that wine the French drink so much of and it tasted like vinegar to me.'

Jory hid a smile. He'd downed many a bottle of wine in France, more interested in the temporary oblivion than the taste. Setting his glass down, he began to fiddle with the edge of the table. 'How's your Ellen? She hurried away before I could speak to her after church.'

Bevan scowled and his cheeks flushed. 'I saw her do it. Bad manners, and so I told her. She's worse than ever, the uppity young madam.' He took another swig, his chest swelling with indignation. 'She wants her hash settling good and proper, that one does. These young women have had the wrong ideas put into their heads by this war. And what a mess she looks!'

Jory grinned. 'She looked all right to me on Sunday.'

'What? You can't mean that. She's had her hair cut short like a man's and her skirts are nearly up to her knees. Indecent, I call that. I don't know what you see in her, I really don't.'

'Same as you saw in her mother, I reckon. Some women are . . .' he waved his left hand in an effort to find the words, but wound up by adding lamely, 'right.'

'Well, I pity you. She'll make a terrible wife.'

'Not her. She's a hard worker, will bring me a motorcycle and I bet she's got money saved too. She always was careful with her pennies, Ellen was.'

Bevan stared at him. 'You reckon she's got money saved?'

'Must have a decent amount or she'd be rushing out to find a job.' Jory added pointedly, 'I'll be happy to get her and the motorcycle. You can keep the money if you help me to what I want.'

'And how will you get her to marry you?'

'I'll find a way to persuade her.'

Bevan emptied his glass of beer, opened the second bottle and refilled his and his companion's glasses, frowning in thought. 'You really think she's got money saved?'

'Course she has. Bound to have.' Jory raised his glass. 'To us fellows helping one another. And there's no one I'd rather have on my side than you, Mr Halsopp.' He waited a minute then changed the subject, 'Now, my dad has an extra sheep for you, if you're interested? Newly killed today.'

'I'd have to see it first. I don't take damaged beasts or those that have died from sickness.'

'I know that. Dad's never sold you anything that wasn't good and I shan't, either. Halsopp's is famous for quality meat and rightly so, best butcher's in town.'

Bevan allowed himself a slight smile in acknowledgement of this compliment. 'Time was I'd have beasts waiting to be slaughtered in the back field behind my shop. Now it's all dug up for potatoes and I have to buy what beasts are allotted to me and let the farmers slaughter them – unless some poor creature just happens to get itself killed.' He winked at Jory. 'Have you taken over that side of things from your dad, then?'

'Yes. He's getting on, glad to have me back to help out with the heavier work. I was coming to see you anyway, so I said I'd tell you about the sheep.'

'You make sure I only get healthy beasts, then.'

'I will, Mr Halsopp. You can rely on us Nelsons.'

Bevan nodded. 'We were lads together, your father and me. It'd be a poor lookout if we couldn't help one another when times are hard.'

That afternoon Ellen walked over to see her Uncle Martin. She found him working on her motorcycle. 'How's it going?'

'Be as good as new in a few minutes, love, with this new chain.'

'Let me know how much it costs.'

He smiled.

'I mean that.'

'You can try to force money on me, but you won't succeed.'

So she had to go and give him a big hug. 'Can I leave the bike in your yard after it's mended?'

'Oh? Don't you want to drive round on it?'

'Sometimes. But I don't want to leave it outside my mother's house. *He* might get ideas about it if he sees it standing around.'

Martin looked at her. 'I had Jory Nelson over here this afternoon asking if I wanted a chicken for the pot. He's soon slipped back into his old ways. He was looking at your bike as if it was his, asking about it with a gloating expression on his face.'

'Well, he's not getting his hands on it. Or me.'

'Can I suggest something?'

She nodded.

'Take off this high tension lead when you park it anywhere. No one can drive it away then. Most folk don't know what to look for when a motor vehicle doesn't work, but I know you do. And it doesn't take long to fit the lead on again.'

'I used to do that in London sometimes when I had to park in the back streets. I didn't think I'd ever need to take such precautions here in Shawcroft, though.'

'Jory's made it pretty obvious he's still interested in you.'

'I hate him.'

The words hung in the air between them for a minute or two as she fought back tears and he patted her shoulder awkwardly. 'He's still interested in you. Me and Jeanie both saw the way he looked at you on Sunday.'

'Well, I'm not interested in him. I can't stand the

man. How can someone like him survive the war when Paul—' Her voice broke off on a sob. 'Oh, Uncle Martin, I do miss him. I was longing to talk to him, just like we used to. He was like a brother to me. I still can't believe Mum didn't tell me he'd been killed, that she let *him* stop her.'

'She was ill by then, not her usual self.'

In the doorway Seth paused, having overheard enough to know he shouldn't intrude. He turned to go back into the house and nearly bumped into Mrs Pugh, whispering, 'I don't think they'd welcome any interruptions just now.'

She looked beyond him, saw Ellen weeping on her uncle's chest and turned abruptly into the kitchen, whisking out her own handkerchief. 'They didn't tell her when my Paul died, but Halsopp told us they had done. I think that's downright cruel. It hurt us when she didn't write and it's been a dreadful shock to her. They were very close, just like a real brother and sister.'

Seth hesitated but she was so distressed he put one arm round her. 'We've all lost people we love,' he said quietly. 'I spent two years training young men to go out as cannon fodder. And then I'd hear that they'd been killed, one after the other it seemed when there was a big offensive on, and sometimes only days after they got to France.'

'How did you bear it?'

'I got angry and stayed angry a lot of the time.'

She pulled back from him. 'Sorry. Losing my Paul still upsets me sometimes.'

'Bound to.'

She gave him a misty smile. 'You're a grand lad.'

'Hardly a lad. I'm nearly thirty.'

'That seems young to me. Seth . . . there's something else I've been wanting to say to you. Don't hurt our Ellen, will you?'

He stilled, staring down at her. 'What do you mean?'

'I can see that you're attracted to one another – well, a blind man could see it – but if you've no intention of doing anything about it, leave her alone.'

'It's taken me by surprise, it happened so quickly. She's a grand lass.' He was surprised that it was so noticeable, though. 'I try not to hurt anyone if I can help it, Mrs Pugh. There's been enough pain in the past few years. I'm looking forward to a quiet life when I come back to Shawcroft. As for Ellen, well, we'll see how things go, eh?' But his pulse had speeded up at the mere thought of her and he'd seen colour come into her face at the sight of him on Sunday.

Jeanie smiled. 'I hope it goes well for you both. But as for a quiet life, it's not always quiet in Shawcroft, so don't expect too much peace. We have a few bad pennies like any other town.'

He waited for her to continue, but she didn't give him any details of who might be considered a bad penny, just changed the subject again.

'You must come round to tea sometimes when you're settled into the police house. And if you want help finding someone to clean and cook for you, just ask me. I know most folk in Shawcroft and there are a few hard-working women who'd be glad to earn a bit extra.'

'Thank you. It'll be nice to have friends to visit and I'd appreciate any help you can give me about the house. In Manchester I lived in lodgings, but here the police station has the bobby's cottage attached. They prefer their country bobbies to be married, but they made an exception for me.'

'Have you never wanted to get married before, Seth?'

'Once or twice. But nothing came of it and somehow I didn't want to marry during the war. It felt wrong to leave someone at risk of being widowed, especially if there were children.'

When Wes Cobbley went into the cottage at the rear of the small police station for his tea, he found an official letter waiting for him. 'Why didn't you bring this through?' he asked his wife.

'You were busy with that Jory Nelson. I don't like them Nelsons, don't know what you see in them. And I didn't want the young one poking his nose into our business. Anyway, we both know what this letter is. It would only have upset you to give it to you.'

He read and reread it, scowling mightily as he did so. He had indeed been expecting this, but it didn't make it any easier to accept what it said. He didn't *want* to stop being a bobby. Why should he? He might not run as fast as a younger man, but he knew a damn sight more about life and how to keep his little town peaceful.

'Well, is it what I think?' his wife asked.

He handed it over to her and she read it then smiled at him.

'I'm so glad, Wesley love. Two weeks will give you time to say goodbye to everyone and clear the police station up. I've been itching to get my hands on the cupboards in there.'

'You're not to touch those. They're full of official documents, they are, not for outsiders.'

'Then *you* can clear them out. You're far too old to be working this hard, anyway. I've been worried you'd drop dead on me. I'll go and give the tenants notice this very evening. One week's notice we said when you went back to work because of the war and we let them rent our cottage. I never thought we'd be gone from it for years, but the rent's given us a nice little nest egg at least. There'll be a few things to set to rights after we move back, but they've looked after things very nicely.'

He sought desperately for excuses to delay things. 'It's a bit short notice for the tenants. I could write and ask if we can wait another month before bringing the new fellow in.'

'Oh no, it isn't short notice. They can move back in with her parents now that her sister's gone to live in Bury. That'll give me time to bring in the painter and get the place distempered all through. We can easily move in by the twenty-eighth.'

'But I won't be earning anything if I give this up.'

'We've enough saved to see us out, though you will have to cut down on your drinking, but you'll have your police pension. And if you drink less beer, that's all to the good.' She gave his large belly one of her severe looks. 'I want to live in our retirement cottage and enjoy the nice big garden, Wesley. This place is cramped and old-fashioned. So don't you *dare* do anything to stop me getting back to my own house. I've waited long enough.' She put the letter down in front of him and tapped it with her forefinger. 'You can write a reply now and I'll drop it in the post on my way to give our tenants notice.'

She wouldn't let him wriggle out of it and stood over him as he wrote to confirm that he'd received the letter and would do as it said, vacating the premises on the Friday of the following week.

The only thing the letter hadn't said was who would be taking over. Would it be some young whippersnapper back from the war, or a fellow who'd sat things out in comfort? Wes wondered. A married chap would be best. They didn't take as many risks, didn't like upsetting the townsfolk.

Whoever it was had better not rock the boat. Folk in Shawcroft stuck together and were wary of outsiders. Rightly so. You had to look after your own and see your friends right. As he had done.

Ronnie was not only hungry and thirsty, she was cold. The day passed slowly with nothing to do and she spent most of the afternoon in bed just to keep warm.

In the early evening footsteps came towards the room and she jumped out of bed, straightening her hair and tying the sash of her dressing-gown more firmly.

When the door opened, her mother came in

accompanied by Dr Hilliam. Edwina had a triumphant expression in her eyes.

'Now, then,' the elderly doctor said. 'What's this I
hear about you not being well, young lady?'

'I'm perfectly well, thank you.' Ronnie bit back
further words, wanting to find out what her mother
had said about her.

'That's not what your mother says.'

'Oh?'

'Let me examine you.'

'No, thank you. I'm perfectly all right. What I want
is my clothes and to be allowed to return to my job
at the farm.'

'You see what she's like?' Edwina said, dabbing at
her eyes with a handkerchief. 'The farmer had to call
me to take her away and she's still pretending she
works there.'

Ronnie took a deep breath. So that was the story,
was it? 'You can ring Mr Tilling up and check that,
Dr Hilliam. It isn't true.' She saw by his face that he
didn't believe her and the words escaped her before
she could stop them. 'Why will you not even *try*?'

The doctor pulled out a phial of liquid. 'I think
we'll give you a few drops of this to calm you down.'

'No! She's already done that.'

'I think I know best, young lady.' He and her mother
advanced towards the bed.

Ronnie knew it was hopeless but she still fought,
protesting loudly that she didn't want to be drugged
and her mother was telling lies. When they'd forced
the drops down her she lay back on the bed, panting,

glad to see that she'd planted a few scratches on her mother's arm as well as one on the doctor's hand.

'She's quite strong,' he muttered as he stood staring down at Ronnie. 'I do think you'd better get some professional help, my dear lady. And as for you, young woman, you'd better . . .'

'What would *you* do if your own mother was telling lies about you, if there was nothing at all wrong with you and yet people kept drugging you?' she demanded. 'Wouldn't you struggle and fight, Dr Hilliam?'

He blinked at her in shock.

'I'm not out of my wits, I'm angry at being locked up and drugged, that's all.'

'She's persuasive, isn't she?' Edwina murmured. 'But she behaves very foolishly and has embarrassed the poor people she used to work for.'

'I haven't!' Ronnie yelled. 'You only have to ask them if they want me back.' She repeated their name and address.

'She can't even get their address right,' her mother said, trying to keep a sad expression on her face, but not hiding her annoyance.

'I've got it perfectly correct.'

Edwina laid one hand on the doctor's arm. 'I don't want this known. Please, Dr Hilliam, can we keep it between ourselves. It may only be a temporary problem. Let's see if she calms down. I'm sure she will now she's got me to look after her.'

Ronnie felt the room start to waver around her. 'She's lying to you. I can't believe you're so trusting! It'd take so little to check.'

She turned her back on them so that they wouldn't see the tears of despair in her eyes, summoned up an image of Giles and clung to that. Surely he'd guess where she was, come and find her, rescue her?

A storm had started outside, with rain beating against the window panes and thunder rumbling in the distance. She listened to the sound of the rain as she grew drowsy.

She didn't notice her mother and the doctor leaving and soon slipped into an uneasy sleep.

6

When Bevan came home from the shop that evening, the way he looked at Ellen worried her. It was an assessing sort of look, the same kind of inspection he gave a beast before he decided to buy it.

Sure enough, after she'd cleared the tea things away and washed up, he pointed to a chair.

'Sit down, Ellen. I want to speak to you.'

She glanced at her mother, who seemed as puzzled as she was by this request, then did as she was told.

'You know how happy your mother is to have you back in Shawcroft?' He raised one eyebrow, waiting for an answer.

'Yes.'

'And you need a proper job, now that this stupid Aides thing has ended.'

Ellen didn't wait for him to finish this sentence. 'If you're going to start insulting Lady Bingram and what she and the Aides did for our country, then I'm afraid I'm not going to listen to you. I have a testimonial from General Lutchenson himself acknowledging what I did and thanking me for my service to my country.'

His face went deep red and he glared at her, opening his mouth as if to speak, then closing it again. After a deep breath or two, he went on, 'That's as may be, but you still need another job now.'

'Eventually, yes.'

Ah, he thought. So she's not short of money. 'Well, you're a very fortunate young woman, because Mrs Shipton was in the shop today asking if you'd be interested in having your old job back.'

'Well, I wouldn't. It's a form of slavery, being a housemaid, especially in that household.'

He gaped at her and even her mother looked surprised at what she'd said.

'If I go back into any sort of service, it'll be in a hotel where you get better paid and better treated too. My friend Mary Ann was telling me about it. There are plenty of jobs for experienced workers in Blackpool, London, Bournemouth—'

'You're not going gallivanting off again, young woman! The war is over now and it's time you realised that. It's not decent for single women to leave home until they get married.'

'Well, I'm afraid I have no plans to get married and I'm not coming back to live here permanently. The only reason I'm here now – *temporarily* – is to see my mother.'

Anger boiled over in him and he thumped his fist down on the wooden table. 'Be quiet or I'll give you the back of my hand. I'm not taking cheek from you in my own house.'

She jumped to her feet. 'If you lay one finger on

me *ever again*, I'll not only leave the house, but I'll go to the police and charge you with assault.'

He laughed in her face. 'Wes won't even listen to you.'

She opened her mouth to tell him Wes's days were numbered, but Dorothy's thin, breathless voice cut into the angry silence.

'Please. Oh, please don't! You know how it upsets me.' Dorothy pushed herself to her feet then gasped and crumpled to the floor.

Bevan was there at once, scooping up his wife and carrying her through to her bedroom. 'Now see what you've done,' he tossed over his shoulder. 'I hope you're proud of yourself!'

Ellen closed her eyes and took a long, shuddering breath, then opened her eyes again and forced herself to unclench her fists. She went to get a glass of water and carried it through to the front room, where Bevan was sitting by the bed, patting his wife's hand, begging her to wake up, speak to him.

Setting the glass down by the bed, Ellen reached out towards her mother.

'What are you doing now?' he demanded.

'Sitting her up. It'll be easier for her to breathe.' She saw his dubious expression and added, 'I did a first aid course as part of my training. I know what I'm doing.'

With a grunt that she took for assent, he stepped backwards, watching suspiciously as she made sure her mother was in a sitting position.

Ignoring him, she took the smelling salts from the

bedside table and waved them under the unconscious woman's nose. She didn't like the pungent aroma, but her mother had always used them for headaches, saying they cleared her head.

After a minute or two, Dorothy made a soft noise and opened her eyes. 'What has—?' She looked from one to the other and tears came into her eyes. 'Don't quarrel any more. *Please!*'

'We've stopped arguing,' Ellen said gently. 'But we can't always agree, you know that.' She saw her stepfather scowl at that remark, but she didn't intend to let him use this episode as a way of forcing her to keep quiet while he continued to bark out orders.

'But you'll take the job?' Dorothy fumbled for her daughter's hand. 'Please. I know I shouldn't be asking you, but I'd like you to stay so that we can see one another . . . while there's time.' She closed her eyes again. 'I'm so tired. Could you help me undress, please, dear? I think I'll stay in bed now.'

Ellen watched as Bevan bent to kiss her mother's cheek and stroke it with one pudgy fingertip, a surprisingly tender gesture from a man like him. Then he left the two women alone.

When her mother was settled, Ellen sat on the edge of the bed. 'I'll go and see what Mrs Gresham is offering in pay and conditions, but there's no use my taking the job if I only get one day a month off, is there? I'd hardly see anything of you then. And I'm not taking it on a permanent basis, not for anything. Three months is the most I'll consider.

They might not want me for that short time.'

'Thank you.' Dorothy closed her eyes.

Ellen waited a moment or two then went back into the kitchen.

He looked up. 'Is she comfortable?'

'Yes.' She hesitated. 'I'll tell you the same as I told her . . . I'm *never* going back to such work permanently and I'm only considering it now for my mother's sake. I'll go and see if Mrs Shipton wants help for a few months.'

He looked at her sourly then nodded.

'I'm going to bed now. I'm tired.' Ellen wasn't in the slightest bit tired. In fact, she was full of suppressed energy, not being used to leading such an idle life. But she didn't want to sit with him and risk another argument that would upset her mother.

Perhaps a temporary job at the Hall was the best way to stay nearby. With a motorcycle at her disposal, she could make some arrangement about time off and easily drive into Shawcroft to visit her mother two or three times a week.

She definitely couldn't live with *him* for more than a few days.

As she was falling asleep, she remembered her savings and came wide awake again. She really did need to get them into a bank. But the savings bank in Shawcroft was a branch of the same one she'd used in London and she knew the manager. He was another who regarded women as inferior beings and he'd probably tell her stepfather how much she had in her account. She hated dealing with men like him.

She'd have to go into the next town and open up an account there, would do it before she started at the Hall . . . *if* she started work there. In the meantime the money was safely locked in her tin trunk, even if it wasn't earning her interest.

The following morning Ellen dressed with care then went round to her Uncle Martin's to get her motorcycle.

'I'm going out to the Hall to see about a temporary job.'

He looked at her in surprise. 'You said you'd never go back there.'

'It's for my mother. I don't think she's got very long to live, so I need to be nearby. Only I can't live with *him*.' No need to explain to her uncle who she meant.

'You could always stay with us, love.'

'I know. And if I ever get stuck I will come to you. But I may as well be earning some money as sitting around.'

He went into his workshop and came out with the high tension lead. 'I took this off last night, just to make certain no one stole your bike.'

'Thank you.'

She fitted the lead on and pushed the motorcycle out of the back of his workshop and round into the road. He stood and watched but didn't offer to help her, which she appreciated. She'd been dealing with motorcycles for years, after all.

As she got out of the alley, Jory Nelson came

strolling along the street, whistling in that tuneless way that always irritated her. Ignoring him, she switched on the fuel and kick-started the bike. The engine started easily and she smiled as she pulled on the leather bonnet. When she'd fastened it, she turned to mount the bike and found Jory standing in front of her.

'Nice to see you again, Ellen.'

His eyes roved up and down her body and she felt her muscles tighten in disgust. She hated being so close to him. How she could have walked out with him for several months without realising what he was like, she didn't understand now. But she'd been young and flattered to be chosen by the man half her friends dreamed about. 'Well, it's not nice to see you. Will you get out of my way, please?'

'Haven't you got a kind word for an old friend?'

'You're no friend of mine.'

'I want to be more than your friend. I've never forgotten our last – meeting.'

She tensed from head to toe. 'Neither have I. I tried to report you for rape and if Wes Cobbley had been a *real* policeman, you'd have stood trial for it.'

'It's not rape when two young people make love.'

'There was no love involved. You hurt me badly and I can't bear even the sight of you now.'

His expression grew ugly. 'You'd better not go around saying that. I can be a bad enemy.'

She glared at him. 'So can I. I'm not the naïve young girl you attacked last time.'

'I'm still bigger than you.'

He laid one hand on her arm, smirking, and she knocked him aside in the quick twisting way she'd been taught in the self-defence lessons Lady Bingram had insisted all her Aides received to protect themselves in the dark streets of London. *Don't wait, attack them before they realise you're going to fight back*, the instructor had always said. *Surprise them.*

As Jory stumbled and fell, he yelled out in shock and she rolled the motorcycle forward, putting it into gear and driving off without a backward glance.

He got up, cursing, yelling after her, 'You stupid bitch! I could have you up for assault.'

'You'd be the one up for assault,' a voice said behind him. 'You were blocking that young woman's way and you laid hands on her.'

He turned to see the man who was lodging with the Pughs glaring at him. 'Mind your own bloody business, you.'

'It's everyone's business when decent young women are accosted in the street.'

'Decent! That one! I've had her spread-eagled beneath me many a time and I'll have her again. She's just playing hard to get. She likes a bit of rough play, Ellen Dawson does. Her and me have known one another for years and we'd be married now if it wasn't for the damned war, so don't poke your nose in where it's not wanted.' He turned and strode off down the street, hands thrust deep into his pockets, shoulders stiff with anger.

Seth watched him go, then picked up his knapsack

and started walking again. He'd miss the train if he didn't get a move on.

As he sat in the compartment on the way to Manchester, he couldn't get the other man's words out of his mind. 'Spread-eagled beneath me' and 'likes a bit of rough stuff'. Was that true? Surely not? His instinct was to say no, the man was lying. He couldn't see Ellen being that sort, she seemed decent to the core and was well thought of by decent people.

But even with his wide experience, Seth had been fooled once or twice before by women. You couldn't always tell. Some people were born liars.

The happy feeling he'd had about meeting Ellen seemed tarnished now. He stared blindly out of the carriage window, his thoughts in turmoil. Surely, surely the fellow had been lying?

As he neared Manchester, he pushed his worries aside. He'd be living in Shawcroft soon, would have plenty of opportunities to get to know her better and find out the truth.

Ellen drove along the lane that led to the Hall, feeling dirtied by her encounter with Jory. Bile rose in her throat as she remembered *that day*. She was tall and strong for a woman and had fought fiercely, but he had been stronger . . . still was. Her eyes filled with tears and she had to stop the motorcycle to get control of her emotions. How many times had she vowed to get on with her life, not let that one evening spoil it? Times without number.

But it was hard to forget something as terrible as being raped by someone you were courting, someone who'd been pleasant enough before, if a bit bossy. And Jory had chosen the time and place so carefully she knew he'd planned it, not acted on impulse, because if there had been anyone within earshot they'd have come running at the sound of her screams.

She shuddered and gripped the handlebars tightly. *Stop it!* she told herself. *Stop it this minute. If you don't, he'll win.* She'd known it would be difficult to come back, that it would revive old memories to meet him again. Well, she'd got the first confrontation over and done with now, hadn't she? She'd be more in control of herself next time. And if Jory thought she was going to start seeing him again he'd got a shock or two coming. She'd as soon walk out with a venomous reptile.

Suddenly she remembered that she had made him fall over today and that cheered her up a little. She hadn't needed to put her self-defence lessons to use before. She'd better go over what the old soldier had told them and practise the moves. She must be ready to act next time she saw Jory.

She allowed herself a few minutes in that quiet lane, sitting listening to a lark. High above her, the tiny bird was trilling away and the sounds cascading down seemed so clean and pure, she could feel herself relaxing. Sunlight warmed her face and dried her tears, seeming to promise better things to come. Well, everyone had promised people a brighter tomorrow after the privations of the war, hadn't they?

By the time she kick-started the engine again, she felt calm and confident. Mrs Shipton was in for a few surprises today. Ellen felt decades older, not a mere five years, and was far more experienced than the girl who'd worked as a maid. As a young girl she'd been terrified of Mrs Gresham and hadn't known how to escape from a job she hated – or how to escape from her stepfather, either.

Thank you, Daphne, she thought, as she had thought so many times before. *You gave me so much.*

There wasn't one of Lady Bingram's Aides who wouldn't agree with Ellen about that.

Ronnie woke up in a tangle of sheets, feeling heavy-headed and unable to think clearly. She pulled the chamber pot from under the bed and used it, grimacing at its stinking contents. She kept expecting her mother to come and gloat over her helplessness, but no one so much as walked past the door.

She was so desperately thirsty she found it hard to concentrate on anything else and went to sit by the window in an effort to distract herself. Not that much was happening at the rear of the house. Glenys walked out with the peelings from the kitchen, putting them into the pig bin. She stopped on the way back to have a word with Gerry, the farm manager who had helped Tadwyn hold Ronnie when they brought her here. He had looked surprised when asked to hold her, but he'd done it. He'd been second in command of the grounds when she left. Had he come back from the war or had he managed to stay here in an essential job?

Finally footsteps approached and instinctively Ronnie got to her feet. The door opened and her mother came in. Tadwyn stayed in the doorway again, arms folded.

Her mother studied her. 'You look dreadful. Are you going to behave sensibly or must we continue to treat you like a foolish child?'

Ronnie closed her eyes for a moment, willing herself to be convincing. The window only opened a few inches, she'd tried it, the door was solid oak and although she had grown stronger through her work in the Land Army, she'd already proved that she couldn't win against her mother's massive strength. She had to use her wits.

'Well?'

By thinking of Giles, Ronnie managed to squeeze out a tear or two. 'What do you want me to do?'

'What I said: be sensible about Algie. Think of your inheritance.' She gestured widely around them. 'You owe this place a duty. As a Gresham, you can't simply please yourself.'

'If I married Algie, I'd not be a Gresham any more.'

'He can change his name. His parents wouldn't object. And it's not as if you don't get on well with him. The two of you were good friends as children. I can't see why you shouldn't be perfectly happy together.'

Except that Algie had never aroused that sort of

feeling in her. Ronnie bent her head, thinking furiously. She wished she could see him, talk to him, find out whether he really wanted to marry her . . . If he didn't, maybe he'd help her escape. He was a rather gentle person, though, who hated upsets and quarrels, so she couldn't even be sure of that. 'I can't think straight.' She was glad her voice came out husky from thirst. 'I haven't had anything to drink since yesterday.'

'We can send for some food and drink the minute you agree to behave yourself.'

'It'll be drugged!'

'I'll give you my word that it won't be drugged if you'll promise me not to try to escape.'

Ronnie wrapped her arms round herself and went over to the window. It was, she found, quite easy to cry when she needed to. The mere thought of losing Giles brought tears to her eyes. Her mother followed her over to the window and she tensed.

'Let's call a truce for today, Veronica. We need to get some food and drink into you – and I promise it'll not be drugged. Once you're feeling better we can discuss matters calmly. You *do* owe a duty to your name, to this estate, you know you do.'

Ronnie let her shoulders sag. 'All right. A truce.'

'Good. I'll send Glenys up with some water and food.' Her voice grew harsher. 'But Tadwyn will be with her. There will be no opportunity for you to escape, not until I am certain that you really have decided to be sensible.'

She walked out and the door closed behind her, the big, old-fashioned key turning loudly in the lock.

Were promises binding when extracted by threats and bullying? Ronnie wondered. She had been brought up always to keep her word, but if it came to a choice between that and keeping Giles, she knew what she would do.

It seemed to be taking a long time for Glenys to bring up something to drink. Ronnie began to pace up and down the room, feeling quite desperate with thirst.

A sound outside drew her back to the window and she watched as a motorbike and sidecar drew up behind the house, coming to a halt near the stables. She couldn't see things close to her, they were just a blur, but she could see quite clearly at this distance.

When the engine stopped, the driver got off and removed a leather bonnet, shaking out her short, curly hair. It was a woman! Ronnie's hand went up instinctively to her own hair. She'd have liked to have it cut short, but hadn't dared because her mother had always said it was her best feature, soft and dark blond in colour, waving gently about her face.

Then she recognised the visitor: Ellen Dawson, who had been a maid here for a few years before going off to London to work as one of Lady Bingram's Aides. Ronnie would have loved to do that, but her ladyship hadn't invited her. In fact, it had taken until 1917 for Ronnie to pluck up the courage to do something that would take her away from her mother. When she'd joined the Women's Land Army she'd done it secretly, then had made sure it was so widely known that even her mother would not have dared pull strings to get her out of doing it. Her mother had washed her hands of her, prophesying that the rough conditions would teach her not to be defiant. But she'd been wrong. Ronnie had loved living and working on the farm.

Outside Ellen was looking up at the house and she didn't seem to be very happy. She sighed then squared her shoulders and walked towards the kitchen door as if about to do something she didn't like.

Was she coming back to work here? If so, perhaps there was a chance of her posting a letter for Ronnie. They'd chatted sometimes in the old days, in spite of their differences, because they had been the only two young women in a house full of older folk.

Hope trickled through Ronnie, just a tiny thread of it.

A key turned in the lock and Glenys brought in a tray. Ronnie went to snatch the glass of water off it and drained it straight away.

'I was so thirsty,' she explained, seeing the elderly maid gaping at her. 'Haven't had anything to eat or drink since yesterday. Do you think you could bring me another glass of water, in fact a whole jugful?'

'Yes, miss.' She set down the tray and went out.

Tadwyn went with her locking the door.

Ronnie sat down to eat, ravenous now. She regarded the food with suspicion, then shrugged and put a forkful of scrambled eggs into her mouth.

She would soon find out what her mother's promises were worth.

Ellen couldn't put it off any longer, so walked towards the house. She hadn't expected to feel quite so nervous. She could remember all too clearly being a scared girl of fourteen just starting on her new job here. And yet the whole place looked smaller than she'd remembered – shabbier too. Was that the war or a lack of money?

She knocked on the kitchen door, which was half open, and footsteps came towards her. It was Glenys who opened it and the elderly maid stood looking at her as if she was a stranger.

'Can I help you, miss?'

'Don't you recognise me, Glenys?'

The other woman frowned then her face cleared suddenly. 'Ellen! Is it really you? Eh, you look bonny with your hair short like that. Have you come home now?'

'I'm back for a while but not to stay.'

Glenys glanced towards the motorbike. 'It was never you driving that thing?'

'Yes. The bike's mine. I learned to drive it in London.'

'Well, I never! Is it safe?'

'If you drive it carefully, which I do.' People were always surprised that a woman could drive a motorcycle and yet it wasn't hard, though a smaller woman might have trouble pushing it and kick-starting it. 'I'll take you for a ride on it one day, if you like.'

Glenys goggled at her. 'Eeh!' She put up one hand to cover her mouth, then straightened up and said in a rush, 'I'd like that. I've never rid on one before.' She lowered her voice to add, 'I envied you going away to London. All I've ever known was housework and I've never been anywhere but my auntie's in Blackpool.'

A voice from inside the kitchen yelled, 'Are you going to stand there all day nattering, Glenys? Who is it?'

'It's Ellen Dawson, come back from London.'

They went inside and Cook turned to study the newcomer. 'You've grown up, lass.'

'I hope so. It's been nearly five years, after all. You haven't changed at all.'

Cook smiled down at herself. 'Not an ounce different to when you worked here. Some get fatter as they get older. I'm lucky.'

'Ellen's driven herself here on a motorcycle and she's going to give me a ride on it,' Glenys said.

The older woman stared for a moment, then drew herself up. 'Can I have a ride on that thing too, Ellen? If Glenys can do it, so can I.'

'Yes, of course.' She was amused by their reaction. Apparently the war had changed them, too, because they'd never have done anything half as daring in the old days. The two of them were close friends, had been kind to her when they found her crying her eyes out in the early days. She'd always got on well with *them*. It was the housekeeper who'd been the tyrant, the mistress's eyes and ears below stairs. 'Mrs Shipton left a message for me to call. Is this a convenient time?'

'Are you coming back to work here?'

'I may be, but only for a while.'

Cook's face softened. 'It's your mother, isn't it? I heard she was ill.'

Ellen nodded, a lump coming into her throat so that she couldn't speak.

'I'll go and see if Mrs Shipton's free,' Glenys said with one of her quick little pats on the arm.

'Thank you.'

Glenys was back almost immediately. 'She'll see you in five minutes.'

Mrs Shipton did that sort of thing, kept you waiting on purpose to try to make you feel nervous. Well, it wouldn't work now, Ellen wouldn't let it. 'Is there a cup of tea in that pot, Cook?'

'Yes. Made only a few minutes ago. Get her a cup, Glenys.'

It was as if time had stood still here.

It seemed even more like the old days when a young girl came in, looking scared, her uniform too big for her.

Cook smiled encouragingly at the girl. 'This is Millie. She started work here last year. She's a very hard worker.'

Millie's anxious expression relaxed a little at this praise. 'I've finished, Cook.'

'Well, you sit down with us and have a cup of tea, then afterwards Glenys will find you another job.'

From the conversation during the next few

minutes, it was soon obvious that Millie was rather slow-witted.

Poor thing, Ellen thought. She hoped Mrs Shipton and Mrs Gresham didn't shout at her. She sipped her tea and accepted one of Cook's scones, eating it quickly, waiting for the summons.

7

Jory scowled as he walked down the street. Halsopp had said he should find himself another woman to take his mind off Ellen. There were plenty of spare ones about nowadays because of the number of men killed in the war. But it had always been Ellen for him, he'd known that right from school. He'd never understood why, because she wasn't the easiest of women, but there it was.

He'd been courting her for over a year when he was drafted into the Army and he came home on leave expecting her to treat him differently. A lot of the lads said their girls had given in to them because they might be killed. But no, not Ellen bloody Dawson! She'd refused him yet again, would hardly let him touch her, apart from a kiss or two.

He stopped walking to stare into his memories for the hundredth time. He could see the evening as clearly as if it had happened yesterday. It'd been warm enough for them to sit in a sheltered space looking down on the town. But his need had risen urgently and this time he'd refused to take no for an answer. He'd enjoyed holding her down, seeing the fear in her eyes, feeling her soft body beneath his. He'd gone wild that night because like the other lads, he knew this might be his last chance to have a woman. There were a lot of men being killed out there.

Afterwards, when it was over, she'd lain utterly still beneath him, eyes closed, tears leaking down her cheeks, silver streaks of moisture showing clearly in the moonlight. Suddenly his feeling of pleasure had drained away. When he got off her, intending to apologise, she jumped up and ran down the hill so quickly he couldn't pull his trousers up in time to catch her.

The following morning he decided he'd better go round and apologise. It was Sunday, her monthly day off, and she'd be at home. He still felt women owed it to soldiers to be kind to them, but he was sorry he'd been so rough. He ought to have been more gentle, it being her first time.

To his relief, Ellen herself had answered the door. She looked terrible, her face white and drawn, her lips a thin, bloodless line.

'What do *you* want, Jory Nelson?'

'To see you. Ellen love, I—'

'Don't you "Ellen love" me!' She glanced quickly over her shoulder then back at him. 'My mother's in the kitchen, so if you lay one finger on me, I'll scream for help and she'll come running. I'll just say this once: I'm finished with you, Jory. I don't want to see you or speak to you ever again. Find yourself another girl stupid enough to trust you, because I never could after what you did to me last night.'

She started to close the door and he put out one hand to stop her. 'You can't mean it!'

'Oh, I do.' She jerked away from him with a look of revulsion. 'If you touch me, I'll be sick.'

'But Ellen, I don't want us to break up. Surely you realise – I want to marry you. Look, let's get married next time I'm on leave, then we can—'

'I'd not marry you now if you were the last man alive in the whole world.'

'It was because I might get killed at the front. You don't know how that makes a man feel.'

'I hope you *do* get killed. In fact, I'll be praying for it every single night from now on.'

He breathed deeply. You didn't need that sort of thing weighing down your mind. You needed all the luck you could get. 'What if you're expecting?'

'If I get a child out of this, I'll leave town and keep it well away from you. Fine father you'd make!'

He flinched. Her voice had a hard edge to it, her eyes were burning with hatred. She didn't look like the Ellen he knew. 'I said I was sorry and . . .'

'That doesn't change things. Do you honestly think I'd marry a man who could hurt me like this?' She pushed up her sleeves to show him the bruising.

He stared at the big blue patches in shock. 'I didn't do that!'

'Who else raped me last night? There are more bruises on my legs, too, just as big. If you've done it once, you'll do it again. I've seen Mrs Flamstead pretending she's clumsy and bumps into things, when everyone knows her husband beats her. I'm not getting into that sort of life. I'll make sure you never have the chance to hurt me again.'

'Shh!' He glanced round but there was no one nearby. 'Ellen, I'll make it up to you. I swear.'

As he reached out towards her she jerked out of reach, yelling, 'Mum!'

A voice answered from the kitchen so he took a quick step backwards.

'It's all right,' Ellen called.

'Look, I'll talk to you again next time I come on leave, after you've calmed down, had time to recover.'

'I'll never recover as far as you're concerned. Didn't you hear what I said? It's over between us, Jory.'

She'd told her mother and Mr Halsopp the same day that she wasn't walking out with him any more, the bitch. Thank god, she'd not told them why, or Mr Halsopp would have come after him. As it was, he tried to find out what had happened between them and—

'Hoy!'

Jory swung round to see Mr Cobbley beckoning to him, which jerked him abruptly back into the present.

'Have you gone deaf, lad?'

'Sorry. I was miles away, remembering something.'

'I've got something to tell you. Better come inside.'

He followed the old man into the small police station and waited patiently until Wes had puffed his way round to sit on the stool behind the counter.

'They're bringing in a new man. I've to retire permanently.'

'Who is it? Anyone you know?'

'They didn't say who, only that he'll be arriving in the middle of the week and I'm to vacate the house by the end of the following week and be ready to hand things over. We're to work together until I leave then he'll take over completely.' He sighed gustily. 'Turned out to pasture, after all I've done.'

'We'll have to hope the new fellow knows which side his bread is buttered on, then.'

Wes shook his head sadly. 'Can't rely on it. They train them to be too persnickety these days. And he'll be an outsider, with no feeling for the town. I wouldn't trust him, if I were you.'

'I'd better go and tell Dad. He'll want to sort out a few things, just in case. Have you told Mr Halsopp yet? He'll need to know as well.'

'No. You can do that for me.' Wes looked cautiously over his shoulder, then added in an undertone, 'I daren't leave the place. *She* wants to clear it up for the new man and she keeps popping in and out. Can't call my soul my own today. Won't be able to after I've retired, either.'

Even as he spoke, Mrs Cobbley came bustling in. She gave Jory her usual disapproving look then ignored him. 'We'll go through the things in your inner office now, Wesley.'

'Yes, dear.'

Grinning at how meek Mr Cobbley always became in the presence of his plump, bustling wife, Jory walked away. But the grin soon faded. Having a new bobby in Shawcroft could put a big dent into certain profitable enterprises his father had set up during the war.

★   ★   ★

When Seth got back to Manchester, Bert took him out for a pint. 'What did you think of Shawcroft, then?'

'Nice enough little town. More of a village, really.'

'Did you meet Cobbley?'

'No. I didn't want to draw attention to myself. But I saw him at church and heard people talk about him. I reckon there's definitely something going on, though no one said what.' He waited and when Bert didn't say anything, prompted, 'Aren't you going to tell me what you were hinting at before I went?'

'I'll leave that to the inspector. We've an appointment with him tomorrow. He's got a few things he wants to discuss with you before you take over.'

Seth's heart sank. 'This isn't going to be an easy posting, is it?'

'It can be as easy or hard as you make it. But be careful who you make friends with because you'll be expected to uphold the law without fear or favour.'

And beyond that comment, Bert wouldn't be drawn. When he clamped his lips together in just that way, it was no use pressing him, so Seth let things ride and enjoyed the quiet stroll back to the house followed by a pleasant evening with Bert and his wife.

When he went to bed, he tried not to think about Ellen, but it was no use. He kept seeing her face, feeling the warmth of her back pressing against him on that motorcycle, seeing the way her eyes sparkled with life when she smiled.

Then he remembered what Nelson had said about her. She ignored the conventions to drive the motorcycle. Did she ignore them in other ways as well? He scowled into the darkness. It *couldn't* be true! Surely, it couldn't?

A restful posting to the country? Hah!

The bell rang in the kitchen and Glenys got up to answer it. She was back a minute later. 'Mrs Shipton will see you now, love.'

Ellen drained the last inch of tea and put her cup down. She went up to the housekeeper's room, which was just above the kitchen, and knocked on the door.

'Come!'

As she walked in, Mrs Shipton stared at her as if she'd never seen her before in her life and Ellen stared back. She waited to be asked to sit down, but she wasn't.

'Step forward so that I can see you properly.'

Starting to feel angry at this treatment, Ellen waited a few seconds then moved forward one slow pace. Mrs Shipton seemed older, with extra lines on her forehead and down the sides of her mouth, as well as an air of worry, but she still spoke as sharply and looked down her nose at you.

'You've come about taking up your old position, I presume?'

'Not quite.'

'What do you mean? Why else would you come to see me after I'd spoken to Mr Halsopp?'

'My stepfather said you were short of staff and my mother's dying, so I want to stay near her as long as I can. But I *don't* want my old job back permanently. I'm just looking around for a *temporary* job. If that would be any use to you, I'm happy to come and work here for a while.'

'I'm very disappointed in you, Ellen, after all we did for you, all we taught you. You knew nothing when you came to work here. Modern young women have no sense of gratitude. We need someone permanent, as you must surely realise. We've only Glenys and *that fool of a girl.*'

Ellen turned back towards the door. 'Then I won't trouble you any further.'

'Come back this minute!' Mrs Shipton stared at her, bosom heaving beneath its old-fashioned, high-necked blouse. 'And sit down. We do still need help.'

Ellen took the chair.

'What exactly were you doing in London for Lady Bingram?'

'I was a courier mostly, taking documents around London for the War Office, driving senior officers too sometimes.' She opened her handbag and pulled out two pieces of paper that she treasured greatly. 'Perhaps you'd like to read these testimonials? Lady Bingram says she'd be happy to provide further references, if necessary.'

Mrs Shipton took them and there was silence as she read them. 'They seem to think very highly of you.' But she said it sourly, as if she wasn't pleased about that.

Ellen took back the pieces of paper and folded them carefully, putting them in the big envelope she'd bought specially to keep them safe. 'I think a great deal of Lady Bingram, too. She taught me so much.'

'Well . . . it's a bit unusual to take on a temporary maid, but I do need extra help right now, so I'm prepared to hire you on a temporary basis. Though if I find a permanent girl, then I'm afraid I shall have to dismiss you immediately.'

'That's fine with me. There's just one other thing. I shall want to see my mother regularly, so I'll need a couple of hours off two or three times a week to go into Shawcroft, rather than the whole day off one fortnight and a half day off the other fortnight.'

'You won't be able to get into town and back again in that short time. It's a four mile walk.'

'I have a motorcycle. It doesn't take very long on that.'

Mrs Shipton stared at her as if she'd grown two heads. 'A motorcycle?'

'That's what I drove during the war, then afterwards I bought it from Lady Bingram.'

'I don't know what Mrs Gresham will say about that. And I certainly don't approve of women driving, let alone bringing one of those nasty, noisy things out here to the Hall.'

'I'd have to bring it with me to keep it safe. And I couldn't work here without it.' Ellen waited as the silence stretched out, praying for patience. She'd forgotten how much grumbling Mrs Shipton did, how you had to bite your tongue and let her get it out of her system.

'Well, I suppose we could let you put it in a shed somewhere. We can't pay you as much as Lady Bingram did, though, especially as you'll be taking extra time off. Fifteen shillings a week, all found.'

Mean old devil! Ellen thought, pursing her lips, wondering if it was worth it. 'All right. But payable weekly, not monthly.' She wanted to put her savings into a bank and not need to draw any money out to tide her through the first month, but would still have to buy petrol. Surely someone round here sold it?

'We have always paid quarterly. Even monthly is a departure.'

'I need the money weekly to buy petrol and little treats for my mother.'

Mrs Shipton breathed deeply. 'Very well. As long as you can start straight away, by which I mean this very afternoon. The place is in a terrible mess.'

'Could I not start tomorrow? There's some business I need to take care of.'

'We need you today. And since we're making an exception about how we employ you, you can surely do that for us.'

Ellen sighed. She'd have to lodge the money in the savings bank another time. Still, it was locked in her trunk at her mother's and should be quite safe, since the house was never left unattended. She'd leave her trunk there and just bring enough clothes here to manage on. 'I'll go back and get my things, then.'

'Do you have your old uniform?'

'No. But I have a dark dress which will do for best if I'm answering the door or anything and it won't matter what I wear to do the cleaning, surely?'

'We have certain standards to maintain.'

'Even if my mother still has my outfit, I've grown

since I was last here and it won't fit me. But I suppose the aprons should still be wearable.'

'And the caps.'

There was a pregnant silence. The housekeeper must be aware that modern young women hated those badges of servitude.

Mrs Shipton looked at her. 'Though how they'll look on you with that short hair, I don't know. If you were staying on, we'd insist on you growing it again. It's not decent, such short hair.'

'I'll see if I can find the caps.' After all, she'd only have to wear the horrible things for a few weeks.

The housekeeper gave a thin smile of triumph then looked at the clock on her mantelpiece. 'It's lunchtime. If you'd care to stay for a meal, you're welcome to.'

'Thank you. I am hungry, I must admit.'

Mrs Shipton watched Ellen go then went to inform her mistress that she'd hired another maid, even if only temporarily. She found Mrs Gresham in the dining room just finishing her lunch, which she always took early when she was on her own, and was graciously invited to sit down and have a cup of tea.

'I hope I'm doing the right thing, ma'am,' she finished. 'But Ellen's the only maid I've been able to find and we do need someone else.'

'Is she a good worker?'

'Very good. Don't you remember her?'

'Goodness me, no. Those young girls all look alike when they've got their uniforms on. Except for this new one, of course. Please continue to keep *her* out of sight of visitors.'

'Yes, ma'am. And to answer your question, Ellen was an excellent worker, one of the best maids I've ever had. I never needed to stand over her to get things done properly. Her mother trained her well.'

'Then we'll give her a month's trial. Make that plain to her when she starts. It'll keep her on her toes.'

As if there was a need to keep that girl on her toes, the housekeeper thought as she walked down to the kitchen. She felt a bit wary of the new Ellen, who had seen more of the world than she had, by the sounds of it. The testimonials spoke of her war work in glowing terms and it seemed she'd even been abroad a few times.

Mrs Shipton prayed that Mrs Gresham wouldn't do anything to make Ellen leave. You could never tell with the mistress, who could be difficult, spiteful even. Look at the way she was treating poor Miss Veronica. It wasn't a housekeeper's place to protest, but really, it wasn't right to kidnap the poor girl just because she wanted a life of her own. From what Tadwyn said, Miss Veronica had found someone to marry, but he reckoned that she'd be forced to marry young Mr St Corbin in the end, as her mother wanted, and they all knew the problems that would arise from that. Surely Mrs Gresham realised what he was like? No, perhaps not. Mrs Gresham only ever realised the things she wanted to.

And servants always knew more than their employers, didn't they?

The master would never have allowed such treatment of the child he'd loved so much, though, nor would he have allowed her to marry a young man like that. He must be turning in his grave.

Seth and Bert were shown into Inspector Dunham's office. Seth had only met him a few times before, but remembered him clearly. Though he looked as brisk and efficient as ever, he'd aged, lost that robust look, as men do when they grow older. His hair was quite silver now, but he still had a very piercing gaze and was the sort of officer you instinctively trusted.

Dunham didn't speak at first, except to invite them to sit down, but he studied Seth just as carefully as Seth was studying him, nodding once or twice as if he approved of what he saw.

'I believe the sergeant has given you some hints about your new job, eh, Talbot?' he said at last.

Seth nodded. 'He hasn't said anything specific, but I gather you're not happy with how things have been run in Shawcroft.'

'That's putting it mildly. We're extremely *un*happy and would have done something about it before now, if it hadn't been for the war throwing up a few more important crises. The persons concerned might have got away with it, because they're not the only ones selling black-market stuff, only they've not stopped their little games even now that the war has ended.'

The inspector went on to explain what had roused suspicions, the things Seth should watch out for, how he was to react. 'Given the murder last month, these men would be desperate if they realised how much we suspect, so I don't want you tackling them on your own. The phone lines run out that way, because of a certain lady's help with top secret groups, so we'll install a telephone in the police station. That way you'll be able to call for reinforcements if you need them.'

'What exactly happened last month?'

The inspector hesitated. 'A man was killed and even though this didn't happen in Shawcross, we think it's connected to the group there. That's why I want you to be extremely careful.'

This was far worse than Seth had expected.

'There's a young lawyer looking to settle somewhere nearby, well, he's my godson, actually. He was doing intelligence work in the Army and is still doing the odd job for the government even now – there's a lot to clear up after a war. Giles Covington, he's called and I've recommended him to contact my friend Monnings, who has the only legal practice in Shawcross. I'll tell them both about you, so if you have any need of their help, don't hesitate to contact them. Covington's a good bloke, very highly thought of in Whitehall.'

'Giles Covington,' Seth repeated, to fix the name in his mind.

'In addition, considering your excellent wartime record, we've decided to promote you to senior constable, firstly because you deserve it and secondly because that will make you senior in rank to the man who has been acting as the local policeman and directing the special constables in that area. We don't want anyone letting things slide, out of mistaken friendship and an assumption that an older man has more authority than you do – though you might keep that under your hat unless you really need to wield a big stick.'

'Thank you, sir. I appreciate that.'

'You deserve your promotion. You were, after all, a Sergeant in the Army and you come highly recommended, not only by Sergeant Roswell, but by your last commanding officer. We're hoping later to get your help in training a new generation of policemen.'

Seth could feel his cheeks grow warm with pleasure and he had to admit that the prospect of this pleased him greatly.

After they'd left the building, Bert stopped and held out one hand. 'Congratulations, lad.'

They shook solemnly, then Seth gave him a wry look. 'Didn't I write to tell you that I was looking for a nice quiet life?'

'Ah, you'd be bored within a couple of months. You're not the quiet sort.'

'Would I?' Seth wasn't so sure. He'd seen too much trouble in the past few years, too many deaths, too much pain. He felt old and weary sometimes. But still, training new policemen was something that did attract him. He enjoyed moulding lads, teaching them how to deal with the world, making men of them as some people called it.

Veronica finished every scrap of food because she was so hungry she felt hollow. Then she waited for the now-familiar blurred feeling to take over. But it didn't, so it seemed her mother had been telling the truth for once.

But that didn't change the fact that she was still a prisoner. And bored.

The door opened and Glenys came in with a book. 'Mrs Gresham thought you might like something to read, so I brought it straight up.'

Ronnie looked past her quickly, but Tadwyn was there again. 'Thank you, but since my mother deliberately smashed my spectacles, everything up close is just a blur. I can only really see clearly at a distance.'

Glenys looked so uncomfortable Ronnie regretted saying that. The poor woman wasn't to blame. All she was doing was obeying orders. 'Thanks anyway.'

After that no one came to see her until lunchtime, when Tadwyn carried in a tray and her mother accompanied him. He set the tray down and returned to the doorway again, watching them.

'I hope you enjoyed having something to read,' Edwina said brightly.

'How could I? I can't read without my spectacles.'

'If you'd not started wearing them so often, you'd not have weakened your eyes. Going without will soon strengthen them.'

'Mother, it won't! Do you think I *want* to wear spectacles? Of course I don't. But at this distance your face is little more than a blur, though I could look out of the window and see exactly what's happening in the copse.'

Edwina scowled at her. 'You're exaggerating.'

'I'm not! I give you my word as a Gresham that I'm telling the truth. The optician I saw said I should have been wearing spectacles for years, that not having them was making me squint. And that's unattractive too.'

There was a moment's silence, then her mother said grudgingly, 'There's an old pair of glasses in your room. I'll send those in. But you're not to wear them except when you're alone and want to read or sew. Do you understand?'

'Yes, Mother.' How she hated saying those two words. But she'd say and do anything at the moment to stop them drugging her again. They couldn't watch her every second of every day. Eventually they'd slip up and she'd escape. 'Can I move back into my old bedroom?'

'No. You're out of the way here. If you start being silly again, no one will hear you.'

Only the maids who used this corridor as a short cut, but then her mother didn't know about that. Anyway, she never seemed to consider that servants could see and hear everything that was going on in a house, or that they might tell someone what she was doing.

Edwina returned a short time later with her daughter's old spectacles, handing them over with a distasteful expression on her face. 'I shall take you to an optician, one of my own choosing, and discuss ways of making your eyes stronger.'

'Thank you.' Ronnie knew exactly what the man would say. Perhaps that would convince her mother.

When she was on her own she put on the glasses and picked up the book. But the prescription didn't suit her now and after half an hour, her eyes were aching. She pushed the spectacles to the top of her head and went to gaze out of the window again.

As she watched, Ellen came out of the house and strode across to the motorcycle. Ronnie felt envious as their former maid got it ready and then kick-started it. She wished she could jump on the back of it and spin away down the lane like that, wished most of all for a few minutes alone with Giles. He always made her feel braver, somehow.

Was he missing her? Surely he didn't think she'd left him voluntarily? As she was driven away from the farm she'd seen the Tillings and Cora come to the door and stare after the car. They must have told him she'd been taken away forcibly.

But what could he do against her mother if Dr Hilliam supported her claim that Ronnie had had a breakdown?

The man was tall and thin, wearing shabby clothes with an old Army greatcoat over the top of them in spite of the warmth of the day. He was carrying an old knapsack slung over one shoulder and he hitched this up as he turned into the drive of the Hall and made his way round the side towards the rear. Before he got there, Gerry stopped him.

'What do you want?'

'I'm looking for work.'

'Oh? What sort of work?'

The vagrant shrugged. 'Anything. Can't afford to be choosy. I've only been out of the Army for a month or two, but I can't settle, can't seem to understand that it's all over.'

Someone at the rear of the house dropped some-thing with a loud, clattering noise and the stranger flung himself flat on the ground, face down, hands protecting his head. In an instant he was shaking all over and whimpering.

Gerry watched him in amazement, then suddenly realised what this was. He'd read about it in the papers but hadn't expected to see it with his own eyes. Shellshock, they called it. His dad said soldiers were too soft these days and should pull their socks up. Fellows imagining themselves ill wouldn't have been allowed in *his* day. But this was no trick, it was real. The man was all too clearly terrified.

Suddenly Gerry was even more relieved than before that he'd been classified as in a reserved occupation, that Mrs Gresham had pulled strings to make sure he hadn't had to go into the Army. This was what war could do to a grown man and his dad was wrong. It wasn't a case of being soft. This poor chap must have been driven to the edge of desperation by horrors they had only heard whispered about – and all the while fighting to protect Gerry and his family.

He stepped forward, speaking gently. 'It's all right, just someone dropping a pail.' He knelt to pat the shaking shoulder, continuing to pat it as he talked in a soothing voice, the same way he did to his little daughter when she'd had a nightmare.

Gradually the man stopped shivering and began taking deep gulping breaths. When he raised his head, he stared all round, a wild-eyed look like a terrified animal being dragged to slaughter. And that's what this poor chap had been, Gerry realised suddenly, a human animal sent to the equivalent of a slaughter-house.

'Let me help you up, then we'll see if Cook can find you a cup of tea, eh? Nothing like a nice hot drink to settle the nerves. And about the job . . . I could do with a bit of help around the place, all sorts of general labouring jobs. But it'll be up to the mistress whether you're taken on. She's the one holding the purse strings.'

'I'd do it just for my keep and a few bob a week. I'm not – not up to much these days, but I'd try my hardest.'

'I'm sure you would.' With one arm round the man's shoulder, Gerry guided him to the back of the house, left him sitting on the bench near the kitchen door and went inside to explain to Cook.

Tadwyn was sitting at the servants' table drinking a cup of tea. People watched what they said when he was around, because he spent so much time with the mistress, but he'd always been perfectly civil to Gerry.

'You're sure this fellow is what he seems?' Tadwyn asked abruptly.

'You can't fake something like that.'

'Well, he won't be much use to us then, will he?'

'We should give him a chance, at least, and be proud to help men like him!' Gerry said angrily. 'And them as can't do that shouldn't call themselves Christians. I'll ask the mistress myself if no one else will. Find out if she'll see me, Glenys love, will you?'

Glenys had been peering out of the window, her

soft heart touched by how thin the man was, how shabby. 'Shall I take him a cup of tea first? We want him to calm down before she sees him, don't we?'

'You're right. Thanks, love. And if there's one going . . . ?' Gerry grinned at them.

She poured him a cup, then filled an enamel beaker with tea and when Cook handed her a piece of cake to go with it, Tadwyn rolled his eyes. Grumpy old devil, Glenys thought. He should be grateful to men like the one outside.

She stopped just outside the back door, closing it gently behind her, but he didn't even notice her. Pity flooded through her because the stranger was weeping now, silently and desperately, wiping away tears, taking deep breaths and muttering, 'Got to calm down. Stay calm.'

'I've brought you a cup of tea, love,' she announced.

He jumped as if he'd been shot and flinched away from her.

'It's only me. My name's Glenys and I'm a maid here. I've brought you a cup of tea and a piece of cake. Lovely fruit cake, it is.'

He stared at her, then turned his head to wipe away more tears, seeming unable to stop weeping.

She set the cup and plate down on the window sill and sat down beside him on the bench. 'Is there anything I can do to help you, love?'

He shook his head, still avoiding her eyes, and a sob escaped him.

'Eh, lad! My poor lad, what have they done to you?' And without thinking she put her arms round him and let him weep on her shoulder, great racking sobs that brought tears to her eyes too. It seemed to go on for a long time and she hoped no one would come out and interrupt them.

Eventually, however, the flood of tears subsided.

'Sorry,' he muttered from close to her ear.

'I should think you've a lot to be upset about, after what you've been through,' she said, patting his shoulder then giving him a hug for good measure. 'It'll do you good to cry it out.'

'Grown men sh-shouldn't cry.'

'Not in a normal life, but what you've seen isn't normal, is it? And it *will* help you to get it out of your system, well, it always helps me.'

He pulled away from her, but his face was still quite close to hers. 'You're a wonderful woman, do you know that? And you're right. I needed a bit of comfort just then and it did me a lot of good to cry it out.'

She fumbled for her handkerchief and helped him dry his tears. 'The tea will be cold now.'

'Doesn't matter. It'll still taste good to me. Please. Don't go back inside. Not just yet.'

She shot a glance towards the window, but there was no one signalling to her so she stayed where she was. Picking up the beaker she handed it to him. 'There. Have a good sup of that, then you can see how you like Cook's cake.'

They sat in the sunshine for a few minutes and he ate ravenously, as if he'd been starved for days, picking up every crumb with his fingertip, before handing her the empty plate and beaker. 'Thanks for everything.'

He sighed. 'They won't want to employ me now after that exhibition.'

'They'd better. You just sit there and I'll have a word with Cook.'

Glenys marched into the kitchen, closed the door behind her and set her hands on her hips. 'He needs a job and he *deserves* a chance. Let me speak to Mrs Shipton or Mrs Gresham about him. I'm sure I can persuade them. Which one should I see, do you think, Cook?'

'Mrs Shipton first.'

'Tell her I can find him all sorts of jobs to do,' Gerry said. 'She doesn't have to pay him a full wage, he knows he won't be up to doing a normal week's work, but it would be very useful to have another pair of hands just now.'

'Ask Mrs Shipton to tell the mistress it'll look good to the ladies she knows, her being kind to an ex-soldier,' Tadwyn said unexpectedly.

Glenys gaped at him. She hadn't expected any help from *him*.

He shrugged. 'It's the only reason she'll listen to you.'

'Go up and ask Mrs Shipton now,' Cook said. 'No time like the present.'

'All right. And look – he's still hungry. Could you find him something else to eat?'

Cook nodded, straightening up, a martial light in her eyes. 'No ex-soldier goes hungry while I'm in charge of this kitchen.'

*　　*　　*

Edwina Gresham stared at her housekeeper and maid. 'You want me to give this person a job?'

Mrs Shipton spoke first. 'I went to meet him myself before I came to you. He's in a bad way, ma'am, but he seems a decent sort. And if we can't help our lads, after all they've done for us, it's a poor lookout.'

'It'll be setting ever such a good example to the other ladies,' Glenys put in quickly. She usually kept quiet when the mistress was around, but today she'd been moved to the core by the man's plight and was determined to help the poor soul. 'We'll all look out for him, help him settle in.'

Edwina tapped a pencil against her lips, then nodded. 'Very well. But he's to keep himself clean, and you're to make sure he earns his keep.'

Glenys nudged the housekeeper.

'And a few bob a week?' Mrs Shipton pleaded.

'Only if Tadwyn thinks he's worth it.'

Glenys sighed in relief. It seemed as if even grumpy old Tadwyn had a soft spot for a returned soldier.

'What's his name?'

Only then did Glenys realise she didn't know. 'Sorry. I forgot to ask. I'll soon find out, ma'am.'

Mrs Gresham left the room and Glenys turned to the housekeeper. 'Can I be the one who tells him?'

'Yes. I'm far too busy to concern myself with him. Tell Gerry he's in charge of the fellow. And if we need anything doing in the house, like filling the coal scuttles, you're in charge of seeing he does things right.'

So Glenys went outside and found the man simply sitting in the sun, his face turned up to it like a flower.

He turned at the sound of the door and got to his feet when he saw her.

'You've got yourself a job,' she announced.

He went perfectly still, except for his mouth falling open in surprise. 'I have?'

'Yes. They'll only be paying you five bob a week, but it's all found, so you'll get your room and food on top of that.'

He closed his eyes and shuddered.

She stepped forward and laid one hand on his arm. 'Are you all right?'

He looked up at her and nodded. 'I was just – relieved. I can't believe it.'

'You'll answer to Gerry, but he's a decent fellow, a good gardener and farmer. He didn't go into the Army, but he worked all the hours, growing food.' She was afraid an ex-soldier would look down on someone who'd escaped being drafted.

'You don't have to worry. I do understand that we needed food as well as guns,' he said softly.

'And if you do jobs in the house, I'll be the one who supervises you. Is that all right?'

'Yes. I'd like that. I'll try not to let you down.'

'What's your name?'

'Didn't I tell you? It's Pel, short for Pelham. Stupid sort of Christian name that, eh? Pelham John Wyler.'

'Pel, then. And I'm Glenys.'

A smile spread slowly across his thin face. 'My grandma was called Glenys. Lovely name, always makes me think of being happy when I was a kid.'

She didn't tell him she'd always hated her name,

which was that of a bossy old aunt who hadn't left her a penny anyway. 'Well, I'd better take you to see Gerry again and he can help you settle in. I'll get a room ready for you in the stables as soon as I have a minute.' She led the way to where she'd seen Gerry working that morning and handed Pel over, then walked slowly back to the house.

Poor man. She'd do everything she could to help him.

As the housekeeper and maid left, Edwina was already working out how she'd mention her charitable gesture oh-so-casually the next time she called on one of the neighbourhood ladies. If it were not for the difficulty of finding decent help, she'd not even have considered the man. It was galling that she had to accept any sort of help she could find to run the estate. A half-wit, an uppity young madam who didn't know her place, and now a man who was half mad. It was so hard to maintain standards these days. Even her own daughter had needed pulling into line.

It was working, though. Veronica was starting to behave more obediently. But Edwina didn't intend to take anything for granted. The girl would be locked in that bedroom with no clothes to escape in and watched carefully every time the door was opened. Sometimes it was a good thing to live out of town, with no neighbours poking their noses into your affairs.

Which reminded her. She'd better get ready to go

and visit her friend Blanche St Corbin, see how dear Algie was getting on. It was time to let them know that Veronica was back home.

8

Ellen drove back into Shawcroft slowly, enjoying the sunny weather so much she started singing 'K-K-K-Katy', one of her favourite songs.

When she got home, she told her mother about her new job, pleased by the joy in the sick woman's face at the news that she would be staying in Shawcroft. Conscious that time was passing and Mrs Shipton wanted her back at the Hall quickly, Ellen chatted only briefly then hurried upstairs to sort out her clothes and see if she could find her old aprons and caps. She wasn't sure whether to be glad or sad when she did. She'd always hated wearing a cap.

Afterwards she locked the trunk carefully, testing the padlock to make sure it was properly closed. She'd have to find a way to get to a bank. She'd probably have to use the one in Shawcroft now. She really shouldn't keep such a huge sum of money lying around. Thank goodness no one knew about it.

Outside the house she hesitated, then decided for the sake of family peace to stop off at her stepfather's shop and let him know she'd taken the job. She started up the bike and drove slowly along Rochdale Road.

She had already half-opened the door of the shop

when she realised he was talking to Jory. So she stayed in the doorway and waited till Bevan turned to her.

'I just popped in to let you know that I'm going to work for Mrs Gresham and she wants me to start this afternoon.'

He gave her a smug smile. 'I thought you would.'

'I've told them it's only temporary.'

The smile vanished instantly. 'What the devil do you mean by that?'

'I'm not staying in Shawcroft . . . afterwards.'

'We'll talk about it when the time comes. In the meantime, make sure you don't upset Mrs Gresham. She's one of my best customers.'

'Want a ride out there in Dad's cart?' Jory asked, moving towards her.

She took a quick step backwards to stay out of his reach, not wanting even to brush against him. 'No, thank you. I have my own transport.'

'You won't need that now.'

'Of course I will. How else will I get back into town to see Mum?'

'I was going to offer you thirty pounds for that bike,' he said. 'It's not the sort of thing a girl should be trying to drive.'

She laughed. 'Tell that to the War Office. They were very glad to have me driving it around London for the past few years.' Turning, she got back on the bike and went towards her Uncle Martin's workshop.

Jory watched her enviously. What he wouldn't give for his own motor transport. He wished suddenly he'd not spent so much of his money on booze.

'I'll see she sells that bike to you,' Bevan said.

'How can you do that?'

'I'll say it's upsetting her mother. Then *you* can bring her into town for visits.'

Jory didn't contradict him, but he couldn't see Ellen selling it. He sometimes wondered at how Mr Halsopp thought the world would do as he wanted. His dad and Mr Cobbley were just the same. They didn't seem to understand anything about the world outside Shawcroft.

'Now, let's get back to business, Jory lad. I'm needing some extra fresh beef next week.'

'I'll ask Dad to find something for you.'

'Good. And did Wes tell you when the new fellow would be arriving?'

'The middle of the week. Mad as fire about that, he is.'

'We'd better all tread carefully till we know what the new bobby's like.'

'Well, he won't know much about slaughtering beasts or where your carcases come from if he's a townie. But you're right. Best to take it easy at first, till we've got his measure. I've got to go now, there's some stuff to load for tomorrow.' Jory went out of the shop, whistling.

The sound died in his throat as he saw Ellen drive away from the workshop, looking confident and attractive. Envy speared through him. He'd have another go at persuading his father to buy a motor lorry for the business. The days of horses and carts were numbered. They were too slow, too limited in what they could do. This was the age of the motor vehicle. He had driven trucks in the Army and he intended to get at least one for carting big stuff within the next year. You had to move with the times or go under.

A voice from behind him said, 'Makes me sick to see her on that thing, showing herself up in public. She's probably driving it wrongly.' Mr Halsopp stood scowling down the street.

'She drives it very well, actually,' Jory admitted reluctantly.

'She never.'

'She does, you know.'

'They must be easy to drive then, if women can handle them.'

Jory realised he'd been standing gaping after her and told himself to snap out of it. 'Got to go now. Bye, Mr Halsopp.'

But he couldn't stop thinking about how bonny she had looked.

Ellen drove back to the Hall slowly and her spirits sank as she arrived at the main gates. She had a sudden urge to turn and drive as far away as she could from this place. She would do if it wasn't for her mother, because after the freedom and stimulation of London, she knew she would hate working here again.

She looked down at the neat wristwatch Lady Bingram had given her after the influenza epidemic. Her stepfather mustn't have noticed it or he'd have been grumbling about this new fashion as well. All the aides had one of these modern wristwatches as a memento and she was very fond of hers. It was so much more practical than a fob.

She looked at the time and exclaimed in annoyance. It had taken longer than she'd expected to pack her things and say goodbye to her mother. Speeding up again, she drove along the drive and turned right down the side track that led to the rear of the house, the servants' area.

While she was sitting on the bike wondering where to leave it, Tadwyn came out of the back door and walked towards her. He'd been in charge of the stables when she first started and she remembered his anger when Mrs Gresham bought a motor car and insisted on him and no one else learning to drive it – that or lose his job.

They'd all had to change in the last few years, hadn't they? She didn't mind, because for her it had been an improvement.

'I was wondering where to put my bike, Mr Tadwyn.'

He stopped to stare disapprovingly at the vehicle.

She knew he was going to make some derogatory comment so forestalled him. 'I not only drive this, I maintain it and do some of the small repairs, have done for years.'

He gaped at her then shook his head slowly, his bafflement obvious. 'I don't know what the world's coming to.'

'I hope it's changing for the better now that the war is over. That's what they promised us.'

'Oh, governments promise you the earth when they want something from you, but the minute they've got it, those promises are put off till tomorrow. I've seen it all before.' He didn't wait for her to reply but changed the subject. 'Now, let's find you somewhere to put that thing, then you can come inside and start work. Mrs Shipton will be watching us from her window, so you'd better not stand here chatting.'

From him this was fairly friendly behaviour. He could be really grumpy sometimes. She glanced sideways at the stables. 'What happened to the horses? I thought you'd have kept one or two.' She knew how much he'd loved them.

'Most of them were requisitioned for the war and the others went to the St Corbins. All our grooms went away for soldiers, you see, no one to look after the poor creatures. Remember Jack Barstead? He died. And Luke Jones lost a leg.' He sighed and started walking. 'Over here.'

She followed him towards the stables, which were open-fronted here, with the doors for the stalls at the back, closed now, no heads poking out. The motor car was standing under cover at the end nearest to the house. Tadwyn walked past it but Ellen stopped to look at the glossy black vehicle standing there in solitary splendour. 'An Austin Landaulette. How did Mrs Gresham get hold of one of those in wartime? She had a much smaller car when I left.'

'She has connections.' He slowed down to scowl at it.

Ellen ran her fingers over the side of the vehicle. 'It's well cared for.'

'The bodywork is. I don't mind polishing it up, but

I don't know anything about engines and she won't let Martin Pugh see to it as often as he wants.'

'Why ever not?'

'Because she wants the car available any time she wishes to go out, says I should be able to manage that. She doesn't realise that it's not like a horse, that it has to have things *done* to it, things I can't manage.' He scowled at the vehicle. 'We've been lucky so far. It's not broken down on me. But it's not pulling like it should do.'

'You don't enjoy driving it, do you?'

'No. Give me a horse any day. If you fall asleep behind a horse, it'll find its own way home. And if you care for it properly, it'll grow fond of you. If I fell asleep driving that thing, I'd crash into a wall or tree and kill myself.'

He'd never spoken to her so freely before. 'I love driving,' she said, 'and I love messing about with motors, actually.'

He gave her a quick wintry smile. 'You're young enough to enjoy change. I've had enough of it lately, just want to see out my time here in peace.'

'The car probably just needs a regular service. I could do that if my Uncle Martin let you have some oil and if you had a few tools.'

'You could?'

'Yes.' She hid a smile because he was looking at her as if she'd suddenly sprouted horns.

'I don't think *she* would approve of a woman touching it. I do put oil in, though. Martin showed me how to do that, and I fill it up with petrol, too.

We keep a few cans in stock.' He pointed towards a pile of square cans stacked by the wall.

He moved on a few paces and pointed. 'If you put your motorcycle at this end and cover it with a tarpaulin, she won't even see it, not that she comes out here very often. But I think it's best if you keep it out of her sight. Mrs Shipton says she doesn't really approve of your bringing it here, so best not to remind her.'

When Ellen had brought the motorcycle into the old stable area, she detached the lead and stuffed it into her pocket. Tadwyn didn't comment or look surprised, so perhaps he didn't realise the significance of that. Then she took her old carpet bag out of the sidecar and set it down so that they could cover the bike with a tarpaulin.

Without another word Tadwyn led the way back into the house.

As she entered the kitchen, the house seemed to close in round Ellen, as it had in the old days, giving her a tight, suffocating feeling. *It's only for a few months*, she told herself.

Glenys greeted her with a beaming smile and showed her up to an attic bedroom. 'Mrs Shipton wasn't sure you'd have a proper uniform, so she found these for you.'

Ellen pulled a face as she stared at the bed, on which lay a very old-fashioned black dress, some aprons and a couple of caps. 'I hate wearing those things,' she muttered. 'But I did find my own caps at my mother's, so I won't have to wear hers. These must be twenty years old at least. Why do they always insist on maids wearing caps?'

Glenys reached up to touch hers and shrugged. 'I never notice it. I think I'd feel strange without it. What's it like having your hair so short?'

'Wonderful. So much easier to manage, especially with curly hair like mine.'

'I think you'd be wise to tie it back. They won't like it looking so fluffy and attractive.'

'It's too short to tie back.'

'They'll make you grow it long again.'

'Oh, no, they won't. I'm never doing that. Besides, I won't be here for long enough to grow it. I'm only staying because of my mother.'

Glenys's voice softened. 'How is she?'

Ellen's throat suddenly thickened with tears and she couldn't speak so just shook her head and turned to lift the carpet bag on to the bed. 'I suppose I—' her voice cracked with anguish and it was a minute before she could continue, 'I'd better unpack and change. Mrs Shipton wanted me to start work this afternoon.'

'It'll be good to have another pair of hands. And you'll be kind to poor Millie, I know. She's a bit slow, but she's a really hard worker if you explain what you want carefully.' Glenys turned to leave, then swung round. 'I nearly forgot.' She explained about the other new member of staff who had just started work. 'Gerry said when he heard a loud clatter, Pel dropped to the ground and covered his head with his hands. He was still shaking when I took him out a cup of tea and—' She looked over her shoulder before lowering her voice and telling Ellen how Pel had wept against her.

'Poor fellow. They went through some terrible times in the trenches. I've met quite a few men with shell-shock. If we can all befriend this Pel of yours, having a job somewhere peaceful may help him get better slowly.'

Glenys blushed. 'He's not *my* Pel. But as I told the others, we ought to look after him because he fought for us. It's only fair. Well, I'll leave you to unpack. It's nice each having our own bedroom, isn't it? In the old days we'd have had to share beds.'

Ellen was still smiling as she put away her things. Glenys had always had a simple view of life, accepting what happened to her cheerfully.

When the bag was empty, she shoved it under the bed and started to put on the hated uniform. The hemline was low and unflattering. She'd take a few inches off that at the first opportunity. It was so much easier to work and be active in shorter skirts.

When she went down to the kitchen, Cook looked up and chuckled. 'That cap of yours looks like it's going to fall off at any minute.'

Ellen wagged her head from side to side and grinned at her reflection in the mirror. 'No, it'll stay on all right. I put some hair pins in it.'

'Mrs Shipton wants to see you.'

'All right.'

'Can you take up her tea tray as you go?'

'Yes, of course.'

Ellen felt as though invisible shackles had snapped shut round her ankles and wrists as she went up the stairs to the housekeeper's room. In this house, it was as if the war years hadn't happened.

Giles was torn between investigating the possibility of setting up his new legal practice in Shawcroft and concentrating on the search for Ronnie. He couldn't neglect his future for too long because he had a family to support, but he couldn't stop worrying about her, knowing how afraid she was of her mother and how Mrs Gresham had bullied her. And it was a ticklish situation. As a lawyer, he'd have to be particularly careful how he intervened.

His godfather, James Dunham, was a police inspector and had not only told him that an old friend called Septimus Monnings was looking for a junior partner, but had also intimated that there was a serious problem of organised lawbreaking in the Shawcroft district. He hoped that if Giles settled there, he'd be able to help sort that out. Things hadn't always been peaceful on the home front during the war, it seemed. Strange to think of their own people taking advantage of the hostilities like that. He knew what he'd do with such traitors.

His godfather had given him the name of the new constable who was about to take charge in Shawcroft, a capable man apparently, who had already been briefed on the local problems. Talbot had an outstanding record in the Army, had been a sergeant, decorated several times. That was enough recommendation for Giles.

The town was an attractive little place and he'd

taken a liking to it. A pity Mrs Gresham lived nearby but he was sure he could protect Ronnie from her mother once she was his wife.

The first thing to do if he was to rescue Ronnie was to go out to the Hall and check out the building and its surroundings in more detail. He'd have to do that at night, preferably on a moonlit night and in fine weather. You left trails of drips if you went inside a house when it was raining, not to mention making footprints in muddy ground.

The next day was fine until teatime then dark clouds began to gather and soon it was not only raining but thundering and lightning as well. After tea, Giles paced up and down the living room, unable to settle. No use going out on a night like this.

'Is something wrong, dear?' his mother-in-law asked.

'Just a case I'm concerned about.' He didn't intend to tell her about Ronnie's predicament because she might let something slip to one of her many friends. She was well-connected in the county, unlike his own family.

Pouring a whisky, he tried to settle down with a book, but found himself staring into space instead of reading, wondering what Ronnie was doing, if she knew he would come and rescue her.

In the end he tossed aside the novel, which was stupid and unbelievable, went into the dining room, got out some paperwork and occupied himself with that. The more of this simple stuff he cleared off his desk, the freer he'd be to hunt for Ronnie. The new senior partner had hinted that he wasn't putting in enough hours and he'd told him roundly that it wouldn't do.

Well, it was the new senior partner who wouldn't do, as far as Giles was concerned. There was something about him that raised Giles's hackles. A sly type, who didn't quite look you in the eye.

Another day without knowing how you are, my love! he thought as he got ready for bed. *I've not forgotten you, never that.*

Edwina stared across her friend Blanche's drawing room at Algie, who still looked pale and dispirited. He wasn't really the kind of man she'd have chosen for Veronica. He was too weedy, the result of generations of inbreeding, no doubt. Veronica was a much sturdier sort, in spite of being so small. But this was a good family for them to ally with, old county stock, of higher status than the Greshams, but with less money. And money spoke loudly. The war had made no difference to that. 'How are you adjusting to civilian life, Algernon?'

He jerked at the sound of his name. 'Sorry. I was miles away, I'm afraid.'

She repeated her question, trying to hide her irritation and seem patient and amused.

'It'll take a while to adjust, I dare say, Mrs Gresham. I feel as if I need some peace and quiet. It was a bit – difficult out there.'

Peace and quiet! she thought scornfully. He'd had months of peace and quiet now and he still looked a mess.

'Dear Algernon has been awarded a second medal.' Blanche gazed proudly at her younger son. 'For bravery in the face of the enemy.'

He scowled at her. 'Please don't brag, Ma. I only did what anyone else would do. And in spite of that, the man I rescued died.'

His last words were choked and Edwina was surprised to see tears rise in his eyes. He walked over to the window and stood staring out at the rain-swept gardens. When he turned back, she hoped she looked concerned, but in her opinion, Blanche ought to tell her son to snap out of it. Edwina would have done.

'How's Ronnie?' he asked as the silence continued.

'I do wish you young people wouldn't keep shortening names. As far as I'm concerned Ronnie is a man's name and my daughter is called Veronica.'

'Sorry, Mrs Gresham. That's what I've always called her, though, and how she signed herself in her letters.'

Edwina pounced on that. 'She's continued to write to you?'

'Oh, yes. Even after she joined the Land Army, she still found time for me. It was good to receive letters from home, cheered you up no end. We've always been good pals, Ron— Veronica and me. How is she? Has she come home yet? She said she was staying on at the farm for a bit longer.'

'Yes, she's back. She's not been well, poor dear, but she's recovering now.'

'I'll ride across to see her tomorrow then, if that's all right with you.'

It would look strange if she told him not to, so

Edwina smiled brightly. 'That'll be lovely. Come to tea. But perhaps not tomorrow. She's still a bit tired. I'll telephone you.' She could always say Ronnie had taken a turn for the worse if the girl refused to be sensible.

'Thanks. It'll be good to see her again.'

As she was driven home, Edwina sat lost in thought and only realised they'd arrived when the car stopped and Tadwyn opened the door for her.

'Thank you.' She walked slowly inside. If possible, Veronica must be persuaded to take tea with Algie and behave herself, but she wouldn't be allowed out of her mother's sight or hearing.

And then, the stupid girl must also be persuaded to let Algernon court her. It was the most suitable match they were likely to find these days.

How could she have bred such an impractical daughter? It must come from her father's side of the family.

Desperately bored, Ronnie spent most of her time gazing out of the window. Later in the day she heard the sound of an engine and watched as Tadwyn brought the car round to the back of the house, parked it clumsily under cover and got out. He slammed the car door hard and stood scowling at the vehicle. Poor Tadwyn. His heart was still with horses. Well, Ronnie loved them too, but she had no doubt that more people would be driving around in motor cars now that the war was over.

Had her mother been out in the car paying calls?

It didn't take much to guess where she'd have gone: to see Blanche St Corbin. And Algie too, if he was home. Ronnie frowned at the mere thought of that. She could never marry Algie, not now she knew how it felt when a man you truly loved took you in his arms and kissed you till your whole body melted against his. Algie had kissed her once or twice when they were younger, experimentally, but there had been no feeling behind it on his side and it had evoked no response in her.

Where was Giles? What was he doing and thinking? Surely he must realise that something was preventing her from being with him? Of course he did and she must never let anyone tell her differently. He had other responsibilities and a living to earn. But he'd come to find her and rescue her soon. He would, he must!

Some time later the motorbike and sidecar chugged slowly round to the rear of the house again and Ronnie saw Ellen looking round as if wondering where to park it. She was glad to have something to distract her, so stood close to the window, watching.

Tadwyn walked outside and beckoned to Ellen to take the bike to the far end of the stable block. After she'd parked it Ellen bent over and fiddled with something. When she straightened up she had a thin piece of what looked from this distance like black wire in her hands. You took wires off to disable machines, Ronnie had learned from Giles. The motors wouldn't start if everything wasn't connected, apparently.

Intrigued, she wondered why the maid was disabling the bike. When Ellen took a carpet bag out of the sidecar, set it down and helped Tadwyn cover the bike with a tarpaulin, Ronnie realised she was definitely coming to work here.

The rear yard was deserted now. Nothing happened outside for ages, nothing at all. Bored because she'd finished the book a while ago, Ronnie began to pace up and down the room, trying to work out yet again how to escape.

After a busy life for the past year she was going mad with nothing to do. She considered hammering on the door, or breaking the window and shouting for help. But the only ones who'd hear her were people who depended on her mother for their livelihoods and homes.

And anyway, her mother had persuaded the doctor that Ronnie had had a breakdown. Smashing windows would only reinforce that.

Tears came into her eyes but she didn't let herself cry because she didn't want to betray any weakness. She was hungry again and wondered if her mother would drug the food tonight. She would never be able to tell.

The following day Ellen was given the task of preparing the drawing room for visitors. It hadn't been used for a while because of lack of staff, and had a neglected air and smell to it.

'I want it cleaned from top to bottom and aired out,' Mrs Shipton said. 'Mrs Gresham is expecting the St Corbins to tea tomorrow and she wants to entertain them properly.'

'Mr Algie survived the war, then?'

'Yes. Got himself a medal or two as well, I heard.'

'Has Miss Veronica moved out?'

Mrs Shipton hesitated. 'She did for a while, worked as a Land Girl, but she's back now.'

'Good for her.' Something in the housekeeper's voice made Ellen feel suspicious. 'Is she in her old room? Will I have to start cleaning that again? I always used to do her room before and help with her clothes.'

'Um – no. She's in the west wing, on the third floor. She's – not been well. Mrs Gresham told me Miss Veronica had had a nervous breakdown from over-work. She's locked in her bedroom for her own safety and you're not to go in there alone, and under no circumstances are you to speak to her or let her out.'

'Oh.' Ellen began moving the furniture to the edges of the room, ostensibly so that she could sweep the carpet but actually to avoid looking at Mrs Shipton. 'Has she been back long?'

'Just a few days. But that really isn't any of your business. Glenys is the one who takes trays up to her and Tadwyn always goes too in case she's – difficult.'

Ellen didn't pursue the matter any further. Something about this explanation sounded wrong. Veronica Gresham had always seemed a lot saner to her than the mistress, who was obsessed by status and doing the right thing and who got bees in her bonnet about things that didn't matter to anyone else.

The housekeeper left and Ellen continued with her work, fetching some damp tealeaves from the box in the kitchen. These would keep the dust down as she got down on hands and knees to brush the carpet with a stiff hand brush. Even so, dust flew up and made her sneeze and in the end she tied a handkerchief round her mouth and nose. She used men's handkerchiefs now, because they were so much more practical than filmy bits of lawn. She grinned at the thought because quite a few of her handkerchiefs seemed to end up with oil on them from her bike.

As she was finishing brushing the square of carpet, it occurred to her that Glenys usually knew everything that was going on and delighted in sharing all the latest gossip. But Glenys hadn't even hinted that Miss Veronica was back. What was going on here? Ellen knew she'd find out sooner or later. It was impossible to keep anything secret when you all lived under the same roof.

It took her until teatime to finish the room but by that time she was pleased with what she'd done. It smelled of beeswax and fresh air, and all the woodwork gleamed. She'd washed the ornaments, too, something no one had done for ages from the look of them.

When Glenys came to fetch her to tea, she looked round with a smile. 'It's so nice to see this room looking right again, Ellen. It's my favourite in the whole house, only I've not had time to keep it up as well as do other things. Mrs Gresham had to entertain her friends in the small sitting room at the back while the war was on. She didn't like that.'

'I'm not surprised you didn't have time to keep everything up. I don't know how you managed to do so much with only you and Cook.'

'We had someone from the village to do the rough scrubbing and she still comes in – Mrs Porton, a newcomer. She's a good worker, but she's only one pair of hands. And Millie started here last year, which helped a lot. But I miss the old days, when there were six indoor servants and we could have a bit of fun. Here, I'll carry the basket of polishing things. You take the brushes.'

Ellen followed her out, tired now. They'd all shared the household chores in London, but Lady Bingram had not only had a Ewbank carpet sweeper, she had bought a portable bellows cleaner as well. Although it took two people to work the bellows to get enough suction, it kept the dust down and did a pretty good job on the carpets, so had been used every month to give them a thorough bottoming. But then, Daphne loved modern gadgets. Mrs Gresham would never have dreamed of spending money merely to make her servants' work easier.

It wasn't till the two women were going upstairs to bed that Ellen dared to ask, 'I gather *you* are looking after Miss Veronica now? Why didn't you tell me she was back? You know I always did her room. I'd like to see her again.'

Glenys shot a quick glance at her, then jerked her head towards Millie and mimed keeping quiet.

When Ellen went into her bedroom she sat on the bed and waited. Sure enough, a few minutes later Glenys came in and sat next to her.

'Oh, it is lovely to have you back again! I missed having someone to chat to after work.'

Ellen couldn't say it was lovely to be back, because it wasn't, so she compromised with, 'It's lovely to see you again too. Now, tell me about Miss Veronica.'

'Well, they brought her back in the car, but she was struggling and shouting, trying to get away from them. Even though she's not very big, Tadwyn had to call Gerry over to help carry her into the house.'

'You mean they kidnapped her?'

'It's not really kidnapping if it's for her own good, is it? Though she doesn't seen mad to me, just unhappy.'

'So you look after her?'

'Yes. I have to empty the chamber pot and take up the hot water, and the trays of food sometimes.' She giggled suddenly. 'You can't imagine Mrs Gresham or Tadwyn doing the dirty jobs, can you?' She paused, head on one side. 'Miss Veronica didn't say much but the way she glared at Tadwyn, it was as if . . .'

'As if what?'

'As if she blamed him about something.'

'How exciting!'

'Isn't it? Now, let me tell you about Pel.'

Glenys was obviously much taken by the shell-shocked ex-soldier, so Ellen let her talk for a while, then pretended to yawn. 'I'm out of practice at hard physical work. I've been mostly driving during the war. I must tell you about my trips to Belgium another time. I was a stewardess on a ship bringing refugees back and we were fired on. It was very exciting.'

'You went abroad? Ooh, you lucky thing! I've never been further than Blackpool.'

At last Glenys took herself off and Ellen had a quick wash before slipping between the sheets, which felt a bit damp. The bed was an old one, like all the furniture in the servants' area, and the mattress was lumpy.

She couldn't get the thought of Miss Veronica out of her mind. Why would the daughter of the house be locked up in the west wing? Was she really suffering an affliction of the nerves? That didn't seem like the girl Ellen had known.

It seemed more likely that she had done something to upset her mother, who had locked her daughter in her room a few times when she was younger as punishment.

9

The next day dawned bright and sunny, all traces of rain gone and the sun beaming happily down on a newly washed world. Giles smiled as he walked to his rooms. If the fine weather held, it would be an excellent night for reconnoitring. He stayed away from his new senior partner as much as he could, and passed the day trying to clear up the various small cases that had been allotted to him, so that he could leave quite quickly if the opportunity arose.

At regular intervals he went to stare out of the window, praying that the weather would stay fine. To his relief it did, so he went round to his friend's house during the afternoon and arranged to borrow his car again.

As soon as he got home, he asked his mother-in-law for a quick snack. 'I'm going off to play cards with some chaps I know. I'll probably be staying overnight. How about packing me some sandwiches to take with me? It's a bachelor household and I doubt there will be any food provided.'

Bernice smiled at him. 'The war didn't make you lose your appetite, did it?'

'Nothing ever does.' He looked down at himself

ruefully. 'Though I always look as if I'm half-starved.'

'It's how nature made you. Now my side of the family go the other way. I don't eat half as much as you do, but I'm plump and I dare say I always will be.'

He went up to pack some things in a knapsack, chatted to her while he wolfed down some scrambled eggs on toast, then left.

This time he avoided the centre of Shawcroft, driving straight out to the Hall, slowing down as he went past it, then parking the car further along the road in a gateway whose rusted, sagging gate didn't look to have been opened for years.

When it was dark he walked back to the road outside the Hall and stood watching. Not until the last light had gone out did he make a careful circuit of the building, just to be sure there was no one still awake at the rear. There appeared to be a light left burning low in the hall and another on the landing, but otherwise the house was dark.

A dog barked somewhere and shortly afterwards the animal came pattering towards him through the bushes. Damn! He looked in the direction it'd come from and saw a lighted doorway to the rear of the stables. It had been hidden from him until now by the outbuildings. It must be one of the staff cottages. He'd remember to check those as well next time he came. Anxiety for Ronnie was making him careless.

The moonlight was bright enough for him to recognise the dog as it moved towards him growling in its throat. It was the one that had come to be stroked when he'd been sitting in the car. 'Hello, Tinker,' he said quietly. 'How are you, old boy?' He bent and offered his hand for the animal to sniff. It recognised him, butting him with its head for a cuddle and wagging its tail against his leg.

When a voice called 'Tinker! Here, boy!' he gave it a shove in that direction. As it went running off, he smiled. Fine watchdog that one was!

He waited a bit longer to be sure the man from the cottage wasn't coming out again. Every rustle had him jerking his head round to try to peer through the darkness in that direction. Then the light went out in the house behind the stables.

Still he waited, his senses so alert he was sure he'd have heard a leaf drop from a tree. But there were no more sounds of human or dog, no lights showing in the rear of the building, nothing but a light breeze and a million rustling leaves. Satisfied that he'd not been detected, he turned his attention back to the house.

Walking softly round it, he tried all the doors and windows, smiling in the darkness as he found a french window unlocked. Slipping off his shoes, he stuffed them into his capacious pockets, took out his torch and strolled into the house in his stockinged feet.

He'd done this before when in France on a reconnaissance mission, and felt just as he had done then. His heart was pounding and he felt as if all his senses were extended to the full. Finding Ronnie, getting her back was so important to him. Padding round the house, he memorised the layout of the ground floor, grateful for the lamp burning low in the hall, then trod noiselessly up the stairs.

There was another lamp burning low on the landing but nothing shone down from the second floor and attics, presumably the area where the servants slept. He padded up the stairs, waiting for his eyes to get used to the darkness.

When he came down to the entrance hall again, he knew the layout of the whole house and had mentally tied it in to the outside shape of the building. That was all he could hope for tonight. The only rooms he'd gone into were those whose doors were already open and of course they'd been empty. How galling it was to be sure that Ronnie was here somewhere and not be able to find her! But he knew it was better to err on the side of caution on missions such as this. Her mother had too much money and influence to be taken lightly and his reputation as a lawyer was too important to be jeopardised.

The next step would be to watch the place in daytime and find out where they were keeping Ronnie. Should he find a hidey-hole inside the house? No, that would limit what he could see and be much riskier because there'd be several people moving about. He studied the outbuildings. A position in one of these would give him a good view of the comings and goings of those who lived at the Hall, though he'd need to find somewhere that wasn't being used.

If Mrs Gresham thought she could keep Ronnie from him, she was wrong.

He put his rubber-soled shoes back on, taking his

time, and started to walk away. On an afterthought he went back and pulled the key out of the lock of the french window, slipping it into his pocket. They'd blame one another for it going missing – if they even noticed. He was pretty sure he hadn't left any traces of his visit behind.

He checked the outbuildings carefully: washhouse, coal store, junk store, privies, stables – the latter empty of horses, with the lower part used as a garage for a motor car and a motorcycle – and there would be sleeping quarters for grooms above them . . . only there wouldn't be any grooms now, would there? Unless the chauffeur who'd helped kidnap Ronnie slept out here? No, there was a narrow cottage to one side of the stables that looked occupied, with curtains drawn and a potted plant just to one side of the door. He'd bet the chauffeur slept there.

Making as little noise as possible, Giles crept up the stairs to the grooms' quarters, which proved to be little more than cubicles. Most of the doors to these were open, but one was closed. When he stopped outside it, he heard a man in the throes of a nightmare, the sort of nightmare many men had brought home with them from the war.

Sympathy flooded through him. There but for the grace of God . . .

He went on past that room. None of the other cubicles was occupied and there was a dusty smell to them that said they hadn't been used for some time. This place would do perfectly. He'd come back tomorrow night and take the end room for a lookout because from it he could see along the side of the house as well as most of the rear yard.

Giles made his way back to the road and walked along it to the place where he'd left his car. He needed to find somewhere out of sight to leave it, but didn't want anyone to find it and wonder why it was there. Perhaps he could pretend it'd broken down? Yes, that might be best.

He waited until dawn then started the car up and drove away slowly, filled with determination to gather all the threads of his life together, not into a knot but into a big, beautiful bow.

As Ronnie was falling asleep she heard some distant sound and then found it impossible to get back to sleep because she couldn't work out what the sound had been. She tossed and turned for a while then drifted off to sleep again.

The same sound woke her at dawn and this time she realised what the noise was: a car engine! Why would anyone be driving around in the middle of the night and so early that it wasn't even fully dawn?

What if it was . . . *Don't be silly!* she told herself.

But she couldn't help wondering if it was Giles looking for her. No, that was just wishful thinking. Why would he creep around during the night? Surely he'd come openly in the daytime, hammer on the door and demand to see her.

Only he hadn't done that so far.

It was better not to rely on being rescued, better if she got herself away from here with Algie's help or with Ellen's, or even without anyone's help.

Her mother couldn't keep her locked up for ever and didn't want to. She just wanted Ronnie to marry Algie and provide the Greshams with an heir. So the first step was to allay her mother's suspicions by behaving meekly. She wasn't sure how good an actress she was, but she would have to do her best.

As long as her mother didn't touch her. For some reason, she simply couldn't bear that.

When Seth got off the train in Shawcroft he looked round for a lad with a handcart to take his luggage to the Pughs' house. There were usually a few lads or old men hanging around stations trying to earn a few pence.

He was wearing the new police uniform, which had been introduced into the area just after the war. It was navy blue and had a hard, high helmet with a small brim. The helmet was made of cork with a cloth covering and was supposed to protect the head from both attacks and weather. It also made the wearer very conspicuous and he wasn't sure he liked that. People were staring at him already, because they'd not have seen the uniform here in Shawcroft. That made him feel self-conscious, besides which, he'd got the chin strap too tight and it was the devil to adjust.

Ah! There was a lad. He signalled and the boy quickly trundled his handcart across.

'Carry your luggage, sir?'

'Yes, please.'

'You the new bobby?'

'Yes.'

'You look a lot smarter than old Cobbley.'

Seth thought it better not to comment on that. 'I want you to take my luggage to Mr Pugh's house. Do you know where it is? Good. And do you have a friend, who'd like to earn sixpence as well? Yes? Then take him along to help carry the trunk inside. Mrs Pugh is expecting it. Tell her I've gone straight to work. She'll understand.'

'Yessir! Gone straight to work. Thank you, sir.' He pocketed the shilling with a grin and with Seth's help got the trunk and suitcase on to the handcart, then whistled a friend across to help him.

Straightening his jacket and running a finger inside the stand-up collar which was very stiff and new, Seth turned in the direction of the police station. People stopped to stare, a couple of urchins started to walk alongside him, trying to imitate his long stride. He ignored them and made his way along the main street. He'd found out where the police station was on his first visit, though he hadn't gone inside it. Turning right just after a small, untidy-looking park, he went up a gentle slope to the police station and cottage, which looked down on the town.

He walked inside the building with a low growl of relief. How was it you could sense people watching you? You didn't have eyes in the back of the head, but there was still something that told you.

An old man, who looked like an over-stuffed pillow in a very old-fashioned uniform that was too tight for him, glanced up from behind the counter and scowled, saying in a cracked, husky voice, 'You must be my new police officer.'

'Your replacement, yes.'

'I'm still in charge for this week and next, son, and don't you forget it. My instructions are to show you the ropes.'

'Yes, so they told me, Mr Cobbley.' The message was loud and clear: you're not wanted here. The other man didn't offer to shake hands. 'I'm Seth Talbot.'

'They didn't tell me your name. Must have had trouble finding someone suitable. You weren't a Special Constable during the war by any chance?'

This was an outright insult, because all sorts of people had been roped in as Special Constables to replace the policemen conscripted into the forces. 'No. I was a fully trained police officer in Manchester before the war, and a Sergeant in the Army during it.' Cobbley's scowl deepened if anything at this information.

'I see they've given you one of the new uniforms. You'll never keep warm with such a short jacket. They should have kept 'em knee length.' He peered at Seth's belt. 'Is that an electric hand lamp?'

'Yes.'

'Not as reliable as oil, if you ask me. And where's your rattle?'

'They give you whistles now, have done since well before the war.'

'I've kept my rattle. People can hear a good rattle for miles and they know what it means. Anyone can whistle. And you can use a rattle as a weapon if you need to, as well. But they never think to ask our opinion about what they're doing.'

Seth filtered in a long breath and prayed for patience. What was all this grumbling about?

Cobbley sucked at a hole in a back tooth, poked something out of it then said, 'You'll be out of touch with policing if you've been in the Army. The best thing to do will be for you to sit in the office and observe what goes on. That way you'll learn how we do things in Shawcroft.'

The man was a fool to be so rude to his replacement and Seth had had enough of it. 'I don't agree.'

'*What?*'

'I'm not used to sitting around. I'll start by going through the paperwork from the last few months. That'll give me a better idea of what's been happening round here.'

'Now look here. You don't walk in and tell me what to do—'

'It was the other way round, Cobbley. *You* told me what to do. And if what you'd told me had made sense, I'd have been happy to do it. But I'm not wasting over a week sitting in a corner looking like a beginner. Because I'm *not* a beginner.'

Cobbley glared at him. Seth kept his face expressionless, something you quickly learned to do in the Army if you wanted to stay out of trouble.

A young man came strolling into the police station, the fellow who'd been annoying Ellen Dawson. He looked from one to the other, then looked again as he recognised Seth.

'This is the new policeman,' Cobbley said in a grudging tone of voice.

'We've already met.'

'Oh?'

'Yes. He was in Shawcroft last week. Didn't he introduce himself to you then?'

'No, he did not.'

As Cobbley opened his mouth to say something else, Seth gave him the sort of look he would have given a troublesome new recruit, and the older man shut his mouth again. You did not bicker in front of outsiders.

'It's always good for a stranger to get to know the territory,' Seth said mildly, 'and since I happened to have friends here I came for a visit.'

'Welcome to Shawcroft.'

He held out a hand and Seth took it reluctantly, feeling his hand squeezed in a way that would have hurt a weaker man. He smiled blandly and squeezed back even harder until Jory was the one to let go. A childish trick. It seemed this was another person who resented his arrival on the scene. 'Nice to see you again, Mr . . . ?'

'Nelson. Jory Nelson.'

'The same Nelsons as are carters?'

'Yes. How do you know about that?'

'I saw a cart with the name on it. Not difficult to put two and two together. You've just been demobbed, I take it?'

Jory nodded.

'That makes two of us. I'd have been out sooner,

but I've been in charge of an emergency influenza hospital since soon after the war ended.' To his surprise, the hostility in Jory's expression eased a little.

'You're a braver man than I am, then.'

'I couldn't let men die untended.'

'He says he was a sergeant,' Cobbley put in.

'I *was* a sergeant,' Seth corrected sharply.

Jory grinned. 'I got made up to corporal once, but lost my stripe for insolence.' He turned back to the old man. 'Dad says he'll have to pick up your furniture next Thursday as we've got another job on Friday and Saturday.'

'You'd better go through and tell the wife. She's the one organising the damned move.'

After Nelson had left, Seth said, 'I'd better move in next Thursday then. Won't do to leave the place unoccupied.'

Wes scowled even more deeply. 'I suppose not.'

'Good. I'm looking forward to having my own place.'

'You married?'

'No.'

'They'll be after you, then. The women. They can't abide to let a young fellow stay single.'

'Will they? Well, I'm not looking for a wife.' Which wasn't quite true. He was more than ready to settle down now. And he'd thought about Ellen Dawson a few times, wondered about getting to know her better. 'Now, about those records . . .'

Going through the records didn't take him more than a couple of hours, even though he went back through the last two years. Either there was virtually no crime in Shawcroft or Cobbley didn't bother keeping records or – even worse – he didn't bother keeping down crime. There were, to Seth's surprise, no accounts of black-market dealers being charged and fined. That was significant for a start.

At one stage, Mrs Cobbley came in from the cottage to ask her husband about something and she, at least, seemed friendly.

'You must have your dinner with us today, Mr Talbot. It's only rabbit stew, but I'm a good cook, if I say so myself.'

'Thank you for the offer, but I have to go and see the Pughs. I sent my luggage straight there when I arrived, didn't have time to call in and I don't want to seem rude.' He turned to her husband. 'What time would you like me to take my dinner break?'

'Half-past one to half-past two.'

Mrs Cobbley was leaving but spun round. 'You'll do no such thing, Wesley. The poor lad will die of hunger if he has to wait that long to eat. You usually have your meal at twelve o'clock, so why do you need to change that? Mr Talbot can easily take his dinner break at one. And in the meantime I'll bring you both a cup of tea and a piece of my parkin to put you on.'

When he'd finished the tea and the generous chunk of sticky, gingery cake, Seth took the plates and cups back to the house.

She invited him in. 'You'll want to have a quick look round before you move in. Have you got some furniture?'

'No. I'll have to buy some. I can manage with a few bits and pieces at first. The Pughs said they'd lend me some things. You get used to living rough in the army.'

She showed him round the cottage, which had two rooms, a kitchen and scullery downstairs and three bedrooms upstairs.

When Seth went back into the station, Cobbley said, 'You took long enough.'

'Your wife kindly showed me round the house, since I'll be moving in next week.' He went into the inner office and began to go through the various drawers and cupboards.

Cobbley followed him to the doorway. 'What the hell do you think you're doing going through my drawers?'

'What I said I'd do: familiarising myself with the station. These aren't your personal drawers. Is there a lock-up?'

'Yes. Two cells. Not that they're used much. Peaceful town, Shawcroft. The cells are out the back there.' He jerked his thumb, staying where he was, sitting on his stool behind the counter as if glued to it.

Seth went to check them, wondering if Cobbley ever went out on patrol.

The cells were spotlessly clean and smelled of disinfectant, no doubt due to Mrs Cobbley's efforts. Mind you, if no one was being locked up, it was easy to keep a place clean. The cells in his last Manchester station had sometimes been in a right old mess, especially after the weekend influx of drunks.

He went into each cell, though there wasn't much

to see. Door keys were hanging on the wall outside. Inside, blankets were folded neatly at the bottom of the narrow bunks. Each cell also contained an enamel bucket, jug and chamber pot.

There was a cupboard in the corridor, but it was locked. Seth strolled back into the station. 'What's in the cupboard out there?'

'Personal stuff. I'll clear it out before I leave, then you can put what you want in it.'

At twelve o'clock Wes heaved himself to his feet and lumbered off to eat his dinner without a word. He took his bunch of keys with him.

Seth gave him a few minutes to settle then went out to the back to study the lock of the cupboard. With a smile, he fetched the collection of odd keys he'd found at the back of a drawer full of miscellaneous oddments, and tried them one by one till he found the correct key.

A quick glance inside the cupboard revealed a pile of packing cases containing tins of food and other non-perishable foodstuffs. Items like corned beef were still in short supply because of the war, so how had Cobbley got hold of these? Had they been confiscated? No, there'd have been paperwork.

Or were they a nice little sideline for Cobbley?

Even more thoughtful now, Seth locked the door and put the keys back where he'd found them.

When the front door opened, he looked up to see the lad who'd carried his trunk and suitcase for him. 'Nothing wrong, is there? You got my things to the Pughs all right?'

Anna Jacobs

'Yes. And Mr Pugh give me a job for the rest of the day, helping out in the workshop. He sent me to ask if you were going there for your dinner. He says to tell you there's plenty.'

'Well, in that case I will. Tell him thank you.'

'Mrs Pugh says I can have some dinner too.' The lad licked his lips. 'She's already give me a jam butty. Real thick slice of bread it was, too.'

Seth smiled. 'They're kind people. Tell them I'll be there just after one o'clock.'

'Yessir.' The boy went out, whistling cheerfully.

Seth sat thinking about his first morning. There was definitely something going on here and he'd bet the Nelsons were involved. Jory had walked into the station as if he was at home there.

Had that man really been Ellen's lover? Seth could not stop thinking about that boast, picturing Ellen's pretty, fresh face, wondering what she was doing now . . . wondering whether she had been involved with Nelson?

Maybe the Pughs would be able to tell him more about her.

Edwina carried up her daughter's breakfast, followed by Glenys with a ewer of hot water and a towel, also a cloth to cover and remove the chamber pot. Tadwyn stood guard in the doorway. Really, she thought, he was the most loyal of her staff. She didn't know what she'd do without him.

'How long are you going to keep me shut up here for no reason?' Ronnie asked as the things were being set down. 'There's nothing whatsoever wrong with me and well you know it.'

Glenys threw her a startled glance and Edwina clicked her tongue in annoyance. Not until the maid had left did she speak. 'If you want to keep eating food which isn't drugged, you'll hold your tongue in future when a servant is in the room.'

'Tadwyn's still here.'

'*He* won't say a word. Maids always gossip about their betters. I'll have to ask Mrs Shipton to have a word with Glenys.' She looked at Ronnie's tangled hair. 'After you've had your wash I'll bring you a brush and comb.'

'I'm bored here doing nothing.'

'Behave yourself and I may let you out. We'll discuss that after you've eaten and tidied yourself up.'

Ronnie ate her breakfast, had a wash and waited. She had to wait over an hour and guessed that her mother was delaying her return on purpose to re-inforce her point. When she heard footsteps in the corridor, she stood up facing the door.

It opened to show Ellen standing behind her mother. Beyond a quick glance, Ronnie didn't look at the maid or say anything, only watched out of the corner of her eye as she picked up the bowl of dirty water, emptied it into the bucket, cleaned out the wash bowl quickly with the towel, then took away the dirty water and towel.

'Close the door, Tadwyn, but stay nearby,' Edwina ordered, then turned to her daughter. 'Let me do your hair for you.'

Ronnie took an involuntary step backwards. 'I'd rather do it myself. You know I don't like anyone else messing with my hair.'

'Very well. Here you are.' Edwina held out the brush and comb and Ronnie took them. There was a small mirror set in each of the wardrobe doors, so she went across to look in one of these as she did her hair, squinting to see properly. Behind her she could see the fuzzy reflection of her mother's outline and hear the impatient tapping of her foot.

'You're squinting.'

'I can't help it. I'm trying to see to do my hair.'

'Hmm.'

When she'd finished, her mother studied her. 'Your hair's gone even fairer. I suppose it must be the sunlight. It looks quite nice, though.' She felt in her pocket. 'I've brought a pot of cream for your face. It'll take a while for that blowsy redness to fade. I'll lend you some rice powder for this afternoon. I don't normally approve of make-up, but we have to do something about your complexion, make you look ladylike again.'

Ronnie tried to keep her voice steady as she asked, 'For this afternoon?'

'Yes. Algernon and his mother are coming round to see you. But unless you give me your word not to be silly, you'll stay up here and I'll tell them you're too ill for visitors. And if you break your word or make any sort of fuss, you'll be drugged for the whole of the coming week. Besides, behaving foolishly would only prove that you're mentally unbalanced.'

Ronnie shivered involuntarily.

Edwina gave her daughter a quick triumphant smile. 'I give you *my* word about the consequences of you breaking *your* word. Now, I want your promise.'

It didn't take much thinking about. Anything was better than staying in the bedroom on her own. And this was the first step towards being trusted again. 'I'll behave.'

For a moment, there was silence then her mother nodded. 'Very well. We'll see how you go. You might as well give up the idea of this man you've met because I'll make very sure you don't marry him.'

It wouldn't do to give in too easily. 'Couldn't you even meet him, see what he's like? He has good prospects.'

'No. I want you to marry Algernon and that's that.'

Ronnie had no need to feign tears. They welled up involuntarily in her eyes and she turned away for a moment, unable to bear that gloating gaze.

'For goodness' sake, try to be practical. You always were too emotional. The estate needs a man to run it, not someone with a separate career of his own. Algernon is perfect for that. He knows what's expected. The estate will bring in as much money as he and you need, and I'll be here to guide you both for some time yet. I am, if I say so myself, a good business-woman. Without me and the money I brought to him, your father would have gone under.'

Ronnie wiped her eyes, hoping she hadn't shown how much the prospect of having her mother control-ling her life from now on horrified her.

'Well? Are you going to behave?'

'I don't have any choice.'

'Good. We'll have you lying on the couch with your feet up, covered by a blanket. You're an invalid at the moment, remember, not able to walk about much.'

Ronnie nodded. One step at a time, she told herself. First get them used to letting her go downstairs, then find a way to escape and go to Giles.

Or maybe he would come and rescue her.

Even if he didn't, there was no way even her mother could force her to marry Algernon.

She just prayed he didn't want to marry her or she'd be fighting on two fronts.

10

Glenys tried to do her work as well as usual, but couldn't help making regular trips to the nearest window to see if she could spot Pel. Several times she had the pleasure of seeing him working. Once she saw him stand up and stretch then turn his face up to the sun as if relishing its warmth on his skin, just as he had done on the bench by the kitchen door.

Ellen came to help her make the beds because it was so much quicker with two and Millie was busy in the kitchen.

'Thanks for letting me take Miss Veronica's things,' Ellen said abruptly. 'I wanted to see her again. Don't look so worried. I didn't try to chat to her.'

Glenys looked quickly over her shoulder. Mrs Shipton had told her in no uncertain terms that she was not to gossip about what was happening in the west wing. In fact, she was a bit worried about what the housekeeper would say when she found out that the other maid had taken her place.

Ellen walked across and shut the door. 'Miss Veronica looked perfectly normal to me. Has she ever looked strange to you?'

'No. In fact, when I carried up her water this

morning, she said there was nothing wrong with her and asked the mistress why they were keeping her locked up. I didn't know what to think, because . . . well . . .' She hesitated.

'Go on.'

'They've been drugging her.'

'*Drugging* her?'

'Yes. I've seen Mrs Gresham putting drops on her food. She does it on the landing, but if I take the short cut to the kitchen, sometimes I can't help seeing what they do.'

Ellen hid a smile. She was quite sure Glenys had eavesdropped and spied on her mistress on purpose. What other excitement did she have in her life?

'I don't know what to think, really. It's none of our business, though, Ellen love.'

'No. And we'll lose our jobs if we try to interfere. But what if they *are* keeping Miss Veronica prisoner? What if there's nothing wrong with her and—' She broke off and put one finger to her lips as footsteps approached, then said loudly. 'There, it's much quicker with the two of us, isn't it?'

'Yes, much faster.'

The door opened and Mrs Shipton peered in. 'No need to close the door when you're working in a room.' She stared round, nodded approval then went away again.

Her discussion with Glenys gave Ellen a lot to think about as she carried on with her duties. She had always got on well with Miss Veronica when she worked here, and didn't think her the sort of woman to fall to pieces, whereas she could well believe that Mrs Gresham would lock her daughter in her room, because she'd done that many times before as punishment. But would she go as far as to drug her?

After some thought, she decided that was possible. Mrs Gresham had been bad enough before the war, irrational even sometimes, but she was now acting as if she were the queen and everyone else a lowly worm. Only what was it she wanted Miss Veronica to do?

It wasn't till nearly lunchtime that Mrs Shipton noticed the skirt hem. 'Have you shortened that skirt, Dawson?'

Ellen looked down. 'Yes. It's much easier to work if you're not catching your foot in your hem all the time.'

'You should have asked permission. It's not your dress.'

'I've only tacked it up roughly. I can pull it down and press it before I leave.'

'When did you have time to alter it?'

'I couldn't get to sleep last night, so I got up and did it then. I'm finding the countryside very quiet after a big city.'

'You should just have gone straight to bed.'

'As long as I do my work to your satisfaction, I don't need to be told what to do when I'm not on duty.'

'Did Lady Bingram allow you to do what you wanted in your free time?'

'Of course she did. All us aides were adults, working together for our country in time of war. They couldn't treat us like children one minute then expect us to think for ourselves the next.'

'Well, it's different here. We definitely don't want you to behave as you please. The very idea of it! It's for the mistress to say how you spend your time.'

Ellen had had enough of being hectored. 'Not my free time.'

'You're living under her roof and what you do reflects on her, so of course she can. And I don't like your attitude. Your stepfather tells me you've no other job to go to, so it's likely you'll be staying here for longer than a few months. You'll still have to earn your living, don't forget. He said your wages were to be paid to him, as we did previously, for safekeeping.'

Ellen stared at her in outrage. 'If you're going to do that, I'm not working here.'

The two women looked at one another and the housekeeper was the first to look away. 'You'll have to take that up with him.'

'No. I'll tell him you'll not be paying anything to him, but I'm taking it up with you here and now. And if you don't give me your solemn word that I'll be paid *all* my wages, I'll pack up and leave this minute.'

There was silence, then, 'Very well. But I trust you'll not spend the money foolishly. Mr Halsopp said you'd been rather – giddy in London.'

Ellen felt as if she'd explode with anger, but somehow managed to control it. 'My stepfather has no idea what I did in London. I'm twenty-six now, not fourteen, let me remind you. And if Daphne Bingram trusted us to—'

'*What* did you call her ladyship?'

'Daphne. She asked us all to call her that while we were working together.'

'I can't believe that.'

'You know I'm not a liar.'

'I don't know what the world's coming to, I really don't.'

'With respect, Mrs Shipton, I think I should make my position clear. I'm working here *temporarily* because I don't get on with my stepfather, so can't live in his house. It's only for my dying mother's sake I'm staying near Shawcroft. I have enough money saved to live on for several months, because contrary to what he's told you I was always very careful with my wages in London. However, I'd rather not dip into my savings, so I prefer to find a job. But the money's there and it gives me a freedom I never had before.'

'Enough money for several months!' The house-keeper stared at her in amazement then said in a brittle voice, 'Very well. You've made your point clear.'

Ellen forced herself to speak in a softer tone. 'You know I'm a hard worker. I'll give you good value for your money while I'm here, I promise you.'

'Yes. You are a good worker.' A wry smile crossed the housekeeper's face. 'And you're clearly a very independent young woman now. The world has changed greatly since I was your age.' She stared into the distance for a moment or two then said briskly, 'Well, you'd better go and get your morning tea now, Dawson. I can't stand here gossiping all day.'

'Yes, Mrs Shipton.' But Ellen's voice came out with a mocking edge to it, try as she would to control it.

Before she sat down for her morning tea, Glenys turned to Cook. 'Can I take a cup out to Pel?'

'The new man? Oh, yes. It's a good thing you reminded me. I'd quite forgotten him. I wonder how he's getting on. You'd better check where he is. It may cheer the poor lad up to have a bit of company, so ask him to join us, because Gerry will be going home to his wife for his cup of tea, and there's no one else working in the gardens.'

Glenys made straight for the kitchen garden, where she had seen Pel working.

When he heard footsteps he turned round quickly, an anxious look on his face.

'It's only me. Cook sent me to ask you if you'd like a cup of tea. She says you can join us, if you like. Mrs Shipton lets us take a break morning and afternoon because no one can work properly without good food inside them.'

'Will that be all right? Won't Gerry mind me stopping work?'

'Not him. He always goes home for a cup of tea round about now.'

Pel smiled at her. 'You're very kind.' Then he looked down at himself. 'Perhaps I'd better sit outside, though. I'm all mucky.'

'There's the bench. I'll join you there. The weather's quite nice today, isn't it?' As he still hesitated, she added, 'Come on. I'm thirsty if you aren't.'

Together they walked back and when he hesitated by the kitchen door, she said, 'You sit down and I'll bring it out to you.'

She brought it on a battered old tray they used in the kitchen, a cup of tea and buttered scone for each of them. Setting it down between them she sat on the end of the bench. Strange, she thought, that she didn't feel shy with him as she did with most men. 'There you are. Get that down you.'

'I've not had such generous butter for years, with all the food shortages.'

'We've not gone short here, what with the farm and all, though there's been less food, of course. I wonder how long it'll be before things get back to normal. What did you miss most during the war?'

And they were off, chatting like old friends.

Cook glanced out of the window. 'Nice that Glenys has taken that poor soul under her wing. Pity she never married and had children. They always come to her and she's wonderful with them.'

Ellen went to join her. 'He'll need a lot of help for the next few months.'

'Do men like him ever recover?'

'I think so, more or less anyway. Though he'll probably do better if he leads a quiet life from now on.' She smiled at the scene in the yard, the spinsterish maid suddenly animated, the nervous man relaxing visibly in her company. 'He'll make a good worker if people treat him right,' she added slyly.

'Who will?'

She turned round to see Mrs Shipton approaching them and dared to put one finger on her lips. 'The new man. The one who's shellshocked. He seems to feel safe with Glenys. Cook said Mrs Gresham has found it difficult to get outdoor staff. Well, gardening is a perfect job for someone like him.'

Mrs Shipton came to stare out, a frown creasing her brow.

'And it's our patriotic duty to help men who were injured fighting for us,' Ellen added.

'I don't need you to tell me about looking after those who fought for us. I'm as patriotic as the next person. And if *you* are not looking after him, Dawson, perhaps you could finish your scone and get back to work. Give Glenys another five minutes, Cook, then tell her to start work again. Oh, and Dawson . . .'

She stopped in the doorway. 'Yes?'

'After you and Glenys have finished the downstairs rooms, I'd like you to help Cook. We're having visitors this afternoon.'

'Yes, Mrs Shipton.'

'Can't you tie that hair of yours back?'

'I've tried, but it just slips out again. It's too short. I pinned the sides back this morning with bobby pins and look at it now.'

With a shake of the head, the housekeeper turned to check on what Millie was doing. 'Where did that dratted girl go?'

'She went back to her work, of course,' Cook said. 'She doesn't need telling once she's learned how to do each job. She only gets muddled if people shout at her. I've not seen such a willing lass for years.'

Ellen decided now was as good a time as any to speak out. Things had been too fraught during her earlier meeting with the housekeeper. 'Um – Mrs Shipton, I'd like to visit my mother tomorrow afternoon if that's all right with you?'

'As long as you don't expect any full days off as well as the half days.'

'No, of course not.'

'I suppose you'll be going into town on that *thing*.'

'Yes.'

'Well, make sure you don't show your legs! We don't want anyone thinking Mrs Gresham employs loose young women. Oh, and you might ask Cook if she needs anything in town. I presume there's plenty of room in that sidecar to bring the odd package back?'

'Yes, plenty. I can easily run errands for you while I'm there.'

Cook winked at Ellen from behind the housekeeper's back. 'Well, I could do with some more cheese, if that's all right with you, Mrs Shipton? Miss Veronica does like her cheese and it's better to buy it fresh than let it go hard. And Ellen could perhaps take me in with her to the market on Fridays, if that's all right with you. It'd be a lot quicker than sending Tadwyn with a list and we'd get better value too, if I could choose things myself.'

'You wish to ride in that thing?'

Cook smiled. 'To tell you the truth, I've been dying to.'

'Very well. Ellen can get a piece of cheese for you from the Emporium tomorrow. Tell her what you need. I'll think about the markets and let you know. Mrs Gresham may not approve.'

When she got up to the bedrooms, Ellen chuckled. It was obvious that Cook was on her side and that even the housekeeper was going to find her visits to town useful. She'd forgotten what it was like to be stuck out in the countryside, far away from the shops and with no omnibuses or trams passing nearby. And there was no stable lad now to nip into town with the horse and trap. No gardener producing miracles of vegetables as old George had done. He'd died early in the war, Glenys said, after which the gardens and greenhouses had gone to pot.

Mrs Shipton was right. The world had changed and no one knew where it would all end. But Ellen found the changes exciting, had enjoyed her new life in London, was determined to make an interesting life for herself in peacetime too.

At three o'clock in the afternoon a carriage turned into the driveway of the Hall and the driver reined in the single horse in front of the house. Algie got out and helped his mother step down.

The coachman clicked his tongue, shook the reins gently and the horse walked on, knowing where to go because it'd been here so many times before.

In the rear yard Tadwyn was waiting to greet the coachman, his long-time friend. 'Nice to see a horse instead of a smelly motor car.'

'We've run out of petrol today, so I had to use Jenny. Mr Algie was supposed to order the petrol, but he forgot.' He went round to the horse. 'I'll just unharness the poor thing. She's too old to be pulling heavy loads round the countryside, aren't you, girl? You and me both need putting out to grass, I reckon.'

Tadwyn lingered to chat. 'How's Mr Algie going?'

The coachman shook his head regretfully. 'Can't settle, poor lad. There's a few come home like that. My nephew's the same.'

'Yes. We've just hired one of them to work in the garden. I think he's from a better background than he's letting on, but he—' he nudged his friend. 'There! That's him.'

They both watched the painfully thin man push a wheelbarrow slowly across the yard.

'Doesn't look up to much.'

'Oh, he does his best, you have to give him that. And they're not paying him full wages. *She* never misses an opportunity to economise, even on a fellow like that. Sticks in my gullet a bit, that does.' Tadwyn sighed and reached out to offer the old horse a wizened apple. 'I'd better get back. *She* wants me to sit in the hallway in case Miss Veronica has one of her turns.'

'Bad, is she?'

'Oh, just a bit run down and won't admit it.'

He went indoors and sat in the hall, arms folded, listening to the voices in the drawing room. He reckoned he knew more about what was going on here than any of the other servants, but he was beginning to worry about what Mrs Gresham was doing – and making him do.

And against his better judgement, because he usually only looked after himself, he had started feeling sorry for Miss Veronica. Mr Algie was a poor, wiffly sort of chap, always had been – even if he had won medals in the war. Mrs Gresham could surely find a better man than that for her daughter to wed. She hadn't even given this fellow Miss Veronica had mentioned a chance. She ought to have done that, at least.

Ronnie lay on the sofa, feeling too warm because of the blanket her mother had insisted they cover her lower body with. As the visitors were shown in, she stifled a gasp at the sight of Algie and could only hope her shock hadn't shown on her face. Her old playmate trailed after his mother, looking not only unwell, but dispirited, like a dog that has been beaten too many times. He seemed twenty years older than the slender lad who had bounced off eagerly with his best friend Pierce to join the Army.

After he'd greeted her mother, Algie came straight across to Ronnie. 'Hello, old girl. I hear you've not been very well.'

'She had a bad bout of flu and hasn't picked up since,' Edwina said quickly, directing her visitors to seats closer to her than Ronnie. 'And of course she was run down after all that heavy physical work. But we're going to feed her up again, aren't we, darling?'

'Yes, Mother.'

Algie sat down where his hostess had indicated and

left it mainly to the two older ladies to maintain a conversation, which they had no trouble doing since they'd been allies for years. Once their attention was distracted, he edged his chair a little closer to Ronnie. 'So, how did you like being a farmer?'

'Very much. I was lucky. The Tillings looked after me well and my fellow land girl pulled her weight. I'm a great milker, you know.'

'Darling, do you *have* to be so bucolic?' Edwina called, pulling a wry face. 'Milking is *not* a skill one should be boasting about.'

Ronnie shut her mouth and counted up to ten before opening it again to draw in a breath of air, because the room felt suddenly stifling.

'And how are you now, Algernon dear?' Edwina said. 'Your mother was just telling me about your medal.'

'I only did what any other chap would do – and it was all in vain because Pierce died.'

His voice was so hoarse with anguish as he brushed aside her congratulations that Ronnie asked gently, 'It was Pierce you rescued?'

'Yes. He'd have done the same for me.'

'I'm sure he would. I'm sorry he's dead. He was always kind to me when I tagged along after you two.'

'He was kind to me, too.'

With a frown Mrs Gresham introduced a more pleasant topic of conversation and politeness forced Algie to reply to her.

'Your Ma keeping you on a short rein?' he whispered to Ronnie when the two older ladies were having an animated discussion on the latest fashions and skirt lengths, and the iniquities of maids who tried to ape their betters.

'Yes. She won't let me out of the house.'

'I'll call again. Maybe we could sit out on the terrace?'

'I'd like that.'

The visit wasn't long, out of consideration for the invalid's supposed state of health. Edwina showed the guests to the door, leaving her daughter on her own for a few minutes.

Ronnie knew better than to try to run away because she'd get nowhere, but when Ellen came in to clear away, she seized her opportunity. 'I'm being kept a prisoner because I won't marry Algie. There's absolutely nothing wrong with me. If I give you a letter, will you post if for me?'

Ellen glanced quickly towards the hallway, which was still echoing to Mrs Gresham's overloud voice. 'Yes. Have you something to write with?'

'No. But I'll find something, somehow, if I've to write in my own blood. I've a friend who'll – look out!' She slid down and closed her eyes and Ellen continued to pile the delicate porcelain cups and plates carefully on two trays.

Mrs Gresham came in, stared at the two young women suspiciously, then turned to her daughter. 'Better get back to bed now, Veronica dear. We don't want to overtire you on your first day up.'

'Can I choose a book from the study first, please? I've finished the other one.'

'If you must. Though you really should rest.'

She followed her daughter to the study then up the stairs, gesturing to Tadwyn to accompany them. Once inside the bedroom she closed the door on her servant. 'Take those clothes off now, Veronica.'

'Can't I keep them? It doesn't feel right sitting around in a nightdress.'

'You can always get into bed if you're cold. Now, take them off or Tadwyn and I will do it for you.'

Ronnie undressed quickly, embarrassed by her mother's assessing stare. Afterwards she looked at the window. 'Could I have it open more than that? It's so hot and stuffy in here, I feel like I'm going to faint.'

'There's enough air coming in, I think.'

When the door closed again, Ronnie sank down on the bed and allowed herself a few tears. It was all very well talking to Ellen about writing a letter, but she had neither pencil nor paper. Then her eye fell on the book she'd brought upstairs and she opened it, flipping to the end. Feeling guilty at damaging it, she carefully tore out the last page, which was completely blank and hid it under the mattress. Then she changed her mind and slipped it underneath the wardrobe.

After which she went back to staring out of the window.

The morning passed very slowly for Giles, who found himself faced yet again with simple legal tasks more suitable for an indentured clerk. He went along to the new senior partner's room just before lunch. 'This work isn't very challenging, Henderson.'

'It's all I have for you.'

'Your uncle used to share the more interesting jobs between us.'

'I'm not my uncle.'

Giles stopped pretending. 'No, you're not at all like him, unfortunately. I don't think you and I are going to get on very well, so it'll be best if I leave the practice. I'll see if I can find someone to buy me out and—'

'Don't bother. I have a friend who may be interested. Leave it to me.'

Giles guessed then that the new owner had been planning to drive him away, so he leaned against the doorpost and smiled. 'Well I give you warning, I shall expect a fair price or I shan't budge – whether I'm bored or not.'

The two stared at one another for a moment or two, and then Henderson looked away.

'Of course.'

'Then the sooner the better, as far as I'm concerned,' Giles added. 'I can leave at the end of the week if the terms are correct.'

Henderson looked at him in shock. 'So soon?'

'What's to keep me?'

'Nothing, I suppose. We're not very busy just now. Very well, I'll see what I can do.'

And that was it, not even a pretence of regret at losing such a capable partner, let alone thanks for all the years Giles had worked in the practice before the war. He had no false modesty about his capabilities because he'd been doing the lion's share of the work before the war and he'd a lot to be proud of in what he'd done in the Army during the war. This man had managed to stay at home, though he didn't look as if there was anything wrong with him physically. Giles knew what he thought of shirkers.

When he went home for lunch, a letter was waiting for him from Septimus Monnings, the lawyer from Shawcroft whom his godfather knew. It asked him to come and discuss the partnership as soon as was convenient, because he was sure anyone recommended by James Dunham would suit him.

Smiling, feeling as if fate had dealt him an unexpected ace, Giles scribbled a quick note and ran down with it to the postbox, just making the second collection. With a bit of luck the letter would be there by morning, but he'd be in Shawcroft before it.

That afternoon he simply informed Henderson that he'd be away for a day or two, investigating certain employment prospects.

The other stared at him sourly. 'You're not wasting any time.'

Giles leaned on the desk. 'I think that'll suit both of us, given your attitude, don't you? But don't think you'll get rid of me more cheaply if I find something. I'm rather stubborn where my own finances are concerned and I can afford to wait you out.' He didn't stay for a response but strolled out, whistling cheerfully.

At home he made his preparations then went to tell his mother-in-law that he might be buying into a new practice and would have to go and investigate a prospect.

'Oh? Where is it?'

'I'd rather not say anything till we see if it's a goer. But it's not too far away. Just wish me luck.' He hesitated. 'You wouldn't mind moving to another town, would you?'

'If you still want me to live with you?'

'I'll always have a place for you, Bernice. You held my home together after Norma died, cared for my children when I couldn't. That's a debt I hold sacred.'

Tears brimmed in her eyes at the mention of her daughter's name and she nodded, not able to speak.

He patted her shoulder. Words weren't necessary between them. They'd both lost their spouses during the war and she a daughter as well. They'd drawn closer because of that. As far as he was concerned she was like a second mother to him now, replacing the one who had died when he was fifteen, and he knew Bernice was not only very fond of him but adored her grandchildren.

Besides, although she came from a good family, Bernice didn't have much money and he wasn't going to leave her to live in genteel poverty.

11

By mid-afternoon, Seth felt as if he was going mad, shut in the police station with Cobbley, who hardly stirred from his high stool behind the counter and seemed to spend a lot of time staring into space. Seth had gone through all the records and there was, quite simply, nothing else for him to do.

To his surprise, no one had come into the place except Nelson, not one single person. Did people in this town not find and hand in items, report loss of property, lay complaints, get arrested for beating their wives or becoming drunk and disorderly? All sorts of things had been going on everywhere else Seth had worked.

'Shall we go out for a stroll round the town centre?' he suggested as the hours ticked slowly past. 'You could introduce me to a few people.'

Cobbley turned a lacklustre gaze on him. 'I suppose we could, but I'm not going far. I've got corns and these boots rub them something shocking, only we haven't been able to get decent new boots during the war, not even those of us on important war work to release the younger men, like I've been doing.'

Seth bit back a sharp comment about the import-ance of what the other was doing.

It took Cobbley ten minutes to get his old-fashioned helmet and button up his jacket, which he'd loosened at dinner time and not fastened up again. The garment was then so tight that Seth wondered the buttons didn't pop off. And it reached right down to his knees, which Seth had always found inconvenient when it rained.

Just when he thought they were ready to leave, Cobbley said he had to go and tell his wife he was going out, then he came back to hunt for a card on which was printed 'BACK IN TEN MINUTES. IF URGENT, LEAVE A MESSAGE AT THE HOUSE'. This he propped on the counter.

'Don't you lock the place up when no one's here?' Seth asked.

'What for? I know everyone in town and they know me. Besides, there's nothing worth stealing here.'

But there were the police records, which anyone could come in and look at. Seth didn't like the thought of that, skimpy as the last few years' records were. But he said nothing. This could all be changed when he took over.

Walking at a snail's pace, Cobbley led the way into town. He didn't introduce Seth to anyone, just nodded to a few people who said 'Good afternoon' and hurried on.

When they started on their way back, Seth decided he'd had enough of this and stopped outside the Town Hall, a small square brick building with no pretensions to anything except keeping the weather off those who went inside. 'Let's see if the Mayor is in. I ought to know who he is, for a start.'

'You can't just walk in off the street and expect to see Mr Flaunden! And anyway, he might not be there. He does have a business to run as well. He's the leading funeral director in this town, you know, handles all the funerals for the better class of people.'

'If he's in, he won't be too busy to stop for five minutes, I'm sure.' Without waiting for an answer, Seth led the way in, holding the door open for his companion, who waddled quickly past him to the counter.

'Is Mr Flaunden in, Joe lad?'

'Yes. Shall I tell him you want to see him, Mr Cobbley?'

'If you will, please.'

Again, he made no attempt to introduce Seth.

The clerk came out from behind the counter and knocked on a door just behind the two policemen, not going in until a deep, plummy voice called, 'Enter'.

Seth studied the entrance hall, thinking it looked more run down than it needed to, even though there had been a shortage of paint and varnish during the war.

When the clerk came out again, he held the door open for them. 'The Mayor will see you now, gentlemen.'

Cobbley led the way into a large, comfortable office. 'Sorry to trouble you, Peter. There's nothing urgent. I've just brought my replacement to meet you. This is Seth Talbot.'

Seth stepped forward, offering his hand, and the mayor gave it a cursory shake.

'We're going to miss Wes,' Flaunden said. 'No one knows this town like he does. If you'll take my advice, young fellow, you'll learn as much as you can from him before he leaves, see how we do things in Shawcroft. He'll be sadly missed.'

'I'll certainly listen to what he has to say,' Seth replied diplomatically, though he had no intention of following Cobbley's example and idling away his days. 'And I hope that once I've settled down and got to know the town a bit, I can make an appointment for a chat with you.'

'A chat? About what?' Flaunden's voice was sharp and his body had suddenly grown tense.

'The town's needs or problems, how the police force can best serve Shawcroft. There should be more than one policeman located here, for a start, and no doubt will be once things settle down again.'

'What we need from you is easy. We just need an eye kept on a few folk who misbehave from time to time. Lads sometimes need knocking into line and we have one or two regular drunks. I'm sure a strong young fellow like you can handle that sort of thing. And then there are strangers to the town. We don't want criminals coming here to prey on our townsfolk. So they'll need keeping an eye on.'

Seth kept a polite expression on his face only with an effort. Clearly Mr Flaunden was a supporter of the status quo and did not have any understanding of modern police work.

Cobbley heaved himself to his feet. 'Well, now you two know one another, we'll be off. I'll see you on Saturday evening, Peter lad.'

The Mayor nodded, hesitated, then looked at Seth. 'We're having a special farewell for Wes here in the Town Hall, if you'd like to come? Seven o'clock till nine.'

Cobbley scowled at his friend and didn't endorse the invitation.

'I'd be delighted.' Seth wouldn't, but he ought to have been invited and was angry with the other for not doing so, as well as for being obstructive, secretive even, rather than helping him settle in.

They got as far as the Town Hall door then Cobbley stopped. 'I'll join you in a minute, Talbot. I just need to tell Peter something private.'

Seth went and stood outside the Town Hall, hands clasped behind him, studying his new kingdom. The whole town seemed to be sagging, somehow. He didn't know what was wrong, but could sense that something was. The people going past either avoided looking at him altogether or gave him quick nods and moved on. Not one paused to pass the time of day. When he'd worked as a policeman in Manchester, even in the poorer areas people had not only greeted him but stopped to chat. He was a stranger here, so there was perhaps some excuse, but they hadn't chatted to Cobbley, either. In fact, the only people who'd wanted to speak to him today had been Nelson and the mayor.

Someone came into view at the far end of the street and Seth had good enough eyesight to recognise Jory Nelson pushing a handcart. The man must have come out from the police station, because there was nothing else up that small cul-de-sac. When he saw Seth,

Nelson stopped for a moment then turned left up the next street. Maybe he'd been intending to turn anyway, but if so why had he only stopped when he noticed Seth?

The door opened behind him and Cobbley came out. He led the way back along Rochdale Road towards the police station at his slow ambling pace. He stopped first at a large public house called the Royal Fleece, which also offered accommodation. The owner was rather stiff with Seth and didn't offer much by way of conversation.

'Stuck-up bugger, that one,' Cobbley said as they walked away. 'Nor I don't believe in allowing women inside pubs, like he does. Not just to eat, think on, but to sit and drink like men in a fancy lounge bar. It's not right, that isn't. I'd not let my wife go out drinking, I can tell you.'

'Don't the poorer women go into pubs?' Seth asked, puzzled, because they had done in Manchester.

'Them! They only go into the snugs and I know what I think of that sort.'

Cobbley stopped just then outside a grocery store which went by the grand title *The Shawcroft Emporium*. 'Best shop in town, this is, but I don't like his prices. Still, I don't mind him taking money off them as can afford to shop here.' He introduced Seth to the proprietor and his wife, who stopped serving customers for a brief chat.

A few doors further along was *Halsopp's Butcher's, Fine meats our speciality*. This was Ellen's stepfather. Seth was introduced to a burly, red-faced man who was an advertisement for hearty eating. Halsopp deigned to have a few words with Seth, but it was Cobbley to whom he directed most of his conversation and the two were clearly old friends.

The two policemen also stopped to speak to the publican of the Black-Faced Sheep, a small public house just off the main road which seemed to cater for the ordinary working man. 'Best beer in town,' Cobbley said as they entered.

'Can I offer you a pint, gentlemen?' the landlord asked, already reaching for two glasses.

'No, thank you, not while I'm on duty,' Seth said.

'I'll pop in later, Fred,' Cobbley said, throwing a dirty look at his companion. 'It's been a thirsty sort of day.'

Then there was the haberdasher, the barber, the ironmonger and the milliner. Cobbley didn't attempt to go into any of the other shops, most of them smaller places, and after a time pulled out a pocket watch and squinted at it. 'Better get back for the last half hour.'

In between the brief calls into shops, he'd not uttered a single unnecessary word and he didn't on the way back, either.

As they were closing for the day, Seth said, 'I'll need some keys to the police station.'

'Not till I move out, you won't.'

'What if I'm needed during the night?'

'I still live at the back, so I'll be the first one to be called and I'll be able to let you in if you're needed – though you won't be. I keep telling you: we have a peaceful town here.'

When Cobbley went out to the back place to attend to a call of nature, Seth opened the bottom drawer and pulled out the bundle of keys. He found the one for the front door and as an afterthought, shoved the whole bunch into his overcoat pocket.

As he walked back towards the Pughs', he was very thoughtful. It was going to be a wearing few days. And the first thing he was going to do after Cobbley handed over the station to him was to change all the locks.

That evening Mrs Gresham called for her car, checked that her daughter was sleeping peacefully with the help of Dr Hilliam's drops, and prepared to go out to dinner with friends.

Tadwyn went out to start the car, but though he swung the starting handle in the correct way, the engine refused to catch. Cursing under his breath he checked that everything was in order and tried again, with the same result.

Ellen had been sitting outside the kitchen, enjoying the evening peace and the pretty patterns cast over the yard by the long slanting shadows. When the car failed to start she strolled across. 'Having trouble?'

'Yes. I can't get a peep out of the damned thing.'

'Let's roll her outside where I can see better. I love these longer evenings, don't you?'

They pushed the vehicle from under its shelter and she lifted the bonnet, checking the wires and connections that were a mystery to Tadwyn. 'You've probably got a blocked fuel line.'

'I have?'

'Mmm. It's the most likely thing, anyway.'

'You couldn't – fix it, could you?'

'Might be able to. I'm supposed to be helping Glenys in a few minutes, though.'

'I'll go and tell Mrs Gresham there's a problem and I need your help.'

Ellen smiled as she bent over the motor again. She didn't envy him. Mrs Gresham would probably have a fit at the thought of a maid fixing her motor car.

Tadwyn found his mistress sitting in the hall, dressed in her best, tapping one foot impatiently.

She looked down her nose at him. 'Is there some reason for your being late in bringing the car round?'

'Yes, ma'am. It won't start.'

Silence. 'Can you not do anything about that?'

'I'm afraid such things are beyond me, ma'am. However, if you'll release her from her other duties, Dawson thinks she knows what is wrong.'

'*Dawson* does? But she's . . . How can she?'

'She said she used to service her own motorcycle during the war. Lady Bingram had them taught, apparently, so that they wouldn't have to trouble any of the men.' He was angry at Mrs Gresham's tone towards him. She spoke as if the car not starting was his fault. He should be used to that by now but lately her selfishness had started to get on his nerves. He stood there, waiting for her answer, trying to appear calm.

'Very well. Let Dawson try. But if she damages it . . .'

'She's less likely to do that than I am. And ma'am
. . .'

'Yes? What now?'

'We really should let Martin Pugh have the car for
a day, so that he can set it to rights. He told me after
church last week that the engine was sounding rough
and I'd hate to have it break down while I was driving
you somewhere.'

'Oh, very well.' She frowned in thought. 'It must
be on Wednesday next, then. I have no engagements
that day.'

He inclined his head and went out to the kitchen.
'She says you can leave your other work and see if
you can fix the motor car,' he told Ellen. 'Will you tell
Mrs Shipton about that if she comes looking for Ellen,
Cook?'

'Yes, of course.'

Ellen looked down at herself. 'I wish I'd brought
my overalls. I don't want to dirty this dress and
apron.'

'There's an old pair of overalls in the garage,' Cook
said. 'One of the gardeners left them behind, so I had
them washed and put them away in the store room.
You never know when things will come in useful.'

'Good. I can change out there.'

'You'll change in here,' Cook said, scandalised. 'Pel
or Gerry might see you in your underwear if you do
it out there. I don't know what they taught you in
London, but here we like to behave modestly.'

Ellen didn't protest. She was delighted at the thought
of getting her hands on a car again because she had

missed fiddling with motors. When Tadwyn brought in the overalls, she changed in the scullery, pulling the hated cap off as well.

Cook shook her head in disapproval as Ellen came out. 'Don't let the mistress see you like that!'

'She's the one who wants me to repair the car. A skirt would catch on things not to mention getting stained with oil and dirt.'

And as it turned out, her guess proved to be correct and it wasn't hard to clear the fuel line.

'There, that's done! See if it'll start now.' She stepped back, wiping her hands on a rag.

Tadwyn stared at her. 'So quickly?'

'It was only a blocked fuel lead. I can show you how to check for that next time and fix it. It's—'

He held up one hand to stop her continuing. 'No, thank you. I don't want to learn anything else about this monster.'

He went to swing the starting handle and the motor started first go. 'Well done. I'd better get ready to take her out now.'

She watched him scowl at the car. 'You don't like driving it, do you?'

He looked over his shoulder to check no one was near. 'No. And I draw the line at repairing it and getting myself covered in oil.' He looked pointedly at her dirty hands.

'I'd love to have a go at driving it sometime.'

He took out a silver pocket watch and squinted at it, then a smile crept slowly over his face and he winked at her. 'I think we ought to take the car for a short run, to check that it's all right before we let Mrs Gresham risk a ride in it, don't you?'

She grinned back at him. 'Won't that make her even later?'

He shrugged. 'She was rather rude to me today.' He bowed and made a sweeping gesture with one hand towards the car. 'You can drive it.'

She got in and drove slowly across the yard.

Glenys came to the kitchen door. 'Madam says how much longer are you going to be?'

'Tell her we're just testing the car to make sure it's safe for her to ride in and won't break down again,' Tadwyn called with another wink at Ellen.

She drove out to the end of the drive, then turned left and went along the road, able to drive faster now. 'It's a lovely car, very easy to drive and holds the road well.'

'If you say so. It's only the second car I've ever driven, so I wouldn't know, and after I finish here, I'm never driving one again.'

She didn't argue with him, wanted to foster this fragile link between them. When they reached a cross-road, she slowed down. 'I suppose we'd better go back now.'

'Yes.' He sighed.

Drawing up in front of the house, she got out of the car and hurried round the back before Mrs Gresham could see her in her overalls.

Tadwyn went to open the front door and let his mistress know the car was all right. She was waiting impatiently in her small sitting room at the rear to the left of the house.

'About time.'

'I couldn't have managed it at all without Dawson. She really seems to understand about motor vehicles.'

'Never mind her, let's get going.' She swept outside without a message of thanks to Ellen and waited for him to open the car door.

He frowned as he walked round to the driver's seat. The war was over now and he was getting tired of Mrs Gresham's rudeness. Very tired. Well, his savings had mounted steadily and one day soon, he would simply give notice and leave. And *she* could like it or lump it.

In the meantime, this was, he decided, the beginning of the end. He'd contact the friend with whom he planned to share a home for their retirement and suggest they start looking for somewhere to live.

As dusk fell, Giles drove slowly along the lanes to the south of Shawcroft, passing the Hall and driving another mile or so further on. The other day he'd noticed a short lane that seemed to lead only to some fields and he pulled in now to inspect the far end of it, nodding in satisfaction as he saw that it was lower than the nearby fields at that end and hidden from the road by a drystone wall. He parked the car and composed himself for a nap, something he'd learned to do at will in the army. He planned to move around midnight and knew he would be able to wake up roughly on time.

Three hours later he came awake with a jerk, quickly realising where he was. He placed the note he'd prepared on the dashboard so that it was visible from outside.

Car broken down, gone for help.

Taking out the knapsack of supplies, he checked from outside to make sure the message on the dashboard was showing clearly and locked the car, starting back towards the Hall on foot. With a half moon shining above him he had no difficulty finding his way along the lane.

When he reached the Hall, he studied the building from a distance, relieved to see that only the night lamps were glowing faintly. Moving cautiously, he went closer, circling the place carefully. No other lights showed anywhere in the big house or the cottages behind it and there was no sign of the dog, either.

The stables weren't locked and he went to the foot of the staircase that led to the old grooms' quarters. Again he paused to take off his shoes and stuff them in his pockets before creeping up. The third one creaked, which he hadn't noticed on his last visit. It sounded loud in the quietness of the night and he froze, waiting to see if anyone had noticed. But there was no sound in this part of the stable block apart from the faint whisper of his own breaths.

As he walked along the short corridor at the top of the stairs, he decided that the man who'd been having nightmares before must be sleeping more soundly tonight, because a slight snore was tickling the air inside that room.

Smiling, Giles moved on to the bedroom he'd chosen, the one nearest the house. The bed had only an ancient, flattened straw mattress, but that would do him. He'd slept in far more uncomfortable places during the war. There was even a rough blanket folded neatly across the bottom of this one. Luxury!

He put on his shoes again in case he had to make a quick exit, and lay down on the bed, which rustled slightly – not enough, he hoped, to alert anyone to his presence. This part had been easy enough. It was daylight with people moving around which would bring the risk of being caught – and also show whether he could pick up any hints as to whether they were keeping Ronnie here, and exactly where.

Some time later he woke with a start, wondering what had disturbed him, then sagged back in relief. The poor sod along the corridor was having another nightmare. Did he have them every night? This one went on for quite a while, then the cries and panicky gasping stopped abruptly. There was dead silence followed by a groan, after which the man got out of bed.

Giles heard a match strike and then saw the flickering light of a candle in the corridor, because he'd left the door of his own cubicle exactly as he'd found it, half-open. When he heard footsteps coming towards him, he rolled quietly off the bed and slid under it. But the man didn't go into any of the other rooms, just walked up and down the corridor in silence for some time before going back to bed.

He didn't seem to sleep again, though, because Giles heard noises at regular intervals: the mattress creaking, a cough, the sound of water being poured into some container, then something small being set down on a hard surface.

Giles didn't sleep either from then onwards, didn't dare.

Once Algie and his mother left, Ronnie wasn't released again that day. Ellen brought her evening meal up on a tray, with the watchful Tadwyn in attendance. The maid winked at her as she set it down and Ronnie hoped this meant she'd hidden something on the tray.

When the door was locked again, she lifted off the cover but disappointment cramped through her when she couldn't see anything special about the meal. Why had Ellen winked, then? She looked at the bowl of soup and the plate of lamb, potatoes and peas without any real interest. She wasn't at all hungry, but they were keeping her short of drinking water so she decided to have the soup at least.

As she dipped the spoon into the bowl, it hit something that felt solid and she pushed the object to the edge. It was a tiny stub of pencil. *Oh, Ellen, thank you!* Relieved, she lifted it out of the bowl, wiped it quickly on her table napkin and slid it into her dressing-gown pocket. The napkin was such a mess, she spilled a bit of soup on to the tray and then wiped some of it up to provide a reason for the mess. There! That wouldn't raise suspicions.

After that she drank the soup slowly and with relish, but couldn't fancy the main course, so just ate the apple pie.

Her heart felt a little lighter in the knowledge that

she'd found an ally inside the house and would be able to write to Giles tonight.

It seemed a long time until they came for the tray and she dozed while waiting. At last Tadwyn picked up the tray then went outside, closing the door behind him.

'You didn't eat much of your food,' her mother commented.

'You don't build up an appetite sitting around doing nothing. I ate some of it.'

'Algernon telephoned. I said you were sleeping. He wants to ride over here tomorrow afternoon to see you. I've agreed, but unless I'm sure you'll behave yourself, he'll find that you've had a relapse.'

'I behaved myself today, didn't I?'

'Yes. We'll see how you are in the morning and I'll decide then. However long it takes, you'll learn to do as I say . . . or you'll suffer the consequences.'

'What do you mean?'

'It'd be easy to keep you drugged and get dear Dr Hilliam to agree that you're not in full possession of your senses.'

'If you do that, the St Corbins won't want Algie to marry me.'

'Yes. But I'd rather keep you locked up for the rest of your life than put up with you disobeying me.'

Her tone was so flat and emphatic Ronnie stared at her in dismay. Her mother definitely meant that.

'You're all I have left now that your brother Edwin's dead and I'm *not* letting you do something stupid. I'm the only practical one in the family. You're too like your father – weak and trusting – so I'm going to keep a firm hand on the reins as far as you're concerned. I didn't save the place for you to lose it again, or to leave us without an heir. Just think about that.' She waited for the words to sink in.

Ronnie thought instead of losing Giles, which made tears well up.

Her mother's voice grew persuasive, 'You've always been good friends with Algernon. It's not as if I'm asking you to marry someone you dislike! I wouldn't do that because it never pays in the long run.'

'He's changed, looks so run down.'

'He needs a woman to look after him and comfort him after what he's been through.'

'I know he does. And I'm very fond of him, but I—' She broke off and buried her face in her hands.

'I'll leave you to think about your alternatives.' Edwina went across to pick up the lamp. 'No sense in leaving this. We don't want you having any accidents.'

'But it's too early to go to sleep!'

'Then lie there and have a good think. And for goodness' sake, be practical about the future, not to mention what you owe to the family!'

Ronnie didn't look up till her mother had left the room. Then she thumped the pillow several times to let out her frustration. She'd have to write her letter very early next morning.

She lay back and the day's images played before her, together with her mother's threats.

Unfortunately, she was fond of Algie and he did

seem in low spirits, in need of comfort. But that didn't mean she wanted to give up her life for him.

Once his wife was asleep Bevan went quietly up to the attic in his slippered feet. He held up the lamp and stared at Ellen's trunk, then set the lamp down and moved forward to examine it more closely. It was locked, of course, but a simple padlock like that could easily be removed. It wouldn't keep a burglar out for two minutes, that wouldn't.

The trouble was, he didn't want to saw it open unless he was sure of finding something worthwhile inside. What children had belonged to their parents, everyone knew that. He was Ellen's stepfather and not only was this her trunk, but it was in *his* attic, so he had every right to know what was inside it. Every right.

Was Jory's guess correct? Did Ellen have money saved? And if so, did she keep it in a savings bank or in this trunk? The mere thought of money always made his fingers itch, but he wasn't showing his hand by breaking open the trunk unless he was sure it'd be worth upsetting Dorothy for.

A prudent person would put their savings in the bank or in a better hiding place than this. The war had changed even sleepy little towns like Shawcroft and there were villains everywhere. You couldn't be too careful with money. His own savings were scattered here and there, in two separate bank accounts and also cash in a special hiding place, just in case anyone queried the extra money he'd made on the

side during the war. He paid enough taxes to the
damned government as it was. Income tax had been
three and sixpence in the pound in 1915 and now it
was six shillings, nearly double. Daylight robbery, that
was. What encouragement was that to a man to work
hard if they took away a third of the money he earned?

His eyes went back to the trunk. Ellen was a woman,
young still, so she might not have been prudent. And
if she hadn't, the money would either be here or in
her things at the Hall. If it was here, he would definitely take it. If it was at the Hall, he'd have to trick
her into bringing it back. After all, he'd had all the
disadvantages of being a father to her; now it was only
fair that he have some of the advantages. Of course
he'd taken her wages when she first started at the Hall,
but that had been a piddling amount, not nearly
enough to recompense him for the trouble she'd given
him.

He went downstairs again and tried to settle to
reading the newspaper. But he couldn't. His thought
kept going to the trunk in the attic.

If only he knew what it contained!

Giles heard the other man get up as soon as it was
light and crept across to the window to watch him
get a bucket of water from a tap in the yard. Thin,
dark rings round his eyes, a haunted expression on
his face. He jerked at the sound of a sharp noise,
standing stock-still for a moment, then pulling himself
together with an obvious effort. He brought the
bucket back inside and had a good wash-down in

the stables from the sounds floating up the stairs, going out a few minutes later to empty the dirty water down the drain. His torso was bare, showing a long scar down one side, his braces were hanging down from his trouser tops and his wet hair was combed back neatly.

He came clumping upstairs again and presumably got dressed before going out again. When Giles next saw him, he was sitting on a bench on the other side of the yard just outside the kitchen door. After a few minutes a maid came out carrying two cups of tea and they sat together on the bench, not saying much, but both smiling slightly as if happy in each other's company.

Giles decided this was a good time to risk nipping down to the privy behind the stables. It was the riskiest part of his mission, getting to a privy, but some things couldn't be postponed indefinitely. Afterwards he regained the little bedroom without being noticed and settled down to observe the activities in the yard and the rear part of the house, thankful that the window of his room was dirty and festooned with cobwebs that helped hide him from sight.

As he'd guessed, the chauffeur came out of the narrow house squeezed between the stables and an outhouse. The man must be well over sixty and was moving stiffly. He stopped for a word with the two on the bench then went into the kitchen.

It was going to be a long and probably boring day – but Giles couldn't think of any other way to gain the necessary information. He didn't intend anything to go wrong when he rescued his darling, for her sake and for his family's sake.

Ronnie got up as soon as it was light. She'd lain awake for ages last night composing a letter in her head and since they didn't usually bring her breakfast and washing water until later than this, she intended to write her letter now, while her thoughts were clear.

Even to write to Giles seemed to bring him nearer. She kept her handwriting as small as she could with the awkward stub of pencil, explaining what had happened and exactly where her room was. She left room at the end and put SEND TO and Giles's address.

When she'd finished she reread the letter quickly, then folded it up small and slipped it into her dressing-gown pocket. Now she just needed Ellen to come with her breakfast and surely she'd be able to find a way to pass the letter on.

But to her disappointment it was Glenys who came, first to bring her breakfast and empty her chamber pot, then to bring back the pot and take away the tray. It was hateful having the maid do this noisome duty for her.

The letter seemed to have grown heavier and to twitch around in her pocket, as if it too was dying to leave this room.

She was too frustrated to settle, but when she heard her mother's footsteps, she sat down quickly by the window and folded her arms.

'How did you sleep?'

'Badly. I'm short of exercise.'

'Well, you'll just have to put up with that,' Edwina said. 'Algernon said he'd call this afternoon. If I let you see him, I want your solemn promise that you won't do anything foolish.'

Ronnie gave a scornful snort. 'He's not exactly the sort to rescue a maiden in distress, is he?'

'Hardly. But he'll make a very manageable husband, and that's worth a lot, believe me.'

You certainly managed my father. For a moment Ronnie thought she'd said the words aloud, then realised with relief that she hadn't.

Her mother's voice grew coaxing in tone, something that had never fooled Ronnie, even when she was a child. 'Poor Algernon does need help and comfort. Blanche told me he's been very down since the war. She thinks that's why they demobbed him early. Who better to comfort him than you?'

'I'd like to talk to him, see if I can help. But that doesn't mean I want to marry him.'

'You will promise not to do anything silly, though, won't you?'

Ronnie sighed, stared down at her dressing-gown then said, 'Yes, I promise.'

'Very well. I'll go and select some clothes for you and you can see him this afternoon. You can go out on the terrace with him, but remember that I shall be in the sitting room with the windows open and I shall hear every word you say. If you move out of earshot, I'll send you straight back to your room.'

'Yes, Mother.'

It was only after her mother had left that Ronnie

realised what she'd promised. She went to stand by the window in a sunlit patch as she thought this through. She'd promised not to do anything silly. Well, it wasn't silly to want to choose your own husband and live your own life. Her conscience, she decided, would be clear if she kept this promise in her own way.

But how much leeway would her mother allow her in future if she behaved meekly? Enough for her to escape?

She *had* to get word to Giles.

If Algie wanted to marry her, she didn't dare entrust her letter to him.

Why had Ellen not returned?

Giles didn't know what made him look up just then, but he did. A figure was standing by the window of a room on the second floor. The window wasn't open to the fresh summer air like the others, which seemed strange, and the woman was just standing there, not cleaning the window or dusting the sill. It was too far away to make out details except that it was a woman. She stayed by the window for a long time watching what was happening in the yard.

Who else in the house would have time to do that? he wondered as excitement rose in him.

He fumbled in his knapsack for his binoculars and didn't find them. Damn! He was sure he'd put them in. They must have fallen out in the car. And without them the mystery woman was just too far away for him to make out the details. Ronnie could see things clearly at a distance and he saw better when things were closer.

Mentally he walked round the house again, as he had done the other night, working out where that particular room was situated. If he got no further information or clues today, he was going to risk going in there in a day or two and finding out who occupied that room. But he wouldn't do that until he had an escape plan worked out which included them getting married. If she was standing by the window, she wasn't in immediate danger.

When he looked back at the window, the figure had vanished.

People came and went in the yard all day and he didn't hear anything useful. He popped out to the privy a couple of times, choosing his moments carefully. Apart from that he simply observed the life of this household. He could be very patient when he needed to be.

The occupant whose looks he liked most was a tall young maid with a mop of curly hair. She had an honest, open sort of face and a warm, generous smile and, best of all, she'd pulled a face at Mrs Gresham behind her back after being spoken to sharply in the yard. He could hear the reprimand because Ronnie's mother had a peculiarly penetrating voice, was probably slightly deaf. What on earth did it matter what a maid wore in her time off? And trousers were far more sensible when driving a motorcycle.

Maybe another way of helping Ronnie would be to catch the maid and make sure that Ronnie was still in the house, then beg her to carry a message for him.

It was galling to be so close, but it didn't do to move hastily, not when his whole life's happiness was at stake.

In the afternoon he heard a horse clopping along slowly and a rider appeared, a rather weedy young man who rode well, but who drooped visibly, as if unhappy. He was known to the servants and familiar with the place, because he waved to them then went to stable his horse himself.

After washing his hands at the tap in the yard the man stood for a moment, reluctance in every line of his body, before squaring his shoulders and going into the kitchen.

Since he must live locally, Giles could make a good guess at who he was: Ronnie's childhood friend Algie. But how good a friend was he to her now? Maybe he had designs on her for himself? This was another person it might be risky to approach, and Giles would only do it if he was desperate.

12

Ellen tried to persuade Glenys to let her take Miss Veronica's tray up, but it seemed Mrs Gresham wanted only Glenys to do it.

So Ellen worked steadily through her chores, winning a rare word of praise from Mrs Shipton about how much she had accomplished in such a short time.

'Have you ever thought of how you could rise in service, Ellen? You're such a good worker, I'm sure you could work your way up to housekeeper. And that's a very comfortable position to be in, I can assure you.'

'I'm sure it is. But the war has changed me. I've grown used to being out and about and I couldn't bear to spend my life shut up in houses. Thank you for your confidence in me, though.'

'I'll have to see if I can change your mind.' Mrs Shipton looked at the clock. 'You'd better get off, then, if you're going to visit your mother. Don't forget the cheese for Cook.'

Ellen went up to change out of the dowdy dress, tossing the hated cap on top of the scuffed chest of drawers and shaking her hair free. After some deliberation, she put on her aide's uniform again because it was more decent for driving a motorcycle.

Unfortunately, she ran into Mrs Gresham as she was going out into the yard.

'What on earth are you wearing, girl?' her mistress demanded.

'The uniform I had in Lady Bingram's Aides, ma'am. It's more respectable than a skirt when one is riding a motorcycle.' She saw the expression of disgust on the older woman's face and wondered why it mattered to her what a maid wore during her free time. But she didn't say that, just waited, hands clasped in front of her, eyes down.

'Please keep yourself as much out of sight as you can when you get into town. I do not approve of women wearing trousers – or driving motorcycles. It's about time you settled down, Dawson, and realised that the war is over.'

Ellen sighed as she watched her walk away. She wished she hadn't come back to work here, because it wasn't a happy house except for the kitchen. Cook and Glenys were fast friends and always cheerful, not seeming to expect more from life than they had already. How many women spent their lives like them in the service of others, giving up even the thought of families and homes of their own? It was a secure job with enough to eat, but that was all you could say for it.

As for the other staff, Millie seemed permanently nervous, Tadwyn was definitely annoyed about something, and poor Pel still twitched at every sudden noise.

Ellen removed the tarpaulin, fitted on the lead and wheeled the motorcycle out into the yard. It started second go and she sighed happily as she drove slowly out towards the road. Freedom! At least for a few hours.

'Mr Algie!' Cook beamed at him across the kitchen. 'Nice to see you safely home again, sir.'

He nodded, forcing a smile to his face though it was even harder than he'd expected because he felt such a strong urge to turn and run away from this sort of life. 'Nice to be back. I certainly missed home cooking like yours, used to dream about it. There was nothing nearly as good in the army.' Which was a lie but you had to say such things to loyal staff. 'I've come to see Ronnie. I arranged it with Mrs Gresham yesterday.'

He noticed Cook shoot an uncertain glance at Glenys and wondered why.

'Better take him in to see the mistress first,' the maid said. 'I don't know if Miss Veronica is receiving guests today.'

Algie looked at her in surprise. 'Of course she is. I saw Ronnie yesterday and she seemed perfectly all right to me. It's a lovely afternoon and it'll do her a world of good to sit out on the terrace.' He watched the two of them carefully and felt from the continuing exchange of glances that something untoward was going on.

What was *that woman* doing to poor Ronnie now? She'd bullied her daughter for as long as he could remember, made her cry often when she was a child. He'd lost count of the times he'd comforted the girl who was like a little sister to him.

When he'd said that to his mother, she'd been furious with him and had told him in no uncertain terms that there wouldn't be a lot of money coming from them and the best way for him to secure his future was to marry Veronica Gresham.

Only he didn't think of Ronnie in that way. Couldn't.

'If you'll come this way, sir?' Glenys said.

'What? Oh yes. Jolly good.'

Ronnie's clothes were brought to her after her lunch, not the ones she'd have chosen, but she had no say in the matter and knew better than to protest. When she was dressed she sat by the window again and saw Algie arrive, riding the old grey mare which had pulled the carriage the previous day. She watched impatiently as he disappeared into the stables to tend the animal. It seemed to take him longer than you'd expect. And even after he'd gone into the house, no one came to fetch her.

She hated being without a clock or watch.

Most of all, she hated her mother.

She'd tried all her life not to hate her, because it was wrong, everyone knew that. But she'd been pushed too far this time and she wasn't going to pretend to herself any longer. Indeed, she was seriously beginning to wonder if her brother's death in the war had unhinged her mother or else why would she be behaving like this? Surely she didn't think she could keep Ronnie a prisoner for ever? Or force her to marry Algie?

Her brother Edwin had always been the favourite

and it was not too much to say that her mother had doted on him. Ronnie had liked him too, because he had a sunny nature. And while he was alive, her mother had given her some freedom, at least. Now, it seemed, she was to be chained here permanently to produce an heir.

When she heard footsteps coming up the stairs, her heart started thumping and she went to sit on the chair by the window, trying to appear calm.

It was Tadwyn who opened the door and he was on his own.

'Your mother would like you to join her and Mr Algernon downstairs, Miss Veronica. I'm to give you my arm, since you're too weak to walk very far.'

She stood up but didn't move towards the door. 'How is your conscience, Tadwyn? Does it make you feel good to help her keep me a prisoner?'

'I'm merely following my employer's orders.'

She let her disgust for him show on her face and wondered if she'd seen a flicker of shame in his eyes. 'I don't need to hold your arm till we get down to the next floor. I don't like touching people who've been criminally unkind to me.' Hah! That was definitely a look of shame on his face, quickly replaced by his glassy-eyed expression, but she knew she wasn't mistaken. It was Tadwyn who'd taught her to ride and she had some fond memories of him as a child. She might try to play on them.

'Remember my first pony? Who'd have thought the man who taught me to ride would now become my enemy?'

He took a deep breath before saying, 'Better come now, miss.'

Without another word she followed him down the stairs, laid her arm lightly on his at the top of the next flight and walked slowly down them with him.

He took her into the small sitting room at the side, where her mother was waiting with Algie, and ushered her to a chair as if she couldn't walk on her own. Her mother leaped up to help her sit down but when Edwina touched her, Ronnie stiffened and drew back, hissing, 'Stay away! I can manage on my own.'

The two stared at one another for a moment, then Edwina stepped to one side. 'I can't help being over-solicitous, darling. You've been so very ill.'

'I'm all right now.'

'You must allow me to know better.'

When they were all sitting down, Edwina led them in a little light conversation. Ronnie replied only when she had to.

After a few minutes Algie said, 'I wonder if I could tempt you outside, Ronnie. I'm sure the fresh air would be good for you.'

Edwina made a play of opening the french windows and studying the weather. 'Only if you sit where I can keep an eye on you. I don't want Veronica tiring herself. She's been *very* ill, you know. We nearly lost her.'

So Ronnie went outside for the first time since she'd been brought here, pausing just outside the door to breathe deeply and look at the flowers in the bed under the window. Such a sun-warmed bed, that one, always the first to produce flowers.

Algie sat beside her on the bench and luckily this meantthey had their backs to the house. When her mother had gone inside, he turned his head slightly and raised his eyebrows questioningly.

'Can't talk. She's listening,' Ronnie whispered. 'Tell me how you are,' she said aloud. 'You don't look at all well.'

He shrugged. 'It was a hard war.'

'I was sorry about Pierce. So sad that he was killed close to the end.' To her surprise, Algie's eyes filled with tears.

'We were together all through the war,' he said in a voice thick with anguish, 'and he was killed only a few days before it ended. I managed to bring him back when he was shot, but he died anyway. Breathed his last in my arms.' And had extracted a promise from Algie which he had tried to keep. 'Now they're giving me a medal for it. As if I damned well want one!' He dashed away the tears with the back of one hand.

She took hold of the hand and patted it. That simple touch was enough to make her realise she could never marry this man. When Giles touched her it set warmth humming round her body. When he kissed her she forgot the rest of the world. With Algie, there were no special feelings at all. 'What are you going to do with yourself now?'

'I don't know.' He winked as he pulled a small note-book and pencil out of his pocket, hiding them under a handkerchief, which he made play of wiping his nose with. When he'd put it back in his pocket he picked up the pencil and scribbled. *What's really going on?*

She took the pencil and scrawled, *She's keeping me prisoner till I agree to marry you.*

He stilled, staring at the words, then at her. 'I suppose I'll just work on the estate,' he said for the benefit of the listener nearby. After a moment or two he took the pencil back and added, *Surely marrying me would be better than staying here?*

I've met someone else and anyway, Mother wants us to live here.

'My brother's going to breed horses. Says there will be a shortage till we've made up for the ones that were killed in the war. It'd make more sense to go into motor cars, which is what I'd do if I had the chance.'

They fell silent, Algie staring down at the notebook and Ronnie into the distance.

They both came out of their reveries at the sound of a chair scraping inside the room. He quickly slipped the notebook and pencil into his jacket pocket.

Edwina came out of the sitting room. 'I don't want Ronnie staying out here too long. She tires easily. You've been quiet for so long I'm sure she must be exhausted.'

'It's not tiring to sit with an old friend,' he said in his old easy way. 'And this always was a sheltered, sunny spot. Ronnie's the only person I know who can enjoy a bit of companionable silence. Everyone else fills each second with babble.' After a pause, he added almost to himself, 'I can't tell you how much I enjoy silence after the noise of the war.'

Ronnie clasped his hand in both hers briefly. The

last words had been a cry from the heart.

'Well, I still think I must put my foot down for now and send Ronnie up to lie down. We don't want her having a relapse.'

'Can't I stay here just a bit longer?' It was out before Ronnie could prevent herself.

'Not this time, darling. Perhaps another day, when we see that you're not exhausted by this first outing.'

'I'll escort you up to your room, then,' he said in his easy way. 'You can lean on my strong, young arm.'

Edwina shook her head decisively. 'Tadwyn can do that, Algernon. I'm rather old-fashioned about men going up to young women's bedrooms.'

There was nothing he could do after that but say his farewells and promise to ride over the next day to cheer Ronnie up.

Her mother came up with her and Tadwyn, insisting on her daughter getting undressed again and handing over her clothes.

Ronnie was left with a new worry on her list. Algie. The poor fellow sounded really down in the dumps. If only Pierce had survived the war! He'd always known how to make them both laugh. The three of them had been inseparable as young children, then they'd all been sent to boarding school. But the two boys had been together, at least, while Ronnie had been on her own. She'd always envied them the extra closeness that brought.

And once she escaped from her mother and learned a little more about the world, she'd wondered about their friendship.

*   *   *

Ellen took her time driving into town, enjoying the fine day and the feeling of freedom. People stared at her as she drove slowly down Rochdale Road, so she pretended not to see them. Just as she was turning off towards her mother's house, Jory stepped to the edge of the pavement and signalled to her to stop. Shaking her head, she drove on. The last thing she wanted was another confrontation with him.

She parked outside her mother's house, hesitated, then pulled off the lead, just to be safe.

Knocking on the door, she poked her head inside and called, 'It's me!'

'I'm in here.'

She went into the downstairs bedroom, shocked all over again by how ill her mother looked. 'I've been given permission to visit you three times a week. Isn't that marvellous?'

'Wonderful. Why don't you make us both a cup of tea and bring it in here?'

'All right. And something to eat, perhaps?'

Her mother pulled a face. 'I'm not hungry, darling.'

'Just a little something to please me?'

'I'll try.'

The kitchen looked tidy, but had that neglected air rooms get when the mistress of the house isn't tending to details. With a brand new gas cooker it didn't take long to boil a kettle. They didn't have such a convenience at the Hall because the gas pipes didn't go out there. They didn't have electric lights either, well, few people did in Shawcroft. She'd grown used to switching on a light in Lady Bingram's house and had forgotten how messy candles and lamps were.

When she came back into the bedroom, her mother looked at her and grimaced. 'Do you have to wear trousers?'

'A skirt would fly up and reveal my legs. Besides, I'm proud of this uniform. Lady Bingram designed it herself.'

Her mother looked unconvinced but let the matter drop and they chatted for a time, Ellen telling her about what she'd been doing at the Hall and who else was working there, though she didn't mention Miss Veronica.

'The housekeeper's right: if you're not going to marry, you could have a good future in service,' her mother said, but sighed.

'Who said I won't get married one day?'

'But you told me you weren't interested in Jory.'

'I'm not and I never will be. *Never!* There are other men in the world, though, and—'

'Not so many now that you're getting older.'

'At twenty-six?' Ellen laughed. 'Not quite in my dotage yet, Mum. And before you ask, there's no way I'd stay on at the Hall permanently. I'll never work permanently as a maid again. It's only for you that I'm doing it now.'

'I know, and I'm grateful, but I'd die happier if I knew what was going to happen to you. If you won't marry Jory, I can't see what else you *can* do but go back into service. I know you and Bevan don't get on and you'll still have to earn your keep.'

'There are other sorts of jobs. I did lots of different things during the war. I could even open up a business of my own if I wanted to. My friend Mary Ann was going to open up a tea shop. She says it's just a question of getting to know how a business runs and keeping everything well organised.'

'It takes a lot of money to open a tea shop.'

'I have enough saved.' She could see that her mother didn't believe her and to reassure her, added, 'It's sitting upstairs in my trunk at this very moment, though I'm going to put it in the bank as soon as I can. I was going to do it today but I didn't get away as early as I expected and the bank will be closed now. Besides, I wanted to see you first, just the two of us. Anyway, I'll do it on Monday, pop in here to get the money, then come back after I've put it in the bank. You won't mind, will you?'

Dorothy sighed. 'Young women shouldn't be running businesses. They should be getting married and having children.'

Ellen sighed and changed the subject, feeling only a sense of relief when she glanced at the clock. She wanted to see her mother, felt it was her duty, but they had so little in common now it was hard to maintain a conversation for long. 'I'm sorry, Mum. I have to do some shopping for Cook before I go back. I'll come and see you again on Monday.'

'You'll know where to find me.'

When Ellen got to the end of the garden path she saw Jory sitting on her motorbike, fiddling with the handbrake attached to the handlebar. 'Get off that at once!' she yelled. 'How dare you mess around with my motor-cycle?'

'It's a good thing I did. It won't start, so you're going to need a ride back to the Hall.'

Anger blazed through her that he had dared to try and start it. 'I know exactly what's wrong with it.' She decided to keep the lead in her pocket because she didn't want him knowing her secret. He might be able to drive but he couldn't be mechanically minded if he hadn't noticed the missing lead. 'I know how to fiddle with it to get it going, there's a trick to it. In the mean-time I have to buy some things for Cook from the Emporium.'

She turned and started walking down the street but to her annoyance he fell in beside her. 'Go away! I don't want to talk to you.'

'Aw, a fellow should be able to walk beside his favourite girl.' He tried to pull her arm into his and she shoved him away so violently he tripped and fell over.

As he scrambled to his feet, face red with indigna-tion, a voice said, 'Are you having trouble, miss?'

She turned to see Seth standing beside them wearing his policeman's uniform. He looked so handsome and well turned out, he took her breath away and she had trouble speaking for a few seconds. 'Yes. This man won't leave me alone.'

'I'm her fellow. We had a quarrel and I'm trying to make it up,' Jory said at once.

'He's *not* my fellow and he never will be. I hate the

very sight of him, but he won't stop pestering me.'

Seth turned to Jory. 'It sounds as if you should go on your way, Mr Nelson.'

His words were quiet and polite, but there was a firm tone to them that said to Ellen he wasn't a man to be messed with.

For a moment the two men eyed one another, like two dogs spoiling for a fight. Anger emanated from Jory, who started to say something then stopped. With a muttered exclamation he began walking down the street, turning at the corner to yell, 'I'll see you next time, Ellen love, when you've got over your huff!'

She shuddered and muttered, 'I'll never do that.'

'*Is* he your fellow?'

'No, and hasn't been since just after the war started. I wouldn't go out with him again if he was the last unmarried man in England! I hate the very sight of him.'

'He must have really upset you.'

'He did. Beyond forgiveness.' Ellen took a deep breath and tried to smile at him. 'Sorry. There's no reason you should get caught up in my quarrels, Mr Talbot. But I am grateful to you for coming to my help. I couldn't get rid of him.'

'If he continues to pester you, I might have to get caught up in your quarrels as part of my duties. Young women should be able to walk down the street without being accosted.'

She nodded and set off walking again.

'I'll come with you, just in case he tries anything else.' He smiled as he added, 'Unless you'd prefer to be rid of me as well?'

'I'd welcome your company.' It was out before she could stop herself and she flushed in embarrassment at betraying her feelings, but he was walking along beside her, not looking at her face.

'I'd welcome your company, too,' he said quietly. 'I've been thinking of you a lot lately.'

'I've been thinking about you, too.'

They didn't say anything else personal, but she felt happiness swirl inside her.

As they turned the corner she saw Jory waiting further down the street, stopped and looked at Seth. 'See what he's like. Won't take no for an answer when he wants something. Um – I just have to buy a couple of things for Cook then I'll go back to my motorcycle. If you've nothing else you have to do, I'd be really grateful for your continued company.'

He smiled at her. 'I'm glad of the excuse to be with you longer.'

The words hung in the air between them for a moment and she looked at him in wonderment. His smile was warm and didn't falter as she stared at him. 'That's – nice.' She was annoyed with herself for sounding so feeble, so turned to go inside.

'I'll wait for you here.'

Seth watched her go into the shop, admiring her upright carriage, her short bouncy hair, her rosy cheeks. Suddenly, what Jory had said about her seemed an utter fabrication. She wasn't the sort to let men make free with her, she just wasn't. Then he remembered her saying 'won't take no for an answer' and he had to wonder if that could mean . . .

He waited outside the Emporium, his thoughts on her and not his job, until she came out carrying two packets in a string bag. 'I can't carry them for you while I'm in uniform, I'm afraid. It'd look bad.'

'I know.' She chuckled. 'But they're not exactly heavy and I'm not exactly weak.'

They walked back to the motorcycle, chatting happily about what they wanted now the war was over. He watched her put her shopping in the sidecar then pull out the missing lead. He didn't offer to help her, just watched, admiring the capable way she fitted it and started up the bike.

She smiled down at it. 'My mother's horrified that I ride this, says it's an unfeminine thing to do.'

'No one was horrified during the war when women helped out and they shouldn't be now.'

'I love this bike.' She patted it affectionately. 'I even know how to do the minor repairs.'

'I spent most of my time servicing guns and training lads to be blown to pieces.' His voice thickened as he said the last words. He could never think of those many fine young men who'd been killed without getting upset.

She leaned forward to lay one hand on the clenched fist nearest to her. 'That must have been dreadful.'

He clasped that hand in both his for a moment. 'It was. Most civilians don't understand, but you must have seen more than most.'

'Yes. I saw some dreadful things after the air raids and on the refugee boats. I helped the injured sometimes because Lady Bingram had made sure we all learned First Aid.'

'You must tell me about what you did.'

They exchanged another of those long but warm looks, then she turned her attention to her bike.

'Well, thank you for your help, Mr Talbot.'

'Seth.'

'Seth,' she echoed. 'And I'm Ellen.'

He watched her drive away, then continued to walk the streets. It was as if they'd settled something between them. She hadn't played hard to get, just been straightforward about making her interest in him plain, once he'd shown his own interest. That pleased him. He didn't like women who fussed and pretended and had to be cajoled even to talk to you, never had.

Gradually he settled down again to the task he'd set himself, getting to know every twist and turn of the town, not just the streets, but the alleys and the little ginnels between houses. Doing this got him out of the police station and away from Wes, and besides, it was basic common sense to know your territory.

When he got back to the main street, he saw Jory Nelson coming out of the butcher's shop and the man gave him a dirty look, crossing the road to avoid him.

Halsopp was standing at the doorway of the shop and he too gave Seth a dirty look as he passed.

Two close allies, were they? And Halsopp was a friend of Cobbley's as well. Seth filed that information neatly in his brain as he continued on his way, making it his business to call in at all the shops and businesses Cobbley had missed out last time and introduce himself.

The people he met were clearly surprised at this

and wary. One man said bluntly, 'Friend of Cobbley's, are you?'

'No. I never met him till I got this job. Why do you ask?'

'No reason. Just wondered.'

'I'm an officer of the law and I'll be taking over here next week. I'll do my job without fear or favour.'

The man nodded, but didn't say anything else and Seth didn't press the point. He'd meant every word he'd said, but he'd have to prove it, of course.

When Bevan got home that night, he questioned his wife closely about Ellen's visit.

'You seem angry about something, dear.'

'I am. She got that new policeman to send Jory away when all he was doing was walking along with her.'

'She seems very set against Jory. I don't think she'll walk out with him again whatever he does. Maybe she'll find someone else to marry instead. A policeman has a nice, steady job.'

'She'll damned well do as I wish, and that doesn't include marrying an uppity newcomer of a policeman who doesn't understand a thing about our town. It's marry or continue to work as a maid and she doesn't seem to like doing that, from what you told me. In fact, going to London has put a lot of fancy ideas into her head, just as I said it would, and the sooner she's brought down to earth, the better.'

'She's a sensible girl, Bevan love, and she *is* twenty-six, so maybe we should leave her to make her own decisions.'

'Sensible! Treating a good man like that! Sensible is the last word I'd use to describe *her*.'

'But she is. Look at all the money she's saved, enough to open her own business.'

He stiffened. 'How do you know that?'

'I was talking to her about the future today, just as you said I should, and she told me then. The money's upstairs in her trunk, though she's going to put it in the bank when she comes into town next. She didn't want me to worry about her, you see, that's why she told me. So now you won't need to worry, either, because you'll know she isn't foolish at all and won't be a burden on you.'

'She'll probably fritter everything away once the shops get filled with things to buy again.'

'I'm sure she won't, dear. If my Ellen was the frittering sort, she wouldn't have saved it in the first place.'

He changed the subject, fussing over Dorothy till she went to bed. Then he went out to his shed to get some tools and crept up to the attic, carrying a lamp. He stood for a minute looking at the trunk then set down the lamp, got out a small hacksaw and cut through the padlock. When he lifted the lid, he saw more of her fancy London clothes and looked at them sourly. Short hair and short skirts. He didn't know what the young women of today were thinking of, trying to ape men.

He fumbled through the clothes until he came to

a bulky envelope. 'Aaah!' He picked it up and looked inside, his mouth dropping open in surprise when he saw the thick pile of banknotes. How much had that impudent bitch saved?

Sitting down on a chair he counted them slowly and carefully, muttering each number under his breath. 'Sixty-three pounds ten shillings!' He raised the banknotes to his lips and gave them a smacking kiss. Whatever Dorothy said, Ellen would only fritter it away on rubbish. Women were always doing that, changing the curtains or buying new cushions for no reason but a whim. Well, he wasn't having anyone waste good money, couldn't bear even the thought of that.

Closing the lid, leaving the trunk's contents in disarray, he went back downstairs, not bothering to tread quietly because Dorothy would be asleep by now.

In the kitchen he sat down to count the money again, loving the crisp feel of the notes beneath his fingers as he flipped the corners of the neat pile. Then he looked round thoughtfully. This needed keeping somewhere safe until he had time to work out what to do with it.

The first thing was to decide how to deal with Ellen. She was bound to be angry when she found out he'd taken her money, but there was no way he was letting her have it back. And when she married Jory, the lad would stop her driving round on that damned motorcycle too. Yes, between the two of them they'd knock her into shape. She was a big, fine girl and would probably breed well, unlike her mother.

Feeling he had reason to celebrate, he poured himself a glass of beer, sat by the fire drinking it and lost himself in his favourite daydream: retiring to the seaside, somewhere like Blackpool or Southport. He wasn't going to work as a butcher until he dropped dead. It was heavy work dealing with those carcases and already they were taking their toll on him. It gave him a pain in the chest to haul a cow around these days.

It was a pity Dorothy wouldn't be with him when he retired. She'd been a good wife, in spite of not giving him children. A man couldn't have found a better one. He didn't like to see her in pain, didn't want to lose her, but even the doctor was helpless now. Bevan blinked furiously and took another pull of beer.

He'd started saving hard in the first place because Dorothy loved the sea and he'd promised her she'd live beside it one day. But he'd continued to save because he'd grown to like the seaside too on their annual holidays. That bracing air really set you up, made you feel on top of the world, almost as if you were young again. He'd missed going last year because Dorothy had been too ill, and anyway, things weren't the same with a war on, as they'd discovered the year before.

He still hadn't decided whether to settle in Blackpool or Southport, but he wasn't going to the east coast, which was a lot cooler. Both the Lancashire resorts had their good points and he enjoyed mulling over which to choose.

When the time came, he'd spend a few days in each, look at house prices and make up his mind . . . sell his business . . . move . . . perhaps even find himself another wife to comfort him in his old age. Why not? He was still a fine figure of a man, even if he said so himself, not shrivelled with age like his friend Eddie Nelson. You'd never think the man had fathered a fine young fellow like Jory.

13

Just before dawn Giles slipped out of the stables and made his way through the quiet countryside to his car. The birds were only beginning to wake and perform a sleepy overture to their dawn chorus, the flower petals were still closed protectively and the only animal he saw was a rabbit sitting quietly under a hedge, seeming only half awake.

Today he would visit the elderly lawyer in Shawcroft – well, he would if the man was in his rooms on a Saturday. But he'd have to smarten himself up first, get a shave and have a good meal to fill the echoing cavern in his belly. Sandwiches were all very well, but his last two were stale now and though he'd sneaked a drink of water from a tap, he'd a strong desire for a big pot of tea with a thick slice of ham topped by two fried eggs.

The car was standing where he'd left it and didn't seem to have been touched. He stopped a few paces away to peer at the ground to see if there were any footprints other than his near it and there weren't. Good.

He sat in the car until eight o'clock, then started it up and drove sedately into town. He didn't meet any other vehicles on the way and most of the shops were still closed when he parked in front of the Royal Fleece. The front door was open, probably to air the place out. He went to tap on it. 'Hello! Is anyone there?'

The landlord poked his head out of a door at the back of the room. 'We're not open until lunchtime, except for residents.'

'I was wondering if you could rent me a room for the day and let me freshen up there now. I was coming here yesterday but my car broke down miles from anywhere and I had to sleep in it. I managed to fix it this morning when it got light, though.'

The landlord came forward. 'Didn't you come in the other day with a young lady?'

'Yes. We had a jolly good luncheon here. I've come back to see Mr Monnings.'

'Ah. Nice fellow, he is. Help anyone he will, whether they can pay him or not. I'll just go and fetch the missus. She deals with residents.'

The landlady came out, delighted to have a paying guest, even if only for a few hours. She fussed over Giles, providing him with hot water and when he came down, a huge breakfast in the residents' dining room.

'I've not eaten so well for years,' he said when he'd cleared his plate. 'How on earth do you get such good food?'

She winked. 'We have to look after our guests, don't we? And the war is over now, so I don't feel it's unpatriotic to buy a few extras on the side.'

He'd guess she'd been eating well all through the war, because she and her husband both looked plump and well fed, but that was water under the bridge now.

Leaving his knapsack in his room, he set off down the main street and promptly at ten o'clock knocked on the door of Monnings' rooms. He was ushered in to see the principal by a weedy young clerk who breathed wheezily and didn't have the bearing of one who'd served in the armed forces.

Septimus Monnings must have been at least seventy, silver-haired and with that very thin, bleached look to him that elderly men often got. He came out from behind his desk to shake Giles's hand and each man assessed the other as they made contact. Monnings had an alert expression on his face and a twinkle in his faded blue eyes. Nobody's fool, was Giles's judgement.

'Sit down, Covington, make yourself comfortable. I'll get Pidgeon to fetch us some tea.' When he'd given the order for this to his young clerk, he came back to sit behind his desk, steepling his hands together. 'Dunham wrote to me about you, said you were looking to join a new practice. Tell me why – and be frank about your reasons, if you please.'

'Well, my senior partner died recently and his nephew has inherited. I don't get on with Henderson or share his money-grubbing morals.'

Monnings grinned. 'That's frank, all right.'

'You did ask.'

'Yes. And I'll be equally frank. My grandson was killed in '17 by a damned sniper's bullet, so there's no one in the family to take over this business. My son's a university lecturer, not interested in anything but

Egyptian History.' A sad look came over the old man's face. 'It's a hard thing to outlive your grandson. But I'd rather close down entirely than hand over to someone who doesn't care what's right and wrong, and only considers what's profitable or not. So when I heard from Dunham that his nephew was looking for a partnership, I made a few enquiries about you. I hope that doesn't offend you?'

'Of course not.'

'Your commanding officer speaks well of you, but didn't go into details about what you'd been doing.'

Giles explained what he could. 'I'm afraid some of my work was top secret, sometimes behind enemy lines. The fact that I'm alive speaks for how successfully I performed my duties.'

'Yes. And we beat the Hun in the end, didn't we? Whatever the cost. Your letter was very timely because I was about to advertise. Tell me about your experience before the war . . . what sort of legal work you enjoy most.'

By the time they'd finished their tea, the two men were well into a discussion about Monnings' business and were even in a fair way to agreeing terms.

'This all seems too easy,' Giles said wryly. He decided suddenly to take the old man into his confidence. 'There's just one other thing you should perhaps know . . .' He explained about Ronnie and the way her mother had taken her away by force from the Tillings' farm. 'You presumably know Mrs Gresham?'

Monnings pulled a face. 'Dreadful woman. Voice

like a foghorn. Don't envy you having her as a mother-in-law.'

'It's Ronnie I want. Unfortunately I may have to break into the Hall to free her.'

The old man's grin took several years off his face. 'Don't tell me any details, but if you get into trouble, you can come to me for help.' He looked at his watch. 'Got the new police chappie coming to see me shortly. Why don't you stay and meet him? We're getting a few new brooms in Shawcroft and the town needs them. Don't be fooled by the peaceful look of the place. There are villains here, as there are everywhere else, and some of them did rather well out of the war, damn them. And if Dunham's right and they killed that chappie found shot in a field a couple of villages away, well, it's about time they were brought to book.'

There was a knock on the door and Pidgeon poked his head in. 'Constable Talbot to see you, sir.'

'Show him in.' Monnings got up from the desk and went to offer his hand to Seth, studying the newcomer as openly as he'd studied Giles. 'Dunham wasn't wrong.'

Seth looked at him in surprise.

'He said he'd send me someone they couldn't corrupt. You've got that look to you, Talbot. Honest.'

'I wasn't aware Inspector Dunham's plans were common knowledge in town,' Seth said.

'They're not. But his father was a close friend of mine and we've always kept in touch. I've alerted him to a few problems here over the years, but you know what it was like during the war, what with staffing shortages and special constables blundering around.' He turned to include Giles in the conversation, introducing the two younger men and then waving them to seats.

As their conversation drew to a close, he said thoughtfully, 'It might be very helpful for you to move here as soon as possible, Covington, given your military background and the problems we're facing.'

'I shall need to find a largish house to rent first. I have a mother-in-law, two sons and soon, I hope, a wife.'

Monnings looked at him, eyes narrowed. 'You could move in with me temporarily, while you look for somewhere suitable. If the boys don't mind sharing a room, that is.'

'I couldn't impose.'

'To be frank, I'd enjoy some company. It's dashed quiet in the evening at my place. Housekeeper goes home, then there's just me rattling around the place.'

'Little boys can be rather noisy.'

'I like that sort of noise. I've got an old dog, too. He'll think he's in heaven having someone to play with and he's good with children.'

'Then if you're sure . . . I accept your offer with pleasure.'

The two men shook hands.

As the younger men stood on the steps outside, Giles said, 'He's a grand old fellow, salt of the earth.'

'He is. Reminds me of a major I knew in France.' Seth glanced across at the town hall clock. 'But I'll tell you about him another day. I have to get back to the police station or Cobbley will be complaining. He doesn't see the point in going out to the people, expects them to come to him – and doesn't make them welcome when they do, from what I've discovered.'

As Seth had predicted, Cobbley met him with grumbles about wasting time wandering round town, instead of being here on duty. He listened without comment then Cobbley went home for his dinner and he was free to examine the cupboard near the cells.

It had been full, was now completely empty. No sign that it had held anything and it had obviously been swept out recently.

A voice called, 'Hello there!' from the front office and he locked the door and went back to the counter.

Jory Nelson stood there, fingers tapping impatiently on the counter.

'Can I help you?'

'You certainly can. This isn't an official call. I'm here to tell you to stop coming between me and my lass. Just because she and I have quarrelled doesn't mean she's available to anyone else.' He glared at Seth. 'If you take my meaning.'

'Oh, I take your meaning all right. I also take her meaning and she swears she wants nothing to do with you, hasn't seen you for years. So if she asks me for help again, I'll give it. And if you continue to pester her, I'll be down on you like a ton of bricks.'

'You're not going to do well in this town with an attitude like that.'

'Aren't I? That remains to be seen.'

'Well, don't say I haven't warned you. She blows hot and cold, that one does. I don't know why I bother with her, but I've known her since we were children and I've always intended to marry her. It's what her family wants too.'

Seth made no comment, waiting patiently behind his bland official face. When the other continued to stare at him as if expecting a response, he waited a little longer then asked, 'Is there anything else, *sir*? Or can I get on with my work?'

Jory breathed deeply. 'Nothing at the moment. Just remember what I said.'

Seth was surprised that the other man would act like this. If he really was walking out with Ellen, he should be speaking to her not to a policeman. But she swore she'd not been with Jory since soon after the war began and Seth believed her. There was something he didn't trust about Jory Nelson – and that wasn't because of how the fellow had treated Ellen Dawson, it was something intrinsic to Nelson's character.

When Cobbley came back after dinner he glared at Seth.

Not another one who's angry with me, Seth thought wearily. What next?

'I hear you've been getting between Jory and his lass, so I'm telling you straight, *as your senior officer*, to stay away from Ellen Dawson. Everyone knows she's going to marry Jory and we don't want any incomers stealing our girls.'

'*She* says she isn't going to marry him.'

'Well, she's stringing you along, because she is. Just ask her stepfather. He can tell you. It's a lovers' tiff, that's all.'

'I'll continue to listen to all sides of the case, but if I'm asked for help by a young lady who is being pestered by a fellow in the street, then as far as I'm concerned, I'm duty-bound to help her.'

'You'll only be making a fool of yourself, then. She's using you to make him jealous.'

They were interrupted by a man coming into the reception area. 'I'm here to install the telephone.'

Cobbley gaped at him for a moment. 'What telephone? No one said anything to me about putting a phone in.'

'Been sent to do it, so someone must have ordered the installation.'

'Well, you can just go away again until I receive notification.'

Seth judged it time to intervene. 'Excuse me, but I know about the phone being installed. I thought you'd have been informed.'

'You're not in charge here yet,' Cobbley snapped.

'Are you intending to prevent this man from doing his job?'

After much deep breathing and a few huffs of angry air, Cobbley stood up. 'Think you're going to have everything your own way when you take over here, don't you? Well, you may find yourself getting a few shocks before you're done.' He stalked out of the station and his heavy footsteps echoed from the side path that led to his house.

'What's got into him?' the man wondered. 'You'd think he'd want a telephone. Saves a lot of legwork, a phone does.'

'He finishes work here next week and doesn't want to retire, so he's a bit touchy,' Seth said. 'Now, you set to work and if you need any help, you've only to ask.'

By mid-afternoon, the phone was set up in the inside office and they'd been given their phone number, which was Shawcroft 39. Cobbley didn't even look at the telephone, let alone pick it up. He went back to sitting on his stool in the outside office but he didn't speak to Seth again.

At the end of the day, he looked at the clock. 'You can go now.'

'I still have fifteen minutes left of this shift.'

'I can hold the fort here. And I don't want you at my farewell party.'

'The Mayor invited me.'

'Only because he felt obliged. I'd as soon you stayed away. As far as I'm concerned you're a stranger and this party is for my friends.' He turned away and began to fiddle with some papers.

'I'll do a quick patrol of the main street before I knock off,' Seth said. 'I don't like to cheat my employers.' He was glad to get out of the office and leave the cloud of anger behind. It was frustrating to be shut in an office with a grumpy old man and nothing to do.

But the day wasn't over yet. As Seth walked along Rochdale Road, Halsopp came to the door of the butcher's shop and called out, 'Hey, you!'

Seth turned round. 'Can I help you, Mr Halsopp?'

'You certainly can. You can stop interfering between my daughter and Jory.'

Not another one! Seth took a deep breath and summoned up his official dealing-with-problem-people face again. 'Miss Dawson asked for my help.'

'She's just using you to get back at her fellow after a quarrel. The two of them are as good as engaged, but it's not easy settling down after they've both been away. So I'm telling you now. Leave them to get on with it.'

'And I'll tell you the same as I told Nelson himself. If a young lady asks for help because a man won't leave her alone, then I shall, of course, give her that help. What's more, your stepdaughter denies any relationship with Nelson.'

'You want to think what you're doing. It only takes a few of the prominent citizens getting annoyed and a policeman can find himself getting transferred – or worse.'

'Indeed? You surprise me. I didn't know the inhabitants of Shawcroft were running the police force for this region.'

'Question of public interest. If enough people complain they get listened to.' One blood-stained finger stabbed out towards Seth. 'Just think about that before you act stupidly from now on.'

This did indeed give him a lot to think about, Seth decided, but not quite in the way Halsopp had meant.

Why were two of the town's leading citizens going out of their way to warn him off Ellen? It didn't make sense. And the threats Halsopp had made seemed stupid – unless they were looking for some excuse for complaining about him to his superiors.

After some hesitation, he asked Martin Pugh's opinion that evening, but his host could offer no explanation beyond a firm belief that Ellen would never go out with Jory again.

Jeanie said the same thing, stopping clearing away the pudding dishes to declare, 'Ellen hasn't even seen that Jory for four years, so how can she possibly still be his girl?'

'Are you sure of that?' Seth asked. 'They could have met in London.'

'If she says they haven't, I'd take her word against his any time. She's not a liar and he is. Nasty little boy he was, and the sort of young man I'd warn my daughters about if I had any.' She hesitated, then added, 'He didn't treat her well, that I know for certain. Why should she go back to him?'

Martin rustled his newspaper and shook his head at her in a warning gesture.

She closed her lips and didn't say anything else.

What secret were they hiding? Seth wondered. He lay awake for a long time that night trying to work out what was going on in the town. Why should this small group of citizens feel confident enough to threaten him openly?

Only a few more days to work with Cobbley then he'd be able to start sorting out the policing in this town, something it clearly needed. Inspector Dunham had promised him another constable as soon as one became available, but what with the losses from influenza and some policemen still being in the army, the force remained short of trained, experienced men.

14

On the Saturday evening Seth dressed in his best suit and made his way along to the Town Hall. Cobbley might not want him to attend the farewell party, but he was determined to do so. To his surprise, Martin had advised against it.

'Only certain people have been invited,' he said earnestly to Seth. 'We haven't, because we stay away from that group of people. You'll find yourself among enemies and it'll be an uncomfortable night.'

'I've been uncomfortable before now. You don't die of that. Besides, I want to see who's attending. It'll teach me a lot about the groups I'm dealing with.' He hadn't asked Martin much about that, because he wanted to make up his own mind. Sometimes a fresh view of things made a difference.

'Be careful how you go, then.'

Seth didn't arrive until ten minutes past seven, by which time the party sounded to be well under way. He found a burly man he didn't recognise guarding the entrance.

'Can I see your invitation, sir?'

'I don't have a written one, but Mr Flaunden invited me. You've only to ask him.'

'If you'll wait a minute, sir, we'll do that.' He beckoned to another man standing just inside the doorway, whispered in his ear and came back to stand near the entrance again, arms folded. 'Won't be long.'

The mayor himself appeared in the doorway of the big inner room where the function was being held. 'Ah, Talbot. I thought you weren't coming or I'd have sent you a proper invitation.'

'Why would you think that?'

'Wes said – but he must have been mistaken. Anyway, do come in.'

Flaunden seemed nervous as he led the way back inside. 'You won't know anyone so I'd – um – better introduce you to one or two people.'

A young woman came up and linked her arm in his.

'This is my wife. My dear, this is the new police officer.'

She held out her hand, her eyes assessing Seth in a frankly sexual way.

'Pleased to meet you, Mrs Flaunden.' He shook her hand and quickly let go. He'd never been attracted to that sort of woman, let alone this one was married to a man he suspected of some involvement in the goings-on here.

The mayor frowned at his wife and pulled her firmly to one side. 'If you'll just excuse me for a moment, dear. Come this way, Talbot.'

He introduced the newcomer to the landlord of the Royal Fleece. 'Oh, you've met already, have you?

Good, good. Then I'll leave the constable with you, John.'

The landlord looked uncomfortable, but his wife held out her hand to Seth. 'I'm Mavis Deane. Why don't you get the constable a drink, John, and I'll introduce him to some other people.'

But when she looked round, those nearby had edged away from them. 'I'm sorry about that. It's – difficult for some of us. We have to – tread carefully.'

'It'd perhaps be better if I left you in peace,' Seth offered. 'I'm clearly not welcome here. I don't mind standing on my own. You do it all the time as a policeman.'

'No, don't go. They're not telling me who to speak to, just because—' she broke off, then completed the sentence awkwardly with, 'because I do business with them. Ah, there's my friend.' She beckoned to a woman across the corner of the room, who looked sideways at her husband and hesitated.

Mavis beckoned again, with more force, and the woman came across to talk to them, followed with obvious reluctance by her husband.

John returned with a glass of beer for Seth then they made awkward conversation for a few minutes.

Seth drained the glass and smiled at the group. 'Thank you for your support, but I'll be all right.' Setting his empty glass down on the drinks table at one side of the room, refusing the offer of a refill from the man behind it with a shake of the head, he wandered slowly round. Several people greeted him, but no one maintained a conversation for long. Some people moved away before he reached them. He noted which.

At the far end of the room he came face to face with Jory Nelson.

'Enjoying your evening, Constable?'

'Very much. You can learn a lot from how people behave at parties.' Seth moved on without waiting for an answer.

There was the sound of someone clapping their hands for attention and the Mayor stepped up on to a small podium. It took a lot of shushing before he got silence, because given that the drinks were free, quite a few men had been imbibing freely.

'Friends and neighbours, we are gathered here to say a fond farewell to our long-time police constable, Wes Cobbley.' Flaunden stopped for a moment to allow the whistles and cheers to die down.

Seth turned his head slightly so that he could watch the audience rather than the speaker. Mrs Cobbley was standing beside her husband dabbing at her eyes and Wes was smiling in a vacant way that said he too had consumed a few drinks.

'Wes has been our local watchdog for a good many years now, and came out of retirement when his country needed him.'

The second round of cheers and applause came mainly from one group of men, Seth noted. If it hadn't been for them, the speech would have been received quietly. Other people, who included some of the small shopkeepers he'd visited, had polite expressions pinned to their faces. Some of their wives weren't even looking at the speaker, but fiddling with handbags or clothing.

The speech ended to more applause and foot stamping, then Wes got up to thank them, which he did very briefly, his words slurred. He ended with an assurance that he would always be there to help them should the need arise again.

Then the ceremony was over and some of the audience turned back to drinking, while others fidgeted and consulted their watches as if wanting to leave.

Seth sauntered round the room twice then went to find the mayor and Wes. 'Thank you for inviting me. It was very – illuminating.'

The mayor muttered something incomprehensible, Wes scowled and turned away.

Seth went outside. He'd seen enough, made his presence felt, and now he wanted some clean fresh air. Pity it was raining, but a bit of water didn't hurt you.

He hadn't gone very far when he heard footsteps behind him. Someone was trying to move quietly but failing. He turned the next corner, scanned the street behind him quickly and saw two dark figures, so stepped into the nearest garden, crouching behind a neatly trimmed hedge to see who went past.

The two young men who'd been guarding the door walked slowly past, clearly searching for him.

'Where's that sod gone?' one asked the other.

'Can't have gone far. We'll soon catch him then he'll learn a hard lesson.'

Seth had heard enough. He moved back in the direction he'd come, reaching the low wall dividing this garden from the next. He swung quietly over it into the next garden which took him back round the corner. A figure materialised out of the darkness beyond the street lamp. Jory Nelson. Seth tensed. He'd not stand much chance against three of them.

For a minute the two men stared at one another then Nelson said quietly, 'I'd not ambush a fellow soldier. If you and I ever fight, it'll be man to man.'

'I'm grateful for that.'

A shout from round the corner was followed by feet pounding along the pavement. The two men skidded to a halt when they saw Jory and Seth standing together.

'We've got him!' one of them crowed.

Seth tensed, looking at Jory. Had it been a ruse to detain him?

Jory pushed in front of him, facing the two men. 'No, you haven't.'

'We promised Wes we'd teach him a lesson,' one of them said. 'You get off home if you're too cowardly to show who you support.'

Jory took another step forward. 'If you ever call me cowardly again, I'll beat you senseless.'

The man who'd spoken fell back a step, looking to the other for support. But he did nothing.

Jory turned to Seth. 'They'd need another six to beat us. I'll walk home with you.'

'Thank you.'

They left the two men muttering.

'Hotheads,' Jory said contemptuously.

'They seemed to think they were speaking for Wes.'

'He'd not have set them on to attack you.'

Seth stopped to stare at him in surprise for a moment.

'He wouldn't, because he has respect for the police. They must just have heard him talking about not wanting you here and set off after you without thinking what they were doing. Not that *I* want you here in Shawcroft, either. You'll not fit in.'

'So people keep telling me. That surprises me when they've not even given me a chance to show what sort of a policeman I am.'

'Sometimes towns find their own balance, as Shawcroft has. Wes understands what's needed. We're doing no one any harm but we like to do things our own way.'

'Oh? I heard differently. I heard someone had been killed. To me, that's doing serious harm.'

Jory stopped walking even though the rain had grown stronger. 'That wasn't in Shawcroft.'

'Not *in* the town but near it.'

'Nothing to do with us.' Jory fell silent and began walking again, hands thrust deep into pockets, a scowl on his face.

Seth continued beside his unlikely rescuer, puzzling over Nelson's reaction. Had the other man really not known about the murder? If he hadn't, who did know what had happened?

When they got to the Pughs' house, he held out one hand. 'Thank you.'

Jory shook it briefly. But his smile had vanished and a grim look had replaced it. 'I won't always be your ally, think on.'

'But you won't be stabbing me in the back, you'll be punching me in the face – or trying to. I understand that.'

With a nod, Jory turned and walked swiftly off into the darkness.

Seth went into the house quietly, meaning to slip up to his room and change.

Jeanie opened the kitchen door, took one look at his rain-wet face and snapped, 'Get those damp clothes off then bring them down to dry. You don't want to catch a chill, so I'm putting on some milk. We'll have a nice hot drink.'

When he came back downstairs Jeanie had the ceiling airer lowered. She held out her arms for his clothes and began to hang them over the wooden rails, then wound the airer up again.

Martin held out a steaming cup of cocoa. 'What happened to keep you out in the rain?'

Seth took a sip, cradling the beaker in his hands, needing its warmth. He explained what had happened, punctuating his talk with sips of the hot drink.

'*Jory Nelson* saved you?'

'Yes. It surprised me, too.'

'Who were the two others?'

'I don't know their names – yet. But I will. I never forget a face and I saw them clearly enough under the street lamp.'

'What are you going to do about it?'

'I haven't decided.'

In fact, he was puzzled by the whole incident. Surely

the two men hadn't expected to get away with an open attack on him?

And why had Jory been surprised about the murder? He seemed to be in the thick of everything else that was going on.

If he went out at night from now on, Seth decided, it might be prudent to take with him a revolver he'd picked up in France – and make sure it was loaded, too.

He didn't intend to make a martyr of himself and if someone in the town had killed once, they might do so again.

Suddenly the problems he was likely to encounter here seemed greater than he'd expected, and the culprits not nearly as obvious.

He would, he decided, report the latest developments to the Inspector as soon as he got the phone to himself.

The following Sunday morning Ellen watched the other servants get ready for church and wished she was going with them. But she had been told to stay behind to keep an eye on things.

A large car drove up to the front door just before the servants set off, and Mrs Gresham was picked up to attend a nearby village church with the St Corbins.

When the mistress had left, the housekeeper came into the kitchen dressed in her Sunday finery and looked at Ellen very severely. 'While we're away, you're to stay here in the kitchen and keep an eye on that joint for Cook, Dawson. You're not to go up to the west wing under any circumstances. Is that clear? Miss Veronica had a bad night and is still sleeping, so we don't want anything to disturb her. Is that clear?'

'Yes, Mrs Shipton.'

'And you can get on with the mending while we're away. I expect to see a difference in that pile when I come back.'

'Yes, Mrs Shipton.' Ellen watched the servants file out and get into the car. Pel wasn't with them, but Glenys said he'd refused to go because he could no longer believe in a loving God after what he'd seen in France.

When Tadwyn had driven them all away in the car, Ellen sat for a minute or two simply enjoying the silence, the feeling of freedom from control. Then she went to look for the spare key to Miss Veronica's room. She was sure they'd have removed the key from the door of the room itself, but had hoped to find the spare on its numbered hook in the storeroom. It wasn't there.

She stood for a minute or two in the kitchen, wondering if this was worth the risk, then pulled herself together. Of course it was! Mrs Gresham had no right to keep anyone prisoner.

Ellen used the main front stairs to go up to the east wing, smiling as she committed this minor crime. As she'd expected, the key to Miss Veronica's room wasn't in the lock. Tiptoeing up to the door, she listened and thought she could hear some faint sounds of movement. Well, she thought, in for a penny, in for a pound, and knocked on the door. 'Miss Veronica? Are you there?'

Footsteps came across to the door. 'Who's that?'

'It's me, Ellen.'

'I thought everyone had gone to church. Can you get the spare key and let me out? *Please!* This would be an ideal time for me to escape.'

'They've taken all the keys.'

'Oh, no! What am I going to do? There's no way I could break down the door.'

'I wondered if you'd managed to write that note?'

'Yes.'

'I could post that for you if you push it under the door.'

'Yes. Wait a minute.'

Ellen went along to the end of the landing to peer out of the window, but there was no sign of anyone coming up the drive to the Hall. When she got back to the locked door, she saw a piece of crumpled paper sticking out underneath it and pulled it out.

'I've got it.'

'Giles's address is on the bottom, but I've no stamps or envelopes, I'm afraid. I'll pay you back one day.'

'I can afford a stamp, Miss Veronica. And the address is very clear.'

'You'll post it for me as soon as you can?'

'Yes. I'm going into town tomorrow to see my mother. I can easily post it then without anyone finding out. How are you keeping?'

'I'm going mad from boredom.'

'I'm sorry. Look, I'd better get back to the kitchen. They've left me some mending and they'll be suspicious if none of it's done. I *will* post your letter, though, I promise.'

'Thank you.'

Ellen ran up to her bedroom, slipped the note into the pocket of her Aides uniform then went back down to the kitchen. She took the mending outside, sitting in the sun to work on it.

But her thoughts wandered here and there: to poor Miss Veronica, imprisoned by her mother . . . to her own mother, dying slowly . . . to her stepfather, bullying people as usual . . . to her own future, which wasn't at all clear . . . and to Seth Talbot, who had walked through her dreams last night. He was a lovely fellow.

When the sound of footsteps had faded into the distance, Ronnie burst into tears and went to sit on the bed. She didn't let herself weep for long because she didn't want her mother to see how upset she was. After a few minutes she patted her eyes dry, took a few slow, steady breaths and went to sit by the window. Not that there was anything to see, except birds and insects and flowers. Sunlight shone through the panes of glass, warming them and the air inside the room, but its brightness made her feel worse because it seemed to emphasise how helpless she was.

After she'd seen the servants setting out without Ellen, she'd hoped desperately that the maid would be able to free her. But of course her mother had thought of everything.

Nearly everything! She didn't know about the letter. *Oh please, let Ellen post it safely!*

If Giles got the note, he'd know exactly what had happened to her and where she was. Then he'd come and rescue her, she had to believe in that. But he had other calls on his time, his children and work to attend to as well as her.

Ronnie remembered suddenly how he'd told her about reconnoitring carefully when going on one of his missions. The sound of that car in the night might have been him checking the Hall. But the only way he'd know for sure that Ronnie was here was if he got that letter.

It all hinged on that. Whatever else she thought about, she couldn't help realising that he was her best chance for escaping. She was so carefully locked up and watched, she didn't see how she could get away herself.

Ellen wouldn't let her down, surely she wouldn't?

Jory woke up on the Sunday with a start as someone shook him. He opened his eyes to see his mother standing over him.

'Are you coming to church or not?'

He started to say no, then remembered that it might be his only chance to see Ellen. 'Yes.'

'Good. Your dad's not feeling well, so I'll be glad of your company.'

'Drank a lot last night, didn't he?'

'Yes. Too much. You know what he's like.'

'He didn't drink this much before the war.'

'He always drank.'

'Yes, but he used to wait till after tea to start, now he's drinking at dinner-time too.'

'I know. He's turned into an old sot. But if there's a way to stop him, I've not found it, so I'm leaving him to go to hell in his own way.' With a toss of her head she left the room.

He got up and went down for a quick wash and shave in the scullery, then ate a hearty breakfast, the eggs fried just as he liked them.

'No one cooks half as well as you, Mum.'

She smiled fondly at him. 'Flatterer. It's good to have you back safe. I wish Ted—' Her eyes filled with tears at the thought of the son she'd lost. She picked up Jory's empty plate and busied herself taking it into the scullery. When she came back she looked at the clock. 'Finish that cup of tea and get ready, son.'

They walked to church through a golden haze of sunlight. He was lost in his own thoughts, and she didn't prod him into speech. She'd always been the quiet one of the family, his mum had.

Who had set Dennis and Keith to beat up Talbot last night? It was a stupid thing to do, attack a policeman. Was it Wes? Had he changed that much? Or was it his father? Or even Halsopp? Jory intended to find out.

And what had Talbot meant about someone getting killed? No one had said anything to him about a death in the district. He'd find out about that, too.

He'd come home hoping for a bit of peace and quiet, but it didn't look as if he was going to get it.

What with waiting for his brother Don to get demobbed, quarrelling with his father about the business, because he couldn't bear to watch the old man bumble along in the old-fashioned way, and trying to make it up with Ellen, he hadn't found much peace.

Once settled in church, he looked round, hoping for a sight of her, but she wasn't among the worshippers. The rest of the servants from the Hall were in their usual pew, and a prim, ugly bunch they were, but there was no sign of her. She must have stayed behind today in case Mrs bloody Gresham wanted her arse wiping.

The sermon went on for too long and his thoughts kept wandering. It was a good thing he'd come back or his father would have drunk the business into the ground. He'd been doing favours for friends and not charging them. Not going out looking for new business. Look at the way he'd intended to turn down a well-paying job just to help Wes Cobbley move house. One stupid old fool helping another! Well, Jory had sorted that one out.

He would have to take over, whatever his father said, and the first thing he'd do would be buy a motor lorry. His father must have a comfortable sum of money stashed away after his wartime black-market activities.

If he and his brother Don both threatened to leave unless their dad handed over the running of the business, that should convince the stupid fool to let go of the reins. And his mother would be on their side, he had no doubt. She was no one's fool. Anyway, his father didn't look very well these days, had a pasty colour to him.

After church Jory looked round for Wes, but couldn't see him. He went across to speak to Mrs Cobbley. 'Wes not here today?'

She gave him an unfriendly glance. 'No, he isn't. And I'm surprised you're here, actually, given the amount everyone drank last night. You shouldn't have encouraged him! He can't take his beer like he used to. He'll be in a foul mood all day. Older men don't have hard heads like you young folk, you know.'

Jory looked at her in surprise. She was normally a pleasant woman and had never complained about her husband like that before, though he and Jory's father had got drunk together regularly. 'Is Wes at home?'

'Yes. Nursing an aching head and serve him right.'

'I'll go round to see him, shall I? Cheer him up a bit.'

'As long as you don't take any beer with you. I'm going round to my friend's for dinner so don't expect to be fed, either.'

He nodded and strode away, grinning. If a man couldn't celebrate with his friends when he retired on a pension, what point was there in living?

When he banged on the door of the police cottage, he was answered by a groan that could be heard clearly through the open window to the right of the door. Grinning he pushed the door open and called, 'It's only me.'

'I'm in here.'

Wes was lying on the sofa in the front room, surrounded by packing cases and tea chests full of stuff ready for the move. A damp white cloth adorned his forehead and the curtains were drawn.

'What are you sitting in the dark for?' Jory went to pull back one of the curtains, surprised at Wes's sickly, yellow-white colour.

The older man gave him an unfriendly look and pulled the cloth down to cover his eyes. 'You shouldn't have kept filling my glass. I lost count of what I'd had to drink.'

'Ah, give over! You wanted it filled. And you'll be right as rain tomorrow. It *was* your party, after all. And a good one, too, after that new bobby left.' He hesitated, then added, 'A couple of the lads went after him to beat him up, did you know that?'

Wes shifted the cloth to stare at Jory. 'No, I didn't. I don't approve of anyone attacking the police and I never shall, not even *him*. But you can't blame folk for feeling angry with this new bobby.'

'I thought you might have arranged it.'

'Well, you thought wrong. And I don't feel like chatting, so tell me what you've come for and then bugger off.'

'Just came round to see if you were all right.' And to find out whose idea it had been to attack Talbot. Somehow Wes's words rang true, which meant it had been Jory's father or Halsopp who'd arranged it. One down, two to check.

'Well, I'm not all right, so you can leave me in peace.'

Jory grinned. No point in talking to Wes today. Pity. He wanted to find out more about what had been going on during the past year or two and about this death. 'I'll leave you to recover in peace then.'

'Fat chance of that with my wife due home any minute.'

'No, she isn't. She told me she was going to dinner at her friend's house.'

Wes jerked bolt upright. 'She said what? The bitch!' He thrust himself unsteadily to his feet and tottered into the kitchen, still holding the damp cloth to his forehead. Glaring round he said in tones of outrage, 'She hasn't left me any dinner!'

Jory grinned. 'You'll have to get something yourself.' He left Wes still grumbling and went straight home. But his mother had got there before him. He'd have to catch his father at the yard in the morning. He didn't want her overhearing their conversation.

But he was damned well going to find out what had been going on.

And if Talbot was on the same trail, Jory would have to do something to throw him off the scent. He wasn't seeing his dad locked up, however much he deserved it.

Greedy, that's what his father and Cobbley had been, even though Jory had told them to be satisfied with a modest extra profit from their black-market activities. No, they'd had to extend their efforts, which meant a lot more people knew about them. Fools, all of them!

* * *

Edwina Gresham allowed Algernon to help her out of the St Corbins' motor car outside the little country church, feeling pleasantly superior to the other worshippers.

'I forgot to tell you: we've been invited round for a quick sherry with my friend Gloria after the service,' Blanche said as she took Edwina's arm and led the way into the shadowy grey interior.

'That'll be very pleasant.'

The service dragged on, but Edwina was used to occupying herself with her own thoughts during sermons, which were always boring. As if she'd allow anyone else to tell her how to think and behave.

Blanche's friend Gloria lived in a pleasant villa set in manicured gardens a mile from the church and was waiting to introduce them to her other friend, who was staying with her.

'Gresham,' the friend, Diana, said later as the conversation faltered. 'Now, where do I know that name from?' She waggled one finger triumphantly. 'I have it. There's a Gresham serving as a land girl at Overlea Farm. Slender, fair hair, pretty.'

'My daughter Veronica. She was very keen to play her part during the war. She's back home with me now, though. The poor girl wore herself out and the doctor insists on a period of strict rest.'

'How sad! You'll have met her young man, then. Giles Covington lives near us. It was lovely to see them together.'

'No, I haven't. She's not allowed visitors yet. Do tell me about him.'

'He's a lawyer. Was an officer during the war, working on something very hush-hush. His wife died early in the war and his mother-in-law looks after his children – you did know he'd been married before?'

'Yes, of course. Two sons, aren't they? I don't know the family though.'

Diana pulled a face. 'Shopkeepers, my dear. Grocery store, I believe. No one knows them. They live in Halifax. He was a scholarship boy, but he did well, you have to grant him that. And he's very gentlemanly. I suppose Oxford knocked the rough edges off him.'

'Yes, that sort of place usually does.'

When they got into the car to drive back, Blanche looked at her. 'You didn't know about this Covington fellow, did you?'

'I knew he existed, not what he was called. She's already regretting meeting him.' She turned to Algernon with a smile. 'Once she'd met you again, a real gentleman, she realised what a vulgar sham he was.'

He gave her a faint smile and turned to look out of the window.

Blanche changed the subject to arranging a whist evening soon.

Edwina kept her fury under control until Blanche dropped her at the front door of the Hall. She even agreed that it'd be nice if Algernon popped over the following day to see Veronica and stood waving goodbye until the car was out of sight. Only then did she let the smile slip.

How dare Veronica act so vulgarly as to be seen in

public holding hands with this nobody? She'd been behaving like a housemaid. That's what came of joining the Land Army and mixing with riff-raff.

The peace was broken again for Wes a few minutes later by someone knocking on the front door. He sat at the kitchen table, holding his head in his hands and made no attempt to answer, hoping they'd go away again.

But the front door opened and a voice called, 'You there, Wes?'

'Yes.'

Bevan came into the kitchen. 'Feeling bad?'

'Yes.'

The visitor grinned. 'You never could take your drink.'

'And you always did have a hard head.' Wes moved incautiously and groaned. 'What the hell do you want? Can't a man get any peace today?'

'I need to talk to you.'

Wes sighed. 'Can't it wait till tomorrow?'

'No, it can't. What I came about is my stepdaughter . . .' Bevan explained about the money and what he wanted to do, by which time Wes had cast aside the damp cloth and was listening intently.

'I can't help you steal her money!'

'It's not stealing. Parents have a right to their children's earnings.'

'Not after the children turn twenty-one, they don't.'

'She won't know that. And it's worth five pounds to you to back me up.'

Wes eased himself cautiously upright. 'Five, you say?'

'Yes. She's bound to come and complain to you, and if you just tell her it *is* my right and you refuse to do anything about it, there'll be nothing else she can do. You could even threaten to lock her up for slandering me if she persists. In fact, it might be a good idea to shut her in a cell and send for me. It'll only be pretending, just to frighten her a bit, no need to charge her with anything.' He paused to scowl. 'She needs a bit of a shake-up, that one does.'

'I could have done it for you before, but Talbot's here now and he won't oblige, I'm sure.'

Bevan made little sucking noises through a hole in one of his teeth as he gave this some consideration. 'You could send him away somewhere tomorrow afternoon – she's not coming to see her mother till then. Say you've had a message about a burglary in an outlying farm – White Walls would be just the place. It'll take him all afternoon to walk out there and back. *He* hasn't got a motorcycle.'

'He'll find out there hasn't been a burglary when he gets there.'

'So when he gets back you can pretend the message was a trick and get angry at someone for wasting police time. Say if you find out who did it, you'll give them what for. She'll have agreed to behave herself by then. There's nothing like being shut in a cell for making someone see reason. By the time he gets back, it'll all be over and done with.'

'I'm not so sure. She's stubborn lass, that one.'

'We'll soon knock that out of her. And without the money behind her, she'll turn to Jory, won't have any other choice. She hates working at the Hall.'

Wes pursed his lips, started to shake his head then looked at him. 'Five guineas, did you say?'

Bevan grinned. 'I said pounds, but all right. Make it guineas.'

'Done. Jory's a good lad. Came round to see how I was just now. I don't know why he's set his heart on your Ellen, but since he has, I'll help him in any way I can. And it's the last thing I'll be able to do for you, now they're putting me out to grass. If you can't help out a friend, you're a poor sort, I reckon.'

Bevan walked home filled with satisfaction. He'd got it all organised now. 'Just you wait, Ellen Dawson! You're in for a few shocks, you are. I wish I could be there to see your face when you find the money's gone.'

He smiled. He might just do that – go home around the time she was due to visit her mother. He'd see that damned motorcycle coming down Rochdale Road, so he'd know when she arrived.

15

Glenys was just giving the entrance hall a quick dust through when she heard a car come down the drive. She peeped out of the side window near the front door and muttered, 'Oh, no!' Her mistress had the sort of expression on her face that made all the servants take great care what they did and said.

She hurried into the kitchen. 'She's back and she's in one of her moods.'

Cook sighed, Millie gasped and clapped one hand to her mouth, Tadwyn muttered something under his breath.

Only Ellen appeared unmoved. 'Does she still get them?'

'Worse than ever!' Glenys said.

She put the duster away and went to open the front door. 'Shall I take your coat and hat, ma'am?'

'No, I'll leave them on my bed as I go up.'

'Would you like me to fetch you a tea tray?'

'Not just yet. I have to go and see my daughter first. Tell Tadwyn to go straight up and wait for me outside Miss Veronica's room.'

As Glenys hurried off, Edwina walked slowly up the stairs to her bedroom. Tossing her hat and coat on her bed, she stared at herself in the dressing-table mirror. Then she took the key out of her handbag and went up the next flight of stairs to the east wing. Tadwyn was there already outside the locked door.

'Wait outside, but be ready to come and help me if she's troublesome.'

She opened the door and went inside.

Ronnie, who'd heard her mother's loud voice and recognised that strident tone to mean she was angry, was standing by the window facing the door.

Edwina looked across at her then gave a slow, nasty smile. 'I've found out who your young man is.'

Ronnie stared at her in shock. 'I don't know what you mean.'

'Oh, but you do. Does the name Giles Covington mean anything to you?' She laughed aloud as her daughter lost every vestige of colour in her face. 'Clearly it does, so don't bother to lie to me.'

'How did you find out?'

'Oh, a little tête-à-tête after church with a lady who was visiting the neighbourhood. She lives in Little Fairworthy near that farm where you were working and knows you by sight. She'd seen you with Covington a few times. She knows him as well and actually thought I'd be pleased with the match.'

She waited for her daughter to say something and when she didn't, added provocatively, 'Giles Covington, widower, two sons. Comes from a shop-keeping background, won a scholarship to university. Clever enough to see the advantage of marrying a Gresham, no doubt, but I shall make sure that doesn't happen.' She waited again, foot tapping. 'Well, what have you to say for yourself?'

'Nothing.'

'Then I'll tell you what's going to happen. You're going to write him a note, and it'd better be a very convincing one, telling him that you no longer wish to marry him and are going to marry Algernon St Corbin. If you don't do that, I'll make it my business to ruin Covington professionally. Believe me, I can blacken his name in such a way that no decent person will ever do business with him again.'

She waited for this to sink in, delighted at how terrified her daughter was looking now.

'No one can blacken someone's name when he's done nothing wrong,' Ronnie said at last.

'Oh, but *I* can. I have excellent connections in this county – as you well know – and I won't scruple to use them to protect my only daughter. I can be very convincing when I want something.'

'I still won't do it.'

'You will, you know. But I'll give you a couple of hours to think about it, then I'll bring the writing paper and dictate the note.' Edwina turned round and left the room. She looked back from the doorway to see Ronnie standing by the window, frozen in place.

Weakling! was her only thought. How had she ever bred such an ineffectual daughter? Even her son had disappointed her, refusing the safe posting she could have obtained for him then getting himself killed.

As for this Covington person, he'd rue the day he'd tried to marry a Gresham. She knew where he worked, would telephone his senior partner, make a complaint, threaten more trouble if they continued to employ him.

She wasn't going to risk him popping up again and upsetting the apple cart once she'd got Ronnie safely married to Algernon.

When Edwina went downstairs, she told Tadwyn that she didn't want to be disturbed, then went into her sitting room. She unhooked the telephone receiver and waited for the operator to respond. After a short discussion she had the phone number she wanted, scribbled it down, then said, 'Will you connect me to that number now, please?'

The phone rang several times before a man picked it up.

Edwina's voice changed now, softening, taking on a cajoling tone as she explained her predicament.

'My dear lady, leave it with me. I am not without connections in this county. You must be very worried about your poor daughter.'

'I am, Basil, I am.'

Not until she had heard the key turn in the lock did Ronnie stumble across to the bed and sink down on it, wrapping her arms round herself as she was racked by shudders. This was what she'd feared when her mother found out, what she'd tried to explain to Giles.

He hadn't believed her, but she knew her mother was capable of anything.

She began rocking slightly because the pain inside her seemed too great to be borne. If she gave in on this, she'd have to give in on everything else and marry Algie.

And she couldn't, she just couldn't.

An image of Giles shivered into being in front of her and she remembered his kindness, his gentle wit, the love he showed for her and the way he talked about his sons.

She couldn't be the cause of his ruin, only if she agreed to write the letter, she was certain it wouldn't end there. Her mother would find some way to drive him out of the county.

Trust me, he'd said.

Could she? Could she trust him enough to defy her mother?

She would have to, because she definitely wasn't going to write that note.

Ellen watched the other servants take immense pains with everything they did, even tiptoeing when they walked into the main part of the house. She couldn't imagine Daphne Bingram inspiring this fear – or wanting to. She was glad her duties didn't take her into Mrs Gresham's company much.

And she smiled in satisfaction at the thought of the letter tucked away safely in her pocket, waiting to be posted.

There was a knock on the back door, which was standing open to let the fresh air in. Pel poked his head through. 'Can I speak to Glenys for a minute, please?'

Ellen looked at Cook who shrugged then turned

back to Pel. 'I'll go and find her for you.' No one ever worked as hard on Sundays, or they hadn't when she was last here, and anyway, why shouldn't Glenys have a minute or two with the man she had helped rescue?

She found the older maid clearing the breakfast room, where the mistress had eaten a very late luncheon. 'I'll finish this. Pel wants to see you.'

'Thanks.' Glenys blushed and carried out a tray of dirty crockery.

Ellen picked up two serving dishes and turned to follow her, jumping in shock when she found Mrs Gresham in the doorway staring at her. 'Can I get you anything, ma'am?'

'No. I just wanted to see what London had done to you and I must say I don't like what I see. Can't you do anything about that hair of yours?'

'Sorry, ma'am, but it's too short to tie back and though I put hair grips in it every morning, they work loose because my hair is so curly.'

'I don't know what the world is coming to when we have to employ untidy creatures like you, who try to ape their betters.'

If this rudeness continued, Ellen decided, she'd not be working here for long.

'What happened to Glenys? I thought she dealt with this part of the house?'

'She's just carried a tray through, ma'am. I'm helping clear up to get things done more quickly. We thought you'd prefer that.'

Mrs Gresham gave her another of those disapproving stares. 'Do you know what Lady Bingram's

plans are for Clough Lodge? Is she intending to reno-
vate the place and live there again?'

'I don't know, ma'am.'

'Surely there were better places to house such
deformed creatures than in a good neighbourhood like
this?'

Fury sizzled through Ellen, but she didn't give way
to it because she had a feeling that Mrs Gresham was
trying to provoke her and would enjoy giving her a
dressing down, or even sacking her. And if she lost
her job, who would help Miss Veronica to escape? 'We
all knew that Lady Bingram was happy to give those
men a home, ma'am, somewhere they could recover
in privacy and peace. We aides were all very proud of
how much her ladyship contributed to the war effort.
I gather she's to be given a medal, and will go and
take tea with Her Majesty after she receives it.'

Mrs Gresham's expression turned very sour and
she left without a further word.

Ellen allowed herself a smile then picked up the
dishes again and carried them through to the kitchen.
But the smile soon faded. What an unhappy household this was! A bitter woman trying to bend everyone
to her will and keeping her only daughter a prisoner,
away from the man she loved.

Not if Ellen had any say in things.

She was glad she'd be going into Shawcroft for a
few hours the following day. The atmosphere at the
Hall pulled your spirits down, somehow – except in
the kitchen.

*   *   *

Two hours after her visit to her daughter, Mrs Gresham summoned Tadwyn and led the way up to the second floor. 'Have you come to your senses yet, Veronica?' she asked.

'If you mean am I going to write to Giles and convince him I've changed my mind, then no. I love him and I'm going to marry him, not Algie.'

'Then I shall have to persuade you, shan't I?' She stepped quickly forward and slapped her daughter's face, hitting her so hard she sent the girl spinning across the room to land on the floor in a crumpled heap.

Picking her daughter up, she shook her hard, hit her again then threw her on the bed. '*Will you – do as – I ask?*'

'Never.'

For once, Edwina let her temper rule her head and began to beat her daughter, slapping any part of her she could reach. Though Ronnie tried to get away from her, it was easy enough for such a large woman to pull back her much smaller daughter.

In the end the beating went on for so long that Tadwyn stepped forward and caught his mistress's arm. 'I think she's had enough, ma'am.'

Panting, Edwina glared at him, then took a deep breath and stepped back. 'I'll leave you to think about it, Veronica. And be sure there will be other beatings if you don't do as I ask.'

When she left the room, Tadwyn followed her, saying nothing.

Veronica curled up on the bed and wept. Then she

pulled herself to her feet and went to peer at herself in the tiny mirror on the wardrobe door. She would have a black eye. Her lip was cut. And she could feel bruises on several parts of her body. Her mother had gone mad.

But the beating only strengthened her determination not to give in to her mother's demands.

When Tadwyn went downstairs he told Cook he was fetching something from his house. He walked across the yard and let himself in, then reaction set in and he sagged back against the door.

He'd thought the mistress was going to kill Miss Veronica. Had she run mad? He was beginning to think so. He went to his cash box, unlocked it and took out his bank book. Had he enough? Just about.

This incident had made up his mind. He was going to give notice. It was almost quarter day and as soon as he'd been paid, he was going to leave. He didn't intend to work his notice, didn't want to stay another minute here.

Then, as he was about to go back to the big house, he stopped. If he left now, who would stop her from killing Miss Veronica next time?

When he went back into the kitchen, Glenys looked at him. 'You all right, Mr Tadwyn?'

'No. I'm a bit shaken, to tell the truth.' He hesitated, then beckoned her and Ellen across. 'She started beating Miss Veronica just now. If I hadn't stopped her, I think she'd have killed the girl. She went mad, that's the only way to describe it.'

They both gaped at him.

'Don't say anything. I just – wanted someone else to know. It's not right to beat the girl like that. She's a gentle sort, Miss Veronica is. I just – wanted someone else to know till I can think what to do.'

When Mr Tadwyn had gone about his work, it was time for Glenys to take some time off. She went outside, as she and Pel had arranged, and found him waiting for her. 'Hello. You're looking better. Did you have a nice rest while we were at church?'

'I just got on with the weeding. Some of those flowers are coming up so fast they need air. But I was thinking . . . do you get any time off, Glenys?'

'One Sunday a month and an hour or two here and there, like this afternoon.'

'Would you walk out with me on your day off?'

She looked at him questioningly, not sure whether she'd heard this properly. It sounded like . . . 'Walk out with you?'

'Yes. I want to do things properly.'

Delight ran through her and she nodded. 'I'd like that.'

'Is there somewhere quiet we can go? I'm – not much good at meeting people yet and you've seen what I'm like with sudden noises.'

'You'll get better, bit by bit.'

'Will I?'

She nodded. 'Oh, yes. Ellen says a quiet job like this is just the thing for you, but it all takes time.' She hesitated, then added in a rush, 'If I can help in any way, any way at all, I'd be glad to.'

'Just being with you helps. You're the most restful woman I've ever met in my life.'

They stood smiling at one another, caught in a sunbeam, not moving until they heard a voice behind them. Glenys turned to see Ellen standing in the doorway. 'Sorry, what did you say, Ellen?'

'Sorry to interrupt, but Mrs Gresham is ringing for you. She doesn't take any notice of people's time off, does she? I don't think you should keep her waiting today, though.'

Glenys grimaced. 'She's had me on the hop ever since she got back from church. She never seems to think we get tired, does she? I wonder what made her so angry?'

'Who knows? She was asking me about Lady Bingram's old home just now, didn't like disabled men living there.'

Pel had turned to walk away, but turned and looked sharply at her as she said that. 'Lads who're disfigured need somewhere private till they're used to themselves, and some will never be able to live proper lives again. Your Lady Bingram sounds wonderful, but what did Mrs Gresham do during the war?'

Glenys looked over her shoulder, then whispered, 'She did nothing, really. Me and Cook knitted for the soldiers and sent off parcels of comforts and wrote letters to lads who'd no one to care for them, but *she* only arranged tea parties to raise money – and she said some really unkind things about the ladies who came to them, claimed it was just a way for them to get inside the Hall, said she'd never have invited them in peacetime. Only it was me and Cook who did the organising, really, *she* just gave orders and forgot about it till the day.'

Cook rapped on the window and beckoned.

'I'd better go.' Glenys hurried inside.

Ellen smiled at Pel. 'You're doing a good job on those gardens. Don't let Mrs Gresham get you down. She's very loud but you can always walk away from here if she pushes you too far.'

'I'd miss Glenys if I did that.'

'You like her, don't you?'

He couldn't help smiling. 'She's so restful, she makes me feel more like my old self than I have for a long time.'

'Pity you haven't got somewhere to take her. It'd do her good to get away from here and see a bit of the world. Mrs Gresham is not – an easy person to deal with.'

He looked at her for a moment. Was she giving him a hint? She went back into the house, so he went up to his room, forgot what he'd come for and stood by the window looking out into the sun-filled stable yard. It ought to be paradise here, could be so beautiful if the gardens were restored, but one wicked woman was making everyone's lives miserable. He knew quite a lot about what Mrs Gresham was doing with her daughter because he overheard more than anyone realised. When windows were left open on a still day, sound carried a long way.

Earlier today he'd heard the cries, the involuntary yelps of pain and pleas to stop the beating. He'd been able to do nothing but stand and shiver because the cries reminded him of the way wounded men had cried out. But he hadn't gone to pieces completely this time. No, he was definitely regaining control of himself, had something to live for now.

He began pacing up and down the corridor, knowing he ought to go outside again and carry on with his work, Sunday or no Sunday, there was so much to do in the garden. What he'd really like was to sit and be peaceful with Glenys. Fat chance of anyone getting any peace today.

It was on his second trip to the far end of the corridor that he noticed the footprints in the dust. They weren't his because there were imprints of stockinged feet and he never walked around in his stockinged feet. The marks hadn't been here when he moved in, so someone had come here during the past day or two. These were a man's footprints, so it couldn't be anyone from the house. And it certainly wasn't Tadwyn, who had his own cosy little cottage squashed in next to the stables and retired there as soon as he decently could after the evening meal.

So who was it?

He followed the footprints into the end room and noticed a depression in the old straw mattress, as if someone had lain on it. And the blanket at the bottom had been folded perfectly. After years in the Army, Pel was an expert at folding blankets this way. He went to the window and found it looked out over the side of the house and the back yard.

He went into the other rooms and studied the blankets there. Not folded in the Army way.

So it was an ex-soldier who'd been here.

Was it somebody on the tramp, somebody who'd sought shelter for the night? If so, Pel would never give him away.

He'd have to keep his eyes open and see what else happened. He was getting better at thinking what to do since he'd come here. It was as if he'd found himself a home and his mind had settled down.

Which was silly. This wasn't his home and never would be.

But it was a good place to rest and get better – or it could be if Mrs Gresham stopped hurting people.

And best of all, coming here had brought him to Glenys. He wasn't going to let anything take him away from her, though how he was to provide for her he hadn't yet worked out.

Glenys watched in puzzlement as Mrs Gresham took the tray of food for Miss Veronica into the small sitting room she used and told her to wait by the foot of the stairs. After hesitating for a moment, because she didn't usually eavesdrop, she crept across the hall and peered through the crack in the half-open door.

Her employer set the tray down and opened one of the small drawers in the inside part of the bureau where she wrote her letters each day. From it she removed a small bottle, held it up to the light and frowned, then took a medicine dropper and dropped several drops on to the food.

What was in the bottle? Glenys wondered. As Mrs Gresham screwed the stopper back on the bottle and picked up the tray again, she hurried back to the foot of the stairs, where she stood with eyes lowered and hands clasped in front of her.

'Fetch Tadwyn! I think it's better if he accompanies us. Miss Veronica has been somewhat agitated today. You can come back with him and take away her slops.'

Glenys hurried out the kitchen and told Tadwyn he was wanted, then got the things she needed to clean up Miss Veronica's room.

Mrs Gresham thrust the tray into Tadwyn's hands and led the way up the stairs, with that expression on her face that said someone was in for trouble.

Glenys stood by the door as the tray was deposited on the small table and Tadwyn came back to stand by the door. Then she went across to pick up the chamber pot and cover it up, before leaving the room, eyes still lowered. But she'd seen enough. Miss Veronica's face was battered and bruised, one of her eyes was blackened and swollen. No wonder Tadwyn had been shocked.

She went to the servants' stairs, hesitated, then opened the door. Setting down the chamber pot on the landing she crept back to eavesdrop, glad she was wearing her soft house shoes.

'Will you write that letter?' Mrs Gresham demanded.

'Never.'

Glenys had never heard quite that note in Miss Veronica's voice. It sounded firm, not like Mrs Gresham's, just quietly firm. It suddenly came to her that Mr Edwin had sounded like that on his last leave. And when he'd quarrelled with his mother, she'd been the one to shout and he'd gone on speaking softly, not losing control of himself.

'Give me the dressing-gown, Veronica.'

'I need it.'

There was the sound of a tussle. The dressing-gown was tossed out through the door.

Glenys clapped one hand to her mouth. What was happening now? Surely they weren't going to beat that poor girl again?

The blankets followed and the sheets.

'Take the tray away, Tadwyn. No, on second thoughts, remove the soup and the dessert. We don't want her to starve, do we? I'll take the water jug. We shan't be coming back for the tray until morning, Veronica. Maybe that'll give you time to think what you're doing,' Mrs Gresham finished triumphantly.

Glenys hurried along to the stairs door and slipped through the door, then stared down at the chamber pot in horror. Poor Miss Veronica hadn't got anywhere to relieve herself now – or anything to drink. And she was always thirsty, drank up the whole jug of water each time.

Things were getting worse. It wasn't right, it simply wasn't right.

*   *   *

When Tadwyn backed into the kitchen carrying the untouched dessert sitting on top of the soup bowl in one hand and the water jug in the other hand, Cook stared at him. 'Didn't she want her dinner?'

'Mrs Gresham decided to keep her on short rations,' he said in a low voice.

'I saw how badly she'd beaten Miss Veronica,' Glenys added. 'Shocking, it is.'

Tadwyn plumped down on the nearest chair as if his legs wouldn't hold him any longer. 'I think she's gone mad.'

'What are we going to do?' Ellen asked when no one else spoke.

He shook his head sadly. 'There's nothing we can do at the moment but she doesn't go up to see Miss Veronica on her own, so I'll be able to make sure she doesn't go too far.'

Ellen's voice was scornful. 'You don't think she's already gone too far, imprisoning her daughter and now beating her.'

'We'll lose our jobs if we try to interfere.'

'I don't think I want a job like this,' Ellen said.

Footsteps approached and Mrs Shipton came in. She looked round, pursed her lips, but said only, 'You're to go up and put away the blankets and sheets from Miss Veronica's room, Glenys. Mrs Gresham says she kept tearing them off the bed.'

Tadwyn looked at the housekeeper. 'She didn't. It was Madam who tore them off. She took Miss Veronica's dressing-gown too. That poor girl will be cold tonight.'

Mrs Shipton shot a quick, surprised glance at him, shook her head and said, 'It's not our business.' She walked out without another word.

Tadwyn went across to the cupboard where he kept a little bottle of whisky for when his rheumatism was bad and took a big swig.

'Are your knees aching?' Glenys asked sympathetically.

'No. I'm heart sore.'

'Mrs Gresham put something on the dinner,' Glenys said suddenly. She'd been dying to confide in someone. 'Some drops she keeps in her bureau. She's not – poisoning Miss Veronica, is she?'

It was only the thought of the letter she was to post the next day that kept Ellen quiet.

Tadwyn was staring down at a teacup half-filled with whisky.

Glenys had tears in her eyes.

Cook was banging her pots around.

'If things get worse, we'll have to intervene,' Ellen told them. But they avoided her eyes and she wondered if they would do anything. Tadwyn said he'd already stopped Mrs Gresham beating her daughter, so maybe he'd make sure Miss Veronica's life wasn't at risk, but Ellen felt really worried.

Could she smuggle in a blanket to Miss Veronica after everyone had gone to bed?

No, the key wasn't kept in the lock any more.

After she'd posted that letter, she'd have a word with Seth Talbot, ask his advice.

*   *   *

Ronnie looked round the room. She had only a short-sleeved nightdress and a bare mattress and it was already growing cooler. But the thing she resented most was that her mother hadn't left her a chamber pot. That had been done deliberately, she was sure.

All she could do was listen to the sounds of people settling down for the night and hold firm to her faith in Giles.

Then, just as she decided that everyone must be asleep she heard someone creeping along towards her bedroom. Was her mother coming to torture her again? No, it sounded like two people. And they were trying to keep quiet. She'd only heard them because she was awake and listening. A light flickered beneath the door and whoever it was stopped there.

For one wild and glorious moment she thought it was Giles come to rescue her, then the key turned in the lock and the door opened to reveal Tadwyn holding up a lighted candle. She sank back down on the bed, biting back the exclamation of joy that had been hovering on her lips.

He put one finger to his lips and she looked at him wearily. 'What does my mother want now?'

'Shh!'

Glenys pushed past him, carrying a blanket and a jug of water. 'You must be chilled through, Miss Veronica.' She wrapped the blanket round Ronnie's shoulders. 'I didn't dare bring a glass as well, in case it rattled, so you'll have to drink from the jug. Sorry.'

Veronica gave her a quick hug which flustered Glenys. 'Thank you.'

'You're welcome. And miss . . .'

'Yes?'

'Don't eat the food.'

Tadwyn put the candlestick down on the small table and deposited a covered chamber pot on the floor, looking embarrassed. 'You'll need this, too.'

'I wanted to let you out,' Glenys said, throwing an angry glance at Tadwyn, 'but he won't. I'm that sorry, miss. I'll be back for these in the morning before madam wakes up.'

'How did you get in?'

'Mr Tadwyn has a spare key.'

The door closed and Ronnie felt tears rise in her eyes. At least this would save her the humiliation of emptying her bladder on to the floor. She was surprised that Tadwyn would do even this much. He'd always seemed very devoted to her mother.

When she'd used the pot, she went to the window, wrapping the blanket round herself as she stared out. Moonlight silvered the world outside, but it made the shadows inside the room seem even darker. She didn't feel sleepy, just deep down weary.

What if she never did manage to escape from her mother?

Pel was woken by another of his nightmares. When he'd walked around a bit, he calmed down as usual, then went to stand by the window and look at the darkened house. Only it wasn't completely dark. A light was flickering in the bedroom on the second floor, the one where Mrs Gresham was keeping her daughter locked up.

As he watched, the light went out and he saw it flickering here and there as the person carrying it came downstairs.

When the kitchen door opened, the candle blew out, but not before he'd seen that it was Mr Tadwyn. The old man made his way across to his cottage and then the world became silent again.

But when Pel looked up, she was standing by the window. There was enough moonlight to see a pale face pressed against it.

On an impulse he got out the binoculars he'd found one day in the garden and put them to his eyes. They were good ones, very good, bringing the figure into sharp focus, showing the droop of the woman's shoulders and, he thought, a glitter of something on her cheeks. Tears. What else could it be?

He'd have to ask Glenys about her. He didn't like to think of anyone being kept a prisoner, not after so many decent chaps had given their lives for freedom.

16

Glenys and Tadwyn came soon after dawn to take away the things they'd brought. The maid muttered an apology. 'I'm sorry, Miss Veronica, I really am.' She looked at the plate of congealed food. 'You didn't eat it then. I'm so glad.' She hesitated, then whispered, 'I saw your mother put some drops on it.'

'Sleeping drops. She's been putting them in my food sometimes.' Ronnie looked at the plate and shivered. If she'd eaten it, she'd have been drugged and might have soiled herself.

'I'd better leave it here.'

'Yes.'

Tadwyn had said nothing, but he looked drawn, as if he hadn't slept well.

Ronnie looked across at him and he stared down at his feet to avoid her gaze, keeping his eyes averted as he left the room. The key turned in the lock and was withdrawn from it.

The door closed and Ronnie was on her own again. Soon she felt cold. The hours passed slowly and no one came. She tried walking up and down or running on the spot, but she grew more and more chilled in spite of these efforts.

When it was fully light again, she went to the window to see an overcast sky and a world whose colours seemed muted.

'What is she up to?' she muttered once, then realised she'd spoken aloud and vowed to be more careful about that in future. She wasn't giving them any excuse to say she was out of her mind.

Some time later, about ten o'clock to judge by the activity that came and went in the back yard, she heard the sound of a motor car coming towards the house. It stopped at the front, so she couldn't see who it was. Who would be coming to see her mother at this hour of the morning?

She resumed her pacing for a time, then went to huddle on the bed again, curling up into a ball.

No doubt she'd find out what her mother wanted in time.

On the Monday, Cobbley was already sitting on his stool in the police station when Seth arrived. He glared at the younger man.

'Who asked you to come to *my* party on Saturday?'

'The Mayor did.'

'You knew I didn't want you there.'

Obviously, there was to be no further pretence of any sort of co-operation from Cobbley. 'The rest of the town was going and it'd have looked strange for me not to be there.'

'Not to me, it wouldn't.'

Seth wasn't going to stand and argue. 'Is there anything I should be doing today?'

'No. You can just stay out of my way and mind your own business, let me enjoy my last week of work.'

'I could take over compeltely. We could telephone Inspector Dunham and I'm sure he'd approve. Then you could start enjoying your retirement.'

'I'm not giving you the reins till I have to, because I don't trust you!'

'I see.' Seth didn't say that feeling was mutual, because it would do no good to reveal his suspicions at this stage. He went into the inner office and sat down at the desk, starting to draw up a list of things he'd need when he was in charge here. Office supplies, for a start. The cupboards were nearly bare.

There was silence for a few minutes, then Cobbley called out, 'You can take an early lunch today. I've someone coming to see me about a private matter and I don't want you poking your nose in.'

'I'll have to find someone to take a message to my landlady, then.'

'Why don't you go yourself? Do one of your *little patrols*. No need to hurry back, either.'

This made Seth suspicious so he walked quickly down to Rochdale Road, beckoned to one of the many youths who seemed to loiter round the town ready to run errands and offered him a penny to take a note to Jeanie that he'd be home for dinner at twelve.

After that he went back to the station, where he found Cobbley making a phone call. The older man put the phone down the minute he came through the door and said nothing about who he'd been talking to. Wondering who it had been, sure it wasn't police business, Seth went back to making his list. After that he began to reorganise the records that had been kept, of which there were very few. 'I think we need a new account book,' he told Cobbley, showing him an ancient, leather-bound volume that had disintegrated in his hands. 'I'll go and buy one after dinner.'

'When you're in charge, you can waste the petty cash. Until then, you'll have to put up with how I've arranged things. *I* didn't need any fancy books and since no one's going to be reading that one, we can tie it together with string when it's not being used. I don't waste my time on paperwork, just do my job and keep the town peaceful, which is more than an outsider like you will ever manage.'

Seth closed his eyes and prayed for patience. He suddenly remembered the attack and went back into the front office. 'That reminds me. I want to report two men for trying to attack me on Saturday night after I left the Town Hall.' He watched Wes smirk. The man definitely smirked, so he must know about the attack, even though Jory said he hadn't arranged it.

'You don't look as if anyone's given you a thumping.'

'They didn't get that far, thanks to Jory Nelson.'

'Ah, I heard he came to your rescue. It's a poor lookout, having a bobby who can't protect himself, someone lads feel they can attack.'

'These weren't lads, they were grown men.'

'Jory said they were lads.' Cobbley smirked again. Seth stepped forward till he was nose to nose with

Cobbley. 'If I find that *you* arranged that assault on me, I'll make sure your pension's revoked.'

The other man's face turned puce. 'I'd *never* do anything to put the police in disrepute. *Never!*'

Seth studied him and for some reason, believed him. Who did that leave wanting to hurt him – or worse? He'd have said Jory, except that he'd been the rescuer. Halsopp, then? And what about Jory's father? He'd been dealing in black-market stuff all through the war, if Inspector Dunham's information was correct. Seth frowned. He hadn't seen much of Jory's father, come to think of it. Eddie Nelson must be keeping out of sight. Now, why would he do that?

'Are you going to stand there all day staring into space?' Cobbley asked with mighty sarcasm.

Seth smiled. 'Sorry. You'd just given me an idea.'

'About what?'

'Something I'd been wondering about. Anyway, I'll write up a report about the attack and get a statement from Nelson, then you can sign it as officer in charge.'

'Waste of time. No one's going to own up to attacking you.'

'I saw their faces. I never, ever forget a face.'

'Maybe you'd do better to let the matter drop. I can have a quiet word in certain circles and make sure it doesn't happen again.'

'Can you, now?'

'Yes, I bloody can! I know the town. They know me, know I won't put up with attacks on the police, even on you. There's no *need* for a report.'

'Nonetheless I wish to make one.'

'You're more interested in bits of paper, you are, than in being a real bobby. Now, since I'm still in charge, you get back in there and play with your paper and I'll deal with the public.'

Seth was tempted to pull rank on him and take over there and then, but managed to hold back the angry words. Cobbley clearly knew quite a lot about what was going on in town, so he'd give the man a chance to let something drop. And Seth only had to put up with him for a week. Not much was likely to happen except that he'd go mad with boredom.

The atmosphere in the small station was so filled with anger that he was glad to leave for his dinner at noon. He walked outside to find it had clouded over and was threatening rain.

Algie found the letter in the wastepaper basket in his mother's private sitting room. He was looking for pieces of scrap paper – no one knew he'd started writing poetry so he did his early drafts on any scrap of old paper he could find, then burned them, which meant raiding the wastepaper baskets before the servants emptied them. He knew that was silly and he had nothing to be ashamed of, especially as he'd had a few poems published. But his family would never understand. They thought only of doing the right thing and preserving the estate. He was strongly tempted to leave, make his own way in the world – only he loved the old house and the woods around it, had ached to come back here during the war.

He pulled what looked like a nice large piece of paper out of the basket and found it was a letter, with a matching envelope crumpled beneath it. Both were the cheap sort you could buy anywhere, the letter paper being lined. He smiled. This was not the sort of letter his mother usually received. Who could have sent her this?

Then he noticed the name on the front of the envelope and his fingers jerked on the paper, tearing one edge. *The letter had been addressed to him!* His mother must have opened it then thrown it away. How dare she open his mail!

After smoothing out the paper he found it was in French, looked at the signature and blinked his eyes furiously. Monique! He hadn't thought to hear from her again, not after what had been said at their last meeting. What could she want from him? It must be serious or she'd never have written.

Before he could read it, he heard footsteps approaching along the parquet floor of the hall. Only his mother clicked her heels in just that way. He shoved the mass of papers back into the basket and stuffed the letter in his inner jacket pocket, but didn't have time to move away from the bureau.

Blanche came in and snapped, 'What are you doing in my room, Algernon?' Her eyes narrowed. 'And what's upset you?'

His heart sank. She always seemed to be able to tell what he was thinking. Then he thought of Monique and found the courage to stand up for himself for once, something he'd always found difficult with his mother. Well, even his father did as she told him. 'Did you open my letter, Mother?'

'How did you find that out?'

'I was looking in the wastepaper basket for scraps of paper to scribble on and I found it. That was *my* letter. You'd no right to open it.'

'I could tell it was from a woman, and not the sort of woman I want you dealing with, either, so I had every right. Don't forget you're still dependent on us.'

As if she'd ever let him forget! It wasn't strictly true, though.

'Presumably this Monique is someone you met in France?'

He inclined his head.

'Is the baby really yours, do you think?'

He stared at her, open-mouthed.

She looked at him in annoyance. 'You haven't read it yet, have you? It doesn't matter. Give it to me and I'll deal with it for you.'

'No. The letter was for me and I'll deal with it. She should have told me . . .' His voice broke and he turned away trying to control his emotions.

Her voice grew quieter, but it sliced through the air between them like a sharp knife. 'Algernon, do as you're told this minute!'

For the first time since he'd got back, he defied her openly, swinging round and staring right back at her. 'Not this time. It's my letter and . . . and my baby. I'll sort it out.'

She hesitated. 'You won't go marrying a woman like this?'

'She's already turned me down.'

'She must be stupid.'

'No. She's very intelligent, actually. But she loves her home and village, doesn't want to come and live in England.' It was as good an excuse as any. He certainly wasn't telling his mother the truth, which would upset her even more and provoke what he and Pierce used to call one of her 'royal rages'.

'If it *is* yours, I suppose we can pay her something, help support the child. That should shut her up and leave your conscience clear. It needn't be very much. These peasants can live very cheaply.'

He ignored her sneers. 'I'll go to France, see her, talk to her myself.'

She shook her head. 'Oh, no. At the moment, you're courting Veronica Gresham. This is *not* the time to go running off to France.'

'It won't take me more than three or four days.'

'I'm not paying for you to go and see *that creature* until after you're engaged to Veronica, better still, after you're married to her.'

'I don't need you to pay. I have some money of my own.'

She snorted. 'That piddling little inheritance. How long do you think that will last? Have a bit of sense for once in your life, Algernon! Stop moodling around and dreaming. As for this poetry of yours, it's trite stuff and you're wasting your time on it.'

Anger sizzled through him. If she knew about the poetry, she must have gone through the cupboard where he'd hidden his writing. Suddenly it was easier to do what he wanted, but he didn't intend to leave poor Ronnie in trouble. 'I'll go and see Ronnie before I leave, but only if *you* will make sure Mrs Gresham lets us talk in private. A chap doesn't like to propose in public.'

Her face was instantly wreathed in smiles. 'You *are* going to propose to Veronica then?'

He nodded, hating to think how angry Mrs Gresham would be with poor old Ronnie when she found out he wasn't going to marry her. Because suddenly, he knew that he couldn't. He'd always known that and so had she. It'd be like marrying your own sister and the thought of touching her in an intimate way made him shudder, as did the thought of touching any woman like that. Pierce had been one for the women. Algie had just strung along and chatted to girls to be with Pierce. It had been a frustrating situation.

His mother continued to smile. 'We'll go over to see them this very afternoon. I'll keep Edwina out of the way and you can talk to dear Veronica. There couldn't be a better match for you. You'll be comfortable for life and have your own estate. Edwina has plenty of money and no one to leave it to but Veronica now.'

He nodded and smiled – well, he hoped he smiled convincingly – then went up to his bedroom and smoothed the letter out, reading it carefully, reading behind the lines, too. The paper was blistered near the bottom. He touched the spots. She'd wept as she wrote and it took a lot to make Monique cry. She mustn't have known she was carrying Pierce's child when he last saw her.

He sat down to have a good think about how best to do this, but his fingers kept going back to the letter, because touching it gave him strength to go against all his upbringing.

He knew he would love any child of Pierce's like his own son or daughter.

Giles started the day feeling pleased that he'd bought his friend's motor car the previous day, just in time to take his sons back to their weekly boarding school in it, a treat they'd all enjoyed. Owning the vehicle would give him the ability to go and free Ronnie at a time of his own choosing. If only there hadn't been so many other matters claiming his attention, he'd have done it by now.

He went down to breakfast and found his mother-in-law there before him, which usually meant she wanted to talk to him about something. He went to choose from the food laid out on the sideboard then brought his plate to the table.

'You look a bit down in the mouth, Giles dear. Have you still not heard from your young lady?'

'No, but I've found out what happened to her.'

'Oh?'

He hesitated, but Bernice wasn't acquainted with Ronnie's mother and he wanted her to think well of Ronnie, so he told her briefly what Mrs Gresham had done.

She gaped at him in shock. 'You must be mistaken.

I mean, it sounds just like one of those Mack Sennett films you and the boys enjoy so much. That sort of thing doesn't happen in real life.'

'I'm afraid it's happened this time.'

'Would you like me to ask my friends about this Gresham woman?'

'No, definitely not. What I've told you is in confidence, not to be told to anyone. Promise me, Bernice. Not a single other person is to know.'

'If you insist.' She ate a forkful of scrambled eggs in that neat way she had, then wiped the corner of her mouth with her table napkin. 'I was wondering if you could take me and the children out for a ride in your new motor car on Saturday. They did enjoy going back to school in it and the poor little dears haven't spent much time with you lately.'

He immediately felt guilty. 'I know I've been neglecting them, but once I've sorted out Ronnie's problems and changed jobs, I'll be able to see much more of them. I hope after we move to find a good day school for them, then we'll all settle down into a much happier life, I'm sure.' He pushed his half-eaten meal aside, saw her frown at it and said apologetically, 'I know we shouldn't waste good food, but I'm not really hungry. Today I have to give my notice in at the practice and it's not likely to be pleasant.'

'So soon?'

'Yes. I think you should begin planning the actual move, packing the ornaments and so on. I want to try to take a day off tomorrow, so that I can drive over and see what Monnings' house is like.' But most important of all, he wanted to rescue Ronnie. He had a friend in Cheshire he could leave her with while he sorted out the formalities for them to get married.

'Very well, dear.'

When Giles got to work the elderly clerk looked up to say, 'Mr Henderson wishes to see you as soon as you come in, sir.'

Giles shrugged and went to put his briefcase on his desk, then stopped and looked round the room. There was something different . . . the books were leaning in the opposite direction, just slightly, but enough for him to notice. He turned round on the spot, his eyes raking every corner. The vase on the mantelpiece wasn't quite where he'd left it. He knew he was fussy about details, but attention to detail was something that had paid off during the war, and was paying off again now. He opened the desk drawer and that too was not quite as he'd left it.

Someone had been going through his things! When he looked, every single drawer had been disturbed.

As usual, anger made him even calmer, but it was a stillness at the heart of a raging storm. Picking up a pad he walked across to the senior partner's office. He didn't knock on the door because it was open just a crack, enough to let him hear Henderson speaking to someone on the telephone.

'I can't believe it of Covington,' Henderson was saying in a distinctly gloating tone, 'but if Mrs Gresham vouches for the truth of the matter, I'll have to take this very seriously indeed, Brigadier. Maybe I should even make a complaint about him to the

Law Society. Yes, yes. I'll definitely take action. Is there anything else I should know before I . . . ?'

Giles moved very quietly into the office and took the earpiece from Henderson's hand. 'Covington here. If you try to spread any more slander about me, Brigadier, I'll sue you – and I promise you I'll win because I've done nothing untoward.' He didn't wait for the man at the other end to stop spluttering in shock but hung the earpiece up, leaving it rocking to and fro.

Turning round, he shot out words like bullets. 'And the same applies to you, Henderson. You shouldn't listen to slander. And if you repeat anything *that woman* has been saying about me to anyone else, it's you who'll be answering questions in a more formal setting. In fact, I'll consult one of my legal mentors about it this morning as soon as I'm finished here.'

Henderson had been staring at him open-mouthed but he closed his mouth now and simply scowled.

'I have something serious to report,' Giles said. He went to the door and called the clerk in. 'I need you to join us because there's been a break-in and I want witnesses.'

The clerk goggled at him. 'But nothing was out of order when I opened up this morning, sir!'

'On the contrary, someone went through all the drawers and cupboards in my office during the weekend. We'd better call in the police to investigate.' He smiled as a dull flush stained Henderson's cheeks. 'Unless it was you?'

'Dewbridge, you can go back to the front office.'

'He's not going anywhere until we get to the bottom of this matter. I still think I should get the police in.' Giles picked up the telephone earpiece.

'There was no break-in!' Henderson shouted, snatching it from him. 'I was simply making myself familiar with my new business.'

'In other words, you went through my things.'

'I have the right. I'm the senior partner here.'

'*You* may feel you have the right, but no professional person would treat a colleague in that way.' Out of the corner of his eye, he saw Dewbridge moving towards the door and snapped, 'Stay.' He turned back to Henderson. 'If you wish me to keep quiet about your grossly unprofessional behaviour, you'll tell me who has been spreading lies about me and what exactly those lies are.'

Henderson collapsed in his chair like a punctured balloon. 'It was Brigadier Westing and he'd heard from Mrs Gresham that you tried to trick her daughter into marrying you in order to get hold of her inheritance, the details of which you must have found out about from our records, since my uncle administered the trust and it's been kept a close secret.'

'That's not true.'

Henderson looked at him disbelievingly.

Dewbridge cleared his throat. 'If I may say something, sir?'

'Well?'

'Mr Covington has never dealt with that particular trust. I could swear to that in court if I had to, because I'm the only one who gets those records out and files them away. Your uncle always kept the details to himself.'

'Covington could have found them on his own.'

Dewbridge gave a tight smile. 'Not possible, sir. I have a particular way of putting things away. I would know at a glance if the papers had been moved or opened.'

There was silence, then Giles repeated, 'What trust is this?'

Henderson scowled at him. 'None of your business.'

'We'll definitely call in the police, then. I'm not going to be accused of something I haven't done without understanding the ramifications. For the record, Dewbridge, I solemnly declare that I want to marry Ronnie Gresham because I love her and she loves me, not because of any inheritance. Now, what's this about? What has she inherited?'

Henderson gave a scornful laugh. 'Oh, don't pretend that you don't know she's an heiress! A very rich heiress. You must have known that.'

'I haven't the faintest idea whether she is or is not an heiress, and it doesn't matter to me either way, because I love her.' He saw Henderson wince as he used this word again. It was no use talking to this spiteful little man about Ronnie. He needed to spell out carefully what he would do if any of these lies were spread by his senior partner. He did this succinctly and with accurate reference to a couple of other slander cases that had set useful precedents.

'You can't be sure you'd win,' Henderson said sulkily.

'Oh, but I am. I happen to have a photographic memory which is why I was employed in intelligence work during the war. And if there are any queries about my character, you may refer them to Inspector Dunham or to General Lutchenson, both of whom will be happy to speak for me.'

'You know Lutchenson?' Henderson whispered, awed in spite of himself.

'I know him well. My section answered directly to him during the war.' Giles waited a minute. 'Have I made myself clear?'

'Yes.'

'Now, make sure you don't spread Mrs Gresham's calumnies!' He stared fixedly at the other man, who shifted uncomfortably, then nodded agreement. 'And finally, I'd like to know what this trust is that you've mentioned . . .'

When he became aware of the facts of Ronnie's inheritance and the way the trust had been extended, Giles could see at once why her mother didn't want her marrying a lawyer.

After asking a question or two, he changed the subject abruptly. 'Given the circumstances, I shall leave immediately, taking all my personal books and papers with me. Dewbridge knows what's happening with the very minor cases I've been dealing with and can find you my notes, which are all up to date. I'll have Septimus Monnings of Shawcroft draw up a contract for the sale of my share in this business and send it on to you. He'll be acting for me.'

He turned on his heel and left Henderson's office without waiting for an answer.

Within two hours he had found boxes, packed up everything that belonged to him, enlisting Dewbridge's help so that no one could accuse him of taking what wasn't his, and carried those boxes out to the motor car, which had come in useful sooner than he'd expected.

He turned to Dewbridge and offered his hand, which the other shook. 'If you ever need a reference or a job, come to me. I've greatly appreciated your efficiency over the years.'

Then he drove home, even more worried about Ronnie. She'd been right that her mother would stop at nothing to come between them, and now he knew why. As to the slander, he had confidence that his war work and the connections he'd made through it would be enough to see him through.

What he didn't understand was why Ronnie herself knew nothing about this inheritance. She'd once told him the estate had gone to her mother on her husband's death and he knew Ronnie wouldn't lie to him.

He couldn't help smiling at the thought of her. As if he cared whether she was an heiress or not!

By the time he got home, he'd decided to go straight across to Shawcroft and speak to Monnings about the whole situation. The sooner he got Ronnie out of that woman's hands, the better.

He picked up the telephone to ring his new associate. He'd had this one installed when he went away to war, so that his wife could summon help if she needed it and had kept it on for his mother-in-law, for the same reason.

17

At last came the sound Ronnie had both hoped for and dreaded, footsteps coming towards her room. Her mother's voice rang out down the corridor, the words quite clear in spite of the closed door.

'. . . and we've been unable to do anything with her. She tore up her bedding so we were obliged to take it away from her and she was so violent she hurt herself. And she's started soiling herself. I'm so upset about all this. I don't know—'

As the key turned in the lock, Ronnie stood up, smoothing her hair as best she could and facing the door, arms folded in front of her flimsy nightdress.

Her mother stopped dead in the doorway and stared round, her mouth falling open in shock. Tadwyn stood impassively behind her, not betraying by so much as a twitch that he had intervened.

Dr Hilliam moved forward on his own, studying the room as he did so then her battered face. 'How are you this morning, Veronica?'

'Very cold and hungry. My mother took away all my bedding.'

He looked towards the plate. 'You didn't eat your food last night.'

'I was worried she'd drugged it again. She's been doing that for the past few days and keeping me locked up here.'

He stared at her in surprise, then asked slowly, 'How did you get injured?'

'My mother beat me. She's stronger than I am. I couldn't stop her.' His eyes narrowed and he looked her up and down again, but she met his gaze squarely, without flinching.

'How are you feeling today otherwise?'

'I'm in great need of relieving myself. She didn't leave me a chamber pot.'

He bent to peer under the bed, opened the wardrobe door and turned to look questioningly at Mrs Gresham.

For once, Ronnie's mother seemed at a loss for words, then she said, 'An oversight. Tadwyn, go and find something for her to use. And take that food away with you.'

'Don't!' Ronnie cried. She turned to the doctor. 'If you have that food analysed, or even give some of it to a dog or cat, it'll prove that I'm not making all this up. Isn't there any law against locking people up when there's nothing wrong with them?'

He pursed his lips. 'Sometimes we have to lock people up for their own good. Sometimes they don't understand that there's something wrong with them.'

'Then tell me what I must do to prove I'm in full possession of my wits?'

Mrs Gresham came across the room and picked up the plate, turning quickly as if to get out of Ronnie's reach and seeming to trip. The plate smashed and the food was scattered across the floor. She shot a quick, triumphant glance at her daughter before turning to face Dr Hilliam. 'So careless of me.'

Tadwyn came back with a chamber pot and slipped it under the bed.

'Could you send Glenys to tidy this mess up?' Edwina said.

'Certainly, madam.'

'And put the food in a dish so that I can take it away and analyse it,' the doctor said.

'Will you do that yourself, Tadwyn?' Edwina asked in her softest voice. 'We don't want it tampering with before the good doctor has checked it.'

Ronnie watched him give his mistress a little nod, as if to say he understood what she really wanted, and knew with a sinking heart that the food would be changed. She looked back at the doctor. 'I'm cold and hungry but I'm not eating anything that's brought to me because sometimes it's drugged and then I can't help appearing disoriented.'

'I could take you away, but I'd have to lock you in the asylum until your state of mind was investigated.'

'I'd be happy to go with you. I think I'd get treated more fairly in an asylum than here.'

Edwina glared at them both. 'Well, I shan't allow you to take her away. If anyone is going to look after my daughter, the only child I have left now, it's going to be me.'

'Then I shan't dare eat or drink anything,' Ronnie said.

Dr Hilliam looked from one woman to the other, his face betraying nothing of his thoughts. 'I'll return this evening and bring something for you to eat, Miss Gresham. In the meantime, if I draw some water from the tap myself, would you drink it?'

'Yes.'

He turned towards the door. 'Let's leave her in privacy for a few moments, Mrs Gresham. She needs to relieve herself.'

He returned a few minutes later with a jug of water, two apples, a piece of buttered bread and a wedge of cheese. 'I selected the fruit myself from a bowl in the kitchen and watched as your Cook cut the bread and cheese. I give you my word that it hasn't left my sight since. Do you think you can eat it?'

'Oh, yes. Thank you very much. I'm ravenous.'

He continued to watch as she took a long drink before starting to eat, then he turned to Mrs Gresham, who was standing in the doorway scowling. 'I'll return this evening. You did say you'd find some blankets and clothes for your daughter, did you not?'

'Just the bedding, I think. I don't want her to run away.'

He raised his eyebrows. 'Very well. Give me a minute with your daughter, please.'

When Edwina had gone, he said quietly to Ronnie, 'You'd better eat these things quickly, in case they're taken away or exchanged.'

'You believe me, then?'

'I'm not sure which of you is telling the truth, but

I intend to make certain you're properly looked after, young woman, until I can prove it one way or the other.'

While she was eating he peered under the bed at the chamber pot. 'You seem able to use the amenities like anyone else.'

'When they're provided.'

Her mother returned with an armful of bedding which she threw on the end of the bed as if afraid to go closer to her daughter.

With a nod to Ronnie, the doctor left.

Edwina followed without even a look at her daughter, locking the door behind her.

Ronnie didn't stop eating, but rolled one apple under the wardrobe for later.

Sure enough, as soon as the sound of the car had faded into the distance, her mother came back with Tadwyn again in attendance.

'You'll never prove anything, you fool. Tadwyn packed up some other food for the doctor. He's very loyal to me, is Tadwyn.' She walked across the room and picked up the half-empty jug of water and the plate with the remaining piece of bread on it. 'I'll take these. You won't need them. And if you continue to defy me, perhaps I will let them take you to the asylum. I'm on the Board of Governors and can be assured of all the help I need for you there. I shall be *so* distressed if they have to confine you in a straitjacket to stop you harming yourself.'

Ronnie hoped she'd kept her fear of that off her face while her mother was there, but after the door had closed she slumped down on the bed, feeling as if there was no hope of ever defeating her mother.

Had Tadwyn really changed the drugged food? Whose side was he on? Last night he'd helped her. Now, she didn't know whether she could trust him or not.

And the doctor? Would he be shrewd enough to prevent her mother pulling the wool over his eyes? Would he even be prepared to alienate someone as influential as Mrs Gresham? After all, he and his wife came to dinner regularly and moved in the best circles because of her mother's social sponsorship.

No, Ronnie's main hope of escape, possibly her only hope, was the letter Ellen was going to post for her. In it, she'd begged Giles to come and rescue her immediately. If that letter went astray, she was indeed lost.

Glenys looked at Tadwyn. 'You changed the food round, didn't you, gave him other stuff?'

He sighed. 'I had to. I have wages owing to me and I need as much money as I can to retire on.'

'It's not fair.'

'Life isn't fair. Surely you've learned that by now? We did what we could for her last night. And I'll make sure madam doesn't go too far.'

When Glenys had finished her chores, she went outside to sit in a rickety arbour no one else used in the garden. She couldn't help shedding a few tears because she felt Mr Tadwyn had betrayed her and Miss Veronica both.

Suddenly a twig broke under someone's foot and she turned her head to see Pel standing there, looking anxious and uneasy. She couldn't hold back another sob, because the sight of him brought home to her that if she did anything to get herself sacked, no one else here would look after Pel like she did. And worst of all, she wouldn't see him again.

He was there beside her in a second, putting his arms round her and she couldn't help it, she put her head on his shoulder and sobbed her heart out.

When the storm of weeping ended, he pulled out a handkerchief and used it to wipe her eyes. The square of cotton was grubby, but she didn't care, because she was entranced by his clumsy tenderness. No man had ever treated her like this before.

'Shh, my little love, shhh,' he crooned, wiping the tears. 'Stop crying now and tell me what's wrong.'

So the whole story came out.

He listened intently, nodding encouragement from time to time. When she'd finished he said, 'I've seen her at the window, poor girl, and I've heard her weeping, too. Sound carries at night and I sometimes go outside for a bit of fresh air if I've had nightmares.'

He rocked Glenys slightly, his brow still furrowed in thought and with a sigh she abandoned herself to the joy of having a man hold her. This man. The only one who had ever noticed her. Had he really called her 'my little love'?

When she felt him pull away a little she looked up and found him smiling down at her.

'Do you mind?' he asked.

'Mind what?'

'What I called you. My little love.'

'I like it.'

'I'm not much of a catch, you know, Glenys.'

'You're just – injured. You'll get better bit by bit. You need peace and quiet for that, so we'd better not do anything to upset Mrs Gresham. I'm sorry for Miss Veronica, I really am. But you matter more to me than she does.' She could feel the heat rising in her cheeks as she added, 'I'm not much of a catch either. I'm middle-aged and plain, never was much of a looker.'

'You make me feel good. I like being with you. That's what matters to me.'

She smiled mistily at him. 'You make me feel good, too.' Then she sighed. 'I do feel guilty about Miss Veronica, though.'

'Maybe we can find some way to help her without Mrs Gresham knowing it's us.'

She brightened. 'I'll keep my eyes open and you do the same.'

He pulled her to him. 'May I kiss you?'

She nodded and lost herself in his kiss, the first she'd received since she was seventeen. In it, she forgot everything except the fact that she'd found a fellow who loved her as much as she loved him.

It was nothing less than a miracle.

But she wasn't telling anyone about it. Not yet. Not even Cook. Their love was so bright and new, she wanted to hug the thought of it to herself, keep it safe and hidden from nasty people who might try to interfere.

When the bedroom door opened again, Ronnie's mother came in with Tadwyn, smiling in the way that meant she was about to do something unkind.

She pulled out a bottle and dropper and Ronnie fled instinctively to the far end of the room, standing pressed against the window.

'You might as well be sensible. We're going to give you your medicine, whether you struggle or not.'

But this time Ronnie fought with everything that was in her, screaming at the top of her voice, flailing about, scratching, biting, kicking.

It took a lot longer for them to subdue her this time and when the hated drops had slid down her throat she pretended to slump back then attacked her mother trying desperately to hurt her where it'd show.

Tadwyn had to drag her off and push her down on the bed while her mother ran out of the room.

'That was foolish,' he said in a low voice. 'She'll use it as proof that you're not in your right mind.'

'How can you live with yourself?' she asked.

She watched him go out then she looked for something to break the window with but there was nothing in the room and she didn't want to cut herself and bleed to death. So she stood by the window and yelled as loudly as she could, pleading with someone to help her, to tell Dr Hilliam her mother was drugging her.

Only when the room began to lurch around her

and her voice was hoarse did she go and lie on the bed.

Black misery overwhelmed her as she sank towards oblivion.

Ellen changed out of her maid's clothing as quickly as she could, not bothering to stay for lunch, because she had so much to do in Shawcroft. Today she was going to put that money in the bank before she did anything else. It was foolish to leave it lying round in someone else's house, even locked in her trunk. If she hadn't been so upset about her mother's illness and coming to work here again, she'd never have done that.

It wasn't until she opened the outer kitchen door that she realised it was raining. 'Drat!' She ran back upstairs to fetch her raincoat and was shrugging into it at the top of the attic stairs when she heard Mrs Gresham's voice, raised in anger.

She crept down the stairs, listening.

'When we go into that room, you are to hold her down, Tadwyn, while I insert some drops. I want Dr Hilliam to find her disoriented.'

There was silence, then he said, 'Is that really necessary, madam?'

Mrs Gresham's voice rose to a shriek. 'Are you daring to question my orders? If so, you can leave this minute and I'll not be paying you your wages, not when you're dismissed for disobedience and inefficiency.'

'Sorry, madam.'

There was the sound of a key turning in a lock and then Ronnie began screaming for help, clearly struggling against the two of them.

Ellen hesitated, but she knew she was only one person and could do nothing to get Miss Veronica away when there were other servants who could be called in to help, including Gerry, who was working outside today. With tears in her eyes, she went on down the stairs.

'You'll get soaked, riding on that motor—' Glenys began, then saw her expression. 'What's up?'

'They're drugging her again. Can't you hear it?'

'I thought that was a cat.'

'Come outside and listen. You too, Cook.'

The three of them stood by the kitchen door and though the window of Ronnie's room was only open a crack, they could hear her pleas, hear what she was claiming.

'I'm getting help for her,' Ellen said.

'How can you do that?'

'I'm going to see that new policeman. This is 1919, for heaven's sake, not the dark ages. We can't let Mrs Gresham get away with this.'

Ellen waited for them to say something, but when they didn't, when they both looked at the ground, she went outside to pull the tarpaulin off the motorcycle, angry that no one else seemed prepared to do anything to help.

Pel materialised from the shadows and began to help her without a word.

'Thanks. It's so much easier with two.' She pulled

the lead out of her pocket and began to attach it.

'You're sensible to do that. You can't trust some of the people in *this* house.'

She looked at him in surprise. He didn't usually volunteer information. 'Why do you say that?'

Another scream rang out from the bedroom where Ronnie was being kept and Pel jerked and cowered back, hands over his ears. 'What are they doing to her now?' he whispered. 'What are they *doing*?'

'Drugging her again so that she'll appear disoriented when the doctor comes to see her.'

'I thought I wanted to stay here, but now I don't think it'd be a good thing. I wonder if Glenys would come away with me.' He took a few deep, ragged breaths and looked at Ellen, as wide-eyed and trusting as a child. 'Do you think she would if I asked her to marry me?'

Ellen smiled at him. At least one thing was going right in this world of broken promises. 'Yes, of course she would. But how will you support her?'

'I'll find a way. My family will help. They wanted to before but I was too ashamed.'

'Then take their help. You don't want to stay here or leave Glenys on her own here.'

The screams were growing hoarser and Ellen couldn't seem to move until they stopped. She waited a minute longer, then as the silence continued she kick-started the motor. It throbbed and bubbled gently, as if itching to be away. Well, she was itching to leave this place too.

With a wave she drove slowly out of the stable yard.

The air felt fresher away from the house, even though it was starting to rain and the black clouds promised more to come. But the worries about Miss Veronica followed her all the way into town.

Seth was glad to leave at noon for his dinner because Cobbley had been tossing nasty remarks at him all morning. If nothing was happening after the other man came back from lunch, Seth decided that he'd go out and do a patrol of the town centre.

This week couldn't pass quickly enough for him.

It was a relief to enjoy the sane conversation of his hosts as they ate together for once, since Martin was now employing the lad who'd taken a message a few days ago and he was watching the workshop.

'You send him across for some lunch after you get back, love,' Jeanie said. 'You know how hungry lads get. Another helping of pudding, Seth?'

'No, thank you. It was lovely, but I'll fall asleep if I eat too much. Not that there's anything to do at the moment. Cobbley just sits and complains whatever I do, and no one seems to come into the police station. I've never worked anywhere like it.'

Martin hesitated, then said, 'He doesn't make them welcome, that's why. They have to have a good reason to complain before he'll deal with anything. I don't like to tell tales on anyone, and it's best you make up your own mind, but I shall be glad when we have a proper policeman in the town again. You can't even register lost property without him making a fuss, these days. We used to have two bobbies before the war, you know.'

Seth shook his head. 'I can't believe he's kept his job, war or no war. He's not earning his money, that's for sure.'

'There was no one else to do it. And I've heard a few tales about special constables not doing the job properly, so he's not alone.'

Seth sighed. 'Yes. So have I. War turns everything upside-down, doesn't it?'

When he got back to the police station, Cobbley growled at him, 'Where have you been? Here's me with a crisis on my hands and you're missing.'

Seth glanced up at the clock. 'I'm three minutes early getting back from my dinner break, actually.'

'Well, it's not early enough. If I were staying on, I'd make sure you ate your lunch here, where I could get you when I needed you.'

Seth prayed for patience. 'What did you need me for?'

'There's been a burglary out at White Walls Farm. They sent a lad into town to tell me. So I want you to go out and investigate.'

'What sort of burglary?'

'How do I know what sort? That's why I need you to go and find out.'

'But surely the message said more than that.'

'It was just a lad and he slipped off once he'd told me. *I* couldn't go running after him, could I? Anyway, Mick Greeley is the farmer out there and he'll no doubt make a lot more sense than that lad did.'

'How do I get there?'

'Go to the end of Rochdale Road, past the railway

station and carry on till you come to some crossroads. Turn left. It's a lane, no turnings, but about three miles further on you'll come to another crossroad. Turn right there. It leads uphill. The farm is at the top of the lane, you can't miss it, the walls on either side of the gate are painted white.'

'Is there a bicycle I can borrow?'

'What's the matter? Not fit enough to walk a few miles?' Cobbley jeered. 'No there isn't a bicycle. You'll have to buy one from the petty cash when you take over.'

With a sigh Seth went to get his raincoat and set off. He wasn't at all sure about this. Surely no one would send a child to make such a serious complaint? And if they did, they'd write a note. But he couldn't call Cobbley a liar. And at least this would get him out of the station for the afternoon.

He grabbed his overcoat from the hook near the door and set off, lost in thought. After a few minutes the air felt so chill and damp on his face he looked up at the sky. It was definitely going to rain in the next few minutes.

It did. With a sigh, he turned up the collar of his overcoat and continued to tramp out of town. It wasn't the first time he'd been drenched and it wouldn't be the last. There were worse things than getting wet.

18

As Ellen was approaching the town it began to rain in earnest, so she drove more slowly. She'd gone past the figure walking along the side of the road before she realised who it was, but she found a gateway in which to turn the motorcycle.

Seth was waiting for her when she got back to him, smiling in spite of the rain trickling down his face.

'Nice day for a stroll,' she said.

'I've been sent out to White Walls Farm. Apparently there's been a burglary there.'

She frowned. 'Are you sure you've got the name right?'

'White Walls Farm, a Mr Mick Greeley.'

'Well, he is the owner, but no one would ever be able to burgle his house because he has the fiercest watchdogs you've ever seen. They don't bite visitors when he lets them in, but they prowl up and down behind the gate, and if anyone is stupid enough to go inside without waiting for him, the dogs trap them against a wall till he comes out to say it's all right. He's famous for it in the town.'

Seth let out a growl of anger. 'I did wonder if

Cobbley was playing some sort of trick on me. But I can't refuse to go and investigate in case there has been a burglary.' He scowled up at the sky. 'I'm going to get very wet indeed, and *not* in a good cause.'

She smiled at him. 'You said you'd driven motor-cycles in the war, didn't you?'

'Yes. I drove them quite often, actually.'

'Why don't you take this one then? You can be out to the farm and back in an hour or so. You only have to prove the message was a trick, then you can come straight back. I can get the bike back from you at the police station when I'm ready to leave in two or three hours.'

'Are you sure?'

'Of course I am. Get on and I'll drive into town, then you can take the bike.' It felt good to have him so close, right even. She tried to be practical, not to let his closeness distract her. 'But Seth . . . if you have to leave the bike anywhere, take the high tension lead off, just to make sure Jo— no one can steal it.'

'Jory Nelson? You're afraid of him stealing it?'

'I found him sitting on it one day and he'd tried to start it. I prefer to be safe.'

'It's very kind of you and I accept with great relief. And of course I'll do as you ask.'

'I'm happy to lend it to you, Seth. I'm automatic-ally on your side because I don't trust Wes Cobbley.'

'What did he do to bring that tone to your voice when you speak of him?'

'It's not something I talk about. But I had a serious complaint against – someone. And Wes refused to believe me or investigate in any way, because the person's father was a friend of his.'

'Jory again,' Seth said softly, from just behind her.

She'd already told him more than she'd intended, but he was so easy to talk to, especially now when they were sitting so closely together. Besides, she had always felt instinctively that she could trust him. She was almost sorry when they arrived at her mother's house and drew to a halt reluctantly, getting off and turning to smile at him.

He sat there for a moment longer, concern in his eyes. 'If you don't want to talk about it, I won't press you. But if you ever do, or you have any more trouble with that same person, remember that I'm not like Cobbley and that I – care about what happens to you on both a personal level and as a policeman.'

In spite of the rain, they looked at one another in silence for a few moments, then he smiled and used one fingertip to trace a raindrop down her cheek.

Her breath caught in her throat and she put up her hand instinctively to catch hold of his, holding it close to her cheek for a minute.

'When this week is over and I've got things sorted out at the police station, I want to start seeing a lot more of you, Ellen Dawson,' he said softly.

It didn't occur to her to act coy. 'Good. I'd like that.'

The wind grew stronger and wailed around them, dashing water in their faces.

She laughed and let go of his hand. 'Look at us

two, standing here like a pair of idiots getting soaking wet.'

He waited till she'd taken her handbag out of the sidecar, then got back on in the driver's seat.

'Do you need anything about the bike explaining?' she asked.

'No. I've driven this model quite a few times before. I'll be careful with it, don't you worry.'

She watched him drive away and nodded approval. Not that she hadn't believed him when he'd said he could drive a motorcycle, but it was good to have that confirmed, because she thought a lot of her bike. It represented freedom and the new life she was going to build for herself.

Only as he turned the corner did she remember that she'd wanted to tell him about Ronnie. She'd have to wait till he got back now. She knew better than to mention it to Wes.

It had sounded as if Seth was getting serious about her. Did she want that?

Sighing, she turned and went inside the house. She thought she did, but didn't want to become just someone's wife, trapped in a house all day.

Her mother was drowsy and when Ellen reminded her that she had to get her money and nip out to the bank, Dorothy smiled. 'You do that. I'll be more awake when you get home. Bevan's had a couple of restless nights. I heard him get up a few times. He doesn't like sleeping on his own, poor love. Of course, I pretended to be asleep, didn't let him know I'd heard him get up. I always do. He doesn't like fussing over when he can't sleep.'

Ellen kept her tongue between her lips. 'Poor love' was the last thing she'd call that man, who was a brute and a bully, even though he hadn't actually thumped her when she was in his power. But he had sent her away to work at the tender age of fourteen, taken most of her wages and not even made her welcome when she came back to see her mother. Oh, the nights she'd cried herself to sleep at the Hall!

She shook away those memories. 'Well, I'd better get the money then.'

She ran up to the attic, humming to herself. But the sound choked to a halt when she saw the sawn-off edge of the brass padlock. Someone had broken into her trunk and she had no doubt who'd done it, no doubt at all.

She opened the lid and knelt down beside it. She had to check but already knew what she'd find. *Her money was missing!* Even the envelope had gone. She felt physically sick and had to spend a few seconds swallowing back the nausea.

Then she checked everything once more, just to be certain before going downstairs. This was something she didn't intend to keep quiet about, not even to protect her mother.

When she stood in the doorway, her mother looked at her in shock and sat bolt upright in the bed. 'Ellen, whatever's the matter? You're white as a sheet.'

She walked across the room on legs that felt to be

made of wood and sat down on the edge of the bed. 'Did you tell him about my money?'

Fear etched itself on her mother's face and she clasped her bed jacket around her with one frail, shaking hand.

Ellen managed to keep her voice quiet, but it trembled as she spoke. She couldn't help that. 'Did you, mother?'

'Yes. Why?' Dorothy reached out and took her daughter's hand. When Ellen didn't speak, she asked again, 'Why do you ask that?'

'Because he's stolen it!'

Dorothy bent her head and tears rolled down her cheeks. 'Oh, no. Oh, no!' She looked up, 'I'm sorry.'

'You know it's him, don't you?'

'Yes. I didn't know what it was, thought he was just pottering about, doing some repairs. He went out to his shed for tools then came back in again. There were noises and a few thuds. Later he went out to the shed again and I drifted off to sleep. I meant to ask him what he'd been doing because I like to know what's happening to my house, even though I can't get upstairs now.'

Ellen took her hand away from her mother's and clapped it across her mouth, drawing in a long, shuddering breath. She wasn't angry so much as sick with disgust. 'It's theft,' she said at last. 'He's stolen my money and I won't let him get away with it.'

Her mother grabbed her hand quickly. 'You're not going to the police. Please, Ellen, don't do that. I'll make him give it back to you, I promise, and—'

'He'll not give it back, you know he won't, even for you, because the thing he loves most in the world is money. I *am* going to the police. It's the only way I'll get the money back.'

Her mother began to weep, begging incoherently for Ellen to give Bevan a chance to return it.

In the end, because she couldn't bear to see such distress, Ellen gave in. 'All right. I'll go and see him at the shop. But only for your sake. I know it's no use. He'll never willingly give me the money back.' She looked at her mother. 'Will you be all right?'

'Yes. Tell him *I* beg him to give it you back, that it means a lot to me.'

Ellen shrugged. It wouldn't do any good. She knew that already.

Giles set off for Shawcroft in the early afternoon, determined to find Ronnie that night, if he had to check every room in the Hall to do so. Halfway there his car began misfiring, jerking forward then slowing down and finally the engine made a coughing noise and stopped completely. He was out in the country, taking a short cut across the moors, so there was nowhere to go for help.

With a great deal of effort he managed to push his car to the side of the road, then took his overnight bag and set off walking. Rain swept across the moors, black clouds scudded across the sky and the rain grew heavier. Gritting his teeth, he turned up the collar of his raincoat and soldiered on, knowing it was at least ten miles to his destination.

A few minutes later a pony trap drew up beside him and a thin-faced clerical gentleman smiled out at him from beneath a rather inadequate canopy. 'Dreadful day, isn't it? Was that your car about half a mile back?'

'Yes. It's broken down, I'm afraid. I'm heading for Shawcroft. You wouldn't be going in that direction, would you?'

'I am and you're welcome to a lift, but I'm afraid I have to call on two more parishioners on my way back. There's a bus stop at the end of the lane where the second one lives, though, and you may be lucky in catching a bus. If not, I'm afraid you'll have to wait. The old gentleman is dying and wants to talk to me.'

'I'm grateful for any help you can offer me.' Giles climbed up into the cart and settled down on the hard, narrow bench seat. It was going to be a while before they got back to Shawcroft, but at least he would be protected from the worst of the rain and it'd be quicker than walking.

Algie's mother looked out at the weather. 'I think we'll wait until tomorrow to go and see dear Edwina. It's a dreadful day.'

'We won't get wet in the car. And I need to go to France, so I want to go and see Ronnie today.'

For a moment Blanche tried to stare him down, then let out an aggrieved sigh. 'Oh, very well. We'll leave at two.'

'All right. I'll go up and start packing.'

'You're not leaving till you're safely engaged to her.'

'No, Ma.'

In his bedroom he got out a suitcase and put a few things into it, for appearance's sake, then fumbled through the big, old-fashioned cupboard built many years ago to hide an uneven corner. He'd kept his toys in it as a boy, had thought it safe to keep his poetry there. Clearly it wasn't.

He found his old knapsack and packed it with a lot of pauses for thought. His poetry, that went without saying. A couple of favourite books, some changes of underclothing and a couple of spare shirts. Damn! You couldn't fit much in. After some thought, he undressed and put on an extra layer of underclothing. Then he got out his overcoat and filled the pockets with more bits and pieces. There was excuse enough for wearing it with weather like today's.

After that he sneaked down to the shed where the motor car was kept and put his knapsack into the boot of the car, covering it with the travel rug that his mother insisted should be kept there, heaven knew why.

Scholes came out as he was closing the boot. 'Is something wrong, sir?'

'No. Just something I want to put in the post on our way back. Did Ma tell you she wants to use the car today?'

'Yes, sir.' He looked out and shook his head. 'Not a good day for driving.'

'I can drive it if you like.'

'No, sir. That's my job and I'll do it to the best of my ability.'

Algie smiled and clapped him on the back. 'But you'd rather have a horse.'

'Yes, sir. I would. But those days seem to be gone.'

When they got to the Hall, Glenys opened the door to them. She seemed flustered and it was clear to Algie that she'd been crying. He wondered why. Probably Mrs Gresham, who must be a brute to work for.

Glenys showed them into the sitting room and said she'd inform madam.

It was ten minutes before Edwina joined them and they both exclaimed in shock at the sight of her face.

'I had a fall,' she said. 'I'm all right. It looks worse than it feels.'

But Algie had seen scratch marks before and wondered what – or rather who – had caused them. He didn't comment, just asked cheerfully, 'Ronnie around? I'd rather like to speak to her privately.'

'He has a certain question to ask her,' Blanche put in coyly.

Edwina breathed deeply as if containing her annoyance, though why she'd be annoyed, Algie couldn't think.

'I'm afraid she's had a relapse. Tried to do too much and fainted on us. We had to call in the doctor. He gave her something to make her sleep, so unfortunately you can't see her. Come back in a day or two. And I'm really sorry, Blanche, but I know you'll excuse me. I need to lie down myself.'

'Where did you fall?'

'Down the stairs. So silly. I tripped on a bit of loose carpet.'

If she got those scratches falling down stairs, I'm a Dutchman's uncle, Algie thought. He said nothing, but as Scholes was driving them back, turned to his mother and said, 'I have to send a telegram. You can drop me in the village and I'll walk back.'

'In this weather? We'll wait for you.'

He brandished an umbrella at her. 'I can take this. I need some exercise, Ma. I've lost the habit of sitting still all day.'

'Oh, very well.'

In the village Scholes stopped the car and Algie got out. He took a step, keeping the car door open, then turned and called, 'The boot's come open. I'll just make sure it's shut properly before you set off again.'

Shutting the car door, he went and fiddled with the handle of the boot, dropping the knapsack on the ground at his feet before slamming the boot lid shut. Then he picked up the knapsack and held it on the other side of his body as he called, 'It's all right now!'

He watched them drive away, then ran across to the village shop which also doubled as Post Office. But he didn't go inside. He stood at the door and made sure the car hadn't turned back for him before setting off walking into Shawcroft. He took footpaths that led across the countryside, heedless of the mud, worried now about Ronnie.

He reckoned she'd fought her mother and given her those scratches. But something would have to be very wrong to make gentle Ronnie fight the woman she'd feared all her life.

He couldn't go to France yet, not till he'd made sure Ronnie was safe.

But he wasn't staying at home any longer, either, having his mother go through his things and treat him like a naughty little boy.

She might not be able to manage on the small private income which was all *he* had, but he was sure Monique would.

England was stifling him.

And without Pierce, there was nothing to keep him here. All that was left of Pierce was in France, growing in Monique's belly. He'd persuade her to marry him and raise that child to the best of his ability.

Bevan saw his stepdaughter driving her motorcycle along Rochdale Road with that uppity new bobby sitting behind her, pressed against her. Shameless hussy! No young woman should have a man sitting so close unless he was her husband, and even then Bevan didn't think it right for them to be pressed together like that in public. Why, their bodies were probably rubbing against one another!

He smiled grimly as he served one of his best customers. If Ellen was going to visit her mother, she'd soon find out what he'd done. And serve her right, too.

It was about a quarter of an hour before she burst into the shop and he was glad it wasn't busy just then. Even though her accusations were false, he didn't want his customers hearing her make them. He held one hand up as she opened her mouth. 'Wait!' He looked meaningfully at the lad standing in the corner.

She glared at him but closed her mouth.

'Take those deliveries out now,' he told his apprentice, then locked the shop door behind him and put up the 'Back in ten minutes' sign before turning round to look at her.

'You've stolen my money,' she said.

'It's not stealing. A parent has a right to a child's earnings.'

'It *is* stealing. I'm not a child. I'm twenty-six years of age and a full adult in the eyes of the law, so unless you give me that money back, I'll go to the police and accuse you officially of theft.'

He shrugged. 'I think you'll find that the law agrees with me.' The law in Shawcroft, anyway. And if the law of the land didn't, then it should.

'My mother knows what you did. It's only for her sake that I'm giving you a chance to return my money.'

He was angry at the scornful way she was talking to him. 'Why did you have to tell *her*? Have you no more sense than to upset a sick woman like that?'

'Some things can't be hidden and shouldn't be. One of them is theft. This is not just a pound or two, but my whole life's savings. So I'll tell the whole town about it if I have to because I intend to get my money back'

'If you say anything, I'll charge you with slander.'

'It's not slander when it's the truth. And by the way, my mother sent you a message.'

'Oh?'

'She said she *begged* you to give it me back, that it would mean a lot to her. So if anyone is going to upset a dying woman's last few months on this earth, it's you.'

'I don't believe she said that, or only because she doesn't understand the situation. She'll be on my side in this when I tell her I'm allowed to do it. Dorothy will *always* be on my side, not yours.'

'Not this time. You've gone too far. It's not even as if you need my money, because everyone in the town knows you've plenty tucked away. My mother won't support your stealing my money.'

'Stop saying that! It isn't stealing.'

'There's no use talking to you.' She swung round and fumbled with the shop door.

He grabbed hold of her and dragged her back, shaking her hard then holding her at arm's length. 'Now listen to me, young woman, and be sensible for once. You have to live in this town. So does your dying mother. Making a fuss about this will only bounce back on your own head. And it'll upset your mother, may even shorten her life.'

'Then give me my money back!'

'It's *not* your money.' He let go of her, opened the door, and flourished a mocking bow, smiling as she walked past him. He watched her stride along the street.

She wouldn't let the matter drop, he was sure, not yet, anyway. But he had outwitted her this time, prepared the path before he'd taken the money. She'd learn that she couldn't go against him and his friends. Everyone else in the town knew that.

Jory saw Ellen hurrying along the street, but she didn't see him and bumped right into him. When he realised those were tears not rain running down her face, he grabbed hold of her to stop her moving on. 'What's wrong? Who's upset you.'

'My stepfather. He's stolen my savings.'

'Is that all?'

She stared at him angrily. 'What do you mean, *is that all?* It's all the money I have in the world and I saved it shilling by shilling during the war.'

'Look, love, a few pounds don't matter. I've plenty for both of us. After we're married—'

'*A few pounds?* There were sixty-three pounds ten shillings locked in my trunk and he took every last penny.'

Jory gaped at her. 'That much?'

'Yes. That much. I'm very careful with my money.'

'What are you going to do about it?'

'I'm going to lay a complaint against him at the police station. I asked him to return it to me – for my mother's sake – and he refused, so now I'm going to tell everyone he's a thief.'

Jory grabbed hold of her again. 'Don't. Let *me*

speak to him. I'll tell him he can keep a few pounds and get the rest back for you.'

'Why should he keep any of it? It's my money.' She tried to shake his hand off, but couldn't. 'I'll do what I think best. You're as bad as he is. There's not much to choose between you. And I am *not* marrying you, not now, not under any circumstances. I hate the mere touch of you after what you did.'

Her voice was burred with so much loathing as she looked down at his hands that he slackened his grip instinctively.

'I'm sorry about that time,' he said desperately. 'I've been sorry ever since I did it. Surely you can give a chap a second chance?'

'Never, ever! What you did was unforgivable. I hate you and I always will.' She shoved him away and walked off along the street, her feet drumming on the damp paving stones, her whole body radiating anger.

Well, he was angry too. It was one thing to let Bevan Halsopp have a few pounds in return for his help in persuading Ellen to marry him, but not that much money. Jory could do a lot with sixty pounds. Only this morning he'd found out how little there was left in the family business kitty, couldn't believe his father had wasted so much when he'd been raking in plenty of money with the black-market stuff. And what did he mean by 'unexpected expenses' and 'paying folk to keep quiet'? If his mother hadn't intervened, Jory would have got the full story out of the stupid old bugger. He'd wait till she was out and try again.

He walked along to the shop and banged open the door. Bevan looked up from the chopping bench behind the counter, smiling at him as if there was nothing wrong. 'You can't keep all the money,' Jory cried. 'Not that much.'

'Finders keepers. I've got it now and I'm not giving it up to anyone. Besides, you said her motorcycle would be enough for you and I could keep the money. We had an agreement.' Bevan didn't stop his meticulous sectioning of a lamb carcase.

'I didn't know she had so much.'

'Well, she hasn't got it now, has she? And a parent has a right to a child's money.'

'She's not your child. I think you'd better change your mind because she's just stormed off to the police station.'

With a smile Bevan continued his precise work. 'Wes knows to expect her. We've agreed what he'll say and do.'

'What about that new policeman? You won't get him on your side.'

'I wouldn't even try. He's been sent out on a fool's errand, won't be back till evening. Before he returns, it'll all be settled. You'll see.' He looked at the window and saw a customer approaching, so went to open the door for her, muttering to Jory, 'You'd better go and get that motorcycle while she's busy. Or was she riding it?'

'No, she was walking.'

'Now's your chance, then. It'll be outside our house. You can drive it away. No one will stop you.'

Jory left the shop but didn't take his advice. He was already in Ellen's bad books, so he wasn't going to add stealing something from her to the list of offences. Anyway, he could wait for the motorcycle. It occurred to him that if he waited a little while, she might need his help in dealing with Wes. She'd see then that he was on her side.

But he still reckoned Halsopp was going too far, taking all her money. She must have been very careful to have put that much away. She'd make a perfect wife, maybe even be able to help him in the business. His mother had no more idea of how to do the accounts than how to fly to the moon. Nor did his fool of a father.

Ellen stopped for a moment at the bottom of the slope that led up to the police station. She wiped the tears away and told herself to calm down, but she couldn't. This was too important to her. It'd do no good to burst into the police station and start shouting at her stepfather's friend. She had to appear calm, even if she was churning with fury inside. Her best plan would be to speak firmly and insist on Cobbley doing something to get her money back.

She knew perfectly well that Bevan had no right to it. Did he think she was stupid? Probably. Or that she'd give in? Well, she wouldn't. Her mother had never stood up to him but Ellen would.

She realised suddenly that people were staring at her as they passed and that it was raining quite heavily again. Still, she didn't move until she felt more in charge of her emotions.

When she opened the door of the police station, she shivered involuntarily, remembering the last time she had come here in tears, hurting from Jory's rough handling. She'd hammered on the house door and Cobbley had sent her to wait outside the police station, had taken his time coming out to her.

He'd listened to her, then laughed and told her she shouldn't have led young Jory on and it was her own fault if things had gone too far. She wouldn't let him dismiss her complaint this time, though. Or at least, if he did, she'd go over his head. Seth would tell her who to see in Manchester, because he wouldn't be able to override Cobbley till the older man stood down. And by then it might be too late to get the money back.

There was a young fellow standing by the counter, someone she didn't know, so she waited her turn behind him.

Cobbley looked at her. 'I won't be a moment.'

He was five minutes, actually, then he smiled at the young man and said, 'If you'll wait over there, Dennis, we'll finish this off later.' Then he turned to Ellen and his smile faded. 'Can I help you?'

'I want to report a theft.'

'Oh? What of?'

'Money. *My* money.'

'Was your handbag stolen?'

'No, the money was locked in my trunk at my mother's house. It was in the attic.'

'Just a moment and I'll get out the form.' He fiddled under the counter for ages, then came up empty-handed. 'That new young fellow must have put them away. Better tell me what happened and I'll write it all down later.'

So she explained in detail then waited.

He looked at her and shook his head as if she was being stupid. 'Bevan Halsopp is your stepfather, isn't he?'

'What has that got to do with anything?'

'Parents have a right to their children's money, always have had, always will. You'll have to take this matter up with him.'

'That's not true and you know it. He's *not* my real parent and anyway, I'm over twenty-one.'

He smiled as he added insult to injury. 'Old maid, you are. You'd do better finding yourself a good man and getting wed, rather than wasting your time on wild-goose chases like this one.'

'Are you going to help me or not?'

'I can't. The law is the law. Better go back and apologise to your stepfather, then start behaving yourself. This isn't London. This is a town where we prefer the old ways, where we look after one another.'

He stared her right in the eye as he said that and she knew with a sick feeling of disgust that once again he was refusing to help her. Bevan must have told him what he'd done.

And because she felt like bursting into tears, she spun round on her heel and rushed out.

There was no sign of Seth and her motorcycle, so

she walked back to her mother's house, taking the back way to avoid passing her stepfather's shop. She went through the gate at the end of the yard, using the kitchen door and leaning against the wall once she was inside, tears running down her face.

'Ellen? Is that you?'

'Yes, Mum.' But her voice broke on the words.

'Come in here and tell me.'

She went into the bedroom and found her mother sitting up in bed.

'What did Bevan say?'

'He said he had a right to the money and he doesn't, Mum, he definitely doesn't.'

'You gave him my message?'

'Yes.'

Dorothy stared down at the bedspread, then looked at her daughter. 'So did you go to the police?'

'Yes. And Wes Cobbley told me Bevan had a right to my money and he couldn't do anything about the theft. I know he was lying, Mum. The law doesn't give Bevan a right to my money.'

'They'll have got together on this. They've been doing business together all through the war, or at least Bevan has been doing business with that Eddie Nelson and Cobbley has been closing his eyes to what they were doing. Black-market food mainly, I think. Wes Cobbley will turn a blind eye to anything if you pay him enough.'

She sighed and closed her eyes, reached out for her daughter's hand, held it tightly. 'I haven't had the energy to say anything for a while now and Bevan wouldn't have listened to me, anyway. He never does.' Another sigh, then she said in a thread of a voice, 'I seem to have been ill for a very long time.'

'I'm sorry for upsetting you, Mum. Don't worry. I'll think of something to do.'

Dorothy opened her eyes. 'I'm not sorry you told me. But I am upset about what Bevan did. He cares about me, I know he does, but I don't like him being a thief, especially when he steals from you.'

She was silent for so long that Ellen had time to wipe her eyes and pull herself together a bit. 'I don't know what to do next,' she confessed. She wasn't sure whether Seth would help her against one of his colleagues. Policemen usually stuck together in her experience.

Dorothy opened her eyes. 'I do. And my plan is probably the best way out for everyone.'

Seth followed the directions carefully, but still got lost on the way, so it took him longer than he'd expected. In the end, he decided that Cobbley must have deliberately misdirected him. When he did at last find White Walls Farm there was no mistaking the place, not only because of the white-painted stretches of wall but also because of the huge black and brown dogs snarling on the other side of the gate. There was no way he was going inside with them there, so he squeezed the bulb of the horn set on one gatepost, producing several loud honks, and waited.

He had to sound the horn several times more

before an irate man came to the gate. 'What are you making that racket for? It's enough to put the hens off laying.'

The dogs quietened down as soon as their owner appeared, so Seth risked getting off the motorcycle. 'Good afternoon, sir. Are you Mick Greeley?'

'I am. What's it to you?'

'I'm Seth Talbot, the new policeman who's taking over in Shawcroft.' He offered his hand and after rubbing his own on his corduroy trousers, the man shook it firmly.

'Wes Cobbley sent me out here to investigate the report of a burglary.'

Mick gaped at Seth. 'Burglary? I always said the man was a half-wit and now he's just proved me right. There's been no burglary here, nor will there be with these two to guard us.' He bent to pat his dogs, then looked at Seth again. 'When does that fellow retire?'

'End of the week, sir.'

'Think you can do any better than him?'

'I'm sure of it.'

'Well, it'd be hard to do worse. We've had sheep stealing and even cattle taken over the past few years. He did nothing, so I stopped reporting it. Us farmers up here took matters into our own hands, so the thieves went further afield.' He stared into the distance for a moment or two, then said gruffly, 'One of my friends was killed defending his stock.'

'I heard something about that, sir, but no details.'

'Come in and have a cup of tea and I'll tell you.

You look as if you've a bit more between the ears than Cobbley. He always was slow-thinking.'

So Seth spent an hour drinking tea, praising Mrs Greeley's cake, and obtaining more details about the murder than Inspector Dunham had given him. He then got on the motorcycle, hoping he hadn't delayed Ellen too long, but it had been too useful an encounter to leave abruptly. If she got in trouble with her mistress, he'd go out to the Hall and explain matters.

The rain had cleared up a bit and Greeley's instructions for getting back to Shawcroft worked perfectly, so he enjoyed the ride back.

19

Ellen stared at her mother in surprise then said firmly, 'What do you mean, best for everyone? Don't tell me to forget it and let him have the money, because I won't.'

'That wasn't what I was going to tell you. Bevan hasn't had time to put the money in the bank. He had to get off to work early because they were delivering some sheep carcasses. It's good that meat is so much more plentiful already, isn't it? Not that we ever suffered during the war, because Bevan was always able to get meat for us . . . What was I saying, dear?'

'That you knew what I should do about the money.'

'Oh, yes. You should just take the money back, forget about accusing Bevan and put your savings straight into the bank.'

'He knows the bank manager, doesn't he?'

'Yes, they're old friends.'

'So if I put it in that bank, his friend will probably take the money out of my account and put it into his.'

'Oh, I don't think they're allowed to do that, dear.'

'I'd have thought policemen were sworn to uphold the law, but they don't do that here, so who knows what the local bank manager does.' Ellen didn't trust any friend of her stepfather's. 'Anyway, how can I take the money back when I don't know where he's put it?'

'That's the whole point. I know.'

'*You?*'

'Yes.' Dorothy coloured slightly and began to fiddle with the bedspread again. 'I used to be a good housewife before . . . this.' She grimaced and waved a hand at herself.

'There was none better,' Ellen agreed, forcing the words past a lump in her throat.

'I even swept out Bevan's workshop every week, couldn't bear anything to be dirty or untidy. So I couldn't help noticing . . .'

'Go on.'

'I feel so disloyal telling you, but then it was because I mentioned your money that Bevan took it, so it's only fair.' She dabbed at a tear.

Ellen held back her impatience. Her mother never could tell a story quickly or get straight to the point.

'Anyway, he's laid bricks on the floor in the workshop to make it cleaner underfoot and one of them wasn't lying flat, so I lifted it up, thinking some dirt had got underneath it. And that's when I saw the cash box. I didn't open it, of course, but since a bit of dirt had indeed fallen in, I scraped it out and put the brick back just as I'd found it. He never knew I'd seen it, well, he never said anything and I think he would have. So that's where he hides his money and yours is probably still there. It's worth a try, anyway.'

A little surge of hope ran through Ellen. She tried

to tell herself not to get too excited. Bevan surely wouldn't have kept her money on the premises? But still, her mother was right: it wouldn't hurt to look. 'Where exactly is this brick?'

'Underneath the workbench, to the left.' Dorothy closed her eyes to picture it. 'Not the brick farthest back, but the one next to the back and it's about two bricks from the left. Or was it three? No, I'm sure it was two.'

Ellen stood up. 'No time like the present, is there?'

'No. Oh, I nearly forgot. There's a key to his cash box. It's hanging in our bedroom, inside Bevan's wardrobe, on a little hook behind his suits.'

Ellen went upstairs, feeling a sense of guilt at searching her stepfather's wardrobe, but then, he'd searched her trunk. She found the key and unhooked it with a hand that trembled, praying this would help her to retrieve her money.

When she went down, she showed it to her mother.

'Yes, that's the one. But be very careful, dear. Put everything back exactly as he left it.'

Bevan was dying to find out what had happened at the police station, but trade had been brisk after Ellen left the shop. So he waited until things went quiet, as they usually did at this time of the afternoon on a Monday, before slipping out to see his friend Wes.

He pulled off his blood-stained apron, washed his hands carefully and grabbed his overcoat and bowler hat. As he strode along Rochdale Road, he felt flushed with success. He hoped Ellen had caused a fuss and

Wes had had to lock her in the cell. She hadn't come past the shop again, that was sure, or he'd have noticed her. He was never too busy to notice who went past.

When he entered the police station, he found his old friend perched on the stool as usual and a young man he recognised as a relative of Jory's sitting yawning in the corner. 'Well, how did it go?'

Wes looked at the young man. 'Could you just go and fetch me a cup of tea from the house, Dennis lad? And one for yourself, of course.' Only when the two older men were alone did Wes tell how Ellen had come in. 'And it all went as you said it would, only more peaceful-like. In the end she just turned and walked away.'

'She didn't make a fuss at all?'

'No. Well, only shouted at me a bit. I had young Dennis here ready to help me if she did get violent – you owe me half a crown for that, by the way – but like I said, she just turned and went out. She looked very upset, though.'

'It's not like her to give up so easily.'

'Well, I haven't seen her since, so she must have gone home. Probably got on that bike of hers and rode back to the Hall to have a good cry. My wife said she saw her standing out in the rain before she came in, looking near to tears.'

Bevan chuckled. 'Well, she won't have found her bike at home, either. I told Jory to take it. When he marries her, it'll be his, so he may as well start using it now. What does a housemaid need with a motor-bike? He can bring her into town on it when she comes to see her mother. It's just sitting there doing nothing the rest of the time. I don't like to see things wasted.'

Wes frowned. 'He should have waited till they were engaged to take it. Talbot will be in charge after this week, and *he* won't hold back if she makes a complaint against Jory. A proper rules merchant, that Talbot is.'

'Ah, you worry too much.' Bevan looked at the clock on the wall. 'I think I've just time to go back home and see how Dorothy is.'

He strode down the street, annoyed when it came on to rain and he realised he'd forgotten his umbrella. He didn't go back for it because he wanted to make sure the money was safe. He should have taken it to work and hidden it there.

Ellen went out to the workshop and soon found the loose brick. She pulled out the cash box and unlocked it, using the key her mother had given her. Inside, lying right on top, was the envelope with her money inside. She counted it quickly, letting out a low groan of relief when she found it was all there.

Shoving the brick back, she hurried into the house clutching the envelope. 'I found it.'

'Good.' Dorothy glanced at the clock. 'Go and put the key back.'

Ellen put the money on the bed and ran upstairs. When she came down she found her mother fingering the money.

'You must have saved really hard. I'm proud of you, dear. But I think you should return to the Hall straight away now, so that he can't catch you.'

'I can't do that yet. I lent my bike to Seth.'

'Seth?'

'The new policeman. He's the one who helped me when I broke down coming over the moors.' She could feel her cheeks growing warmer and hoped her mother hadn't noticed.

'I didn't know you were on such good terms with him.'

Ellen shrugged. 'I've met him a couple of times at Uncle Martin's. I told you, he's lodging there.' She didn't like the knowing look on her mother's face, so stood up. 'You're right, though. I'll go to the police station and wait for Seth to come back, and I'll go there along the back lanes, so that I don't bump into Bevan.' She went to kiss her mother.

'I hope all goes well with you and your young man,' Dorothy said. 'Do try not to be so bossy with him. Men don't like that.'

Ellen didn't reply. She didn't think she was bossy, she just stood up for herself and she was going to continue to do so. She'd never marry a man who wanted to boss her around, never.

After her daughter had left, Dorothy slid down in bed, feeling exhausted now. It was going to be all right. Ellen had got her money back and Dorothy would tell Bevan that he was not to take it from her again.

Algie breathed a sigh of relief as he arrived in Shawcroft without anyone recognising him. He kept his overcoat collar turned up and his hat pulled down as he made his way to the Royal Fleece.

He went round to the kitchen door and rapped on it, relieved when John Deane opened it.

'Mr—'

'Shh.' Algie put one finger to his lips. 'I don't want anyone to know I'm here. I'm a bit old for it, I know, but I'm running away from home and I don't want my mother chasing after me and making one of her grand fusses.'

'Come in. I'll take you up the back stairs.'

When they were in one of the guest bedrooms, John looked at his dripping wet companion. 'You'll want to get out of those wet things.'

'Not yet. I've another errand to run. But when I get back, I'd be grateful if you could lend me a dressing-gown and ask your wife to dry my clothes for me.'

Since John had known Algie since he was a lad, and helped him and Pierce out of scrapes many a time, the publican grinned. 'What crime have you committed this time?'

Algie hesitated then told the truth. 'I don't want to marry Veronica Gresham and I find I can't settle down here. There's a woman back in France who's expecting my baby. Ma tried to keep that information from me. But I found out and I want to marry her.'

John looked at him with a slight frown. 'A woman?'

The air was suddenly filled with tension.

'What do you mean by that?' Algie asked.

'No offence meant, but I've a cousin like you, so I can recognise a man who doesn't fancy women. I guessed it quite a while ago, before the war. Makes no difference to me, but you're right to keep it quiet, the law being what it is.'

Algie stared at the carpet. 'It's Pierce's baby, actually. I loved him but he wasn't – like me. The woman's in trouble and I'm hoping she'll marry me. It's all I can do for him – now.'

John nodded. 'All right, Algie lad. I'll help you get away. I can drive you to the next town, if you like, then no one will see you getting on the train.'

'I accept with gratitude. But I can't get away till I make sure Ronnie is all right. I think that damned mother of hers is keeping her locked up at the Hall.'

More silence, then John frowned. 'I heard Dr Hilliam went out to see her this morning. My wife saw him come back, said he looked upset. We thought it was because Miss Veronica was ill.'

'No, she's all right – or she would be if she could get away from her mother.' He looked down at himself ruefully. 'I'm not the hero type. Never have been strong. But I thought I should talk to the doctor, beg him to help Ronnie. He's a decent fellow, wouldn't you think?'

'Yes, but his wife sets a lot of store on being accepted at the Hall.'

'I'm afraid she won't be after this if he does the right thing by Ronnie. I'll go and see him, but can I come back here and stay the night before I take you up on your offer? I can't leave till I'm sure Ronnie's all right.'

'Yes, of course you can. I'll tell Mavis. And we'll find you some old clothes to wear while we dry those.'

'Thanks. I'll go out the back way, if you don't mind.'

When Bevan didn't see any sign of the motorcycle outside the house, he smiled to think of Jory taking it. Ellen wasn't going to need it for a while, that was sure. She could go into that cell overnight, if she continued to make a fuss. He'd outwitted her today, though that would probably make her lose her job at the Hall. Which wasn't necessarily a bad thing. If she'd no money and no job, she'd have to turn to Jory.

He let himself in quietly via the kitchen door and crept through to peep into his wife's bedroom. But she was still asleep. He stood looking at her, blinking away tears, upset at how thin and frail she was.

He crept out again and went to the shed. He'd go and put the money in the bank this very afternoon. There would just be time if he hurried.

When he knelt beside the workbench the first thing he saw was a smear of dirt on its leg, then he realised that the brick that hid his cash box was crooked. He stiffened for a minute, staring at it. He never put it back carelessly, so someone must have been here. Lifting the brick, he took out the cash box and found it locked as usual. Taking his key from his waistcoat pocket, he unlocked it and cursed long and fluently when he saw that the envelope was no longer there. Somehow she'd found the money and taken it back.

Well, she wasn't keeping it!

Only how had she known where to find it? And how had she got the key?

He realised there was only one way and felt a deep sense of betrayal. Putting the box carefully back into the hole, aligning the brick just so, he went back into the house, this time making no attempt to keep quiet.

He flung open the door of the front room. 'Why did you do it, Dorothy?'

She shrank back, pulling the bedcovers up to her chin.

He took a step forward. 'Why did you tell her where the money was? And how did she get hold of the key?'

'I told her because it wasn't right for you to steal her money. And I've always known where you keep the spare key, just as I heard the noise you made in the attic the night the money vanished. I've not lost my sense of hearing because I'm ill and before that, I used to know what there was in every square inch of my own home.'

'I never thought you'd go against me.'

'I never thought you'd steal from my daughter.'

He thumped one hand down on the bedside table. 'It's *not* stealing. I've been a father to that girl and anything she earns is mine by right.'

Dorothy shook her head, tears running down her wasted cheeks. 'You've never been a father to her, Bevan, we both know that. I've let her down in the past, allowed you to ride roughshod over us both because I'm weak. But I'm not letting her down now. This may be the last thing I can do for her. And if you love me, you'll leave things be from now on.'

'She's not taking my money!'

'It's *her* money, Bevan, *hers*. And I'm pleading with you to—'

He swung round.

'Stop! Where are you going?'

'I'm going after her. I'm going to get my money back!'

'No, Bevan, no! *Bevan!*' She sat up, swung her feet over the edge of the bed and staggered to the door after him, but by the time she got there he'd left the house and although she called down the street, he didn't even turn his head. Clutching the doorpost she began to weep. A neighbour came out and hurried over to her, helping her back inside the house.

'No, I'll be all right now. Thank you so much. Sometimes I forget and try to do too much,' she assured the neighbour. 'Me and Bevan we just – had a little quarrel.'

When she was alone, she fell back on to the pillows, weeping. She knew now that he loved money more than her. Well, if he accused Ellen of theft, she'd testify in court if necessary that she'd heard him stealing her daughter's savings.

But it was a sad way to end your life, falling out with the man you loved, torn between him and the daughter you'd neglected. She wept for a long time then fell into a restless sleep.

Ellen ran along the back lanes behind the houses, ignoring the rain beating in her face. She slowed down a little when she saw a woman huddled under an umbrella stop to stare at her, then speeded up again once she was round the corner. She could get nearly all the way to the police station by this route, just crossing one or two side streets. She was hoping desperately that Seth would be there with her motor-bike.

But he wasn't.

She stopped just inside the back alley, panting, trying to keep out of sight of the police station. There was no shelter nearby, so there was nothing she could do now but wait and put up with the rain.

Surely Seth would be back soon! It didn't take all that long to drive out to White Walls Farm and back.

Jory saw someone dressed in brown hurry across from one back lane to the next in what could only be described as a furtive manner. He recognised that outfit, so stopped and handed the reins of the donkey cart to the lad sitting beside him. 'Take him home. You know how to unharness him and be sure you wipe him down properly. I'll help you unload later.'

He was already running towards the lane even as he issued the last instruction. When he saw Ellen at the far end, running hell for leather, he wondering what was going on. As she disappeared from sight he ran after her, heedless of how much noise he made.

As he turned the corner, he bumped into her, grabbing her or he'd have sent her spinning. 'What's wrong?'

She glared at him and shoved him away. 'Why are you following me? Go away and leave me alone!'

He looked at her face. 'You're upset. I want to help.'

'Whether I'm upset or not is none of your business.'

'Well, I'm making it my business. Aw, come on. I care about you, Ellen love. Let me help.'

'You care only about yourself – and perhaps about money too, if you're anything like the other Nelsons. You lot don't care how you come by it, whether you break the law or not, just as long as you get it. Look at the way your father's been behaving during the war, running black-market goods. I call that being a traitor.'

He wasn't going to listen to her insulting his father. 'Well, we can't all be Miss Perfects like you, can we? Running off to London with titled do-gooders. I haven't asked what you got up to in London, but I'm sure you had a few little adventures down there with the men you were working with. But perhaps you think that sort of thing's *patriotic*?'

She stared at him open-mouthed. 'What do you mean by that?'

'Halsopp told me you'd been enjoying yourself in London. Well, it stands to reason you didn't act like a nun while you were there, doesn't it?'

'He knows nothing of what I did in London, and nor do you.'

'Look, love, things were different during the war. I do understand that. But *you* ought to realise that being in the army, not knowing if I'd be dead the next week, is why I forced you that time. Now the war's over we can start living normal lives once more, and that means you and me getting together again, forgiving one another.' He took hold of her arm and this time wouldn't let go.

'There's nothing for you to forgive me for.' She tried to pull away, panicking for a moment as she remembered that other time, how strong he'd been.

He saw the sudden fear in her face and would have pulled her into his arms to reassure her, only he saw Bevan Halsopp running towards them. Damn the man! He was always poking his nose in where it wasn't wanted, seemed to have got some sort of hold over Jory's father.

'Hold on to her, lad!' Bevan panted, coming to a halt beside them and grabbing her other arm.

She threw Jory an accusing glance. 'Now, see what you've done.'

'What's the matter, Mr Halsopp?'

'She's took my money, the bitch.' He reached out to fumble in Ellen's clothing and when Jory jerked her back away from him, Bevan shouted, 'Let me get it from her.'

'It's not your money, it's mine!' Ellen yelled. 'You're a thief, you are, and if we had a proper policeman in charge of this town, you'd be locked up by now.'

'Let me talk to her, Bevan,' Jory pleaded. 'No need for any violence.'

Bevan lunged at her again. 'You can talk as much as you like after I've got my money back.'

Jory pushed himself in front of her. 'Get your hands off her.'

But their altercation had drawn attention to them and attracted a few spectators. This had alerted Wes, who had puffed out of the police station and was now walking across towards them.

He turned to the bystanders. 'Right, everyone, you can get on with your business now. I'll see to this.'

Some of them moved, others didn't, so he roared at them again, threatening to lock them up for loitering and obstructing police business. Then, when the area near the police station was clear, he turned back to Bevan. 'What's up?'

'She's took my money,' Bevan said at once.

'It's *my* money!' she insisted, but she might as well have been talking to the wall.

Wes smiled. 'Dear me, she has been a silly girl, hasn't she? Bring her inside, Jory lad.'

She pulled backwards away from them. 'I've not done anything and I'm not going anywhere with you two.'

'You were eager enough to come inside earlier,' Wes said. He looked at Jory. 'Keep a-hold of her. We don't want thieves running loose in the town.'

Ellen tried again to pull away. 'I haven't stolen anything. I've only taken my own money back, money I told you about earlier, money *he* stole from me.'

'Resisting arrest is a serious charge,' Wes said. 'Bring her inside.'

'Don't argue with them,' Jory whispered. 'You'll only make it worse. I'll see what I can do to help you.'

'I don't want help from you. You're as bad as them.'

To his dismay she fought them all the way into the station, yelling out at the top of her voice, accusing her stepfather of stealing her money till Bevan put one meaty hand over her mouth. She was a tall woman and strong, and she made it difficult for the two men to move her, but when Wes shouted for Dennis to come and help, a third man came out of the police station. He picked up her feet and then there was nothing she could do to prevent them carrying her inside.

Jory stepped back. He felt sorry for her, didn't want to be part of this, but his father was too deeply involved to upset these men.

'I'll get the handcuffs,' Wes said and pulled them out of the top drawer, where he'd had them ready. 'Hold her arms behind her and I'll fasten them on her.'

When the handcuffs were locked in place, Ellen still stared at them defiantly and when her stepfather laughed, she shouted, 'You *are* a thief, Bevan Halsopp! And my mother knows it now.'

'How dare you upset Dorothy!' He slapped her across the face and drew back his hand to do it again, but Jory grabbed his arm.

'You don't lay another finger on her or you'll have me to answer to.'

Bevan breathed deeply and let his arm fall.

Everyone looked at Wes, who cleared his throat and said formally, 'You say she stole some money from you, Mr Halsopp?'

'Yes. Search her. She's not had time to get rid of it.'

Wes got a gloating look on his face as he took a step forward.

Jory saw her shudder and look as if she felt sick. Wes's smile broadened. Jory suddenly remembered that look on men's faces from the war, the look that said they wanted to use a woman, make free of her body by force. 'You're not touching her.' He turned to Ellen. 'You can tell me where it is and I'll only touch the money, not you. You'd better do it. They'll not treat you as gently.'

A sob escaped her. 'But it *is* my money.'

'Sometimes, love, you can't win. Sometimes the other fellows have all the aces.' Out of the corner of his eye, he saw Bevan stir impatiently. 'Where is it?'

'*My* money is in my coat pocket. And if you take it out, you're helping them steal it from me.'

He sighed and opened her outer coat. He didn't want to do it, but there were three of them to one of him and he still hadn't got to the bottom of what his father was afraid of, so didn't dare cross them at this stage. He hated the way she flinched from his touch and shuddered as he put his fingers into her pocket to pull out the envelope. And as he stood holding it, she looked at him with such loathing and disgust he felt ashamed. What had he come to, stealing a lass's life savings?

'That's it!' Bevan reached out one hand for it.

Jory pulled his hand back, hesitating.

Wes leaned on the counter. 'For your father's sake, you'd better consider what you're doing, lad, and whose side you're on. If we told what we knew about him, he'd hang.'

Jory stared at him in shock. 'What do you mean?'

'He hasn't told you, has he? Well, ask him. In the meantime don't upset us.'

Jory forced a smile to his face. 'I'm on your side, of course I am. I just feel sorry for the poor lass.'

'Well, don't!' Bevan advised him. 'She's got to learn her place. She'll make you a better wife once she does.'

Jory looked at Ellen, shaking his head slightly as if to say he was helpless to do anything.

'Cowards and thieves, the lot of you!' she said.

'Shut up!' Wes said. 'Or we'll gag you. Now, Mr Halsopp, is this your money?'

'Yes, it is. It was stolen from me this afternoon.'

'And we found it on her person, so she must have taken it.'

'Yes.'

Wes looked at Ellen again. 'Well, young woman, are you going to behave sensibly and stop trying to accuse one of the town's leading citizens of theft, or do we have to lock you up for theft *and* slander?'

She stood taller, squared her shoulders and looked them all in the eyes. 'I'll not change my story, not for anything. Because it's true. That's *my* money and I can prove it.'

'You'd better lock her up, Wes,' Bevan said. 'Give her time to come to her senses. When she finds out what it's like to be shut away, thinks of being locked up for years, she'll soon realise what has to be.'

Jory couldn't stop staring at Ellen. She was magnificent. Suddenly he knew she wouldn't cave in and wondered what they would do to her if she didn't withdraw her accusation. He'd better go home and confront his father straight away, find out what they knew about the old man. They'd hurt her enough and he wasn't going to let them hurt her any more if he could help it.

Wes put one hand on Ellen's shoulder and she shook him off. With a nasty smile, he took hold of a fistful of her hair and dragged her towards the side door. 'Someone open that for me, then open the nearest cell door.'

As she continued to struggle, he yanked her head back, banging it on purpose against the door post. It made him feel good to see the tears of pain in her eyes. There were all sorts of ways to tame prisoners. He'd not forgotten how it'd been in the old days. Policemen had some respect then, were in charge, should still be now. Well, he wasn't going to finish his days as a policeman by letting a woman get the better of him. Damned if he was.

He threw Ellen into the cell so hard that she fell, banging her head against the edge of the wooden bench on the way down. 'You'll stay here till you change your mind, young woman,' he said and slammed the door on her.

When Wes went back outside, Bevan and he shook hands, then they both turned to Jory.

'You have to stand by your friends,' Bevan said.

Jory nodded. 'I know. I'm just – a bit fond of her. Well, I'd better get going. I left the lad in charge of the cart.'

After he'd left, Wes reached under the counter. 'Anyone feel like a tot of whisky?'

Both men nodded.

Feeling better about the world than he had for a long time, Wes poured them all a generous measure, lifted his own teacup and said, 'Here's to old friends!'

His second drink was to 'Old ways.'

Bevan winked at Dennis. 'I'll get back to the shop now. You keep an eye on things here – and let me know if there's any more news about *her*.' He jerked his head in the direction of the cells.

When the door of the cell slammed on her, Ellen lay on the floor, half stunned by the fall. It was a few moments before she even tried to move and even longer before she succeeded in pulling herself to her feet because they'd handcuffed her hands behind her.

She leaned sideways against the wall as the room spun round her, panting with the effort. When it stopped spinning she eased herself carefully down on to the end of the hard, narrow bench. She tried to think what to do but her head felt muzzy and it took her a while to admit to herself that there was nothing she *could* do. She was totally in their power.

And if Jory hadn't stopped them, what else would they have done to her? Might still do to her? A wave of revulsion shuddered through her at the look on Wes Cobbley's puffy old face as his wrinkled, age-spotted hand reached out towards her breasts.

Whatever vile things they did to her, did he and Bevan really think they could persuade her to lie about the money? That a court would convict her? That thought made her stop and wonder how she was to prove the money was hers until she could get in touch with Lady Bingram. They'd not let her get messages out, she was sure. What if they had a magistrate in their pay as well? She really could end up in prison.

She shivered and closed her eyes, alone with her dark thoughts.

Jory had helped her, there was no denying that. Even though he hadn't helped her escape, he'd stopped Bevan beating her and stopped Cobbley touching her. But he'd also believed she'd been behaving immorally in London. What had her stepfather been telling people?

Maybe Jory thought she would be so grateful for any help that she'd agree to marry him. Well, she wouldn't. Wild horses wouldn't make her give herself to him.

Footsteps clumped up to the door and she stiffened, turning her head with some difficulty to face whoever came in. But the door didn't open. A small hatch opened outwards and a face peered through the hole, the younger man who'd helped them drag her in here. Then the hatch closed and whoever it was walked away.

What would Seth say when he found out she'd been arrested? Cobbley must be senior to him, so he'd have to do as he was told, wouldn't be able to help her escape.

What would Bevan tell her mother?

Rain beat down against the small window and the sky was so dark that it was like twilight in the cell.

Tears trickled down her face. Her head was hurting

and her arms were feeling numb. She had only once before in her life felt so helpless and humiliated. But this time, things were worse, because the whole town was going to know she'd been arrested for theft.

It was the sudden memory of how brave some of the badly injured soldiers had been that helped her pull herself together. They'd faced horrendous injuries, losing a limb, sometimes more than one. And they'd been so cheerful when she visited them in hospital. If they could keep going so bravely, so could she.

She slipped off the narrow bunk and wriggled round until her back was to the wall and then, laboriously, she set to work to leave proof that she'd been here.

20

Seth saw a man standing at a country bus stop, coat collar turned up, shoulders hunched, and slowed down automatically, wondering whether to offer him a lift. When he realised who the man was he stopped a few yards past the bus stop and shouted back, 'Covington? Is that you?'

Giles ran towards him. 'Talbot. Are you going into Shawcroft?'

'Yes. Climb on the back quickly. I have to get this bike back to the owner. You can tell me what's happened to you when we get somewhere dry. It might be April, but it's still damned cold!'

He drove on through the heavy rain that was coming down at a distinct angle thanks to the wind. When they got into Shawcroft, he called over his shoulder, 'I need to check whether Ellen is waiting for me. I'm a bit later than I expected to be when I borrowed her bike.'

But there was no sign of her near the police station. Well, who in their right minds would stand out in the rain waiting? He couldn't believe she'd have gone inside, or been made welcome if she had, but he had to check. Leaving the engine running, he ran across to the station. But the interior was well lit, due to the dullness of the day, and he could see Wes through the window, slumped on his usual stool, and a young man whom Seth recognised as being one of those who'd tried to attack him after the party. No sign of Ellen.

He could see Wes staring towards the window, but knew how bad his colleague's eyesight was, so ran back to the motorbike without going inside. 'She's not there. Where do you want to go? I'll drop you off then come back and see if she's arrived.'

'I'm heading for Monnings' rooms. I'm hoping he'll give me a bed for the night. If not I'll go to the Fleece. What were you doing out in the middle of nowhere?'

'Pursuing wild geese, courtesy of Cobbley. The sooner that lying sod goes, the happier I'll be.' He explained in a few terse phrases what had happened then drove slowly through the town centre, keeping an eye open for Ellen. *Where the hell was she? Was she all right?* When Covington got off, Seth said, 'You'd better call in at Martin Pugh's once you've had a word with Monnings. He'll know someone who can fetch your car back then he can repair it for you.'

'Good idea. Thanks for the lift.'

'Glad to help.' Seth hauled his pocket watch out and peered at it, shielding it from the rain with one hand. 'At this rate, Ellen's going to be late getting back to the Hall. I do hope her mother isn't ill.' He continued slowly along the main street, noticing Halsopp stop serving a customer to gape through the window at him. Perhaps the butcher had recognised his stepdaughter's motorcycle.

At Halsopp's house, he knocked on the door. When no one answered he opened it, knowing the invalid would be inside. 'Is anyone there?'

A voice called out faintly and he turned into the front room just off the hallway, where he found Mrs Halsopp lying in bed, looking pale and haggard.

'Are you all right?'

'No, I'm not. Oh, Mr Talbot, please go and stop them! They'll hurt her, I know they will.'

Jory went straight home, banging the front door open and marching straight through into the kitchen. 'Where's Dad?'

His mother turned from her cooking. 'In the sitting room, boozing. Has been doing it all afternoon. I don't know what's got into him these past few months. See if *you* can talk any sense into him. I certainly can't and it's not for want of trying.' She gestured to some empty bottles on the floor near the back door. 'He's already got through these.'

From the way she was banging her pans around, Jory realised she was extremely angry. 'I'll go and see him.'

He found his father in the process of pouring beer from a bottle into a glass, his hand unsteady so that some of it missed and splashed over the edge. Three more empty bottles stood on the floor next to the sagging old armchair which Eddie refused to get rid of and which only he ever sat on. One of them had fallen over, spilling beer dregs on the carpet that was his mother's pride and joy. She'd go mad when she saw the mess.

Jory righted the fallen bottle, then took the glass and half-empty bottle out of his father's hands, setting them down on the mantelpiece out of reach. 'What the hell do you think you're doing getting drunk at this hour of the day?'

'Doing what I want. You're home from the war now, aren't you? 'S'all up to you now. It's a poor lookout if a man my age can't take things easy.'

'Man your age! You're only sixty-six. Grandad lived to eighty. Plenty of work left in you yet if you'll only stop the boozing.'

'Give me back my glass,' his father said in a whining tone. 'My rheumatism is bad today and I need a drink.'

'Only if you'll tell me what Wes Cobbley meant. He's been threatening me, saying something about saving you from the hangman.'

Stark terror etched itself across his father's puffy features. 'It was an accident. I didn't mean to hurt anyone. If that fellow hadn't moved suddenly, he'd have been all right.'

'*What – did you – do?*'

His father began to sob. 'I killed him, Jory, killed a man. It was an accident, I swear it was. But since then Cobbley and Halsopp have been asking for money to keep it quiet. They call it "loans" but I know they're not intending to pay me back. I thought they were my friends, but they're not. I've got no friends in the world now. No one. Is it any wonder I drink?'

Jory was so shocked he couldn't think what to say or do. 'You killed a man? You can't have. You're not the violent sort.'

'I've just been telling you: it was an accident.'

'But what were you doing? *How* did you kill him?'

Eddie peered over his son's shoulder as if to check that no one could overhear them, then put one finger to his lips. 'Shh. Mustn't tell *her*. She didn't approve of what I was doing. But it was money for old rope. No one can watch all the sheep, so it was just a question of finding somewhere quiet and taking one here and another there. Farmers don't miss the odd one. Why, the stupid creatures fall and break their legs all the time. Good money, them sheep brought in during the war. And then it was the odd cow as well. They're bigger, bring in even more.'

He half rose out of his chair, stretching his hand up towards the glass of beer on the mantelpiece. Jory shoved him back. 'Never mind the booze. Go on with your tale.'

'Jus' one little sip.'

'Not till you've told me everything. *How* did you kill a man?'

'I shot him.'

'I didn't even know you had a gun.'

'Halsopp got it for me, to kill the animals with. One shot to the brain, quick and painless. I never could cut a creature's throat. Only this fellow turned up just as I was about to shoot his cow. I looked round and he was there and I near died of fright, I can tell you. I don't know how it happened, Jory, only the gun went off and he fell down and Dennis said he was dead. So we left the cow and got out of there quickly.'

'Did *you* check that he was dead?'

'No, Dennis did. Your cousin. Strapping big fellow, but got a heart murmur, so he couldn't pass his medical. Didn't stop him helping me during the war, though. You should be grateful to him. I couldn't have managed without him after your brother Don went and volunteered, the stupid bugger. Anyway, Dennis said there was nothing we could do to help the man, so what was the point in staying there, or calling the police?'

'Were you mad? Why did you need to *steal* animals? There's always a farmer willing to part with one and plenty of money to be made from it on the black market.'

'There weren't many going towards the end of the war. Food regulations were so tight the inspectors counted every beast, damn them, so we did what we had to.'

Jory began pacing up and down, three steps each way. This was far worse than he'd expected. As he passed the old man, he paused to throw at him, 'While I was risking my life fighting the Hun, you were killing our own people. Damn you for a greedy fool, Dad! Where does this leave me now?'

His father clutched his sleeve. 'You aren't going to tell, are you? Promise me you won't tell anyone. You're my son, my eldest son now our Ted's dead. You *can't* turn me in. They'll hang me!'

'Not if it really was a mistake.'

'How the hell can I prove that? Please, son . . . ?'

'I don't know what I'm going to do.' Jory couldn't stand the sight of his old man any longer, so went back into the kitchen, drained the cup of tea his mother had poured for him and tried to think what to do. 'Thanks. I have to go out again.'

She turned round sharply. 'You've only just come in. You're soaking wet. Wait! What about your father?'

Jory paused near the door. 'Did he tell you what he did?'

'I overheard a few things.' She looked at him miserably. 'Killed a man, didn't he?'

'He says it was an accident.'

'That doesn't make the man any less dead, does it?' Tears spilled down her cheeks.

He went and gave her a quick hug, worried even more when his normally cheerful mother clung to him, sobbing. 'I don't like getting involved in this sort of thing, Mum.'

She pulled herself away, looking up at his face. 'And I don't want you involved, love. Accessory after the fact, they call it, and they'd arrest you too, if it came out. Only . . . Wes Cobbley's involved, so who's to stop him, let alone arrest him? Though if he or that Halsopp come here again asking for money, I'll turn Eddie in to the police myself rather than give it to them – or I will once that new bobby starts. Your father's stupid, but Halsopp is downright wicked. There are only two things that man cares about in the world: money and Dorothy. Well, all the money in the world won't save her now, poor soul, then he'll find cold comfort in the other.'

'I'll have to see what I can do, Mum. We can't leave things like this.'

'You should stay clear of them!' She gave him another quick hug, wiped her eyes on a corner of her apron and returned to her cooking.

Jory shrugged his damp overcoat back on and stood in the doorway looking up at the sky. It seemed to have an unending supply of rain to pour down on them lately.

He crammed a cap on his head and pulled his collar up, sighing as he walked back to the police station. He hadn't expected to come home and face this sort of problem. What the hell had his old man been thinking of, stealing sheep and cows?

Some people went stupid in their old age, softening of the brain they called it. He was beginning to wonder if his father was one of them.

Algie went round to the doctor's but was told Dr Hilliam was out visiting a sick patient. 'I'll wait, then. It's urgent.'

Mrs Hilliam looked down her nose at him. He knew that look. She suspected what he was like. 'You can come back later. He'll be at least an hour.'

Annoyed that she'd answered the door and not the maid, he pulled his hat down to hide his face as much as possible and went outside again, cursing under his breath. Today of all days, the doctor had to be out on a call.

What had Mrs Gresham done to poor old Ronnie to make her scratch the old tartar's face like that?

She'd have had to struggle desperately against such a large woman to do it and would have had no chance of escaping her.

He'd once asked his mother how she could be friends with such a dreadful person and she'd gone all stony-faced and only when he'd pressed her, had she said it was 'safer'. She'd refused to explain further.

He was only now beginning to realise now just how ruthless Ronnie's mother could be.

Edwina paced up and down her small sitting room, stopping every now and then to stare at herself in the mirror, outraged at the way Ronnie had scratched her where it showed. She definitely wasn't leaving the house looking like this.

She went to her bureau and unlocked it, reaching for the spare bottle of sleeping drops she kept there, but finding the space empty. She frowned at it. She was sure there had been a spare bottle. She went up to her bedroom and looked at the small blue glass bottle on the mantelpiece. Not much left now. Would there be enough to keep her daughter quiet as well as furnish her with her own nightly drops? She couldn't sleep without the stuff these days, she had so many worries.

She had felt *sure* there was another full bottle, but no one else knew where she kept her drops, let alone had a key to this bureau, so there couldn't have been.

She should have checked this while Dr Hilliam was here. He'd said he'd return later to see Veronica, but if he came after his evening surgery, it would be too late to send Tadwyn into Shawcroft for more drops, so it would be a choice between keeping Veronica quiet and getting her own night's sleep.

She hadn't time to go to her other supplier. Dr Hilliam had emphasised that she wasn't to take too many of the drops, had even said he wouldn't keep giving her them as they were addictive, but she'd found someone else who wasn't so squeamish. She couldn't sleep without them and that was that.

She went to stare out of the window and saw that fool of a fellow who claimed to be shellshocked carrying a pile of wood into the house from the shed. She'd not normally have employed someone like him. Most of those claiming shellshock were just trying to get out of doing their duty. But this fellow wasn't turning out as badly as she'd expected, so perhaps he was one of the genuine cases.

She clapped her hands together as she realised that here was the perfect excuse for asking for more drops. Running quickly downstairs, she rang the bell for Glenys and sent her to find Tadwyn.

'I want you to go into town and call at the doctor's. Ask him for a prescription for some more sleeping drops. The chemist won't give me any without a note. Tell the doctor I gave some to that Pel person, to help him through his nightmares, then call at the chemist's and wait for them to be made up. I must have some more by tonight. I've nearly run out.'

'Yes, madam.'

When he'd gone she began to pace up and down again, unable to settle to anything. It was galling to think that Algernon had come round ready to propose and Veronica hadn't been in a fit state to receive him.

There had to be some way to bring it home to that girl where her duty lay. The stupid creature deserved a good thrashing. Edwina was not going to be defied by her own child.

She flung herself down on the sofa. Her head was throbbing and it was all Veronica's fault.

Tadwyn stopped in the kitchen to let them know where he was going. Glenys looked so upset at what he said that he beckoned her outside. 'Has something happened?'

'Can the mistress just go on getting those horrible sleeping drops? I was sure I'd heard the doctor say he didn't want to give her any more.'

'Glenys?' She didn't reply, was avoiding looking him in the eyes, so Tadwyn took a wild guess. 'You didn't happen to take the last bottle from her bureau, did you?'

She clapped one hand to her mouth, clearly terrified.

'That was very clever of you.'

She looked at him doubtfully.

'I mean it.'

'But if she's getting some more, it'll make no difference. She'll still go on giving them to poor Miss Veronica.'

He grinned. 'Not if I put water in the bottle instead. She won't be able to see any difference because the drops are colourless.'

'Ooh, Mr Tadwyn, you wouldn't!'

'I would too. Have you got an old pop bottle I can fill with water? I'll stop on the way back and do it.'

'I'll go and get you one straight away.'

He watched her go with a slight smile on his face. Who'd have thought Glenys would do something like that? And now here he was going to go against his own best interests and intervening. But he couldn't continue aiding and abetting Mrs Gresham, not after seeing how desperately Miss Veronica had fought last time.

The problem was how to stop her bullying that poor lass once and for all. If Mrs Gresham was thwarted, she could be a terror. And it was no use telling anyone. She knew a great many important people who would undoubtedly believe her before they believed him.

It was such a miserable day that the streets were empty. Who'd think this was April, nearly May? It felt more like winter. Bevan decided to close his shop earlier than usual, something he rarely did. He set the lad to scrubbing down and went into the back, hesitated, then called, 'I'm just going home. I'll be back in a few minutes to check that you've done everything properly.'

He was worried about Dorothy. He'd ignored her pleas, walked out on her, didn't want her making herself worse by fretting about that damned daughter of hers.

When he got to the house he went in the back way

through the kitchen. There was no sign of Madge, who should have been there by now. He'd tear a strip off her next time he saw her.

He strode through to the front room and found Dorothy lying in bed. Her face was puffy with tears and he didn't like to see that, so went round to sit beside her, holding her hand even though she tried to pull it away from him. 'You shouldn't take on so. I'll make sure your daughter is all right. Jory still wants to marry her, so it'll all work out in the end.'

'She doesn't want to marry him and I wouldn't either, if I was her.'

'What do you mean by that?'

'I've thought and thought about it, and I've been sure for a long time that he forced her and that was why she finished with him.'

He was silent. He'd guessed that too. 'Well, he wants to marry her, so that'll make it right.'

'No, it won't. She'll never trust him again, and I wouldn't either. If he'll hurt her once, he'll hurt her again. Besides, I think she's taken a fancy to that new policeman and that'd be a much better match for her, don't you think? A policeman's job is always secure and they get a good pension too. I'd like to see her settled for life before I die.'

Bevan gritted his teeth and said nothing. If that young bobby fancied her, he'd be even more keen to set her free. Damnation, this was all going wrong.

Dorothy frowned then looked at him. 'What are you doing home at this time of day, dear?'

'Came to make it up with you.'

She took hold of his hand and smiled at him. 'I'm glad. I don't like to be at odds with you, or anyone else come to that.'

'I know. You're too soft for your own good, you are, my girl. It's a good thing you've got me to look after you. It's a miserable day and there's hardly anyone about, so I'm shutting up shop early for once. I've got the lad scrubbing the place down, so I'll have to nip back and check he's done it right. I'd expected Madge to be here making a start on the tea and she hasn't even called in for our meat.'

'Oh, I forgot to tell you. Her daughter popped in to say Madge isn't well. She's got a heavy cold and didn't want to give it to me.'

'Well, she's right about that, but she should have let me know, not you. I'll go round to the fish and chip shop later, then, get you a nice bit of hake, eh?'

She snuggled down in bed, smiling at him. 'I knew you wouldn't stay angry with me, Bevan. Now please make things right with Ellen. You really shouldn't have taken her money.'

He didn't contradict her because the thought that she was still taking Ellen's side against him had set anger throbbing through him so strongly he felt like his chest was going to burst with it, particularly the thought of that bitch shouting out to people that he was a thief.

He looked down and saw that Dorothy's eyes were closed, so set her hand down gently on the bedspread and went out again the back way. The anger made him walk so fast that faces around him were a blur and he didn't bother to reply when someone said hello to him.

It wasn't a day for being polite.

As soon as he'd shut up shop, he was going straight to the police station to check on Ellen. And by hell, she'd better have come to her senses or he wouldn't be answerable for what happened to her next. He'd had enough of her coming between him and his wife!

Seth drove the motorcycle round to Martin's and left it there. 'Ellen lent it me and she's been delayed so I want to keep it safe while I look for her.'

Martin stared at him. 'There's something wrong, isn't there?'

'Nothing I can tell you about at present.'

'Look after her and call me if you need help. She hasn't got any family except us to do that.'

'She's got me now as well as you.'

Martin's face lit up. 'My Jeanie said you were taken with Ellen. Have you spoken to her?'

'Yes. She feels the same.' That thought made him feel warm inside – and even more determined to sort this mess out. He strode through the streets, wondering how to do that. If Mrs Halsopp was right, Ellen was in danger.

When he entered the police station, Cobbley stared at him in dismay and jerked to his feet.

'What are you doing back so soon? You haven't had time to get out to the farm and back.'

'I got a lift. And it was all a hoax anyway. There hadn't been a burglary at all.'

Seth watched Cobbley sag down on to the stool again and continue to watch him warily.

'I'll give that lad what for if I catch him,' he muttered.

'Do you know who he was?'

'No. He was from one of the poorer streets by the look of him. But they don't usually play tricks on *me*.' He stared at Seth, chewing one corner of his lip, then said, 'You may as well finish for the day. You'll catch your death of cold if you hang around in them wet clothes.'

Seth looked towards the young man sitting in the corner. 'Is there some other trouble?'

Cobbley's face twitched into anxious lines again. 'Why do you ask?'

'Well, you appear to have a customer.' He jerked his head in the direction of the other man.

'Oh, that's just young Dennis keeping me company. I've known him since he was a lad.'

The other nodded but Seth thought he had a wary look to him as well.

'I know your face, don't I?'

Dennis shook his head.

'Oh, I think I do.' Seth was pleased to see an uneasy expression on the other's face as he turned back to Cobbley. He'd deal with young Dennis later. 'No other trouble today?'

'Bit of a fracas earlier but I soon sorted it out,' Cobbley said. 'Nothing you need worry about. You get off home.'

Ellen could hear voices in the front office, but the walls were thick and she couldn't tell who it was.

Should she risk shouting for help or should she wait until she was sure it was someone who would come to her aid?

She was shivering so violently, she decided she had nothing to lose. If she continued sitting here getting colder and colder, she'd come down with pneumonia.

She went across to the door. With her hands bound behind her she couldn't hammer on it or try to push the flap open, so began kicking it and shouting for help at the top of her voice.

Please let someone hear me! she prayed. *Please!*

21

Algie went back to the doctor's an hour after his first visit and to his relief Dr Hilliam had returned and would see him.

He was shown past a line of patients by the elderly nurse, who'd been here for as long as anyone could remember. 'This way, Mr St Corbin. Hurry up, please. Doctor is a very busy man.'

Did everyone have to shout out who he was? There was no hope of keeping things quiet in this town, so the sooner he left the better. Once his mother found out where he was, she'd come hunting him and he'd rather not have to face her at the moment.

Dr Hilliam gestured to a chair. 'What's wrong with you, Mr St Corbin?'

'There's nothing wrong with me. It's just – I'm worried about Ronnie, Veronica Gresham that is.'

'Oh?'

'Yes. Her mother's keeping her a prisoner and Ronnie's begged me to help her get away. Only I have to leave for France and I can't think what to do. I'm *really* worried about Ronnie, though. She was looking dreadful.'

'I've seen Veronica Gresham myself and can assure

you she's all right. I'm going out to see her again this evening and will continue to keep an eye on her. Now, is that all?'

'No, it isn't. I've made a serious charge here and you've treated it like it's nothing.'

'Believe me, young man, I'm aware of Miss Gresham's claims – and also aware of what her mother is telling me about her illness. I can't take any action until I can see who is in the right. More than that I cannot tell you. Now, I have other patients to see, so if that's all you want to say, consider it said, and let me get on with my work.'

Algie went out feeling he'd failed. Hands thrust deep into his overcoat pockets he made his way slowly back to the Fleece, wondering what to do next. There was no way he could rescue Ronnie single-handed, no way he could bear to leave her in that situation, either.

As he was about to turn the corner into Rochdale Road, he stiffened and stepped quickly back. No mistaking that car. What the hell was his mother doing here?

He stepped into a doorway and watched. It seemed a long time until the front door of the pub opened and his mother came out. The chauffeur jumped out to open the door for her, then got back inside, turning to receive his instructions. With a nod, he drove away, but not in the direction of home.

Worried, Algie stayed where he was and sure enough the big car purred along the street that ran parallel to Rochdale Road. He used the back alleys to make his way towards the Fleece, only to stop dead as he saw that his mother's car had stopped again, this time in a place that had a good view of the rear of the pub.

Even as he stared a man came out of one of the terraced houses nearby and approached the car. He had an earnest conversation with the chauffeur, then held out his hand to receive something, presumably money.

As the car moved away, the man grinned down at the contents of his hand and went back inside the house. But the door stayed open and Algie could see a shadowy figure standing there.

He didn't dare go back to the Fleece until it was fully dark, and then only to pick up his knapsack. Shoulders hunched against the rain, he set off, trying to find somewhere to shelter. But there seemed to be a lot of other people with the same idea and all the good places to shelter were taken.

Well, he'd been wet and cold on many occasions in France, Algie told himself. He could put up with it for an hour or two while he planned his next moves.

It didn't seem likely that he'd be able to help poor Ronnie, though, if his mother was chasing him that determinedly, and for that he was sincerely sorry.

When Algie had left, the doctor sat frowning into space for some time before ringing the handbell for the next patient to come in.

This case at the Hall was not all cut and dried, not by any means. If Veronica's pleas had any truth in them at all, she did need help. But if he helped her,

Hilliam knew he could say goodbye to a lot of the social life his wife enjoyed so much. And possibly worse than that, he'd incur the wrath of a woman who had the ear of many important people. She had only to drop a word here and there, doubting his capability as a doctor and he'd lose a lot of his richer patients – and without them he couldn't do nearly as much to help his poorer ones.

Not that he'd let any of that stop him if Mrs Gresham really was keeping Veronica prisoner. But it seemed so far-fetched that he had to be certain before he could act. Only how to do that beyond doubt was more than he could work out.

Seth heard shouting from the direction of the cells and looked in that direction. 'Who's that?'

Cobbley stood up, moving more quickly than Seth had ever seen him do before, to stand in front of the door to the cells. 'It's just a drunk. He's not getting out till he's calmed down. If he doesn't shut up, I'll go and fettle him.'

'I'll do it for you, if you like,' Dennis volunteered.

'You're not a policeman,' Seth said, turning to frown at him. 'You're not allowed to go near one of our prisoners.' As he listened, he felt certain it was a woman's voice. If it was Ellen . . . if they'd hurt her . . . he'd make very sure they regretted it. 'It sounds like a woman to me.' He started calculating how best to get past Cobbley before Dennis got involved.

Cobbley folded his arms and leaned against the door. 'Well, it's not a woman. He's *my* prisoner, so it's got nothing to do with you. You've not taken over here yet, so I'm still in charge.'

'I'll just go and check that he's all right.'

'I do that at regular intervals.'

The young man stood up and came to join them. 'Look, the prisoner's my uncle. That's why I'm here. My aunt wants me to keep an eye on him and bring him home when he sobers up. Wes tries to keep it quiet whenever my uncle gets drunk. If the old devil's shouting, it means he's not sobered up yet.'

Seth was about to take action when the door opened and Halsopp came in, together with the other young fellow who'd been guarding the door at the party.

Four against one was greater odds than he was prepared to take on.

He studied the newcomers covertly. Their arrival made him even more certain that there was something going on, so he faked a shiver. 'Well, if you're sure your prisoner's all right, I *will* go home and change. I'm chilled to the marrow. There was a freezing wind up on the tops.'

When he got outside he walked briskly down the hill till he was out of sight of the police station then started running, praying that Covington would still be at the lawyer's rooms. He wanted an expert witness with him before he took on that lot.

The lawyer's rooms were still lit, but only the clerk was there. 'Mr Monnings has gone home for the day, I'm afraid, sir.'

'Was Mr Covington with him?'

'Yes.'

'I need to see Giles very urgently indeed – a police matter. I'm new to the town so don't know where your master lives. Could you give me directions to his house, please?'

The clerk picked up the telephone. 'I'll ask him. Mr Monnings has a telephone at home as well as at the office, you know. He's very modern-thinking.'

It took a few minutes for the telephone operator to connect them and for the clerk to speak to his employer. He hung the phone up before Seth could stop him. 'Mr Monnings says you're to go round to his house.'

Seth held back his annoyance at the delay. 'Tell me where he lives.'

When the new bobby had left the police station, Bevan listened to the faint shouts coming from inside the police station, and turned to Dennis. 'Go after him and keep an eye on him and if he seems like he's about to interfere, do something about him.'

'All right if I take Keith with me?' Dennis asked.

'Yes. But don't touch Talbot unless you have to. We want to keep things quiet, not stir up trouble.'

With a nod, the two younger men left.

Wes, who'd been listening open-mouthed, protested, 'You can't go round attacking a police officer. I draw the line at that, I do indeed.'

Bevan scowled at him. 'You're in this as much as we are. I'm not saying he should be killed, am I?'

Wes winced.

'We just need time to get that girl out of here and take her somewhere else.'

'But she thinks she's been arrested.'

'Well, now she can learn that she's in much more serious trouble than that, can't she? *In trouble with me.* On top of everything else, she's upset my wife and I'm not having that under any circumstances.' As the other still looked unconvinced, he added, 'Crossing me is a very dangerous thing to do, believe me.'

Cobbley gulped and made no further protests.

Bevan looked round. 'Where is she?'

'In the cells.'

'Go and tell her to stop making that racket or you'll douse her down with a bucket of cold water.'

Wes shambled off to do that and the noise subsided.

Some time after Algie had left, Tadwyn was shown into the doctor's waiting room and explained to the nurse why he'd come. She indicated the end of the long wooden bench and he sat on it, hoping he wouldn't have to wait long. There was a murmur of voices from inside the consulting room and once a child yelled, 'Ouch!' and began to cry.

When the door opened, a woman shepherded out a little girl who was still sobbing and a man at the other end of the bench stood up.

The nurse called, 'Just a minute. This gentleman needs to see the doctor first.'

Tadwyn walked past a row of scowling faces and into the surgery.

The doctor looked at him in surprise. 'What can I do for you?'

'It's for Mrs Gresham. She's nearly run out of sleeping drops and she forgot to ask you for a note for the chemist.'

'I told her not to use them so freely.' Dr Hilliam frowned and pulled a file out of a cabinet. 'She had three bottles. She should have more than enough to last till next month.'

Tadwyn hesitated. 'She said to tell you she's been giving some to her new employee. He's shellshocked, poor fellow, and has dreadful nightmares.'

Dr Hilliam looked at him, his lips pressed together, brow creased in thought and took a chance. 'What has she really been doing with them?'

There was dead silence in the room.

Tadwyn put up one hand to ease his shirt collar, which suddenly seemed too tight.

'Well?'

'I can't say, sir.'

Dr Hilliam went across to the cupboard and pulled out a plate of food he'd been given that morning. 'This isn't the food that was spilled on the floor in Veronica's room. Yet you gave this to me. Why did you change it?'

Tadwyn sagged against the back of his chair and decided it was too much to keep up this charade. Let alone he was feeling guilty about poor Miss Veronica, he didn't think he could go on deceiving people. 'Mrs Gresham wanted me to.'

'I didn't hear her say anything.'

'It was more how she looked at me. You get to know someone when you've worked for them for as long as I have.'

'Why should she want the food changed?' Silence. *'Tell me!'*

'Because she'd drugged the other.'

'So Veronica Gresham was telling the truth?'

'Yes, sir.'

'You realise you've been aiding and abetting Mrs Gresham to break the law. Kidnapping is a very serious offence.'

Tadwyn stared pleadingly at the doctor. 'I had to. I've my retirement money to think of.'

'Well, now you have me to deal with, so you'd better start thinking about doing what's right instead. Who else knows about what Mrs Gresham is doing to her daughter?'

'All us servants do. You can't keep such things secret.' He hesitated then added, 'If I return without some more drops, she'll go mad at me and maybe take it out on her daughter. Mrs Gresham has been really chancy tempered lately, if truth be told.'

'Then I'm definitely not giving you any more drops. That bad temper may be partly an effect of the drug, though she's never been an easy woman to deal with.'

'Ah. Well, you see, doctor, I was actually going to pour the stuff away and fill the bottle with water. Just to keep the mistress happy till me and Gladys could see how best to help Miss Veronica. Could we maybe do that?'

Dr Hilliam relaxed visibly. 'Good idea. I've got a

bottle of the same sort. I'll fill it with water for you myself.' He opened a cupboard, took the bottle across to the washbasin and filled it, then screwed the top back on and found a label, writing on it carefully. 'There.'

'This won't keep her happy for long,' Tadwyn said nervously. 'She'll soon find out the drops don't work.'

'I'm coming out to see Veronica again later, but I may be delayed. I have a patient who could die at any minute. Can you hold the fort till then? Make sure Mrs Gresham doesn't hurt her daughter?'

'Yes, sir.'

Tadwyn drove home feeling as if a load had been lifted from his shoulders. Well, partly lifted. They just had to get through till the doctor came, then they could leave all this to him.

Luckily, Monnings' house wasn't far away, so Seth hurried through the streets, heedless of the rain, desperate to get help. Covington had been employed in intelligence work during the war and would know how to look after himself. Best of all, he was a lawyer, so a highly reputable witness.

Seth felt sure from what Mrs Halsopp had told him that they'd got Ellen shut up at the police station. It all fitted. They'd even sent him out of town on a pretext. But though it had gone against the grain to leave her there just now, he couldn't have acted against four people, three of them strong men.

Just as he was turning the final corner, he heard footsteps hurrying along behind him. As he was turning to see who it was, something hit him on the head so hard it knocked him to the ground. Instinctively he let himself go limp, as if unconscious, while keeping alert in case they continued to attack him.

'Have you knocked him out?' one asked.

The other peered down at him. 'Yes.'

'Should we tie him up?'

Seth tensed.

'No, we'll just shut him in that old warehouse then go back and help. Those old buggers won't be able to carry her far. She's a big fine lass.'

As they bent to pick him up, Seth swung his fist into the nearest man's face and leaped to his feet, yelling for help at the top of his voice. He wasn't sure he could fight two such sturdy men off, but he'd have a damned good try.

He ducked another blow and danced out of the way as the other man tried to get behind him, yelling again for help.

One of the men bent and picked up a piece of wood, then moved forward, brandishing it, grinning, his face lit up by a nearby street lamp like a devil's mask.

Seth tried to find an opening to run away, because discretion was definitely the better part of valour here, but the two seemed well versed in fighting and were blocking his escape.

He settled grimly into a defensive position, promising himself to sell his freedom at high cost and then suddenly a man's voice yelled out from along the street.

'Hey! What are you doing?'

From the other direction a door opened and light streamed out of it as another voice shouted out, 'Stop that, you young varmints, or I'll fetch the police.'

Seth's two assailants froze, then as footsteps came pounding towards them and the lights from open doors continued to shine, they slipped away into the darkness of an alley behind them.

If he had his way, Seth thought, he'd block off all these damned back alleys.

'Are you all right?'

He turned gratefully to his rescuer. 'Thanks to you, I am. I didn't think anyone would be out in this weather.'

'I'm not out willingly. I'm avoiding my mother.'

'You all right now?' the voice yelled from the other direction.

'Yes, thanks.'

The door shut and the light vanished.

The rescuer stuck out one hand. 'Algie St Corbin.'

'Seth Talbot.'

The two men shook hands.

The name seemed familiar to Algie and he frowned for a minute, then snapped his fingers. 'Ah, you're the new policeman!'

'Yes.'

'I'm delighted to have met you because I've a crime to report.'

'Do you think it could wait until morning? I'm in the middle of sorting out a crime at this very moment and it's urgent. I have to go.'

As Seth began walking, the other man fell in beside him. 'Oh, hell! I'll have left Shawcroft by then.'

A brass number announced Monnings' house and Seth hesitated as he came to a stop outside it. 'Come inside. If you can tell me your problem in two minutes flat, I promise you I'll listen. But I've definitely got to attend to the other business first.' He knocked on the door and didn't wait for it to be opened but went straight inside, calling, 'Mr Monnings, are you there?'

When the elderly lawyer and Giles appeared, Seth took charge, gesturing to them to be quiet while he listened to Algie, then explaining quickly why he was there.

Giles stared from one to the other. 'Small world, isn't it? I was going out to the Hall to rescue Ronnie myself tonight. She and I are engaged.'

Algie beamed at him and shook his hand vigorously.

'Will you come with me first, Covington?' Seth asked. 'I think Ellen's case is desperate. The two who attacked me will have got back to tell them I'm still on the loose.'

'Of course.'

'I'll go and get the local magistrate,' Monnings said. 'He won't dare do anything but uphold the law with me there.'

Algie looked at the group of men standing in the hall. 'Bit like the war, isn't it? Want another person in your platoon, Talbot? If I help you get your young lady free, perhaps we can all go and rescue Ronnie afterwards?'

'Done. Now, we'd better run. This is taking too long.' He didn't wait for them but set off at top speed.

Ellen looked up as the cell door opened and felt bitterly disappointed as she saw her stepfather standing in the doorway with a gloating smile on his face.

'Come to your senses yet, miss?'

'If you mean am I going to let you steal my money without complaining, then no, I haven't.' A shiver racked her but she continued to stare defiantly at him. 'I'll *never* change my mind about that. And don't try to pretend the law says you have a right to my money, because I'm not stupid.'

His smile faded and he glared at her. 'Then we'll have to persuade you to be *sensible*, won't we?'

She saw the man hovering behind him. 'How can you break the law like this, and you a policeman?' she demanded. 'You're no better than a thief, Wes Cobbley.'

'He has a right to the money,' Wes said. 'Why will you not accept that?'

'Because it's not true.'

The outer door banged and a voice called, 'Anyone home?'

Bevan turned round. 'In here, Jory lad.'

Ellen was unable to control her shivers. 'Another thief come to get his share of the loot!'

Jory looked at her then pulled off his jacket and moved to wrap it round her.

Bevan struck his outstretched hand back, knocking the jacket to the floor. 'There's to be no cosseting her.'

'Cosseting! She'll catch her death of cold if you don't get her out of those wet things and into some warm, dry clothes.' He picked up the jacket again.

'She'll be getting wetter still in a minute, so it's a waste of time.'

'What do you mean?'

'We've got to move her.'

'Why?'

'The new bobby,' Wes said. 'I knew he meant trouble as soon as I saw him.'

'The lads are out delaying him a little.' Bevan chuckled. 'He's another one who needs to learn a bit of sense and by hell, I'll see that he does. But when he comes back he'll find the cells are empty.'

'Where are you taking her, then?'

Bevan smiled and tapped his forefinger against his nose. 'You'll find out – that is, if you're with us, Jory lad. But she'll not know where she is.'

'Right.' He put his jacket on again.

Ellen hoped her fear hadn't shown on her face. 'You'll have to kill me to make me change my mind,' she said. 'Are you really prepared to go so far?' It was Jory she was looking at as she said that.

But it was Bevan who answered, and smiled as he said, 'Maybe I am. If you force me to.'

The outer office door banged open just then and Jory turned to see Dennis and Keith, looking the worse for wear. 'What the hell's happened to you two?'

'We had that new bobby nicely boxed up but some bugger came along and saved him and another inter-fering sod came out of his house. We didn't want to be seen, so we slipped away. You'd better get her moved quick.'

'Let me gag her first,' Bevan said. 'I'm not having her calling out for help.'

22

Ronnie came awake so slowly she realised she'd been drugged yet again. She hated the way that stuff made her feel, clouded brain, dry mouth, but most of all she hated not knowing what had happened to her while she was unconscious. She shivered and felt for the blankets, but found that once again, she was lying on a bare matteress clad only in her night-dress.

Why had Giles not come for her? She couldn't keep back the tears. Her hope of rescue had never been at such a low ebb. And she had no faith in the doctor, for all his reassurances. By the time he came back, she was quite sure her mother would have given her another dose and she'd seem stupid and uncoordi-nated.

Had Ellen posted the letter? She must have. She'd left hours ago. But even if Giles got it tomorrow, he'd still got to come to Shawcroft. Who knew what would have happened to her by then?

Lightning slashed across the sky outside and a few seconds later thunder rumbled in the distance. She decided to get up and watch, squinting through the window, trying to see whether the motorbike was back in place. She thought not, but couldn't be sure.

The car wasn't back either. Where had Tadwyn gone? Had he taken her mother out or was her mother downstairs planning how to hurt her next?

Ronnie stayed where she was. Normally she enjoyed a good thunderstorm – as long as she was inside the house. But tonight the weather seemed to add to the unreality of her situation, as flashes lit up the room, then darkness followed, filled with booming noise.

She moved and winced. Her body was a mass of bruises now and her face felt tender in places as well. It was hard to stay defiant when you felt so low.

She stayed by the window for lack of anything else to occupy her, trying not to shiver, trying not to give way to her emotions. The glass was cold beneath her fingertips and was streaming with water outside. Wind shook the panes, rain rattled against them, died down, then beat an even fiercer tattoo.

Below her, light shone from the kitchen windows, streaming across the yard and she wondered what time it was. She must have slept for hours.

So loud was the thunder she let herself weep, leaning against the window and sobbing, making no attempt to keep quiet.

Pel had been crossing the yard when the lightning flashed for the first time. He reacted instinctively to it and to the thunder which followed, cowering back against the nearest wall and letting out those whimpering cries he hated to hear himself making.

'Got to stop this,' he muttered as he tried to regain control of himself. But another flash of lightning had him cringing back before he knew it. At least he no longer threw himself flat on the ground at any sharp, unexpected sound, he thought as he steadied himself against the wall. The rough feel of the bricks under his splayed hands was comforting. Somewhere a cat meowed and that was comforting too.

He stood there and fought his instinctive reactions until he could face the booming noise and bright flashes of light without doing more than twitch slightly. For Glenys, he kept telling himself. He had to get better for her sake.

It was only then that he realised how wet he was, soaked to the skin because he'd not thought of putting on his overcoat just to go to and fro from house to stables. He had his back to the worst of the weather but water was dripping from his hair down his neck, lashing against his back, hitting the skin of his outstretched hands like sharp pinpoints. 'Stupid to stand here in the rain,' he muttered and went inside to his room above the stables to change.

As he was standing by the window of his bedroom, towelling his hair, he saw something pale against the window of the room where they were keeping the poor young woman prisoner. On an impulse he got out his binoculars and focused on it.

She was weeping and even though he couldn't see her features clearly because of the rain blurring everything, her face was a mask of anguish.

He couldn't bear to see that. He'd fought for freedom, not to make it possible for that nasty old biddy to get away with ill-treating her daughter.

Maybe if he could save this Veronica, he could gain some self-respect, know he was still capable of doing the right thing.

This time he remembered to pull his old greatcoat on before he went out and ran down the stairs, fired with determination to act. Just as he was crossing the yard, the car returned from town. Standing in the shelter of the kitchen doorway, he watched Tadwyn get out and dash across to join him.

'What are you doing standing out here, lad?' the older man asked.

'Just been getting some dry clothes on. I saw the car so I waited for you.'

'You all right?' Tadwyn jerked his head towards the sky. 'This storm not bothering you too much?'

'I'm getting used to it. I'm better than I was.'

'Yes, you are. We can all see that. Come on inside, I want my tea, even if you don't.'

'But—' Tadwyn had gone before Pel could speak out.

The kitchen was a haven of warmth and light and he leaned against the door for a minute, relishing it. The fire was burning brightly in the big kitchen range, the side table, where the servants ate, was set for six, and something that smelled good was bubbling on the side of the hotplate. Cook, Glenys and Millie were sitting chatting at the table.

'Ellen not back?' Tadwyn asked. 'No, of course she

isn't. Now I come to think of it, the motorbike wasn't in the stables.'

'I hope that contraption of hers hasn't broken down,' Cook said. 'I'd not like to be out riding on it in a thunderstorm.'

'Perhaps that's why she's late, sheltering from the storm.' Glenys shivered as a sudden rain squall beat against the window panes. 'Did you ever see such an April? It's been more like winter today.'

'Well, if we don't tell madam Ellen's late back, there's no harm done.' Cook looked round for their nods of agreement. 'She's a good worker, is Ellen.'

A bell jangled and they all looked up at it instinctively to see where *she* was.

'Mrs Gresham must have heard me coming down the drive,' Tadwyn said with a sigh.

'Did you get what she wanted?' Glenys asked.

'Yes.' He fumbled in his pocket and pulled out the small bottle.

'It's not right,' Pel said suddenly.

'What's not right?' Glenys asked.

'Drugging that girl.'

There was silence in the kitchen, then Cook said slowly, 'No, it isn't. But if we try to stop her, we'll lose our jobs and that won't do Miss Veronica any good, either.'

Pel scowled at Tadwyn. 'You should throw that stuff away and tell her you couldn't get any.'

Tadwyn winked at him. 'In a manner of speaking, I've already done that.' He smiled at Glenys then looked meaningfully at Millie. 'You tell Pel about our plan later, eh, Glenys love?'

The bell jangled a second time, jumping about furiously on the end of its spring.

Tadwyn realised suddenly that if Miss Veronica didn't know the new drops were harmless, she'd fight them all over again when Mrs Gresham went up to her. 'Keep madam busy for a minute or two, will you, Glenys? I have to go upstairs and do something before I see her.'

'All right.' Glenys went to Pel and whispered, 'We've got a plan, but we don't want Millie to know about it in case she gives something away. I'll tell you when I come back.'

Tadwyn hurried up the narrow servants' stairs and knocked on the door of Miss Veronica's room, remembering suddenly that Mrs Gresham had taken away the blankets. That poor lass must be chilled to the marrow. If he had his spare key, he'd let her out this minute. But his mistress had now taken charge of all the keys, even taking his spares away. Typical of her!

Just as he was about to knock again, a voice called, 'Who's that?'

'It's me, Tadwyn. Look, miss, you'll just have to trust us on this, but me and Glenys have changed the drops. It's just water in the bottle now. Can you please not struggle tonight, because we don't want you to get hurt again. And afterwards, can you pretend to fall asleep?'

Her voice was flat and emphatic. 'I don't trust you. You're just trying to trick me.'

'I don't blame you, but I promise I'm telling the

truth. Dr Hilliam helped me with the drops, gave me the bottle, even wrote on the label. Look, your mother's been ringing for me. I must go to her now. *Please!* Just let her dose you. She'll do it one way or the other, you know she will, so give us a chance to help you.'

When he'd gone Ronnie began to pace up and down the room in a vain effort to keep warm. Was he telling the truth or was he just trying to stop her fighting?

If he was telling the truth, she wasn't on her own any longer.

But maybe this was more of her mother's trickery?

What should she do?

Edwina pulled the bell again. 'Those servants are getting slacker and slacker,' she muttered staring at her face in the mirror and getting angry all over again at the sight of the scratches. 'Ah, there you are at last, Glenys.'

'Would you like a tea tray, madam?'

'No, I wouldn't. I want to see Tadwyn. I heard the car return, saw the headlights. Why hasn't he come to see me?'

'He was very wet, madam. Didn't want to drip all over the house. It's terrible weather outside. Shall I make up the fire for you before I go? You've let it burn right down.' Without waiting for permission, she went across and placed some pieces of coal carefully on the glowing embers.

By that time Mrs Gresham was sitting in her easy chair, fingers drumming on the arm rest. Glenys didn't dare delay any longer.

'I'll send Tadwyn up as soon as he's changed, madam.'

When Glenys got back to the kitchen, Pel was still standing near the door glowering. Worried by the look on his face, she went across to him and whispered, 'Come into the scullery for a minute. We can't talk here.'

As she tugged him across the room, Cook looked at her disapprovingly and Millie gave her the blank stare she usually wore when she wasn't worrying about her current task, then took another bite from a piece of bread and butter.

In the scullery Pel said stubbornly, 'I don't care if we both lose our jobs. I didn't fight that war to come home and see injustice done here, let alone help to hurt some poor lass.'

'No, I know you didn't,' she said soothingly. She moved closer and lowered her voice, keeping one hand on his arm. 'Tadwyn and me agreed before he went into town that he'd replace the drops with water, and from the wink he gave me just now, he's done it. Mrs Gresham won't be able to tell the difference, but Tadwyn had to go up and tell Miss Veronica so that she wouldn't struggle again. She scratched Mrs Gresham's face earlier, you know, fought like a wildcat, Tadwyn said.'

'Good. She deserves scratching, that one does.'

He sounded different today. Glenys studied him. 'You all right, love?'

He smiled suddenly. 'Getting there. Not right yet,

but better than I was. And that's partly thanks to you, love.'

'Thanks to your own courage.'

'Let's leave here tomorrow, you and me.'

She shook her head. 'If we did that, there'd be no one to help Tadwyn. If I had a key, I'd let Miss Veronica out tonight, but I haven't. The mistress has hidden them all. Doesn't even trust us.'

'She's a wicked woman, that one is. We'll be better off working for someone else.'

'Trouble is, jobs aren't easy to find. And I've nowhere else to go till I find something, Pel love. All my family are dead.'

He hesitated. 'We could go to my family till we sort something out. They'd not turn us away.'

'You never said you had family.'

'I've not been back. Didn't want them to see me in such a mess.'

'Tell me about them.'

Cook's voice interrupted them. 'Glenys! Didn't you hear the bell? Madam's ringing again.'

'Drat her,' Glenys muttered. 'What does she want now?' She turned to Pel. 'Wait for me in the kitchen and I'll tell you how it goes.'

He watched her walk out and went back to sit at the table.

'You might as well eat something while you're waiting,' Cook said. 'There's good food going to waste here.'

'Not yet. Not till we see what happens tonight.'

'Whatever it is, I don't want to be part of it.' Her

face crumpled and she whisked up her apron to wipe her eyes. 'I'm too old for all these upsets.'

'You can't help but be part of it. Mrs Gresham is committing a crime.' He went to put his arm round her.

With a sigh she leaned against him for a minute, then sniffed and gave him a tearful smile. 'You're right, really, but when you're older, like me, you just want a peaceful life.'

'Some of us young 'uns want that, too. Those of us who were in the fighting have had enough strife to last us a lifetime.' He looked up at the ceiling. 'I wonder what they're doing up there.'

Someone wrapped a blanket round Ellen's head and she was dragged out of the police station, stumbling and nearly falling headlong because of her hands being cuffed behind her.

A warm hand gripped her arm. 'Steady on.'

Jory. She tried to wrench herself away from him but someone took hold of her other arm and they hurried her on, going downhill then turning left. Going along Rochdale Road, then, she decided. She tripped as often as she dared to slow them down. The hands on her arms didn't slacken though, didn't let her fall when she tried to or slow the pace for more than a step or two.

Then they stopped and someone twirled her round, laughing as she started falling.

Again a strong arm caught her. 'There's no need for that, damn you!' Jory's voice said next to her.

When she felt uneven setts beneath her feet she knew they were in one of the back alleys. All the children played in these alleys, and you never forgot the feel of the crumbling squares of stone under your feet. Where were they taking her? It wasn't far from Rochdale Road. And then she guessed: her stepfather's shop. But she didn't say anything, just tried not to shiver, grateful for the extra warmth the blanket provided, even though it felt airless beneath it with the gag covering her mouth.

The rain seemed to have eased off, but she splashed through puddles several times and her feet were wet and icy cold.

When they went through a gate and on to grass, she was quite certain her guess was correct. His shop was on a corner and it had a larger back yard than the others. He kept some of it as lawn because he still kept an occasional animal there before he killed it himself.

But how would anyone else know how to find her here?

The three men raced through the streets, feet alternately splashing through puddles or clattering on the pavements. The rain had stopped but clouds still covered the sky and everyone else seemed to be indoors.

The police station was locked, no lights showing.

Seth fumbled in his pocket and found the set of keys that he'd filched. It took a few goes to find the correct one, but eventually he got the door open.

Just as he was about to go inside, a voice quavered, 'What are you doing? Where's my Wes?'

They turned to see Mrs Cobbley standing there, shawl huddled round her, slippers on her feet.

'Isn't he at home with you?'

'No. And when I told him tea was ready, he said he didn't want it yet, and that's not like my Wes. I'm that worried about him.'

'He's probably out with Mr Halsopp,' Seth said, keeping his voice gentle because he doubted she was involved in these troubles.

'Well, Bevan did come round earlier with that Keith. I never did like that young fellow. Caught him tormenting a cat once.'

'Oh? Anyone else with them?'

She counted them off on her fingers. 'Dennis and Jory. Oh, and Ellen Dawson was here earlier. Eh, she was crying and shouting, carrying on something shocking, accusing her stepfather of stealing her money. As if he would! They had to drag her into the police station to calm her down. Her mother would be that upset to think of her making such a scene. Perhaps that's why Bevan came round afterwards, to help calm her down. But it's nearly eight o'clock now and if my Wes was going out, he should have let me know. His dinner's ruined, absolutely ruined.'

'We'll keep our eyes open for him, Mrs Cobbley,' Seth said. 'You go back into the warmth now. We don't want you catching cold.' He pushed open the door of the police station and led the way inside, flicking on the light switches, grateful that they had electric light here.

A quick tour of the station showed it to be empty. But the floor inside one cell was still damp in patches, showing the muddy marks of a man's boots.

'This is where they had her locked up,' Seth said.

'They had someone in here, but there's nothing to show it was her,' Giles pointed out.

'What's this?' Algie pointed to some flakes of white on the floor, then looked at the whitewashed wall above the mess.

Marks showed where someone had been scratching. And to one side, in badly misshapen letters was the word *ELLEN*.

'Clever girl!' Seth said approvingly.

'Why are the letters so badly misshapen?' Giles wondered. 'It's as if they'd been written by a child, or someone who couldn't see very well—'

'Just a minute!' Seth dashed out and looked through the cupboard, then came back looking even grimmer. 'There's a pair of handcuffs missing.'

'Bloody cowards!' Algie muttered.

'What else have they done to her?' Seth asked in a voice choked with anger. 'When I get my hands on them . . .'

'You'll do nothing. Leave them to me and Algie here,' Giles said firmly. 'You're too involved.'

Seth looked at him. 'Is it that obvious?'

'Yes.'

'She's a grand lass.'

'I'm sure she is. Let's go and find her.'

'Not yet. I need to make a phone call first.' He had to wait for the operator, who sounded sleepy, and when he gave her the emergency number, she asked him if he was sure.

'I'm certain!' he snapped. 'Put me through to whoever's on duty and as quickly as you can.'

It took him a few precious minutes to explain the situation to the man at the other end. He refused point blank to wait until the Inspector could be fetched and hung the earpiece up.

'The police have known about this little nest of vipers for some time and I was to call if I needed help,' Seth said brusquely, 'but I'm not waiting for reinforcements to come. Those sods have got Ellen. I'm going to get her back.'

'Where do you think they've taken her?'

'It won't be to Halsopp's home, because his wife's there. I saw her earlier. She was very upset about what he was doing.'

'He has a shop.'

'He can't be so stupid, surely?' Algie asked. 'I mean, it's the first place anyone would look.'

'They had to move her in a bit of a hurry.'

'Nelson's family have some large premises on the edge of town. They could have taken her there.'

'If we don't find anything at the shop, we'll go there next,' Seth promised. 'Now, let's not waste any more time.'

'I'll carry her,' a voice said. It wasn't Jory but a man Ellen didn't recognise.

'No, I'll do it.' Jory's voice this time.

She was slung over his shoulder and carried up some stairs. She didn't struggle. What was the point? They were indoors now and there'd be no one to see them. She couldn't even make any noise with the gag in her mouth.

Jory set her down and she started to fall because her hands were still cuffed behind her. Someone shoved her and she tumbled backwards on to a bed, banging her head against the headboard.

'I said, there's no need for that!' Jory shouted.

'Don't be so soft!' someone mocked.

Bevan's voice cut in. 'Ready?'

The blanket was removed and she saw four men watching her. Her clothes were rumpled, showing her legs, one almost up to the thigh. Ellen tried to wriggle into a more decent position and Jory stepped forward to pull her skirt down, helping her to sit up. She sat as straight as she could and glared at them, because that was all she could do with a gag in her mouth.

Bevan pushed Jory aside impatiently. 'Are you going to do as we want?' he demanded. 'The money's mine and it's staying mine, one way or another, and if you've any sense you'll accept that.'

She shook her head but to her surprise he didn't get angry and shout, only smiled. But it was such a gloating, confident smile she felt fear lodge like a piece of lead in her belly as she wondered what he would do to her next.

'Well, it was your choice, Ellen,' he said in the tone he'd always used when disciplining her as a child. 'So

I'll tell you what we're going to do to change your mind. We're going to use your body for our pleasure until you give in.'

She looked at him in horror.

Jory exclaimed and took a hasty step forward.

Bevan held up one hand. 'Let me finish, lad. I'll not touch her. I'd never fancy an uppity bitch like her.' He turned back to Ellen, smiling again. 'But I've seen how these three fine lads have been looking at you, so why don't I give them a treat?'

Icy fear ran through her as the two brothers smirked.

Jory scowled at him. 'She's mine, Bevan. You're not giving her to anyone else.'

'You can have first turn, lad. But if you can't persuade her, if she doesn't agree to behave, I'll have to suppose you've been too gentle with her and then I'll let them try.' He waved one hand towards the bed. 'She's all yours.'

Jory started to speak then closed his mouth with a snap. 'Get out, then. Because I'm not doing it in front of you.'

Laughing softly, Bevan gestured to the two brothers to precede him, then turned back to Jory and Ellen. 'I allus knew you'd had her, you know. Wes told me she'd tried to complain to him about it. You've got him to thank for keeping it all quiet. And she's had plenty of other fellows in London since, I've no doubt. Just make sure you persuade her good and proper this time to keep her mouth shut, or I meant what I said.'

'What's Wes going to do about this? He *is* a policeman, after all.'

'He'll do nothing. He's scared out of his wits I'll tell them what he's been up to if he does.'

'Leave the lamp. I want to see what I'm getting.'

'I need that lamp myself.' Bevan found a candle, pulled a box of matches out of his pocket and lit it, then set it in an old-fashioned candlestick on a tall chest of drawers. 'Best I can manage, I'm afraid. I don't spend money on things for up here because I just use it for storage,' he smiled, 'and when I need a woman. It's surprising what some of 'em will do for a nice piece of meat.'

Ellen couldn't believe that this was her stepfather talking, the one who was supposed to love her mother so much. How had he kept his goings-on quiet in Shawcroft? She was sure her mother didn't suspect anything, hoped she never would.

When Bevan had left the room, Jory went to the door, opened it noiselessly and then closed it again. 'There's no key.' He came across to the bed. 'Don't make a noise till I tell you to.' He took the gag out of Ellen's mouth, then looked at her wrists. 'Damn! I can't do anything about those handcuffs.'

He took one of the chairs and wedged it under the door, then turned back to her.

She cringed away from him, couldn't help it, knew there was nothing she could do to stop him.

23

Edwina took the new bottle of sleeping drops and smiled at Tadwyn. 'Good. Now, where did I put that other bottle? I'll just use that up and—'

'Dr Hilliam says these are a bit weaker than your usual ones,' he said hastily.

She paused. 'I'd better keep the others for myself then. I know exactly how many drops I need to sleep well. Is the doctor still coming out here tonight?'

'He isn't sure. He's got a patient near to death.'

'Well, we can't risk him finding her in her full senses, can we, so we'll have to give her some more in the morning. Come and wake me at six o'clock.'

As she took a lamp and led the way upstairs, Tadwyn followed with a sigh, watching as she took a key out of her pocket and wondering where she kept the spare ones now.

She unlocked the door and held up the lamp, smiling as her daughter spun round to stare at them. 'Chilly in here, isn't it? Never mind, you won't notice soon. But I'll warn you now, if you fight me again, I'll thrash you good and hard after I've given you the dose.' She fingered her cheek with her free hand. 'You'll not do this to me again. Tadwyn, take this lamp.'

Unhappily he took it from her. Behind his mistress's back he mouthed, 'Please trust me.'

Ronnie burst into tears and pressed against the wall.

Edwina advanced on her. 'Open your mouth.'

Still weeping, Ronnie did as she was told.

Holding her daughter by the hair, Edwina dropped the colourless liquid slowly into her mouth, then laughed and stepped back. 'That should be enough to hold you.' She turned to Tadwyn. 'It's cold up here. Let's go back down to the fire.'

When they were outside, he ventured a small protest. 'She'll catch her death of cold, madam.'

'She's tougher than she looks and she'll soon be asleep.' Smiling, Edwina led the way downstairs again. 'She should be drowsy and disoriented soon. Whether the doctor comes tonight or tomorrow, he'll find her very different from the way she was this morning.'

She stopped at the sitting-room door, took the lamp from him and gestured to him to leave.

All without a single word of thanks, he thought bitterly as he watched the door close. On a sudden thought he bent down to peer through the keyhole, but contrary to popular belief it wasn't possible to see much through such a tiny hole. However, from the sounds he heard, he realised that she must be putting the bottle of drops away inside her bureau.

Worried sick about what to do next, he went back to the kitchen. But he couldn't fancy his tea, felt every one of his years weighing down heavily on his shoulders. He agreed with Pel: it wasn't right what Mrs Gresham was doing. She'd taken things too far.

After he'd eaten as much of his meal as he could force down, he tried to answer Pel's urgent questions, explaining what he had seen and heard.

'She'll be frozen on a night like this without any bedding!' Cook said, scandalised.

'If only I knew how to pick locks,' Pel lamented.

'Mrs Gresham takes those drops every night,' Tadwyn said abruptly. 'The doctor prescribed them for her. If we wait until later, we might be able to jemmy open the door without waking madam. I don't care if she finds out. I'm not being responsible for Miss Veronica catching her death of cold.'

Ronnie watched the door close and the line of light fade as her mother and Tadwyn went away. She went and lay down on the bed to wait for the now familiar feeling of weariness.

She shivered and wondered if she was getting sleepy.

After a few more minutes she realised that she was still wide awake and sat up, hugging her knees in the darkness, feeling relief shuddering through her.

Tadwyn was on her side. Surely he'd be coming soon to help her escape?

If only it wasn't so cold.

She didn't dare get out of bed and jump about to keep warm in case someone heard her.

She could only sit and wait, shivering, listening to the wind and rain.

Ellen looked apprehensively at Jory, remembering how strong he'd felt as he carried her upstairs.

'Don't look at me like that!' he said harshly, then lowered his voice and added, 'I'm not going to rape you.'

She couldn't speak for a moment then asked, 'What *are* you going to do then?'

'Buggered if I know.' He went to the window and looked out, tried to open it and found it nailed down. 'I think we'd better give them lot downstairs a bit of a show, though, or they'll be coming up to see what's happening.'

'What do you mean?'

He bounced up and down on the bed, grinning as it creaked loudly. 'If I keep doing this, can you cry out, plead with me not to do it, like those stupid heroines do in the picture shows?'

His bouncing set the bed bumping against the chest of drawers and the candle rocked to and fro, flickering. 'Damn!' He stopped bouncing to pick it up and look for somewhere safe to put it, then set it down on the window sill. 'If all else fails, I'll smash the window and we'll yell for help. There must be someone within earshot. Trouble is, that storm's making a lot of noise. But breaking the window's a final resort. I'd rather not have people finding out I've been involved with them buggers.'

He scowled downwards and began bouncing again. 'Go on, start shouting.'

She felt foolish, but cried out. 'No, no!'

'Louder.'

She yelled it more loudly.

'Plead with me!' he whispered. 'I can't do this on my own.'

'No, please don't do it, Jory.' She pretended to weep. It wouldn't have been hard to turn that pretence into reality because she couldn't quite believe that he was on her side, and even if he was, couldn't see how he could get her safely out of there.

After a minute or two, he muttered, 'For heaven's sake, keep yelling!' So she began begging him not to touch her, then not to hurt her.

The three men stopped outside the front of the butcher's shop. 'No sign of any lights,' Seth commented. 'Let's try round the back. And tread quietly.'

At the rear lights were showing, an oil lamp showing brightly on the ground floor and what looked like a single candle flickering in an upstairs bedroom.

'They're here!' Seth whispered.

'What do we do next?' Algie asked.

'Find out how many there are. Go in and arrest them as long as there aren't too many.'

'Let me have a recce,' Giles said. 'I'm pretty good at it.'

He had no sooner got into a position just outside the window from which he could check the room than an old man stood up and moved towards the door. His voice came floating out to them.

'I've got to use the privy, Bevan. It upsets my stomach, this sort of thing does. I don't know what you wanted me with you for tonight, I really don't.'

As Wes came stumbling out, still grumbling under his breath, Giles drew back into the shadows and watched him stumble across to the far end of the yard. While the old man was using the privy, he went to whisper to Seth, 'I vote we capture him and tie him up. That'll even the odds against us a bit.'

'Good idea. What did you see through the window?'

'There are three other men, another older one and two young brutish looking fellows, but no sign of a woman. See if you can find something to tie this one up with. If not I'll use my tie.' He looked up. 'Is it my imagination or is the storm dying down?'

'It's still raining.'

'Not as hard. And I haven't heard thunder for a few minutes.'

Just then a voice floated out from the bedroom. 'No, no!'

Seth stiffened. 'That's Ellen.'

Giles nudged him. 'Look out.'

As Wes stumbled out of the privy, they grabbed him and before he could do more than gurgle in shock, Giles put a hand across his mouth and Seth forced him against the wall, face towards it, so that he couldn't see his captors.

'Stand still and keep quiet if you value your life,' Giles said.

Wes whimpered and did as he was told.

'What's happening in there?'

He explained in halting tones.

'Fine policeman you are,' his captor snapped.

Ellen's voice floated down to them again, 'Don't hurt me! Please don't hurt me!'

Before Wes could move again, a gag was thrust into

his mouth and fastened there with Giles's tie and he was lowered to the ground, where they tied his arms to the clothes post.

'I've got to get to her!'

Giles held Seth back. 'There's obviously another of them upstairs, so that makes four against three.'

'I'm not very good at hand to hand fighting,' Algie admitted. 'Sorry. I'll do my best, though.'

Giles still kept hold of his companion's arm. 'What if they win? That'll not help her.'

Seth looked up at the window where the frail flame was still flickering. 'I'm not leaving her there!'

'Let's see if we can draw another of them outside, then.' Giles picked up the dustbin lid and tossed it to the ground with a loud clatter.

There was a sudden silence inside the house, then one of the men came towards the door, calling, 'Wes? What the hell's taking you so long?'

As Seth tried to jump him, he seemed to sense he was being attacked and fought back, yelling for help.

The mêlée which followed was short but vicious. The two younger men were experienced fighters and Halsopp was heavy enough to prevent anyone capturing him easily.

In the end, the attackers proved so troublesome that Halsopp knocked Algie flying and got away, crashing down the back alley.

'Don't follow him,' Seth panted. 'Fetch the rest of the clothes line.'

Seth made sure their two captives were secured then pounded up the stairs.

There was silence from inside the room. He tried the door and it gave a little, so he drew back to kick it in.

When the noise of a fight erupted, Jory went to stare out of the window. 'Damn! Can't see who it is.'

'Why don't you go down and find out what's happening?'

'Not till I know who it is.'

'Well, it may be my chance to escape, so I'm going.'

When she tried to get to the door, he shoved her back. 'Stay here till we're sure. There are three big men downstairs and they won't be taken easily. Or do you want to give them an excuse to come and do what I haven't?'

She looked down, trying in vain to make out who was there. 'It'll be Seth, I know it will,' she muttered. When Jory cursed she turned to him and found him looking at her so strangely that she drew away from him. 'What's the matter? Why are you looking at me like that?'

'I'm the one who saves you from being raped, but when you think he's there, your whole face lights up. How do you think that makes me feel?' He took her arm. 'He can't care about you as much as I do. Who do you think I thought about when I was in the trenches? You. Only you! Ellen, you cared for me once, you can care for me again. I'll *make* you care for me.'

She shook her head. 'I stopped caring a long time ago, Jory. I was just a girl then, didn't know myself, let alone you. I've changed, grown up and . . . well,

I'm grateful for what you've done tonight, but it's Seth I care for now – and he cares for me.'

Feet pounded up the stairs and Jory stared at her for another minute, then went to the door, which was being rattled. 'Who's there?'

'The police.'

'Seth?' Ellen called.

'Are you all right? He hasn't hurt you?'

'I'm fine,' Ellen said. 'Let him in, Jory.'

With a final crooked smile in her direction, he opened the door. 'About time you got here.'

Seth punched him as hard as he could and in a minute the two men were rolling about on the floor.

'Stop it!' Ellen screamed. 'Stop it!'

But they didn't seem to hear her.

Another man appeared in the doorway.

'Stop them fighting,' she pleaded. 'Jory saved me. He's not one of that lot.'

Giles nodded and stepped round the struggling pair, grabbing the rough blanket off the bed. He flung it over the two men and caused a temporary halt, yelling, 'Stop it!' at the top of a very loud voice.

They rolled apart, shoving the blanket aside, glaring at one another.

'Jory saved me from them,' Ellen said quickly.

'Which is more than *you* did, Talbot!' Jory taunted.

Seth ignored him. His eyes raked Ellen from head to toe, taking in her bruised and battered appearance. He went and drew her into his arms and she leaned against him with a sigh.

*   *   *

Giles found himself feeling sorry for the young man who was watching the couple with such anguish in his face. He touched Jory on the shoulder and beckoned to him, leading the way downstairs. 'You care about her,' he said quietly as they reached the bottom.

'Aye. But I made a muck-up of it.' Jory stopped in the doorway looking at Dennis and Keith, who were tied up and glowering at the world. 'Where's Halsopp?'

'He got away, but we'll catch him later.' Giles looked upwards. 'I reckon we can afford to give Seth and Ellen a few minutes, then we've got to get these buggers to jail. There's another urgent problem needing attention at the Hall.'

'Why don't you just lock them in the cellar here, then? Very snug, Halsopp's cellar is.'

'Show me.' He nodded to Algie. 'Keep an eye on them and yell out, if they so much as wriggle.'

Algie waved one hand in acknowledgement and picked up a wooden meat mallet. 'I reckon a little love tap with this would sort out any problems.'

Jory showed Giles the cellar, which had two half carcases hanging to one side over a drip tray and a very stout outer door. 'There's another store room hidden over there beyond the coal cellar. It's where he keeps his black-market stuff. Very enterprising fellow, Bevan Halsopp, always finding new ways to get hold of money. He never spends much, though.'

Giles pulled out his watch and flipped the lid open. 'Let's fetch those two villains down here then we'll have to disturb Seth.'

'What's the hurry?'

'We've got to go and rescue my fiancée – Veronica Gresham. Her mother's got her locked up and drugged.'

Jory let out a crack of scornful laughter. 'I come home for a bit of peace after all the fighting and I walk straight into crime and mayhem.'

'We all want peace. But it doesn't mean we'll let villains get away with things.' Giles studied the other man. 'Were you involved in the murder?'

'No.'

'But you knew about it?'

'I found out recently.'

'Who did it?'

'I'm not telling you.'

'Must be someone you're close to, then?'

Jory shrugged.

Upstairs Seth hugged Ellen again, kissed her cheek then fumbled in his pocket. 'Turn round and let me undo those handcuffs. How long have you had them on?'

'Hours.'

He released her hands then began rubbing them and her arms, hearing her stifle a moan. 'It's going to hurt for a while, I'm afraid. Are you really all right, Ellen?'

'Yes. Jory kept the others off me till you came.'

'Are you sure?'

'Of course I am. He's not long been back in Shawcroft so he wasn't involved in whatever they were doing.' She hesitated.

'He used to be your fellow.'

'Once. A long time ago.'

'And you're standing up for him now.'

'I'm telling the truth. That's a bit different. Ouch,' she grimaced as she tried to move normally.

Seth hesitated, then asked stiffly, 'So you've not – made things up with him?'

She looked at him and her whole expression softened. 'Never. I'm just setting the record straight.'

'Your stepfather escaped, but he won't stay free for long.'

'He'll have gone home. He's got money hidden there.' She tried to raise her arms to put them round Seth's neck and winced, so let them drop again, saying in a voice that wobbled, 'I need you to hold me.'

He pulled her to him, feeling her shaking. 'Ah, Ellen darling, you're all right now. It's just reaction. You'll be all right soon. Shh, now. Shh.'

Gradually she stopped shaking and sighed against him.

'I'm sorry I didn't get to you sooner. I heard you calling out for help in the police station, but I was outnumbered, so I went for help. Giles Covington's below and you've met Algie St Corbin, I think.'

'Giles Covington!' She jerked upright as the name sank in. 'I've a letter for him. I never got a chance to post it.' She fumbled in her inner pockets, coming up with a damp, crumpled envelope. 'It's from Veronica Gresham. I smuggled a stub of pencil in to her and she tore a page from a book to write on.'

'We'd better give it to him, find out what it says. She's the next one to be rescued.'

Seth helped Ellen down the stairs, not trusting her to be steady on her feet yet, then found her a seat. She gave the letter to Giles, explaining what it was. 'I'm not sorry now that I didn't get a chance to post it today.'

His face brightened at the mere sound of Ronnie's name and he tore the envelope open, quickly scanning the piece of paper. 'She says her mother has her locked up and is drugging her. How can the woman get away with it in this day and age?'

'There aren't any neighbours at the Hall.'

'There are the servants, though. How could they stand by and let it happen?'

Algie let out a hollow laugh. 'Have you met Mrs Gresham? She's a fire-breathing dragon in human form, and my mother's nearly as bad. I'm so afraid of the pair of them that I'm running away from home to marry a Frenchwoman, who's carrying P— my baby.' He gave a wry smile. 'The pair of them had their hearts set on my marrying Ronnie.'

'I can assure you that *I* am not afraid of Mrs Gresham,' Giles said firmly.

'Well, you ought to be,' Algie told him. 'She's cunning and she's got very influential friends.'

'The servants are afraid for their jobs,' Ellen added. 'Some of them have nowhere else to go, no family left.'

'They still should have helped Ronnie.'

'If you're well enough to walk now, Ellen, we'll take

you round to the Pughs',' Seth said. 'I don't want to delay any longer.'

'I'm coming with you.'

'Not this time, love, you'd be more hindrance than help, the state you're in.'

She sighed. 'I suppose so. How are you going to get out there?'

'We'll need to borrow a car,' Giles said. 'Mine broke down and as far as I know, it's still out on the moors.'

'Take my motorbike,' she said at once.

Jory, who'd been watching them, said quickly, 'We won't all fit into it.'

Everyone looked at him in surprise.

He shrugged. 'I might as well be in at the finish. And Algie here said he's not much good at fighting. I am.'

'Take him with you, Seth,' Ellen said. 'I'll feel better about it all then.'

So they walked her to the Pughs' house, where Seth cut short the exclamations and asked Martin to help him get the bike ready.

'Keep her here,' he said as the engine roared into life, filling the quiet air with an urgent throbbing. 'Don't let her go to her mother and don't let anyone in here. Algie, we need you to go to the police station and wait for the men coming from Manchester.'

'As long as no one else sees me,' Algie said. He went out into the rain again.

'He's terrified of that mother of his,' Jory said scornfully. 'Allus was, even as a lad. But she's not nearly as bad as your lass's mother. We all used to be afraid of

Mrs Gresham, didn't scrump her apples. She's a wicked witch, if ever there was one.'

Jeanie had Ellen into a warm bath within a few minutes, but couldn't persuade her to go to bed, so had to lend her some clothes and let her come down to the sitting room.

'I couldn't sleep,' she insisted. 'Not till I know Seth's all right.'

'You love him, don't you?'

Ellen's smile blossomed like a daisy opening to the sun. 'Oh, yes. And he loves me. It's so wonderful, we don't even have to think about whether we love one another or not. I didn't realise it could be like this.' Then her smile faded. 'I hope he's all right.'

'Well, there's not much trouble they can get into at the Hall, is there? I mean, Mrs Gresham will play up, but they're three great brutes of men, so they'll be able to deal with her all right. Don't you worry.'

24

Bevan ran along the back alleys, pausing for a moment a couple of streets away from his shop to catch his breath. There was no sound of anyone coming after him so he stayed where he was, legs feeling like jelly. It seemed a long time before his heart stopped pounding. He hated running, always had done.

They'd check his house first thing, but he reckoned he had time to slip back and get the money he'd hidden away. Why hadn't Ellen taken it when she retrieved her own money? Because she was stupid, that's why. He would have done.

He began walking again, trying not to make a noise. Through the allotments would be the best route, he decided, then down to his house the back way. He'd be able to make sure no one was there waiting for him before he went in. They probably wouldn't know he had an allotment, because it was rented in Eddie Nelson's name. There was a hut there with a stout lock. Very useful that hut had been during the past few years.

He froze when he heard the sound of a motorbike in the distance. Only one person in town that he knew had a motorbike. Where was she going at this hour of the night? But he relaxed as the sound faded away into the distance. As long as it wasn't coming in this direction, what did it matter?

He shouldn't stand around here like a fool. He had to get a move on, retrieve his money. He'd hide out in the allotment until the following day.

When he got to the rear gate of his house, he stopped to listen again, but the back lanes were quiet and there was no sign of a light in the house. He wished he could wake Dorothy to say goodbye. How would she manage without him? He might never see her again.

He walked quietly along the garden path to his shed and was shocked to see that someone had dug up the cash box. It was sitting on the workbench, gaping empty. Had Ellen come back for it? No, she'd been locked up all day, hadn't been able to. So where was his money? Who had known about it?

He stood on a wooden beer crate and fumbled along the joist, letting out a soft groan of relief when he found the bankbook in its oilskin wrapping. No one knew about that account, not even Dorothy.

But the lack of money in the cash box meant he'd have to go inside the house and see what he could scrape together. He always left the housekeeping money in the pot on the kitchen mantelpiece, had just refilled it. There should be enough there to see him through till he was safe in another town, then he could get some money out of his other savings account, which was in a different name.

It was a good thing he had always been careful and

spread his money around, he thought with satisfaction. He was too smart for them.

He let himself into the kitchen, surprised that the back door was unlocked. Moving cautiously he felt his way towards the mantelpiece. But the pot wasn't there! Had Madge moved it when she was cleaning?

'I can hear you, Bevan!'

He swung round in shock. 'Dorothy?'

'I'm wide awake. Come and tell me what you've been doing.'

He hesitated, but he'd already given himself away, and he did want to say goodbye to her.

As he went into the bedroom he heard her scratching a match and dropping it with a soft exclamation of annoyance, so he hurried forward. 'Let me do that.'

He lit the candle that stood next to the bed and stared at her by its flickering light. She looked as transparent as a ghost.

'Bevan, what on earth's happened to you? Have you been fighting?'

'Yes.' Suddenly he felt so weak he had to sit down on the edge of the bed. 'I'm getting too old for such capers, I can tell you.' He picked up her hand and held it tenderly in both his. She was the only woman in his whole life who hadn't let him down.

'Well, you can go and wash those scratches, make us both a cup of tea then tell me what you've been up to.'

'I can't stay, love. The police are after me.'

'*The police!* Bevan, no! What have you *done*?'

He watched as she jerked her hand away to put it

across her mouth. She always did that when she was upset. 'It's all your Ellen's fault. *She* brought them down on me.'

Dorothy was quiet for a minute or two, then shook her head. 'No, it was the money. That's what brought them down on you. You stole my daughter's savings and that's upset me more than you'll ever understand.'

Anger glowed inside him. 'Well, she's got her own back now, damn her. They're after me, Dorothy, and I need some money to get away. Did you take the money from my cash box?'

'Yes.'

'How did you get out there? You can hardly walk.'

'Anger, Bevan. It drove me on. I was furious with you. So I took your money to show you what it feels like to be robbed. I've hidden it and you'll never find it if you look for a million years.'

'Then tell me, love.'

'No.'

He began to search her drawers, ignoring her attempts to talk to him, tossing things out and letting them lie on the floor. In one drawer he found some small change and scooped it up, shoving it in his pocket, then he rifled through her handbag and took a couple of banknotes out of her purse. But that was all he found.

He turned round to her. 'Please tell me where the other money is, Dorothy. Surely you don't want them to put me in prison?'

'If you admit what you've done, I'll ask Ellen not to press charges. She'll do that for me, I know she will.'

'I'll not beg any favours from that bitch!' He took her by the shoulders and shook her violently, then let go when she cried out in shock. He looked at her aghast, then at his own hands, as if they had a life of their own. 'I'm sorry. I never meant to— Dorothy, forgive me.'

But she was weeping wildly now.

He stood there for a minute, undecided, then sat down beside her, risking a few more minutes to set things right. 'Listen, Dorothy, you keep the money. There should be enough to keep you for a few months.'

'By which time I'll be dead,' she said bitterly. 'Only now I won't have you to comfort me as I die, will I?'

'What else can I do but get away?' he yelled suddenly.

'Confess. Ask Ellen to forgive you.'

'Never. And she wouldn't forgive me, either. They're not putting me in prison. I'd rather kill myself than be caught.'

She began weeping again. He scrubbed his eyes and left her, running upstairs to grab some clothes and stuff them in a carpet bag. At the foot of the stairs he hesitated, then shook his head. He daren't risk staying any longer.

Letting himself out of the back door he made his way quietly up to the allotments. Just as he was opening the gate, he heard the sound of another motor. It carried clearly in the damp air, now that the storm was over, a car engine this time it sounded like. Who the hell was driving around Shawcroft at this hour of the night?

*   *   *

When Bevan went out of the back door without even looking into her bedroom to say goodbye, Dorothy got angry and staggered after him. She stood clutching the doorpost, staring outside into the darkness. The moon came out from behind a cloud and she saw the gate still open. It was so quiet at this time of night she could hear the sound of his feet crunching on gravel in the distance. There was only one gravel path near here so she knew exactly where he had gone. When she heard the faint squeak of metal on metal, she nodded. She'd been right. The allotments. He'd complained so many times about the noise that gate made because no amount of oiling would make it stay silent for long.

She knew so much more about him than he realised. But she didn't know what she was going to do about him – give him away to the police or let him escape?

Feeling weak and dizzy, she stumbled back to bed, pulling the eiderdown up and then began weeping again. It didn't matter how much Bevan loved her or she loved him, he'd committed a crime and wouldn't repent.

But could she turn him in to the police? Could she do that to him? She didn't think so.

'Why could you never be satisfied?' she whispered into the darkness much later as the bedside candle guttered and the flame died. 'You didn't need to steal Ellen's money. You had plenty of your own. Now look where your greed's got you!'

She'd probably never see him again. That thought made her stomach cramp with agony. She wished she could go to sleep and never wake up again, was dreading people finding out what he'd done.

The rain stopped completely as they were driving out to the Hall.

Giles leaned forward to shout in Seth's ear, 'Slow down. I know a place to stop, then we can cut across the fields on foot.'

When they stopped, Jory got out of the sidecar, grumbling at the muddy conditions underfoot. 'I don't know why we don't just drive up to the door and demand to be let in. What's the use of being a policeman if you can't tell folk what to do? Haven't you two had enough of tramping through mud during the past few years? I certainly have.'

'More than enough,' Giles agreed. 'But I'm afraid Mrs Gresham will hurt Ronnie if she hears us coming. She isn't behaving like a rational person.'

There were lights still on in the Hall as the three men made their way quietly across the ploughed fields. Giles led them round to the rear, where they found a lamp had been left burning low in the kitchen, its flame so tiny it barely showed the outline of the window. The door opened and a man made his way across the yard.

Soon afterwards, lights showed in the attics, pale flickering lights of candles rather than the steady glow of oil lamps.

'The servants are going to bed,' Giles whispered.

'There's one room still lit downstairs.'

'It's a small sitting room at the rear. I went inside

the house a few days ago and checked the place out,' Giles said absent-mindedly. 'I've a key for those french doors, but I want to give Mrs Gresham time to get to bed, then try to get Ronnie out without her realising it.'

But as they waited they heard the noise of a motor car.

'Damnation! Who can that be at this hour of the night?' Seth muttered.

They crept along the side of the house and watched a small vehicle chug up to the front of the house.

'I'll go and see who it is,' Seth said. 'You wait here.'

He came back a couple of minutes later. 'It's the doctor. I heard Mrs Gresham greeting him at the door.'

'That's torn it!' Giles said. 'You go and make a diversion at the front and I'll get in through the back. I think I know where they're keeping Ronnie. I'm not giving anyone a chance to drug her again.'

'Ellen said only Mrs Gresham had the keys to the door of Ronnie's room.'

'I'll break the door down if I have to.'

'I'm sorry to disturb you at such a late hour,' Dr Hilliam apologised, 'but I was worried about your daughter.'

Mrs Gresham smiled graciously. 'Do come in. You were right to worry. She's had another turn. I can't get a word of sense out of her.'

He stared at her. 'I'd like to examine her. But first – what happened to your face?'

'Veronica attacked me. If Tadwyn hadn't been with me, I don't know what she'd have done to me.'

He put one finger under her chin, turning her towards the light from the oil lamp she was carrying, tutting under his breath.

'I'll summon Tadwyn before we go up to her,' she said. 'It'll be safer.'

But she had no need to do that because Tadwyn appeared at the rear of the hall, holding up a lamp. 'I heard the doctor's car and thought you might need me, madam.'

'Yes, we do. I was telling the doctor how my daughter attacked me earlier.' She gestured to her face.

Dr Hilliam turned to Tadwyn. 'Did you see this attack?'

'Er – yes.'

'That's very serious. I must have been mistaken in my diagnosis. People suffering from such disorders can be very cunning and persuasive.'

Edwina pretended to dab at her eyes. 'It upset me terribly, I must admit. My own daughter!'

'We'd better go up to see her at once. I'm afraid we may need to lock her away, for her own safety and yours, in the asylum.'

Giles yanked Jory back into the shadows as the door opened and an elderly man hurried across the yard to the house, pulling on his jacket.

They watched as he went inside and then they crept across to peer in the window. He lit another lamp and left the kitchen carrying it.

'Now!' Giles whispered. 'We can go up the servants' stairs to Ronnie's room. How's your night vision?'

'Not bad.'

'Come on then.'

Jory gave him a mock salute, but followed confidently. He recognised this sort of officer, the right sort as far as experienced soldiers were concerned, the sort who didn't expose you to unnecessary danger. He'd prayed for such officers sometimes when he'd had to put his life into the hands of a young lieutenant who was still wet behind the ears.

The two men entered the house and Giles led the way across the kitchen and up the narrow stairs.

Jory followed him, wishing he could stop and have a good look round on what was likely to be his one and only visit to the splendours of the Hall.

When Pel heard the sound of a car he went to the window of his bedroom and stared out across the yard, but the vehicle had stopped at the front and he couldn't see it from here. There was enough moonlight for him to see two men come creeping along the side of the house, however. They drew back to hide in the shadows when Tadwyn went hurrying back to the house.

Were these burglars? Were they the ones who'd stayed in the stable bedroom?

Once the brighter lamp light had vanished from the kitchen the intruders reappeared, darker silhouettes against the wet grey stonework. They paused at the door and when the taller one said something, the other saluted.

Pel was surprised to see that. It had been a proper salute, not one of the flapping imitations so many civilians did, so these must be ex-soldiers. He didn't like to think of them being reduced to burglary. Maybe if he could warn them he'd spotted them, they'd go away and there would be no need for any trouble.

As he entered the kitchen he could hear Mrs Gresham's booming tones from the hall so guessed the men wouldn't have gone that way. There was only one other way up, so he took it, treading very softly.

Ronnie hadn't been able to sleep because she'd been too cold, so when she heard the car she sat up, sure that this would mean trouble for her one way or the other.

She debated pretending to be asleep, then changed her mind. The doctor seemed to be at least partly on her side. She'd simply keep calm – that was most important – and beg him to get her away from here tonight, not leave her in her mother's power again.

But she wished she had her clothes, hated appearing in front of people so scantily clad, dreaded to think how her bruised face would look, and couldn't help shivering from time to time.

Then someone rapped lightly on the door and a voice she'd been longing to hear called, 'Ronnie! Are you in there?'

'Giles!' She flew across to the door, pressing herself against it. 'Giles, is it really you?'

'Are you all right, my darling?'

'I am now, or I will be if you can let me out. My mother's got all the keys to this door, though.'

'Shh. There's someone coming up the stairs.' He gestured to Jory to go into the bedroom on one side and slipped into the door on the other side.

Ronnie stood there with tears streaming down her face then backed away from the door. He'd come. No matter what anyone said or did now, she felt quite sure that Giles would get her out of here.

The door opened and she braced herself as she faced the light that flooded in.

'Are you all right, Miss Gresham?' the doctor asked.

She wiped away a tear. 'I'm very cold. They took away my blankets again.'

Edwina stared at her daughter in angry dismay, then shot an accusing glance at Tadwyn, who was staring fixedly ahead, before saying coldly, 'You started tearing the bedding up. Don't you remember?' She moved towards her daughter.

Ronnie stepped back. 'I don't want her to touch me again, doctor.'

Dr Hilliam opened his bag and took out a syringe he'd already prepared. 'Just let me give you something to calm you down, Veronica.'

She panicked then. What had happened to make the doctor change his mind about helping her? What had her mother been saying? 'Giles! Help me! Giles!' She backed away from the doctor towards the window.

Edwina watched with a triumphant smile on her face, which turned into shock as Giles burst into the room. Tadwyn moved hurriedly out of his way but Edwina stood her ground.

'Who are you? What are you doing in my house?'

'I'm Ronnie's fiancé, Giles Covington,' he said, stepping past the doctor and pulling his beloved into his arms, horrified by her battered face. He ignored the others while he made sure she was all right and when he realised how cold she was, slipped out of his jacket and wrapped it round her. 'Are you trying to kill her?' he demanded, flashing a glance at her mother.

Edwina glared at him. 'What do you know about what we've had to put up with from her? She can put on a good face in company, nearly had the good doctor fooled. But she is *not* safe to be let loose.'

Dr Hilliam cleared his throat. 'That is presumably why you needed the extra sleeping drops, to keep her quiet?'

'Yes.' Mrs Gresham sobbed and used her handkerchief again. 'I didn't want anyone to know how violent she'd become. They had to call me from the farm a while ago to ask me to come and fetch her. I felt so *ashamed*!'

'That's not true!' Ronnie cried.

Dr Hilliam stared from one to the other then turned to her mother. 'I'm sorry, dear lady. I seem to have completely misunderstood the situation. Mr Covington, whether you're the girl's fiancé or not is irrelevant. Have you seen her mother's face? If she did that, Veronica is dangerous and in need of treatment and restraint in an asylum for the insane.' He lifted the syringe again.

Before he could move the knocker sounded on the front door below, used so vigorously it sounded through the whole house.

'What next?' Tadwyn muttered. 'Shall I go and answer that, madam?'

'No, let them knock. I need you here.'

'But it must be important for someone to come out so late at night,' the doctor protested.

'I'll say what's important and what isn't in this house,' she declared. 'I'm the mistress here. And what I want is for my poor deluded daughter to be kept safe. Please do what you need to, doctor. And you, Covington, or whatever you're called, get out of my house this minute or I'll have you thrown out.'

25

At the end of the corridor, Glenys took Pel's hand, glad she had his support. She'd come down and found him eavesdropping, so had joined him. Now, she'd heard more than enough to make up her mind. 'We can't let Mrs Gresham go on like this. We have to tell them all what she's been doing to Miss Veronica. I don't care any more if I lose my job.'

'I agree. Come on, love.' He put his arm round her shoulders and they walked forward together.

Jory who was standing just outside the bedroom, ready to intervene if Covington needed help, turned at the sound of their steps. 'Who the hell are you?'

'We work here and we need to tell that doctor something. It's about Miss Veronica. There's nothing wrong with her.'

He gestured them inside with a mocking bow. 'Go in and join the party then. Things are just getting exciting.'

Inside the room Giles was standing between Dr Hilliam and Ronnie, arguing with the doctor, while Mrs Gresham kept shouting at him to leave her house. At one stage she made a lunge towards her daughter and Dr Hilliam had to pull her away while Giles protected Ronnie.

Far from helping his mistress, Tadwyn was standing motionless just inside the door.

No one seemed to be getting any further towards sorting this confusion out, so Jory put his fingers to his lips and whistled, a piercing sound that had them all stopping short and turning towards him.

'There are two people here who want to tell you something, doctor.' He gestured to Glenys and Pel.

After starting at her maid in frozen astonishment, Edwina snapped, 'Go back to your room at once, Glenys! This has nothing to do with you. And what is that fool doing inside the house?' When they didn't move, she shrieked, 'I said go away, both of you. This minute.'

Still holding Pel's hand, Glenys moved forward. 'Dr Hilliam, I can't keep quiet any longer. I've seen Mrs Gresham forcing those drops on Miss Veronica, ill-treating her, drugging her food, leaving her without clothes or bedding. It's not Miss Veronica who's behaving strangely, it's her mother.'

'Wouldn't you fight back if you knew there was nothing wrong with you and someone was keeping you prisoner and drugging you?' Pel demanded. 'Everyone in the house knew she had her daughter locked up and was tampering with her food.'

Edwina rushed at Glenys and tried to shove her forcibly out of the door. 'You're dismissed! Both of you!' she shouted.

Seth, who had let himself in through the front door, arrived in time to see the attack. Pel moved to protect Glenys, putting up one arm defensively as Mrs

Gresham tried to hit him.

'What the hell is going on?' Seth demanded, pulling Mrs Gresham away.

She turned to the member of staff who hadn't joined in. 'Tadwyn, tell the doctor it isn't true, that we were *protecting* Veronica.'

He shook his head. 'I can't do it, madam. I saw you force her to come home and to my shame, I did nothing to stop you. And I've seen you force those drops down her throat or put them on her food! You even left her without a chamber pot so that she'd soil herself.'

At that betrayal, Edwina turned and attacked him instead, shrieking and clawing at him. It took all Jory and Seth's strength to drag her off him and then she spat obscenities at the doctor, accusing him of misconduct. Spittle dribbled from her mouth as she continued to shriek and struggle against those holding her.

Dr Hilliam used the syringe to inject her with the calming medication. 'Hysteria,' he said curtly. 'Paranoia, I shouldn't be surprised. Had me fooled for a time.'

The drug he'd used took effect quite quickly and Mrs Gresham sagged against the two men holding her captive.

Ronnie had stopped weeping but was still clinging to Giles.

'Who is going to look after Mrs Gresham?' Dr Hilliam asked. 'She will need constant attention, if this is what I think it is.'

Ronnie shivered and shook her head. 'I couldn't. She's too strong for me.'

The doctor looked at the servants, who shook their heads. 'She'll have to be confined in an institution, then. Constable, will you come with me if I drive her to hospital? She may need restraining.'

'Yes, of course. Giles, you'll be staying here, I presume?'

'Of course.'

Seth turned to Jory. 'It'll be up to you to take Ellen's motorbike back, then. Can I trust you to do that?'

Jory gave him a wry smile. 'Yes. Strange the allies you make when there's trouble, eh? What about Halsopp? He's still on the loose.'

'I telephoned for help. It ought to have arrived by now. If it hasn't, you may need to protect Ellen, as well as keeping an eye on the prisoners until Inspector Dunham sends someone.'

'I'll protect her. But afterwards . . . it's you she wants, damn you, so you'd better make her happy!'

The two men looked at one another, a long, searching stare. Each nodded to show understanding of the other's situation, then Seth turned to help the doctor with the practicalities of taking Mrs Gresham away.

Ronnie went across to Glenys. 'Thank you for speaking out. I know what it must have cost you. But please don't leave. I'm going to need your help in the house.'

'I'm happy to help you, miss, I'm sure.'

'Then can you get a room ready for Mr Covington? He'll be staying the night.' She turned to Giles, 'You can phone Mr Monnings from my mother's sitting room, darling. Glenys will show you where it is. I must go and put some clothes on.' She wanted to linger in a warm bath, but there were too many things to sort out. And anyway, most of all, she needed to be with Giles.

She walked down the stairs to where a lamp was burning on the first floor landing, lighting one of the candles standing ready nearby. In her bedroom she held the candle up to look round. She hadn't been here for months and it seemed strange, not hers any more. There were plenty of clothes to choose from but there was nothing she could do about her face. She smiled. Giles wouldn't mind that, she was sure.

When she was dressed, she went downstairs to find Giles waiting for her in the hall. She ran down the last few steps into his arms and rested against him, sighing happily. This was what she needed more than anything else at the moment.

He pushed her to arm's length, studying her face. 'Are you all right now, darling?'

'Yes. Tired, but feeling more myself every minute.'

He folded her back into his arms. 'I'm obtaining a special licence and we're getting married as soon as is practicable.'

'Yes, please.' Joy filled her as she lifted her head for his kiss.

Jory drove slowly back into Shawcroft, not looking forward to more trouble, but knowing this matter wouldn't be settled until Halsopp was caught. He found the police station lit up brightly and a man who had every appearance of being a senior police officer standing behind the counter.

'Who are you?' he barked as Jory went in.

'Jory Nelson, sir, late of the North Lancashire Rifles. Seth Talbot sent me to report in. I've been assisting him. He's been unavoidably delayed, helping Dr Hilliam get a madwoman to the hospital.'

'Oh?' The man eyed him narrowly as if he doubted this.

'Has anyone told you about the prisoners, sir? They're at the butcher's shop.'

'Yes. A Mr St Corbin has taken my three men to get them – I gather Talbot left them locked in the cellar.'

'Yes, sir. But there's still Mr Halsopp to catch. He legged it while the fighting was going on. Has anyone seen him?'

'No. We've only been here an hour or so. Any idea where he might be? If he's got any sense, he'll have left the town.'

'He hasn't got a car, so he can't drive anyway. I'd guess he went back to his home first to get some money. He always has something tucked away, that one does, can always lay his hands on fifty quid if he needs it.' Or so his dad had said a year or two ago when boasting about his black-market activities. Jory looked up at the clock. 'I don't reckon Halsopp will be at his house now. He'll have holed up somewhere.'

Remembering what his father had told him he snapped his fingers. 'I know! He and my dad had a place to hide the black-market stuff, on one of the allotments. It was in my dad's name, not Halsopp's. My dad was involved with him, I'm sorry to say. Halsopp won't think anyone knows except Dad, so maybe you'll be able to catch him there.'

Inspector Dunham nodded. 'As soon as they bring the prisoners back, you'd better show us where to go.'

'There's just one thing.' Jory hesitated. 'My dad was involved with them and there was some trouble. He killed a man by accident. I know my dad. He'd never kill anyone intentionally. Could you – go a bit easy on him?'

'I'll bear it in mind, certainly. You're sure it was an accident?'

Jory nodded. 'I'd stake my life on it.'

'Very well. We'll give that possibility consideration. More I can't promise. In the end, it's up to the courts. Now, where is this allotment?'

Ellen was warm and dry again, after a hot bath and a bowl of Jeanie's broth, but she couldn't settle to sleep. She knew that if she stayed downstairs, they would too, so eventually went to bed, hearing her Uncle Martin and Aunt Jeanie follow soon afterwards. She didn't undress and once her uncle's snores started to rumble out, she crept down to the kitchen again, determined to wait up for Seth.

For some reason she couldn't stop worrying about her mother. She didn't usually have 'feelings' about things, always prided herself on being practical, so she tried to dismiss them. But she couldn't interest herself in her uncle's evening newspaper and the more she sat there, the more worried she became about her mother.

Surely her stepfather would have left the town now? He'd not linger in a place where he could be traced so easily.

In the end she gave in to her feelings and decided to go round to her mother's, just to check that everything was all right. She scribbled a note and left it propped up against the teapot, then slipped on her aunt's coat and headscarf and crept out.

It was strange to walk through the quiet streets at night. The clouds had mostly gone and the moon was shining down, reflecting back at her from puddles or winking briefly from window panes. In one house a light was on and there was the sound of a baby crying.

As she reached the end of her mother's street Ellen stopped moving and stayed in the shadows, waiting, checking that no one was about. But everything was silent and the silvery moon seemed to smile down a blessing, so she pressed on.

She stood outside the bedroom window, which had once been the sitting room, and heard clearly the sound of a woman sobbing inside. Without hesitation she tried the front door and found it unlocked.

'Mum? It's me.'

'Ellen?'

'Yes.' She went into the bedroom. 'Haven't you got a candle?'

'It burned down.'

'Here, let's pull the curtains back so that I can see what I'm doing.' Talking gently she helped her mother sit up, then went to fetch another candle from the shelf in the scullery. It didn't seem a time for bright oil lamps.

She sat on the edge of the bed. 'Has he been to see you? Is that why you were crying?'

'Yes. I begged him to confess, ask your forgiveness, but he wouldn't. I stole his money, Ellen, trying to make him feel what it was like to be robbed, but it did no good.' She mopped her eyes. 'He's always been too fond of money and now he can't seem to think about anything else.'

'But he did come to say goodbye to you, at least. I'm glad of that. Here, lean against me and see if you can sleep a little. You used to hold me like this when I was little, remember?'

Soon, her mother's breathing slowed down and she slept, weightless as a bird, her head on her daughter's shoulder.

In the hut, Bevan tried in vain to settle to sleep on a pile of sacks. He kept hearing Dorothy weeping, seeing her face and feeling her tears on his hands. He could have been gentler with her, should have been.

He turned over again, but the sacks seemed to get lumpier by the minute and he didn't feel in the least bit sleepy.

In the end he stood up and looked out of the tiny window in the door. Everything was quiet. No one had come hunting him. It wasn't even raining now. Should he . . . No, it'd be stupid to go back home. Stupid.

But Dorothy had been weeping and he hadn't taken the time to comfort her, make her understand what it would be like for a man like him to be locked away as if he was a criminal. Anger surged up briefly against his stepdaughter, but it faded quickly, not nearly as important as the thought of his wife.

In the end he opened the door, creeping out down the hill towards his house.

When he opened the back door, he heard voices and froze for a few seconds, till he realised it was only his wife and Ellen. But then Dorothy started crying again, saying she'd never see him again and he couldn't help it. He moved forward noiselessly, not sure what to say or do, only sure that he couldn't leave her like this.

It was Ellen who noticed him first. She gasped and stiffened, which made Dorothy look up.

Her whole face lit up and she cried, 'Bevan!' holding her arms out to him.

So of course he went to her, shoving Ellen out of the way and kneeling by the bed. 'Now then, what are you getting yourself into such a state for?' he scolded fondly. 'Didn't I tell you you'd be all right with Ellen?'

'Yes, but you didn't say goodbye to me.' Her eyes searched his face hopefully. 'You've come back to give yourself up, haven't you? Oh, I'm so glad.'

'Dorothy love, I can't do that, you know I can't.'

'Then why . . . ?'

'I kept worrying about you, wanting to say goodbye properly.'

Ellen started edging towards the door and with an

angry growling sound he grabbed her skirt and tugged her back. 'You're not going anywhere. And before I leave, I'm tying you up. I'm not having you fetching the police to me, missy!'

'Oh, Bevan, don't make things worse!' Dorothy's face crumpled and she pulled away from him.

His anger flared up so brightly it seemed to burn up the whole room. He tried to push himself to his feet, but couldn't. He tried to grab the bedside table, but his hand wouldn't do what he wanted it to.

There was no further sound as he tumbled forward to lie on the bed next to his wife. 'Bevan!' Dorothy began to scream and shake him, begging him to speak to her.

Ellen turned him over, pushing her mother's hands away, but there was no mistaking that look. 'Mum, please. Stop that. He's gone.'

Dorothy stopped screaming to look at her blankly. 'Gone?' Then as she realised what Ellen meant, she gave a gasp and fell back against the pillows, one arm across her eyes.

'Mum, are you all right?'

Dorothy moved her arm and stared at her daughter, then reached out one hand, resting it on her husband's head. 'Better this way,' she said. 'He was a proud man.'

The front door opened and someone came in. Ellen turned and let out a sigh of relief. 'Seth!'

'I found your note so I came round here.' He looked down at the still figure on the bed. 'What happened?'

'I think he had a seizure of some sort. He's dead.'

They both looked at Dorothy who was stroking

Bevan's head, talking quietly to him, promising to join him soon.

So Seth pulled Ellen towards him and put his arms round her. 'Are you all right, love?'

'Yes. And you? Did you save Miss Veronica?'

'Yes.'

There was a knock on the door, hesitant sounding, and they went to answer it together.

It was the neighbour. 'I heard your mother calling out and there's been all sorts of to-ing and fro-ing. I don't want to sound nosy, but is everything all right?'

'Thanks for coming round, Mrs Baines. My stepfather's just died, I'm afraid. Some sort of seizure.'

'Oh dear, dear.'

The back door opened and Jory came in, accompanied by a policeman. He looked at Ellen. 'You found her, I see, Talbot. We've been looking for Halsopp. Thought we saw new footprints in the back garden.'

So Seth repeated the news, with the neighbour nodding as if to corroborate what he was saying. 'He's in there. He just keeled over and died, apparently. Seizure of some sort, we think.'

Jory went to the door of the front room and watched the stranger kneel and check the still figure.

Seth guided Ellen into the kitchen at the rear. 'I was worried sick when I got your note. Didn't you realise how dangerous your stepfather might be?'

'All I knew was my mother needed me.'

'I need you too.'

She smiled at him, a glorious smile that made him feel as if he was king of the world.

He grasped both her hands in his and raised each one in turn to his lips. 'Do we need a long courtship, Ellen?'

'No, love.' She was utterly certain of that.

'Good. Then let's buy a special licence and get married quickly and quietly. I don't want you facing all the fuss about what's happened tonight on your own.'

She put her arms round his neck. 'Getting married is a wonderful idea, but I'm not doing it quietly, Seth. I shan't be in mourning for *him*, so I'm going to invite as many of my friends from London to come as can make it, Lady Bingram too. We'll wait a week or two, for my mother's sake, then we'll do it properly and joyfully.'

'If you insist.' He kissed her then stepped reluctantly away from her because it wouldn't look well to be seen cuddling while a man lay dead in the front room. 'All right, let's get started on sorting things out . . .'

He hoped it would always be like this between them, so simple and straightforward, no need for long explanations or silly fusses. Then something occurred to him. 'Eh, I nearly forgot to tell you I love you.'

She chuckled. 'I'd guessed that. I love you too.'

So they stole one quick kiss to celebrate that.

Giles took Ronnie with him into town as soon as it was light, because he didn't intend to leave her on her own again. He told Tadwyn to take charge of the other servants and said they'd be back that afternoon once a few things had been sorted out.

Septimus Monnings welcomed Ronnie to his home and listened to the tale, then frowned. 'What I don't understand is why you didn't come to me to end the trust if you were having trouble with your mother, Miss Gresham. I got your deposition, assigning the power to run things to her until further notice, and forwarded it to the trustees, as you wished. I must say I wondered why you'd done that.'

She stared at him in shock. 'Deposition? I haven't made any depositions. And what trust are you talking about?'

'The one your father set up, leaving everything to you under your mother's charge until you turned twenty-five.' He leaned back, brow wrinkled. 'Another firm of lawyers dealt with it, I was just your mother's family lawyer. Until the recent deposition I've had little to do with your affairs. I must admit I'm not familiar with everything, only the broad outlines, but I thought – the deposition seemed quite genuine . . . I had no reason to doubt what your mother said. Well, I'll show it to you later.'

'That's why my mother didn't want me to marry you, Giles,' Ronnie said. 'I was surprised at how vehement she was about my marrying Algie, but of course *he* wouldn't have checked on the business side of things, not if she'd told him to leave them to her. He hasn't got a practical bone in his body.'

Giles put his arm round her and looked at his new legal partner. 'What was left to Mrs Gresham then?'

'A life tenancy of the Lodge, a generous allowance

for as long as she lived and her own jewels and personal possessions, but not the jewels and heirlooms that have been passed on down to the females of the family.'

'She'd have hated giving things up,' Ronnie said. 'She always has to be in charge, to be the most important person in a room. As for leaving the Hall, she'd have refused to do that, I'm sure.'

'There were legacies for the servants too, and I wondered why they hadn't been paid, but there were statements saying the servants agreed to wait until after the war ended.'

'How could she cheat them?' Ronnie exclaimed. 'I'm so glad they've been left something. They deserve it, even Tadwyn, because they've given their lives to my family.'

'Well, I can ask to have the trust ended now and you can pay them all.' Septimus smiled at Giles. 'And that solves the problem of where you two are going to live after you're married, I presume?'

'We'll live wherever Ronnie wants to. If the Hall has too many bad memories, we'll find somewhere else.'

Her smile was luminous. 'We'll make good memories there instead, darling. And the best thing about it is that there'll be plenty of room for your mother-in-law and the boys there.'

It wasn't until the afternoon that Dr Hilliam came out to the Hall to see them about Mrs Gresham.

'She's been taking too many of those sleeping drops. She'd got another doctor to prescribe them as well as myself, it seems. It's going to take a while to wean her off them, and there will be side effects. I think you should find her somewhere quiet to live, with someone to look after her.'

'She's never been quiet in her life,' Ronnie said.

'She is now, like a spent storm. She doesn't want to see you, though.'

'I don't want to see her, either. But I'll pay whatever it costs to have her looked after. Is that all right, darling?' She looked at Giles.

'Of course.'

Epilogue

Ellen and Seth got married a few weeks later, with Dorothy watching them fondly from a wheelchair. She was so frail as to seem almost transparent, but her happiness that her daughter was getting married glowed brightly in her eyes.

Beside her sat Lady Bingram, magnificent in a lavender silk gown, with a wide-brimmed hat sporting black feathers.

The new Mr and Mrs Covington were there too, both radiating happiness.

Pel and Glynis sat modestly at the rear, because she still hadn't got over the fact that she had been invited *as a guest* to a Gresham wedding. The two were making their own wedding plans but were intending to settle on the estate and live quietly, working at the Hall.

After much consideration, Jory had been invited but had declined the invitation, to Ellen's relief. He was busy running the family business with his brother, and his sister was keeping an eye on Mrs Cobbley, who had gone to pieces when they put her husband in prison.

'It all ties up very neatly, doesn't it?' said Lady Bingram at the wedding breakfast.

'More neatly than you think.' Dorothy leaned across to whisper, 'When I die, everything will go to Ellen. Bevan had quite a lot of money saved and it all came to me. She doesn't know about it yet, but Mr Monnings has sorted everything out for me.'

In a quiet moment during the celebrations, Lady Bingram congratulated her former aide. 'I suppose you'll be settling down now to running a house and raising a family.'

'Not quite.' Ellen smiled at her. 'It seems a shame to let all my skills go to waste, so Uncle Martin has taken me on to help him run his business. He's going to teach me all he knows about repairing cars and motorbikes.'

'That'll cause a few raised eyebrows in the town.'

Ellen tossed her head. 'Let it. If Seth doesn't mind, why should anyone else?'

'If Seth doesn't mind what?' He came to put his arm round his new wife's shoulders.

'My new job.'

'Oh, that. I wouldn't dare protest, would I? I'm terrified of you.' But he followed his teasing up by saying seriously, 'I don't think a helpless clinging wife would suit me at all. A policeman's wife has to be independent because she can never quite count on her husband being at home to do things.'

'A man like you won't stay in Shawcroft for ever,' Lady Bingram prophesied.

'Well, we'll still find a way to let my Ellen do what she wants.' The kiss he planted on his wife's cheek made her smile at him so tenderly that Lady Bingram was obliged to blow her nose, not once but two or three times.

If you enjoyed Tomorrow's Promises *then read on for an exclusive first chapter of Anna Jacobs' brilliant new saga,* Yesterday's Girl, *out now . . .*

ANNA JACOBS

Yesterday's Girl

HODDER

I

Violet Gill was walking home with a bag full of spoiled fruit and vegetables that she'd got cheaply from the market. She'd just turned a corner when she saw some lads snatch a loaf from an old lady, who was hobbling painfully along. They'd started running towards Vi before they noticed her and tried to swerve, but she didn't hesitate for a minute. Dropping her shopping bag, she flung herself sideways at the lad carrying the booty, shoving him so hard he bounced off the wall and let go of the loaf.

She grabbed him by the neck of his ragged shirt and gave him a couple of good clouts about the ears. 'Don't you dare steal anything again, Frank Pilling, or I'll hand you over to Constable Tucker! And you can be sure I'll tell your mam about this.'

His two companions in crime stopped further along the street to watch.

'I'll be telling your mams too!' she shouted at them, still holding the young thief by his shirt front. 'I know who you are. Brave, aren't you, to steal an old woman's food!' She gave her captive another thump for good measure and then let go of him. She knew how short of food the lad's family was, but it was no excuse.

He half-raised one hand to hit her back and for a minute all hung in the balance.

'Don't – you – dare!' she said softly, and although she wasn't much taller than him, something in her tone made him shrink away. With a yell he ran off down the street towards his companions. Only when the trio had disappeared round the corner did Vi turn to the lads' victim, who was leaning against the wall looking pale and shocked, and put one arm round her.

'You all right, love? See, I've got your loaf back. It's a bit dusty, though.'

'Thank you.' The old woman patted her chest. 'Eh, it give me a right old shock, that did. Made my heart pound. Be all right – in a minute.'

Vi waited patiently for her to pull herself together, then gave her back the loaf and watched her walk slowly and painfully away. The town hall clock struck the hour just then and she clicked her tongue in annoyance at the delay before picking up her own bag and retrieving one or two apples which had fallen out. Hurrying up the street, she turned the corner into the Backhill Terraces, twenty or so narrow streets clustered round the town's two big cotton mills on a slope that led up to the moors. It was here, in the poorest area of Drayforth, that her family's corner shop was situated.

She always enjoyed her outings to the markets, where the stallholders knew she'd pay them for bruised or overripe pieces and saved them for her. She paused at the door, sighing. She didn't enjoy being shut up in the shop all day. But what choice did she have?

What choice had she ever had from the minute she finished her schooling? Her father left most of the running of the shop to her mother and herself, and her mother had been ill for a few years, though she'd been a lot better in the past year, thank goodness.

Vi had been needed while her mother was ill. Without her the shop would have failed.

The two ladies who had stopped to watch this incident from further down the street began walking again.

'Well done, young woman!' Lady Bingram said softly. 'Who is she? Do you know, Freda?'

'I think she works in one of the corner shops. I've seen her when I've been visiting the slums.'

'Can you find out more about her?'

'I suppose so. Why?'

Daphne Bingram grinned, an urchin's grin for all she was in her mid-sixties. 'I'm looking for more young women to join my Aides. The government finds my little group so helpful in the war effort that it's asking me to find more of them, and is even giving me some money towards the costs. I certainly couldn't afford to support a bigger group myself.'

'Surely you don't want women of that class in your group?'

'Snobbery won't win the war, Freda. There are plucky women in all classes, and that's the only sort I want working for me.'

Her companion sniffed. 'Well, rather you than me. Some of those women from the Backhill Terraces have no moral fibre. The things I've seen in my charity work!' She frowned. 'I'd have thought you'd want younger Aides, though. That one must be well over thirty.'

Daphne stopped trying to reason with a woman who had always been a snob and a stick-in-the-mud, and wasn't likely to change now, war or no war. The trouble was, she needed the money her companion was raising to help buy the necessary cars and motor-bikes for those women from her group who were acting as couriers to various offshoots of the War Office. It was so good to be able to contribute to the war effort. It gave a meaning to her life she hadn't had for a long time. She'd do anything she could to keep her Aides going, even be nice to Freda Gilson.

As they were parting company on the main street, she reminded Freda of her promise. 'If you can find out about that young woman for me, I'll be very grateful. I have to get back to London soon.'

'You're still coming to lunch tomorrow, though? The Lady Volunteers are looking forward to meeting you and hearing what you do with the money we've raised.'

'Of course I am. That money is being put to very good use, I promise you. You've done really well.' She'd never liked Freda, who was the daughter of a now-dead friend, but war made for strange bedfellows.

Vi arrived home to find a queue in the shop and her mother telling one impatient customer she'd have to wait. Her father was nowhere to be seen. Grimly, wondering what his excuse would be this time, Vi carried her purchases through to the back room, tied on a pinafore and began serving.

When she went to the till for some change, she was surprised at how few coins there were and looked across at her mother, who flicked her a quick glance then avoided her eyes.

During a lull between customers she asked bluntly, 'Has Dad been at the till again?'

Her mother hesitated then nodded.

'Why didn't you stop him?'

'I tried to. He pushed me away.'

'Oh, Mum!' Vi bit off further protests. Her father was a big man and her mother, like herself, was barely five foot tall. 'How much did he take?'

'About ten shillings.'

'Then I'm not providing him with any food at teatime for the rest of the week.'

'He'll only take ours.'

'Just let him try. We'll eat when he's not there.' Lips pressed together grimly, Vi went to sort out a few greengroceries for themselves from the stuff she'd brought home then set up a small box holding the rest on top of a packing case just outside the door. The less provident women would buy these pieces one or two at a time and she'd make a small profit on what she'd paid for them at market. Every penny helped.

And she wouldn't allow her father to steal any more of her hard-earned money for his drinking.

When the teatime rush had passed, Vi left the shop in her mother's capable hands again and went to seek out her brother. She wasn't particularly close to Eric, well, no one was. He kept his thoughts to himself, always had done. He took after their father in looks, but was much cleverer. Though he no longer lived at home, Eric thought the world of their mother. Vi hoped he'd help them in this constant battle to stop their father drinking away the profits she and her mother worked so hard for.

She found her brother standing by the bar in The Drover's Rest pub. She didn't like going inside, but needs must. 'Could I speak to you outside for a minute, Eric? Me and Mum need your help.'

He set his glass of beer down on the bar and looked at the landlord. 'Keep an eye on that, Den.'

The landlord nodded and placed the half-empty glass on the back shelf.

Outside Eric cocked one eyebrow at her, waiting.

'Dad's been at the till again. If he goes on like this, the shop will fail because we won't be able to pay our suppliers. Could you persuade him to leave the shop money alone? Mum was that upset today.'

Eric nodded. 'Dad's a stupid sod. Can't think beyond the next drink. You were right to come to me. I'm not having our mum upset. I'll pop round tomorrow after tea and have a word with him.'

'Thanks.'

He nodded and went back into the pub without even a goodbye.

He was like that, their Eric was. Didn't waste his time on chat or politeness, just went straight for whatever he wanted. He worked for Mr Kirby, helping

Sully, who was in charge of collecting rents and looking after the many houses Mr Kirby owned. Eric must be earning decent money because he had good lodgings and never seemed short of a bob or two.

If anyone could stop Dad ruining them, it was Eric.

The next evening Vi waited impatiently for her brother, beginning to grow anxious when time passed with no sign of him. He turned up eventually at nine-thirty, waited for the last customer to leave and locked the door behind the woman.

'We don't close for another half hour, love,' his mother said.

'You do tonight. I've got something to say to Dad.' He studied her face. 'You're looking tired, Mum, working too hard.'

'We can't lock the door yet. Your father's not back from the pub.'

'I'll go and fetch him. Where's he drinking these days?'

'He usually goes to The Drover's Rest.'

'Not since I started drinking there, he doesn't.' He patted her arm. 'Don't worry. I'll soon hunt him down. And don't open the shop again. You look tired. If those silly bitches can't remember to buy their food earlier, let them go without.'

May went into the back room and Vi followed Eric to the shop door. 'Thanks.'

He shrugged. 'I'm not letting him do that to her.'

Ten minutes later there was shouting in the street and someone hammered at the door. When Vi opened it, one of the men who worked with Eric shoved their father through and Eric followed him inside.

'Lock up again,' he said curtly as he guided the drunken man through into the back room and pushed him down on a chair.

When Vi went to join them, she found Eric going through his father's pockets and dropping the coins he found on the table.

'Only four and twopence. No, here's another penny.' He slammed his father against the chair back. 'Damned well stay where you are, you!'

Arnie subsided, scowling at his son.

Eric smacked one hand down on the table so hard everyone jumped. 'This is the last time you take money out of the till, Dad. The very last time.'

Arnie was pot valiant still. 'It's my shop, my money.'

'It's Mum and Vi who work in the shop, so I reckon it's their money. You're a lazy sod an' you hardly lift a finger. I don't know how Mum's put up with you all these years.'

'I do my share.'

'You've never done your share.' Eric leaned forward and poked his father in the chest. 'I meant what I said.' He waited a moment and added in a softer voice that was nonetheless chilling, 'If you do pinch any more money from the shop, I'll see you get the beating of your life.'

Arnie shrank away. Eric had a weak heart, so he didn't get into fights himself, but if he said he'd arrange a beating, he'd do it. He never made threats he couldn't carry out. Arnie glared at his wife and daughter.

'Even if Mum doesn't tell me, I'll find out.' Eric gathered up the money and looked at his mother. 'How much did he take?'

'About ten shillings.'

'Here.' He added five shillings out of his own pocket and put all the money into her hand, clasping her fingers round it. Hesitating a moment, he gave her a quick, almost furtive kiss on the cheek and left without another word.

'You went and told him,' Arnie threw at his daughter.

Vi stared back defiantly. 'I certainly did. An' I'll do it again if I have to. We need that money. Takings are down because of war shortages.'

He spat into the fire and heaved himself to his feet. 'I'm going to bed. It's a fine lookout when a daughter's as ungrateful as you. It's me as provides the roof over your head and don't you forget it. Children! Bite the hand that feeds them, they do . . .'

When he'd gone up the stairs, still grumbling, Vi looked at her mother. 'He's getting worse.'

'Yes. I don't know what's got into him lately.'

'You go up to bed, Mum. I'll check the shop and bring the takings in.'

It was another half-hour before Vi got to bed, because she liked to leave things tidy. She rubbed her aching forehead and climbed the stairs to the bedroom she now had for her own. It seemed a long time since she'd shared it with her older sister. Beryl had been married for the past eighteen years to a nice fellow who did what Beryl told him and seemed happy with that state of affairs.

Vi sometimes wished she'd found a fellow to marry, because she'd have liked a family of her own. But what would have happened to her mother if she'd left the shop? Her mother had had several years of ill health, though she was much better these days.

Anyway, no one had asked her to marry them, had they? A couple of lads had asked her to walk out with them when she was much younger, but she hadn't been fussed whether she did or not because they weren't up to much. Her mother said she read too many magazines and books, real men weren't like the heroes in those stories, nor was real life. But if it came to a choice between staying a spinster and marrying someone like her father, Vi would rather stay single any day.

They were dead now, those two lads, poor things. Both killed in the first year of the war. A lot of the fellows she'd grown up with were losing their lives in this dreadful fighting and all she could do was serve in the shop. She'd have liked to make a contribution, join the VADs or something, but her mother had needed her. And anyway, the sight of blood turned her queasy, so she didn't really want to nurse anyone.

But the years of her life were passing so swiftly it shocked her sometimes. What had become of yesterday's lively girl? She was thirty-five, had done nothing, gone nowhere. She was far too old to marry now, though she didn't feel old. Why, her hair wasn't even going grey yet. She had nice hair, her best feature her mother always said, but who was there to notice that now? All the men her age were either away fighting or long married with several children.

The following day Daphne Bingram was driven to Freda Gilson's house for lunch, her last engagement locally before she returned to London. She pinned a smile to her face as the group of women fluttered and fussed over her because of her title. Silly things! She'd come from a much poorer home than theirs. But they weren't too silly to raise money.

During a lull in the conversation she turned to Freda. 'Did you find out about that young woman?'

A sour expression crossed her companion's face. 'Not so young. She's thirty-five.'

'And . . . ?'

'Her family runs a corner shop, a mean little place. She and her mother do most of the work and it isn't thriving because the father is a drunkard. So you see, she's really not suitable to join your Aides.'

Daphne held back a protest and pulled out her little notebook. 'What's her name?'

'Violet Gill, but they call her Vi. I abominate nicknames, don't you?'

'And the address of the shop?'

'Corner of Reservoir Road and Platts Lane.'

'Thank you.' Daphne put the little silver propelling pencil into its holder and slipped the notebook back into her handbag. She endured another half-hour of inane chit-chat, thanked the ladies again for their wonderful contribution to the war effort and took her leave.

'I need to visit someone in the Backhill Terraces,' she told her elderly chauffeur.

After stopping to make enquiries, they pulled up outside the shop and Daphne studied it with a grimace. It looked very run-down, though of course paint was in short supply because of the war. But the window was clean and had a neat little display of tins of food in it.

That young woman had stayed in her mind for the past twenty-four hours. Daphne's instinct about people rarely let her down. 'Wait for me here.'

She got out of the car and stopped at the entrance to the shop, watching for a moment or two as Vi served an awkward customer, jollying her along. Then they both turned round and gaped at the sight of Daphne, who knew she looked like a creature from another world in her elegant clothes, so moved forward, smiling.

The customer stepped hastily back and Vi looked at the newcomer enquiringly.

'Do finish serving this lady first,' Daphne said. 'Then I wonder if you could shut the shop for a few minutes. I'd like to talk to you.'

'I'll come back later,' the customer said and scuttled out with another nervous glance at the newcomer.

Vi followed her to the door, locked it and hung up a sign saying, 'Back in ten minutes'. Then she turned to her visitor and waited.

'Is there somewhere we could sit down for a minute or two? What I'd like to talk to you about is rather important, to do with the war effort.'

'Come through into the back.' She led the way and introduced her mother, who was sitting at the table, weighing quarter pounds of sugar on the kitchen scales and pouring it into triangular blue paper bags.

Daphne held out her hand. 'Pleased to meet you, Mrs Gill. I'm Daphne Bingram.'

'Pleased to meet you too, Mrs Bingram.'

'It's Lady Bingram, actually, but I don't like to stand on ceremony.'

Vi pulled out a chair for their visitor then sat down herself. 'How can we help you, your ladyship?'

Daphne explained about her Aides. 'I saw you in the street yesterday, dealing with those louts and retrieving the old lady's loaf. I knew at once that you were the sort of woman I want in my group. Would you like to come to London and work for me, help win the war? I pay a pound a week all found, and I provide the uniform.'

It was the mother who spoke. 'Eh, that sounds wonderful. You should do it, our Vi.'

'How can I, Mum? I'm needed in the shop.'

May frowned in thought. 'I think I could manage now. I'm a lot better and this is a good chance for you, love. It'd mean a lot to me to give you a better chance than this place. You deserve it.'

Vi stretched out one hand to her and they smiled at one another. Lady Bingram was moved by their obvious closeness, wishing yet again that she'd been blessed with children.

'I reckon Tess Donovan would jump at the chance to help in the shop, Vi. She did all right before when you were helping our Beryl after she miscarried. With her husband away in France, Tess is desperate for money. She's a good worker.' May waited and when her daughter didn't speak, added, 'And now that our Eric's keeping an eye on your father, I'll be all right. Eric won't be going anywhere after failing his medical.'

Daphne nodded approval. 'Well spoken, Mrs Gill. It is a good chance for your daughter to see a bit of life and help win the war.'

May turned to her. 'You'll – look after her properly? She's never been away from Lancashire before. I wouldn't want her to be lonely or unhappy.'

'She'll live in my house and as there will soon be twenty other Aides, she definitely won't be lonely.'

They both turned to Vi, who was looking stunned.

'Well?' Daphne asked gently. 'Do you want to come with me?'

Vi opened and shut her mouth then swallowed hard and looked at her mother. 'Are you sure?'

'Yes. I'll miss you, but it'll make me that happy to see you get a chance like this.' She reached out for her daughter's hand again. 'Do it, love. Don't let this opportunity slip by.'

Vi turned a face glowing with excitement towards Daphne. 'Then I accept, Lady Bingram. And thank you.'

Daphne stood up. 'Can you be ready to leave tomorrow?'

Vi gasped then nodded.

'I'll pick you up tomorrow morning about eight o'clock, then. I'm driving down to London and you'll probably find it easiest to come with me.' She turned to May Gill. 'Thank you so much for letting me have your daughter. I can guess what this will cost you.'

The two older women shook hands.

Vi stood there like someone frozen to the spot till her mother nudged her, then she moved forward to show their visitor out.

After her ladyship's car had driven away, they made no attempt to open the shop. Going back inside they locked the door, then looked at one another.

With a sob, Vi flung her arms round her mother. 'I don't know how I'll ever thank you for this.'

'It's your big chance. I couldn't bear you to turn it down.' May held her daughter at arm's length and studied her face for a moment as if memorising it, then gave her a little push. 'Now, there's a lot to do. You'd better go and fetch Tess to help out. Her mother will look after the little lasses and the son's in school. Then you'll have to do some washing and bring down that old trunk of mine from the attic. It's still sturdy enough, even if it is scratched. And—'

Someone hammered at the shop door and May moved towards it. 'I'll serve in the shop and if there's a rush, they'll just have to wait their turn. It'll take you all your time to get ready.'

For once, Vi let someone else tell her what to do. Bemused, still not believing this could be happening to her, she left the shop and hurried along the street to her friend's.

★   ★   ★

Tess opened the door and smiled at Vi. 'You don't usually come calling at this time of day, love. I hope nothing's wrong.'

'Something's come up – it's good news, though – and we need your help.'

Tess held the door open and Vi walked in. Her friend's little daughter was playing on the rag rug and a baby was crawling nearby. The whole place was immaculately clean, if sparsely furnished.

Vi didn't waste any time but explained what had happened, ending, 'I can only do it if we get someone to help Mam in the shop. Do you want the job?'

Tess gaped at her for a minute. 'You're going to London?'

'Yes.' She gestured to the children. 'Can your mother look after them for you?'

Her friend beamed. 'Yes! We could do with the money an' I like working in the shop.'

'You couldn't start today, could you?'

Tess gave her a cracking hug. 'Give me half an hour to get my mam.'

Vi walked out, feeling as if the world had turned upside down. After a moment's hesitation, she went to find Eric and share the news with him. He was just as important as Tess in her new plans.

He stared at her, lips pursed, then nodded slowly. 'It'll be a good thing for you, that. An' I'll keep an eye on Dad for you, don't worry.'

'Thanks.'

He nodded and walked away.

She smiled as she watched him go. You'd think words

cost money, he was so sparing with them. But it didn't matter. He'd look after their mother and keep their father in check.

She hurried off to call on her sister Beryl and let her know what was happening. Not that Beryl would be much use to Mam, because she and their father didn't get on and she refused to have anything to do with him. But still, it was only right to let her know. Vi didn't see her sister very often because the shop kept her busy till all hours but they'd always been fond of one another.

Joy flooded through her and she stood for a moment beaming at nothing, still unable to believe her luck. She was going to see the world she'd only read about before.

Anna Jacobs grew up in Lancashire and emigrated to Australia, but still visits the UK regularly to see her family and do research, something she loves. She is addicted to writing and she figures she'll have to live to be 120 at least to tell all the stories that keep popping up in her imagination and nagging her to write them down. She's also addicted to her own hero, to whom she's been happily married for many years.